The Guardian Chronicles
Book One: Rising Sun

By Zac Virdee

Paperback ISBN – 978-1-910667-87-3
.epub ISBN – 978-1-910667-59-0
.mobi ISBN – 978-1-910667-58-3

To my family, you kept me on the straight and narrow. Without you guys I doubt I'd still be here. Hope I didn't annoy you all that much.

Prologue: I'm giving him a fighting chance

Broken titanium and ceramic walls discharged electricity as a lone figure walked through the underground tunnels. The once beautiful walls looked falsely weak but in actual fact were able to withstand massive amounts of damage. From what the damage looked like it appeared that something had peeled apart the walls like butter.

Dr Steven Sampson clutched his right arm and cleaned the blood from his jaw. His right arm was dislocated badly. Sampson gritted his teeth and relocated his arm into the socket. His scientific mind began analysing the area around him. The tunnel itself looked as if it could easily break down from the stress it was under. Turning his attention to the back of tunnel he focused through the dirt and deep fog. He heard a deep roaring in the background. Slowly Sampson focused more and saw the figure walk toward him. Though the light was dull he could make out the features of the monster before him. It was at least nine feet tall and weighed around a ton. Moving with inhuman speed Sampson landed three punches into the creature's stomach and then one final uppercut. The creature seemed more annoyed by the blow which would have shattered a human body.

Sampson's real name was Saar-Vaar. He was a science officer from the planet Kord about 17 light years from earth. His body was an absorption unit enabling him to absorb almost any type of energy but solar was the best. This made him far stronger and faster, it granted many other abilities native to his race.

Sampson realised fighting the creature was impossible. He supersped to the last stronghold and sealed the 50 inch titanium reinforced wall. Another man was there but Sampson knew who it was.

"Bernard have you restarted the automatic defences?" he asked.

"Yes sir all defences online," Bernard said in his strong British accent. Bernard Smith was around six feet tall and well muscled for someone his age. He clutched a shotgun and had a bandage around his left arm.

"Is the recorder ready?"

"Yes sir." Sampson turned to look at the test tube which was located further behind the defences and just before a small winding staircase. The child inside was only 18 months old and kicked his legs. A tear ran down Sampson's eye he would never see his son again. He went to the recorder and switched it on.

"My son I am so sorry to be leaving you like this. Earth is a beautiful place, the Guardians were right the people have the power to be upright and kind but they lack a role model, someone to lead them into the light. They will stumble but you can be that role model and you will lead them into the light. I do not have much time, this will be revealed to you soon and you alone will know what to do. Your mother is so sorry she could not be here. She loved you very much. As do I my son. Goodbye and farewell." Sampson rechecked the defences. They were not human defences but special Kord defence turrets; they would hold the enemy for as long as was needed. Sampson looked at some unfinished technology on the table next to him. It hummed with power. He approached and began tinkering with it, moulding it into something else. He then approached his son's test tube. For a brief second he looked up to the staircase; *no such luck for a last minute escape* he thought as he heard the defence systems behind him firing. Sampson placed the device on top of the tube and waited a brief second. The projector at the top of the tube glowed yellow and shot a brilliant light into the tube. Sampson increased the output of the light. He considered briefly the ethics of placing his infant son in the tube. Though he wasn't in any pain, the child was being taught almost everything earth had to offer in terms of knowledge. Languages, concepts, martial arts and other information were being poured into his young mind. Though Sampson wasn't worried about the data overload, he could handle it.

"Master Sampson what are you doing?" Smith asked.

Sampson shifted uneasily on his feet. "Giving my son a better chance at living, I'm infusing him with more sunlight and source energy. And I'm taking the monster somewhere where he cannot escape."

"So what will I teach the boy without you to guide him?" Bernard asked softly.

Steven smiled gently. "I have faith Bernard; teach him how to be human and to learn humility. Teach him restraint and have faith that he will fulfil and he will succeed in his task."

Bernard smiled and checked his shotgun. "Are you absolutely sure you have to leave? The boy needs you." Sampson studied his son with a thoughtful look and pursed his lips.

"There is nothing more that I want than to stay with him to guide and protect him, but for his sake I need go. I know I am leaving him in capable hands," he said as he looked at Bernard.

"Sir, I am not the best choice for this. I don't even get on with my own children," Bernard retorted.

Sampson smiled. "You will give him a human perspective of life. You will protect and care for him." Sampson placed his hand on Bernard's shoulder. "I know that you are the right man for this and in advance thank you for everything that you have done." Bernard smiled and nodded. Suddenly a massive smack shattered the peaceful silence. Sampson checked the defences; all of them had gone down. This was the time, Sampson thought. He finished the bracelet and calibrated it making sure that it had enough power. The bracelet was a teleportation device and it would send both Sampson and the beast away from there. Bernard began reloading shells in his shotgun but Sampson stopped him.

He shook his head in the no fashion and said, "No Bernard. It's time for us to part ways. Know that I am thankful for all you have done. You will always be my friend." Sampson lifted Bernard into the air and threw him up the staircase and into the building above. The door was about to be knocked down. Sampson made some final checks and sealed the lab. With that the door was broken down. Sampson looked at the monster. It walked in and roared at Steven.

"I am and will always be better than you son, and he will be better than you. He will defeat you." Letting out a mighty roar, the beast shattered part of the lab with a telekinetic shock. He knew he had seconds to react before the monster attacked and destroyed the tube behind him. Sampson's eyes turned a darker shade of blue and twin cylindrical beams of energy shot out of his eyes. The beams were hotter than the sun and pushed the beast back. Taking one last look at his son, Saar-Vaar shot forward defying gravity and grabbed the beast flying upward towards space. Saar-Vaar kept increasing speed and blasting the beast with energy beams. He endured punches that could level mountains. They shot out of the atmosphere and Saar-Vaar took one last look at the brilliant sun shining in the black of space. He blinked a tear from his eye and thought, *My son amend my mistakes.* He pressed a button on the bracelet and like the twinkling of the stars around them they disappeared.

Chapter 1: *Just a bad dream*

Lightning engulfed the king-sized bedroom as the occupant jolted awake. Michael Sampson fell into the corner of the room cowering like a wounded animal, he took long ragged breaths until he composed himself. *Just a dream, just a dream*, he thought calming himself down. Sweat poured off his body as he searched his thoughts, desperately exploring his memories for clues of what had just transpired. A sharp rap of the door echoed throughout the room. Michael stood back up, standing at his full height of six foot six. He approached the door and opened it a small amount. He realised that it was Bernard, his trusted friend and butler and the sole tie to his past.

"Master Michael, are you alright?" Bernard asked. Michael relaxed.

"Bernard, I'm fine just-just a bad dream."

"Well sir if there's anything else I'm just downstairs." The thunderstorm outside continued raging, spewing lightning from the heavens. Michael walked over to his bedside table and picked up his watch, it told him that it was 3 a.m. He stretched fully and flexed his muscles. Michael's mansion was in the outskirts of New York. The mansion had been built by Michael's late father. Sleep was something that Michael didn't normally get; there was no reason for him to go back and try. Approaching the en-suite bathroom he splashed water on his face. He stared into the mirror at the reflection. His skin was lightly tanned though appeared pale because he didn't get out much. His black hair was ragged and dirty. His deep black eyes drifted from black to a deep red, a trait he had had since he could remember. Whenever he was in a state of emotion his eyes would turn red. Michael looked at the medicine cabinet and pulled out a small necklace. The necklace resembled a pair of dog tags and had an unidentified coat of arms on it. He had spent years trying to decipher the shield but had not found any background for it.

Michael walked out of the bathroom and to his wardrobe. Picking out a black shirt and trousers he quickly got dressed. Pulling his coat from the hanger he walked towards the window. The weather didn't dissuade him from quickly jumping out. Landing on the lawn he caused a small depression and looked out towards the city of New York. Letting the rain fall on his face he took a deep breath clearing his lungs. Michael began sprinting towards the city and the whole world began melting around him, slowing down according to his perception. Michael was travelling at superspeed, moving at a rate that enabled him to be almost invisible to the human eye. Michael possessed accelerated vision enabling him to perceive things in slow motion. Arriving in Times Square in seconds, he hid himself in an alley away from anyone's view. Michael focused his vision on an apartment building around two blocks away from his current destination. Michael crossed over the still busy road quickly walking towards the apartment block as he did he heard a woman cry out in pain. Michael turned his attention to the woman as his eyes turned red in anger.

The woman was being beaten by a larger man. Every time she went down he brought her back up to beat her again. Michael didn't want to get involved, as he walked towards the building. Suddenly a voice in the back of his head told him to intervene. The voice had been there ever since he was young, driving him to help people. Though he tried to it ignore it, it eventually wore him down.

Alright dammit, he thought, *I'm going.* He entered superspeed and shot towards the thug. Michael appeared behind the man and lifted him up. The man gaped at him in fear; Michael felt no sympathy for the bully.

"You shouldn't hit women," he said, his deep voice inspiring fear in the man as he threw him into a wall, breaking his shoulder. Michael looked back at the woman and flashed his eyes red. He disappeared away and reappeared near the building. Michael sighed with content, he had done his good deed for the day, hopefully that would satisfy the voice.

The apartment complex was known as the "Times Square View" and provided a stunning look at the area of Times Square. Michael crouched down as force gathered around his feet and leapt into the air, landing on the fire escape. He looked at the girl in the window. She was in every sense of the word beautiful and in Michael's eyes the only woman he had ever loved. Her name was Charlotte Phoenix; Michael had known her since the start of elementary school. She had found out about Michael's powers when she saw him save their bus from falling into the Hudson River. Bernard had taught Michael how to handle his powers so that he could keep his secret, but she had seen everything. Like Michael she did not get much sleep so she was up watching her favourite film "The Phantom of the Opera". She mimed playing the piano as she watched the film almost lost in the music. Michael tapped gently on the window just loud enough for her to hear. She looked round and smiled as she walked towards the window. Her brown hair fell to her shoulders as she opened it. She was around five feet seven and had beautiful brown eyes. She had lightly tanned skin that was darker than Michael's because of her Italian heritage. She almost jumped on him, hugging him as tightly as she could.

"I missed you Michael," she said softly.

"I know I missed you too," he said softly as they kissed for what seemed like hours. When they pulled apart Michael asked, "Now that I'm here, were can I take you?" She looked deep in thought as she pondered on where Michael could take her.

"We shared our first kiss there." Michael smiled; he knew where he was going. He hoisted Charlotte off her feet and supersped to the Empire State Building. The rain was getting heavier now so Michael formed a telekinetic shield around them which looked like a blue halo over them. They sat on the edge and watched the stunning city go by. "Thank you for bringing me here, it's always beautiful at this sort of time," she said softly.

"I know that's why I chose to bring you here all those years ago. Only you have properly seen it like this." Michael had put his coat around Charlotte's shoulders to keep her warm. He didn't feel the cold. They lay back slowly and watched the clouds float by. She turned round and felt Michael's necklace, juggling the two tags.

"I love this necklace Michael, it seems so powerful."

Michael smiled and gently placed his hand on top of hers. "I know. I just wish I knew something about it."

She smiled. "What do you know about it?"

"Bernard said it belonged to my father, that it was his most prized possession and that he wanted me to have it. That's about it really."

She examined the tags more closely. "It's beautiful, I'm sure your dad would have been proud that you're wearing it."

Michael frowned. "I don't know." He sat up slowly and looked at the falling rain. "I can't remember anything from before my fourth birthday, Charlotte. It's like I wasn't there one minute and the next I appear. I don't even know when my real birthday is and I can't remember one thing about my father. In truth, I'm alone."

Charlotte sat up and turned his face to hers; they touched heads as she shushed him softly. "I know Michael, I know you'd like to have known him but I'm sure that he loved you. And you're not alone, not ever, because even though you may not have any family you have me and you will always have me."

Michael smiled; he was almost overwhelmed with his love for her. "You just know what to say all the time. I love you, you know that."

She smiled. "I love you Michael, more than anything in this world," she said. She fell asleep slowly and Michael just stared out into the distance.

It was about 6:30 in the morning when Michael woke up. The sun was shining, freed from the confinement of the cold. After Charlotte fell asleep she had remained in Michael's arms for the rest of the night. Michael had managed to fall asleep for an hour or so but he had been bewitched as he had watched her sleep. Michael wrapped her in his coat and supersped to her apartment. He slowly laid her on her bed, making sure that she was covered from the cold. The door slowly creaked opened and Michael immediately turned around. He relaxed when he saw Charlotte's little sister Amy looking at him. She was ten years old, had light brown hair with shining blue eyes. She loved Michael like her older brother since he could always make her laugh. Michael put his finger to his lips to quiet her. He got on his knees and smiled.

"Is Charlotte alright?" she asked softly.

Michael nodded. "Yeah she's fine, did you have a good night's sleep?" he asked.

"No I had a bad dream," she said with a quiver. Michael bent down and wiped a small tear from her eye.

"Don't worry; you've got me to look after you."

Her face suddenly lit up. "I know Mike; you're the strongest boy in the world."

Michael smiled. "That I am, kiddo. Try and get some sleep, I'll see you soon." She nodded and gave Michael a big hug.

Michael made his way out of Charlotte's room and leapt to the roof of the apartment. The sun was now shining brilliantly over the skyline and shone directly on him. Michael closed his eyes as his veins turned yellow and his eyes turned red. The solar energy refreshed Michael like a fresh glass of water. He knew it was time to leave as he superleaped back towards his mansion. Michael landed in the gardens behind the house and approached the back door. As he went to open the door, Bernard abruptly opened it before he had a chance.

"Late night Master Sampson?" he asked dryly.

Michael smiled and shrugged. "Not as late as you think, Bernard."

He smiled as he let Michael enter. "Well I took the liberty of preparing some breakfast and fresh coffee." Michael grabbed a coffee as he walked to the staircase and placed his hand on the wall. A part of the wall shuffled and Michael pushed it open. He walked down the stairs, switching the lights on to illuminate the area beneath. Michael had found this lab when he was ten years old and was utterly in love with the area. It featured everything he could want so that he could build and invent different things. Bernard had said it was a small workshop his father had built years ago before his birth. Michael pressed a small button on the wall and a blue light in the middle of the workshop shone. The light showed off the multiple tools and computers. The workshop had numerous blueprints some of which Michael had made and some which his father had created. Michael turned to a blueprint of an arm and it all came back to him.

Two years ago Michael had been with Charlotte's family at one of her performances. Charlotte had trained for years to be the best ballet dancer ever seen in the world. It was her greatest hobby; Michael had known that she loved it so he always tried to take to her preferences. She had even tried to teach him how to dance, but unfortunately Michael wasn't that flexible. This one performance was her most prestigious and a producer from a famous Russian ballet theatre was there looking for new talent. Michael found his seat next to Charlotte's younger sister; she smiled at Michael and alerted her younger brother Ryan and her mother Mary to his appearance. He waved gently as she smiled at him. The lights dimmed and the performance started. Michael watched Charlotte closely his accelerated vision slowing down time so that he could better see her movements. Michael was almost spellbound by her performance until a sudden ticking caught him off guard.

Michael possessed incredible hearing enabling him to hear even the heartbeat of a human and a whisper from a thousand miles away. Michael stood up gently and quickly walked out; he closed his eyes and focused on the sound. There were two logical places the sound could come from. Entering superspeed he shot towards the roof, desperately searching for the source. Michael could see different spectrums with his incredible eyesight. He blinked as he kept changing his vision from thermal to X-ray and others.

He even began scanning radio waves to see if the sound was linked to some kind of emitter. *Nothing*, he thought as he blurred away to a second location.

Behind the stage, Michael made his way towards the sound. A dancer tried to divert him but Michael simply pushed him out of the way. *Fool*, he thought as he found the source of the sound. Michael analysed the device and quickly came to the conclusion that it was a bomb. His incredible brain contained a vault of knowledge but there was no instruction on how to disarm a bomb. The ticking had increased now and Michael knew that he couldn't get it out, neither could he warn anyone. Focusing, his eyes turned red as he surrounded the bomb in a telekinetic shield. As the bomb's explosion stuttered it clashed with the light blue shield. Michael could feel the pressure and he suddenly came to the horrible realisation that he couldn't stop it. He glanced at Charlotte and tried to yell but the explosion distorted the very air and sound. The blast was not as explosive as the average bomb; rather it was more telekinetic in nature much like his abilities. The explosion burst out of the shield and sent Michael hurtling out of the building. It almost demolished the theatre with the sheer force. Crashing through three buildings, Michael finally landed in an apartment block. The damage was extensive and one the buildings he had hit had almost crumpled from the full energy of Michael smashing into it. The metal of the three buildings groaned from the stress. Michael pushed a pile of rubble off him and groaned softly. The damage hadn't been enough to hurt him properly but he still felt the force. Michael's eyes were blazing red and his skin was cracked and pale from a lack of energy, a side effect of Michael's superhuman abilities, meaning that he had to hide from normal people or wear dark glasses. His extraordinary vision switched so that he could trace any energy sources and he found a small electrical wire jutting out of the damaged building. Michael grabbed the wire and his body began absorbing the electricity. The electrical energy left a metallic taste in his mouth which almost made him vomit. Michael generally preferred solar energy to any other sort, the main reason being that it gave him a better boost and didn't leave any side effects. Shaking off his dizziness he stood and then proceeded to wipe dust off his body.

Michael did a quick check of his surroundings; he was in an apartment building but luckily there had been no one in the room he fell into. A sound like thunder caught Michael's attention as a form appeared in front of him, wearing a hooded cloak, with blazing red eyes. The figure hissed at Michael and rushed him back into a wall. Michael desperately tried to break free from the creature's grip. For the first time in a long time Michael couldn't remove himself from the monster's grip.

"You know not the war that you will bring to those closest to you. Now watch your beloved die," it roared. Michael struggled under the pressure and with his incredible hearing he picked up Charlotte screaming in pain. Michael's eyes hardened red as he roared in anger trying to overpower the figure. He found another gear and punched the creature as hard as he could. The punch sounded like thunder and sent the figure through one of the buildings Michael had crashed into. He leapt towards the monster and headbutted him multiple times. With one last effort, Michael roared and used a telekinetic wave which sent the figure out to sea. Michael relaxed for a brief second; the figure had easily been able to overpower Michael and hurt him. He prepared himself and leapt back towards the now ruined ballet theatre. Bodies littered the area but none of them belonged to Charlotte. Michael's phone began to ring. He picked it up.

"Mary, where is she?" he asked.

"It's all right I'm in the ambulance with her," she said in cut up voice.

"I'm on my way don't worry."

"No, Charlotte said that she wants you to stay there and help."

Michael protested. "No I need to be there for her."

"Michael!" Mary shouted immediately halting Michael in his tracks. "Charlotte is in a tremendous amount of pain and the last thing she said was that she wants you to help. Please, I'm begging you, help the people."

"I'll stay, don't worry I'll help as much as possible. Tell Charlotte I'll see her soon." Michael ended the call. In anger Michael destroyed the wall next to him. He wanted to leave and be by her side, but that voice was there again; driving him to help the people around him. Michael spent the next few hours doing his best to pull people out of the wreckage. The bomb had torn through a few more buildings behind the theatre and threatened the very stability of their foundations. Multiple EMT crews were around doing their best to help the injured. Firefighters stacked up looking for ways clear more wreckage. Michael did his best without revealing himself but managed to help more people. The building frame had almost been completely blown out meaning that Michael had to support most of the structure. Several people had been injured and there had been severe power outages causing lights to simply blow out. After a while Michael began scanning the building for remaining civilians; after three looks he let the building crash gently without harming anyone else. Michael superleaped to the nearest building. Checking his watch, he realised Charlotte would have got to the hospital by now; it was time for him to go. He supersped to the hospital where Charlotte was being treated. He slowly walked to the reception area.

"Hi I'm here to see a patient, Charlotte Phoenix."

The woman looked at her computer and looked back at him. "Are you family?"

"Yes he is." Another voice yelled from the hallway. Mary came running toward Michael and gave him a big hug. "Michael, come with me." Michael had noticed that her eyes were red raw from crying. He felt a deep pang of guilt again as he followed her to Charlotte's room. Amy and Charlotte's younger brother Ryan were sitting outside a room. The children looked pale from what had happened; they looked up at Michael. Both of them gave Michael a big hug as more tears came.

"Hey guys, I'm here now. It's alright." They nodded as they let him go. Mary gently pulled him along into the room; Charlotte lay sleeping on the hospital bed with an IV in her arm. The heart monitor beeped steadily as Mary started crying again.

"Oh god, Michael, they-they had to take her left leg and right arm. They said that the bones were damaged beyond repair and that she was lucky. She'll have to have prosthetics, Michael I don't know if I can afford that."

Michael was emotionless; the only difference was that his eyes were blazing red.

"Don't worry about that." He gave her his credit card. "Get her whatever she needs." He walked towards the bed and held Charlotte's left arm. He whispered gently, "Charlotte, forgive me." He bent down and kissed her softly on her forehead, as he walked out Mary called out for him.

"Michael, Michael where are you going?" He stopped briefly.

"Everywhere I go death follows, you're all better off without me. Take care of her, Mary." Michael kept walking as they entire family began protesting. He disappeared from view and sped back towards his mansion. Michael appeared in the garden; everything hit him as he fell to his knees. He was silent first but then roared in anguish, losing control of his telekinetic abilities, shattering the area around him.

For the next six months Michael fell deeper into an already deep depression, it was something he had tried to deal with since he was younger but this was new. It had broken what little resolve Michael still had. Charlotte was the only thing that helped Michael control himself; it was like she had some sort of aura which protected him from his depression. He had tried to commit suicide but he couldn't find a way to kill himself. Bernard had tried to console him but Michael shut him away. He kept himself away from Charlotte and her family for as long as he could. He had seen Charlotte once; the prosthetics that Mary had been able to afford were barely good enough even with Michael's substantial wealth. Charlotte could barely walk and was rapidly losing the will to live. Michael could almost feel her begging him to help her. He decided to put his intelligence to use. He went through his workshop designing two new prosthetic limbs for her which would give her normal movement again. Michael built the limbs out of a lightweight carbon fibre and titanium material. The key was making sure the heart could run the two new limbs. Michael had decided to design sophisticated nano machines which would form a base where the limbs were to be attached. Then a separate group of nano machines would go into the heart. They would improve the heart and make it damn near impossible for Charlotte to have a heart attack. In addition the limbs would be powered by a hydrogen fuel cell which would run for six months each. Though the prosthetics would be cybernetic they would as flexible as Charlotte's other limbs. They would be driven by thought as the limbs would send electrical impulses to the nervous system giving her a sense of feeling.

The build time for the limbs wasn't as long as Michael had thought. He had both the money and the resources to make them better than his first designs. Michael had told Bernard to bring Charlotte and her family to the mansion so that he could attach the limbs. Charlotte had been devastated from the injuries; she had lost the desire to go on and could barely function. Her entire family had suddenly broken apart from the stress. Worse still, her father had not even bothered to help Mary with medical bills. Michael had wanted to snap the bastard's neck but he had kept control. Charlotte walked gently into the main living room with the aid of Bernard and Mary. Mary took the younger children and Bernard into another room so that Michael could work. Charlotte smiled gently at Michael.

"Hey, I've missed you."

Michael was devastated; he hated himself for not being there for her.

"I'm so sorry Charlotte. I should have been able to help you. But I couldn't; I... I understand if you hate me but I thought this could be something good for you."

Charlotte placed her hand on Michael's face soothing him. "Michael, I don't hate you, I love you. I know you did as much as you could and I know you will help me now. So please, let's get started." Michael smiled as he pulled the cybernetic right arm from a small box. He took a syringe and disconnected the old prosthetic. Injecting the nano machines into her muscle, he enabled his almost X-ray vision to watch them split up and travel to the heart. The rest went to the stump and formed a base. He gently attached the prosthetic and heard a small click, signalling that it had formed a seal with the arm.

"Okay, the arm uses electrical pulses that travel through your nervous system to the brain. All you need to do is think about moving the arm." She gasped slightly as she moved it around.

"Michael I... I can feel it. It's working." He smiled and repeated the process with the left leg.

"Okay, now if you can just stand." She stood up instantly and walked towards him. She laughed with joy and hugged Michael as hard as she could.

"Michael it works, it works!" She said as she held him.

He smiled gently as he lifted her up. "It works." He put her down gently and held her hand. "I promise you that I'll never leave you ever again." She smiled as they kissed deeply.

Chapter 2: *Preparation*

Michael got out of his car, driven by Bernard, and walked towards the driver's window.

"Okay, I've got to meet someone and I'll probably be some time. Take the car home and I'll see you later." Bernard nodded and drove off. Though Michael could break the sound barrier by running, he enjoyed driving sometimes. It gave him time to reflect and think on what he was doing for the day. The tall skyscraper had been built in the early eighties and was taller than the Empire State Building and futuristic in nature. Michael always thought that it looked like something out of a science fiction book. The building had a holographic sign reading "Sampson Industries". The company had been set up by Steven Sampson in the early seventies and was at the forefront in medical and aerospace technology. Though Michael was supposed to take control of it, he really didn't feel that he was worthy. Nevertheless he visited the building from time to time using the labs and taking a look at the research and development wing of the building. Michael entered the building and walked towards the elevator. Since he didn't get out much not many people knew him and paid him no attention. The elevator played a cheesy sort of muzak that Michael's father used to like. He stopped at the top floor and walked to a small empty room. A red light covered him.

"Please say your code word," a computerised voice said.

"Charlotte six delta five," Michael responded. The red light switched off and a set of double doors opened before him. The room was filled with multiple hard drives and computer systems. Various holograms followed him showing different pieces of information. He dismissed them with a wave of a hand.

"Freeze right there mister," a girl said. Michael turned around and saw one of his best friends.

"Sarah Robbie. A pleasure to see you." Sarah kept walking toward him in a huff.

"Yeah, yeah, whatever. How did you get in here?" she asked.

"Well I did build this place," Michael retorted. Sarah smoothed her brow in a mildly annoyed way. Michael had known her since they had been very young, they had formed a brother-sister relationship with each other. In her spare time she was a freelance journalist, she had written for the New Yorker. Michael had read her stuff; it was good but she preferred investigative journalism. Michael had known that she had backed away when he and Charlotte had taken their relationship to the next level. Michael had felt sorry for her but she had brushed him off. He remembered the first time he had met her. It seemed like such a long time ago.

Michael had just moved into the eighth grade and was struggling with mixing with normal children. Due to his superhuman brain he was naturally smarter and more aware. That and his powers were developing faster with every year. The knowledge that had been imbued in him from an early age didn't make much sense but Michael was grasping it better every single day. His thirteenth birthday had been quiet, with Charlotte and her mom being the only others in attendance along with Bernard.

Michael moved through school as he normally did, head down and not trying to draw attention to himself. Michael was still a big guy at a young age, he had thought that it would give him an exempt status from being bullied. It didn't; as Michael was that much smarter he was bullied relentlessly. Though he rarely fought back, he was beginning to realise that it wouldn't be long before someone figured out he was different. By age ten his skin was strong enough to break a bully's arm. He had had to roll with their punches so that he didn't hurt anyone else. However he had declared that enough was enough when a bully was picking on Charlotte for being with him. He had lost his temper and thrown the bully through a solid wood door, breaking the bully's collar bone. Bernard had decided to pay off the parents with a considerable amount if they didn't press charges. Bernard had warned Michael to try and keep his head down and leave everyone else alone. *If only they would leave me alone*, he thought as he walked to his next class. That was until he bumped into her. She was shorter than him with long blond hair and a freckled face. She was carrying a bunch of books each to do with science fiction or something of the nature. Michael bent down to help her pick them up and handed them back to her.

He looked her in the eye and simply said, "Sorry. Wasn't looking were I was going."

She shrugged nonchalantly. "S'okay, I was probably doing the same thing." She looked up. "You're Michael, right?"

Michael cocked his head to left. "You know my name, that's rare not many people notice me."

She smiled softly. "You try too hard. I've noticed you since we first met in elementary school." Again Michael

26

was intrigued he really couldn't remember her. Michael had an incredible memory; he didn't forget people that easily. She smiled again. "I said you were good at hiding." She smiled deviously. "I'm better. I noticed you when you pulled that bus out of the Hudson River. I noticed you when you threw that bully through a solid wood door. There was something special about you and I noticed." Michael felt as if someone had thrown a vault at him. He was completely stumped; he quickly recomposed himself and supersped her out of the busy school to a quiet place on campus. Her cool front had cracked. "That was amazing. Did you just break the sound barrier?"

Michael shook his head. "No I normally keep it under 600 mph when I'm travelling around the city and with company. We were still too fast to be seen. So how did you notice? When I pushed the bus out of the water most of the pupils were either too scared or in shock to tell what had happened."

She nodded. "Okay first of all that's awesome. And second of all I wasn't in the bus, I was walking home. I followed the bus because it takes the route that I do and then I saw it career off the bridge into the water. I was the only person that thought to go down to shore to check it out; I videoed the whole thing."

Michael turned his eyes red on command. "You did what!" This time the blond girl's facade shattered and was replaced with primal fear.

"I... I didn't leak it; I kept it to prove my theory." Michael realised that he had scared the girl out of her wits and turned his eyes back to normal.

"What theory?" he asked almost shaking with anger.

"That there are people among us with superhuman abilities either latent or instinctive. Have you ever seen those documentaries about people who have been able to tap into a pool of superhuman strength or other abilities?"

Michael nodded. "It's adrenalin part of a human's natural ability to deal with flight or fight." She nodded in agreement.

"In the normal case yes but I'm talking about stuff like what you did or other cases. I read about someone who was able to fly and I saw someone crumpling tank armour like it was tinfoil in the first Gulf War."

Michael shook his head in disbelief. "You really believe that sort of stuff?"

She smirked. "You can break 600 mph in your shoes and you don't think someone could do the same thing."

Michael shrugged. "Touché; so what do we do now?"

She smiled. "Now I introduce myself: Hi my name's Sarah Robbie. It's nice to meet you." Michael smiled and shook her outstretched hand. Over the next few years, Michael helped Sarah on different journalism cases. However more than enough had got her in dangerous situations and Michael was normally there to save her. On one case, that occurred when they were both 20 years old, Sarah had got caught by a dangerous gang of gangsters. Michael was checking in on her at her apartment which was always messy but this time he had noticed something was wrong. Michael quickly searched the apartment and realised that she was in danger. He searched the city with his vast superhuman hearing. Filtering each sound Michael could distinguish between all of them. Suddenly he picked up Sarah's cry. Superspeeding to the compound Michael burst through the metal gates, moving with incredible speed he dispatched each of the gangsters. Michael burst into the room were Sarah was being held. Time slowed down as Michael blocked bullets and even stopped one intended for Sarah. Michael had easily taken all the targets down. He approached Sarah and took off her blindfold.

"Sarah, don't worry it's me," he said softly as he untied her and comforted her. She didn't waste time; she jumped on Michael hugging him as hard as she could.

"I knew you'd come, it's always you," she said trying to hold back tears. Michael held her close. He would never let anything happen to her.

That was the beginning of a long friendship. Michael had saved her life multiple times mostly when she was busy endangering her own life. She did that a lot. As a peace offering and a promise on her part to keep out of trouble, Michael built this office where she could redirect satellites and provide logistical support. Sarah was probably a foot shorter than Michael but that didn't stop her from bossing him around all the time.

"Yes you may have built it but you can't come here. You're not a member of The Team," she said. Michael smiled. He supersped past her and began typing in some computer commands. Michael had promised Charlotte that he would take her on vacation. He had seen that the foremost Russian ballet group still had tickets. Michael booked it all. He was going to have his private jet fly them there.

"Hey stop," Sarah said as she tried to pull Michael away from the desktop. But she couldn't as much as she tried. Michael chuckled to himself and typed in more commands on the computer. He was checking flight times. Charlotte loved ballet and Michael was able to find tickets for the prima ballerina in Moscow. A gift Michael thought to himself, as well as a vacation.

Sarah hadn't given up. Michael weighed well over 200 pounds. He'd always been a big guy. Not because of training but because he had always been that way. All doctors Michael had seen had said that he was overweight, but the truth was Michael ate less than most people and even then he had a slightly muscular and husky appearance. *Can't please anyone*, he thought. Michael wasn't getting frustrated with Sarah but he needed to get going so he simply lifted Sarah up and placed her to the side.

"I gotta run so I'll see you when I see ya," Michael said as he walked off.

"Hey wait, the stairs are to the left," she called out.

"Keep your eye on the roof camera," he shouted back. Sarah heard a whoosh and rushed back to the computer screen switching it to the roof camera. Michael walked past the camera. He took a breath and suddenly leapt off the roof.

Sarah smiled and said under her breath so he couldn't hear, "That man is one crazy bastard."

Michael landed back on the mansion grounds causing a slight crater in the ground. He stretched and then walked towards the mansion. Michael loved superleaping; he had first discovered it when he was 12. He and Charlotte had been walking home when they were almost run over. Michael had instinctively picked her up and leapt as high as he could. He landed on an office building just opposite their school. From that day on Michael tried not to jump for joy so much.

As he entered the house the phone began to ring. Before Bernard could pick it up Michael got to it first. "Hello, who is it?"

"Michael is that you?" Mary replied.

"Yep it's me. How can I help?" Michael said.

"Oh thank god I caught you in; work is keeping me back. So is it alright if you pick Amy up from school?" she asked.

"Yeah that's fine. I'll be there in a second," Michael said. He said goodbye and put the phone down. Michael checked his watch; he had around five minutes before Amy finished so he supersped over to her school. When Michael had told Charlotte and Mary about his powers, they had agreed that they wouldn't tell the children until they were older. Though that was a good plan Michael had had to reveal his powers to Amy when he saved her from being run down. Despite the fact that Amy was only ten she had promised not to tell anyone. To Michael's surprise she had kept it a secret and had not told a soul. Amy walked out of her school and spotted Michael standing not too far away. She broke out into a sprint and high-fived Michael who smiled at her.

"Hey Mike, what are you doing here?"

Michael smiled and said, "Well your mom is working late and your sister had to pick up Ryan. So she sent me to get you. How was your day?"

Amy shrugged but let out a small smile. "It was good. I got a new teacher who was really cool and we started learning about history. Mike, do you think it would be alright if we got some ice cream?" she said.

Michael smiled and nodded a little. "Sure, as long as you don't tell your mom." Michael held her tight and supersped towards the nearest ice cream parlour. When Michael supersped with someone, he formed a shield around them which protected the passenger from any danger. After getting ice cream they walked back towards Amy's apartment. Michael took her up to the house and put her down slowly.

Amy looked up at Michael and said, "We're going on holiday tomorrow, aren't we Michael?"

Michael looked down and smiled. "Yep, tomorrow morning. I'll be coming to pick you up and we'll go on my new plane." Amy smiled and finished her ice cream. She gave him a hug and said goodbye to Michael who smiled and returned to his house. Michael had started packing last night but he only needed a few things more. He checked his watch and set his alarm for the following morning. Michael sat down with a glass of Scotch. He began to unwind and wait for their holiday.

Michael was troubled by what he called bad thoughts. Ever since he had suffered from depression he was plagued by suicidal thoughts. It was when Michael realised that due to the incredible toughness of his skin, he couldn't be hurt. *Maybe this time*, he thought as he walked into the kitchen. Bernard was elsewhere so Michael was alone for the moment. Taking one of the sharpest knives he could find he pressed it against his skin. He could feel the cold metal against his skin. Closing his eyes he jabbed it into his wrist; opening his eyes, he was unsurprised to find the knife bent against his skin. In anger Michael tossed the broken blade away and headed back to his Scotch. *Time to drown my sorrows*, he thought; until he heard a scream. It was a woman asking for help somewhere in the distance. Michael tried to ignore it until he realised no one was going to help. The realisation caused Michael to grimace but he decided not to intervene. He took another drink from his glass and knocked it back, he was finally at peace; until the voice started nagging him again. Michael smashed his fist into the wall; one night Michael thought just one night so I can sleep. He stood up and grabbed his coat and then disappeared from view.

The woman was scared; she tried to help her boyfriend back up but there was nothing she could do. She desperately yelled help again but there was no one to help her now. Suddenly a gust of wind blew past them all. Michael arrived in a second. The woman was about to be attacked. Presumably her boyfriend had tried to stop the assault until he was knocked out. Michael supersped into one of the attackers sending him flying into a wall. The other one pulled a gun on Michael. The man fired three shots into Michael's stomach, the bullets bouncing off his hard-as-steel skin. The man looked up in astonishment at him; Michael lifted him up and threw the man away. The last one had guts. Even after Michael had beaten his two other friends the guy wasn't backing down. He had a switchblade and swiped at Michael. He dodged and let the man stab him. The blade bent and crumpled against his skin like the other one. Michael looked up at the man who had a look of fear on his face. Michael smiled and pushed the man away with his telekinesis. *Done,* he thought, making sure that the woman and the man were still too frightened to look. He supersped back home. The time was now 10:30 and Michael went up to his bedroom with another glass of Scotch. Michael examined his glass, the brown liquid glistened in the light. Though Michael was strong he had always enjoyed Scotch. It helped him get on with his life. Charlotte and Bernard had voiced their concerns that he drank too much. Michael had dismissed their claims as stupid. Michael's metabolism burned up the alcohol faster than anyone else on the world. Still he looked at the almost empty bottle of Scotch that he had brought up with him. Maybe he had drunk a bit too much he thought and placed the glass on his bedside table. He lay in his bed and stared at the ceiling. Michael hated sleeping; mainly because he couldn't stop thinking. There was always something new he could make or think about, but it was better if he could just shut his eyes for a few hours at least then he could say he slept. At least that would make him just a bit more normal.

Michael's alarm went off at 5:45; in truth Michael could have stopped the alarm, he had already been awake for around two hours. Getting up, he showered and dressed and made his way to the car waiting outside. Bernard was just placing Michael's case in the trunk as he opened the back seat and sat down. Opening the fridge he poured himself a double Scotch and downed it in seconds. He sighed softly as they set off towards Charlotte's apartment. Michael checked his phone and put in a quick call to the pilots waiting for them.

"Hey guys, I've just set off, so we should be there in around half an hour. Get the jet ready to go."

The pilot's voice crackled over the phone. "Got it Mr Sampson, we'll be ready."

Michael ended the call and smiled stupidly to himself. The private jet was a model Michael had built when he had turned 20. The plane was the size of a business jet and could fly higher and faster than any other passenger jet in service. This meant that a normal flight of nine hours fifty minutes was cut down to six hours. It also meant that the flight would be relaxed and they could get some sleep. The drive was calm and uneventful; there wasn't that much traffic on the road so they arrived in record time. Michael exited the car and saw Charlotte and her family waiting in the lobby. He hugged Charlotte and grabbed their bags disappearing to the car and back. Michael had noticed that Ryan and Amy had fallen asleep while waiting. Charlotte picked up Ryan and Michael gently picked up Amy. They laid them in the back of the car so they could sleep for the rest of the way. Mary had elected to sit in the front with Bernard while Michael and Charlotte were in the back. Amy gently leaned on Michael as the car drove off towards the airport. Charlotte smiled at Michael; they didn't speak to let the younger children sleep.

As the name would suggest, JFK airport was named after John F Kennedy in 1963 in memoriam of the late president. The airport covered 4,930 acres and had six terminals with more than 125 aircraft operating there. Statistically, it was the nineteenth busiest airport in the world and Michael could tell why. Even though it was 6:30 in the morning it was already busy with multiple people trying to get flights. Michael exited the car and helped Charlotte and her mother out. Charlotte's younger brother Ryan and sister Amy crawled out of the limousine. They still looked too tired and were going to be moody.

Michael bent down and said, "You know there are beds on the plane so you can have a nice long sleep." The two children smiled at him and began running forward, Charlotte's mother increased speed to keep up with them. Michael and Charlotte took it slowly and waved off Bernard who was stopping behind. They made their way through airport security and went out to see the private plane.

Ryan's eyes widened as soon as he saw the plane. Michael smiled; he had designed the plane to look as futuristic as possible, he thought that added character. The pilots greeted them as they entered the plane. Michael showed Mary and the kids to their rooms. There were seats on one side of the plane two in a row. The seats were made of the finest leather and were outfitted with an entertainment system. There were three king-sized rooms; each had a bathroom en suite, with a mini bar and a television. The smaller room had two single beds with the same things that were in the larger rooms. The last room was an entertainment room with a projector and games system. Though this was only a prototype; the next one Michael was building would be bigger than the latest jumbo jet. *That would be cool*, Michael thought.

The plane's engines began starting up, Charlotte walked though the cabin. She had just tucked her two younger siblings into bed. Hopefully they would sleep all the way through the flight. Michael saw her as he was walking into his room. Charlotte followed him in and closed the door behind her. Michael looked up at her and smiled slyly.

"You do know your bedroom is the one further down." She looked at him with coy look in her eye.

"Well this looks more comfortable than mine." She walked toward him and kicked her shoes off slowly.

Michael stood up at full height and met her before they got to bed. Michael heard the pilots doing their safety checks and informing the passengers of what to do if there was an emergency. Michael saw Charlotte walk towards him and smiled gently. He reached out with his telekinesis and switched off the lights.

An hour into the flight and Michael was lying in bed with Charlotte in his arms. Sex was a difficult thing for Michael. Not because he couldn't over some sense of morality but because of his physiology and abilities. Michael realised early on when he and Charlotte got deeper into their relationship that he could seriously hurt her. So until Michael learned more of his powers he and Charlotte swore never to go too far. Michael stood up slowly not wanting to disturb Charlotte. Michael opened room doors and walked outside. Suddenly Mary appeared out of nowhere. Michael had checked that Ryan and Amy were asleep and he thought the same of Mary. He was wrong.

"Oh hi, Mrs Phoenix," he said sheepishly.

"First of all put a shirt on," she said looking at Michael's torso. Michael disappeared for second and then reappeared with a T-shirt on. Mary stood there with her arms folded and motioned for him to sit. Mary was fond of Michael but was a bit stricter when it came down to him and Charlotte. Mary was a smart lady mainly because she was a trained psychologist and because with age came experience. She took her seat opposite Michael.

"So what were you doing?" Michael scratched his head slowly.

"Um nothing." She looked at him. "Seriously nothing." She kept looking at him. "No really nothing. We just snuggled for an hour and she fell asleep, nothing."

Mary sighed heavily. "You promised you would find out

where your powers came from. In the last few months you still haven't done anything."

Michael looked down. "I have been looking. There's nothing. No birth certificate, no record of date of birth. I had to make one up. There's not even a record of my mother. I may as well not exist. The only thing I know about my dad is what people have told me and even that's not a lot. There's no needle that can pierce my skin so the blood is out. The swabs I've take from my mouth are almost, I don't know, alien in origin. They feature lipids and proteins that you wouldn't find in a human; that you wouldn't find in any other creature on earth. Other cells that aren't in a human body, even organs. I actually think I have organs that don't have names. I'll have to start making names up for them. The truth is that I don't know what I am. I may be a genetically engineered human or something else." Michael kept looking down at his shoes. Mary took Michael's hands in hers.

"You've never had any parents. Bernard's done his best and he has raised a wonderful boy. You're kind and I can completely tell that you will always love Charlotte. You just have to find out more about your powers. There are other heroes in the world. Marvellous wonders who are helping people daily; but one day I believe you will become our greatest inspiration and hope."

Michael exhaled slowly. "My powers have never been easy. Sometimes I have dreams, horrific dreams of the world burning before me, like I've destroyed it just for fun. I don't want people to fear me but I have to hide what I am. That's why no one outside of us knows Michael Sampson well; I never attend any of these billionaire parties, or dated supermodels because I don't know what I am and how I am. I've tried to ask Bernard about my father and who he was but Bernard can't remember anything about him. I've tried to map my powers; theoretically they should have stopped by age 16. But they haven't they're growing every day; I can break the sound barrier in a second and lift a tank with my pinkie finger. There's nothing normal about this. I-I, I've considered leaving New York to try and get a handle on my powers. But…" He paused for a second and looked into his room. A tear formed in his eye. "She gives me hope. When she had her accident I-I thought I'd never be able to go on, even after I built the new prosthetics. But look at her. She's thriving she still walks and she isn't scared. As much as I draw my power from energy, I draw more of it for her. I-I love her," Michael said with his head in his hands.

Mary kissed him softly on his cheek. "And she loves you. As much as you don't want to admit it she can't go on without you. The same with her brother and sister; you've touched our lives and give us hope. I know you'll figure this out and eventually you'll become the best of us all," she said and went back to her room.

Michael smiled and said under his breath, "Hell of woman." Michael stopped holding back and let his superhearing run wild. He heard everything, from cries of help to a mother singing a song to calm her child. So many people each wanting closure on their lives, trying to find hope in their lives. Michael activated his GPS and looked at the flight time remaining. Three hours left he thought. Michael made his way back to his room. Charlotte was still sleeping. He got in bed next to her and looked at her beautiful face. *I will find out what I am*, he thought and kissed her gently.

Two hours later Michael was dressed and showered. He heard a light yawn and watched as Charlotte woke up. She walked to him and kissed him gently on his forehead and walked into the bathroom. Michael walked out of the room and saw Amy and Ryan watching cartoons. He sat down next to Amy and joined them in watching them. Michael smiled at the cartoons. They were about a superhero flying around saving people. Flying; Michael thought that was silly, though it wasn't the strangest thing he'd ever seen. He ruffled their hair and walked towards the flight deck. The pilots were beginning their checks for landing.

Michael asked, "How we doing up here?" The co-pilot turned round to Michael.

"First let me say that this plane is an incredible piece of engineering; flies perfectly. Anyway, we're about 45 minutes out from Moscow. It's around five °C in Moscow so I'd wear something warm. Oh and it's raining." Michael smiled and nodded. He walked back to his seat and checked the itinerary that he had planned out. First they would go to their hotel. Michael had arranged for them to stay at the best hotel. The first performance was on Thursday and would start at 7:00. Michael had planned for a tour of the Kremlin and the Red Square. This would last till the 6:30. *Perfect*, Michael thought, everything Charlotte wanted for a holiday.

The plane touched down softly. Michael went down to the luggage compartment. The plane had its own X-ray machine fitted so that pictures of the luggage were relayed to airport security. This made it faster to get through. Michael brought the luggage up and quickly checked his case. It contained two hydrogen power cells that ran Charlotte's prosthetics. It had been six months since the last power cells were replaced. Michael knew that any day now the power cells would run out so he had brought a spare set. There was a Sampson Industry in Moscow so Michael had been able to arrange for a pick up as soon as they cleared airport security. The plane door's opened slowly. Charlotte got her stuff off Michael and was the first to disembark. Ryan and Amy followed quickly and then Mary followed them. Michael did one final check of the plane and smiled with approval. He'd built a hell of a plane.

Michael left the plane and caught up with Charlotte and the rest of her family. The security checks were not that long, but Michael could tell that Charlotte and her family were tired. Unlike Michael they possessed no incredible stamina. The limousine pulled up outside the airport, Michael could tell that it was his. He opened the door and let Charlotte and her family climb in. The Russian chauffeur got out of his car. He was around 6ft tall with close-cropped grey hair and piercing blue eyes.

He said in a heavy Russian accent, "Welcome to Russia Mr Sampson."

Michael smiled and replied in Russian, "Thank you for picking us up friend. Do you know the journey?"

This surprised the chauffeur and he replied in Russian, "Your Russian is very good. If you would enter the car please I will be able to get you there as fast as I can." Michael smiled and entered the car. The journey wasn't that long and they arrived at the beautiful Hilton hotel. Charlotte looked at the hotel.

"It's beautiful Michael but we didn't have to stop at a hotel like this."

Michael looked at her. "This is your gift so I made sure everything was perfect." She smiled sweetly at him and kissed him gently on his cheek. Michael helped her out of the car. Thanking the driver he and the rest of Charlotte's family walked into the hotel. Michael had bought the penthouse for him and Charlotte and the other top-floor room for Mary, Ryan and Amy. The elevator ride wasn't long to the top floor and when they disembarked they said goodbye to Mary and the kids. Michael and Charlotte entered the penthouse. Charlotte put her bags neatly down on to the bed and went to the balcony. She looked over the Kremlin and Red Square and looked back at Michael.

"You're the best you know that right?" she said softly.

"Is this because of my money or me?" Michael asked sarcastically. She hit him softly on his arm and they began kissing. Michael was about to lift her up when he suddenly heard his phone beeping in New York. "Aw dammit I forgot my phone," Michael said.

Charlotte looked and said, "You're silly you know that as well."

Michael smiled. "I'll be back in a minute, well less if I want." Michael disappeared from view and went back to New York. He found his phone on a desk and began his trip back when suddenly he saw figure watching him. Michael was travelling at insane speeds but the figure looked at Michael exactly. The figure was tall and slender and reminded Michael of something that he couldn't put his finger on. Michael thought nothing of it and reappeared next to Charlotte in Russia. "Now show will we pick up from where we left off?" Charlotte smiled and so did Michael.

Chapter 3: *Stay here and don't come out*

The tour guide was defiantly earning his money for the tour.

"If you turn to the right you will see the beautiful artwork of our beloved Kremlin." Michael watched as the all of the tourists turned towards the Kremlin. Built in 1485 the Kremlin had stood as the seat of Russian power for the last five hundred years. The word Kremlin meant "fortress" and Michael could see why. The place was defiantly built to last; armed guards patrolled the streets with assault rifles.

He turned back to Charlotte. "Are you enjoying the tour?" he asked.

"It's beautiful. I don't think you could do anything better." She looked at Michael and smiled deeply.

The tour was moving towards the Kremlin for a closer look at the beautiful building. Michael switched his vision and he saw that Charlotte's power cells were about give out. She looked at him and a visible tear formed at the base of her eye. Michael sighed and linked his arm with hers gently walking her to a cafe where they could sit down. Mary, Ryan and Amy followed them. Michael pulled the two new fuel cells out of their case and prepared to switch them. He pressed a part of Charlotte's right arm and the skin lifted and moved back. Michael took the old power cell out and pressed a shutdown button on the back of it. It was a fail-safe that would form a nano shield around the cell so that it could let the cell die by itself.

Michael quickly did the same with her left leg and said, "All good." Colour retuned to Charlotte's arm and leg. She smiled at Michael and mouthed thank you. Suddenly as he turned Amy and Ryan began asking him things at multiple times. Overwhelmed, he said, "Okay, okay one at a time."

Ryan went first. "We saw a toy shop on the other side of the bridge."

Then Amy said, "Can we go there please?" They both put on their best sad faces and their eyes seemed to widen to try and get Michel to go.

He smiled at them. "Yeah come on then let's go." They began jumping up and down rapidly, cheering. Michael turned to Mary. "We'll be back soon. Make sure she doesn't start jumping up and down." Mary nodded and Michael set off.

Michael, Amy and Ryan began walking. They got over the bridge when suddenly Michael saw a figure standing on the river. Michael remembered the figure; it looked like the same one who blew the theatre up, the same one who crippled Charlotte. Michael began walking towards the figure when suddenly it flew upwards and broke the sound barrier. Amy and Ryan came back to see what Michael was doing. Suddenly Michael heard ticking and realised what it was. Michael had to act quickly, he lifted them both up with his telekinesis and threw them back towards the cafe. In the last moment he slowed them so they would survive the fall. Michael forced all of his power into a field around the bomb. The air cracked with his power and seemed to split apart as if the very fabric of reality was being torn to pieces. The sun was out and shining on Michael fully, without a cloud in the sky. His body was absorbing the all the energy and he was roaring with all of his power trying to stop the bomb, but it wasn't enough. Michael was overwhelmed and suddenly he was thrown back into the cafe.

Michael shook off the damage and quickly saw the cafe was about to cave in on Charlotte and her family. Michael quickly rolled under the wall and took the weight. He lifted the wall and quickly scanned Ryan and Amy. There was no damage. A wave of dust rushed towards them and flooded the cafe. Michael quickly formed a shield around them. The dust bounced around the shield but none got in. Michael put his arms down and the shield dissipated. He looked back at Charlotte and her family. They were shaken and looked ill.

"We gotta move. We'll get out and head for the Kremlin. It'll probably be safest." They nodded and they began moving out with Charlotte and Mary carrying the children. The once beautiful Kremlin had been almost ripped apart from the bomb. Again the bomb had not been explosive it had been almost like his telekinetic power. Michael kicked a car out of their path. The area was littered with dead people and wreckage. Michael turned round to Charlotte. "Hide the kid's faces; it's not something they should see." Charlotte nodded and let Amy bury her face into her shoulder. Mary did the same with Ryan. Michael looked through the dust and made a mental note of the amount of dead. It would be important to document all of this.

Out of nowhere a vehicle suddenly burst out of the dust. Michael recognised what it was: a Russian BTR, a heavily armoured personnel carrier. Michael breathed a sigh of relief. It was obviously a Russian army version so they must be looking for civilians he thought. Suddenly the main gun swivelled and aimed at Michael. In the seconds he had to react he supersped Charlotte and her family into the Kremlin.

"Stay here and don't come out," he ordered. Michael ran towards the BTR. Three shots thundered out and smacked into Michael. He was slowed down but he kept going. Michael's eyes tuned solid red as he ran and at the last moment swung on to the gun. He landed and punched the armour cracking it; he pulled the driver out and threw him a metre into the air. As Michael kept dismantling the BTR a blur caught his attention. Thinking nothing of it, Michael leapt back off the broken BTR. Michael looked around and saw a tank coming towards him. The tank had priority; Michael dodged the tank shell and leapt on to it. He grabbed at the turret and pulled it straight off and then overturned the tank. Michael turned his attention to the blur that had flashed by him. He was Michael's height but had a more slender build. The figure's eyes flashed a sharp blue and then switched to a dark green. The figure removed its hood and revealed a scar that stretched from his collarbone to below his chin. His long black hair reached down to his shoulders and a portion of it fell down as his fringe. On his belt was a black sheath that hid a blade of some sort. The figure was not the same one that attacked New York.

"That bomb was used to attack New York two years ago. It is unlike anything I've ever seen. Tell me who you are and I'll pull my punches," Michael said. The figure looked up and revealed an emotionless face.

"You are... amusing child. Even when you are fighting you are slow; I'm surprised you saw me. You are in no position to make demands of me. I stayed my blade from you and your family once before but this time I will remove you from the equation," the figure said in a deadly serious but calm voice. The voice sent shivers down his spin.

"Who are you!" Michael yelled.

"Again you make demands of me; you are not worthy to know my name. But as I was taught to reveal my name to those that will die from my blade, I am Knight Warrior Nor-Veer. I am here for one reason and one reason alone: to kill you and remove you from our mission," Nor-Veer said in his still calm voice as he unsheathed his katana. The katana had ceremonial markings over it and was completely black. Michael had to act quickly as Nor came down with a swipe. Michael dodged and countered the swipe with a quick three-punch combo. Before Nor could react Michael used the overturned tank as a weapon he smashed on Nor. He went for another but Veer sliced straight through it. While Veer was busy getting through the tank Michael landed a kick which sent him back. Nor fell back and at the very last second flipped to a standing position. He remained cool and collected as he prepared to charge Michael again. Nor was relentless, he wouldn't stop; but he was silent, not even grunting when he put effort into his swipes. He was almost faster than Michael and the fighting style he used was unlike anything Michael had seen before. Michael continued to duck and dive but the last swipe moved with incredible speed. Michael had seconds to react and he formed a telekinetic shield to hold the blade back. The air rippled with power as Michael desperately tried to keep the sword there. He couldn't believe the sword was breaking through the shield and Michael's telekinesis was fragmenting the air around him. In the end he couldn't stop the sword. Pushing back, Michael summoned a telekinetic blast which sent Nor back slightly but left no lasting damage. Michael took a breather and wiped a small amount of blood from his mouth. Nor re-engaged Michael and slammed him to the ground; he placed his foot on Michael's neck and dragged his sword towards his dog tags. Nor raised an eyebrow and cut the necklace. "I bet you don't even know what this is, do you?"

Michael grabbed his foot and snorted. "This was my father's and I know he wouldn't have had anything to do with a creep like you."

Nor scoffed at the words. "Child, you can't even begin to understand who I am and who you father was."

His eyes turned red as Michael kicked Nor off him and pushed back. This wasn't working; Nor had the advantage in close quarters combat, maybe he could catch him off guard at long range. Michael leapt into the air trying to get away and break the fight up, but as soon as he got into the air Nor appeared hovering there. He rushed Michael backwards towards the Kremlin and they smashed into the wall. Nor beat Michael and kneed him in the stomach; Michael doubled over in pain. He felt a sharp pain in his back. Nor had brought his elbow down on his back sharply. Michael quickly grabbed Nor's arm and punched him through the structure. Using Nor's momentum they flew through the Kremlin breaking apart concrete and brick. Michael quickly grabbed Nor in a suplex and threw him back down. Michael grabbed on to a ledge and pulled himself up. He took a breath and let sun shine on his body, but suddenly he saw a helicopter coming towards him. The attack helicopter began firing at Michael, the cannon shells bounced off and missiles fired into his body. Quickly Michael leapt on to the helicopter; he telekinetically pulled the pilot into the glass to knock him out. He shoved his hand into the rotors. As soon as the rotor hit his hand it snapped, Michael leapt off and just as he was about land on the ground he felt a sharp pain in his stomach. Michael looked down and saw Nor's blade had run him through. Michael had never felt pain like this before. The pain scared him, for the first time he felt helpless. He heard Nor make an amused chuckle. Blood poured off Nor's sword down his shirt.

"Feel the metal of your world. This metal can split atoms, even your skin is not safe from its sting. The blade has been tempered in the fires of the planet's core." Nor's words were drowned out by the ringing in his ears. Nor looked down at the Kremlin and hesitated for a second. He whispered into Michael's ear, "I didn't want it to come to this." He turned his attention back to the Kremlin. "Fire on the building, full spread." Charlotte was in there.

Michael put both his hands on the blade and began bending it. The metal cut through his hands but Michael continued to bend the blade. Summoning every ounce of strength he had he snapped the blade. He wrenched the one piece out of his abdomen. Nor looked dumbfounded; his normal calm facade was broken for just an instant.

"That's not possible," he said. Michael took the chance while his defences were down and headbutted Nor from behind, he then delivered a sharp kick to Nor's stomach and landed two punches which sent Nor backwards. Michael hit Nor with a telekinetic blast. He hoped that would be the end of him but somehow he knew it would not be the last time today. Michael had not been able to intercept the missiles in time. Michael willed himself down to the Kremlin. For a second he thought he was flying.

The missiles blew apart the Kremlin's last supports and the structure was about to give in. Michael willed himself to increase speed and he fell under the building on his knees. He looked at Charlotte and braced himself for the weight.

"Charlotte on your knees now," he said before the weight hit him. Michael roared as all the weight of the Kremlin fell on his shoulders. There was no light anywhere. Michael could still see perfectly; his extraordinary vision enabling him to see through the dark. Michael could still hear people screaming and crying for help. "Charlotte, press the button on my watch now." Charlotte did so. A small holographic screen appeared out of the watch. Sarah's face appeared. "Wait, how did you get this number?"

"Sarah enough of that we need backup in Russia, something is going down. Send the big guns."

"You got it, the alert is out." The screen switched off.

"Michael why are you bleeding?" Charlotte said with a quiver in her voice. Michael looked down, there was a piece of metal stuck in his stomach and the wound was still fully open. Michael had managed to pull most of the blade out of his stomach but a small shard was left in his abdomen. For some reason it was stopping him from absorbing any energy; not that there was any to absorb down there. His skin tone had become pale and his eyes were burning red but shimmering, a side effect from not having enough energy. Michael winced. The weight was getting more intense.

"Charlotte I need you to pull out the small piece of metal in the wound," he asked. Charlotte wasn't squeamish. She dug her hand into the wound and pulled the metal out. Michael took a deep breath and the wound began healing. "I need to get us out of here but I don't think I can lift this. I'm going to have to blast a way out of here." They looked at him and nodded. Michael didn't feel good about the idea; his telekinesis used a lot of energy and at the moment he barely had any. He focused and sent one blast. There was a sound like thunder as Michael's telekinesis smashed into the rock. There was hardly a crack. Michael tried again and forced himself to put more effort into the next blast. The result was no different. Michael roared and tried again.

"Damn it to hell," Michael yelled. "I can't blast through it. There's no energy for me to absorb."

Mary looked at him quizzically. "What does that mean? Absorbing energy?"

Before Michael could answer Charlotte said, "His body works as absorption unit. He can absorb different types of energy but solar or sunlight is better than anything." Michael smiled, the girl knew everything he thought.

"Alright listen I'm going to have to lift this off us. But it may take time. There's not that much air down here so conserve your oxygen. Take a deep breath and hold it. I don't need to breathe so I'm aright." They all nodded.

Suddenly Amy piped up, "Are you going to save us Michael?"

Michael looked at her and smiled. "Don't worry kiddo super Michael to rescue." Michael began passing the weight to his massive shoulders. He pushed but it wouldn't budge. He tried again. He could feel the wreckage begin to move. "Come on dammit," Michael yelled. He pushed again putting all of his strength into it and began lifting the pile. With one final effort he overturned the structure. Michael looked at the sunlight. His eyes turned red and his veins turned yellow. Michael began feeling better, as he helped Charlotte up and let her get a breather.

Amy turned around to him and said, "You're a superhero."

Michael smiled. "I guess I am."

Michael tore his tattered shirt off and threw it down. He moved some rubble and found his necklace; the chain had been cut apart by the blade. He picked it up and placed it in his pocket for safekeeping. He suddenly heard jet engines; he turned round and looked further using his enhanced vision.

"We got bad news coming our way; a squadron of fighter jets. Stand behind me now." Michael thrust his palm forward and formed a shield that was able to ward off missiles. "I need to deal with them. Stay here within the shield and you'll be fine." Michael switched to battle mode and began analysing the area. He had always had an uncanny sense of how to fight and how to strategise. He isolated the first fighter jet and leapt toward it, ripping the tail fin off. The plane began diving; Michael held on and leapt off at the right moment on to another. He smashed his foot through the plane's fuselage. *Two down*, he thought. Michael saw another jet aim and fire a missile at him. Using his superspeed he grabbed the missile and threw it back at the jet. Michael smiled at his success but he rested too soon. Another jet locked on and fired a missile at him. The explosion sent Michael hurtling back to the ground. More jets suddenly began targeting him. Michael couldn't win this. Suddenly a blur ripped through the remaining planes. The figure landed in front of Michael.

He breathed a sigh of relief and said, "Oh it's you."

Adam Spence looked like the average Californian surfer. He had white sandy hair and an athletic build. He stood at around six foot two and weighed 200 pounds. The only difference was that he possessed a set of white angel wings. His wingspan was exactly 18 feet. The wings could propel him to supersonic speeds. In addition he possessed incredible strength and speed. Another power was his ability to expel a vast source of kinetic energy through his vocal cords. Michael had never seen this ability used but he had heard that it could shatter a mountain at full power. The most outlandish thing about him was the costume which was silver and blue. On his chest were a pair of angel's wings which signified his name.

"Hey Mike good to see you again; Charlotte always a pleasure. Sorry I was late guys, flood in Africa kept me occupied. What can I do for you?" Spence said. Adam's hero name was Angel. He had earned it after people had seen his angelic wings.

"Damn good to see you man. That squadron almost had me beat. There's something else; someone attacked me. He was strong, stronger than anything else I've ever seen," Michael replied. More jets were coming.

"Right, first things first, we take down those planes. But why would the army deploy their own planes against civilians? Strange," Angel said.

Michael nodded. "I don't think they're actually with the army. I think they're more with the guy who attacked me. But you're right let's take care of those jets."

Michael superleaped into air and Angel flew at the jets. Michael threw himself at the plane and ripped the canopy off the top of the jet. The pilot looked in horror at Michael as he reached in and threw the pilot out. Angel flew straight into one jet ripping it into shreds. Another jet doubled back and fired on Angel's wings, the bullets harmlessly bouncing off. Angel turned around and shot through the jet's wings. Michael realised the plane he was on was going down and leapt on to another. He reached into the plane and used telekinesis to rip the plane in two. Three planes flew towards them. Angel grabbed Michael and threw him towards one of the planes. Michael smashed into the plane's cockpit and broke his way through it. Angel flew towards another and cut it from the cockpit all the way to the tail fin. The penultimate plane fired a barrage of missiles at Angel. Before Adam could react, Michael willed himself in front of them and telekinetically crushed the plane. Angel mouthed a quick thank you. The squadron was almost done with. Michael let Angel take the last one down. As he fell back on to the ground he saw Charlotte and her family helping people up through the rubble.

Michael was more concerned with the whereabouts of Nor. Michael suddenly heard a boom and then saw Angel fighting against Nor. Angel was an amazing fighter but he was completely outclassed. With a massive blow from Nor, Angel was sent hurtling towards Michael who leapt in towards him and caught Angel. His chest was bloodied. Michael helped him sit up.

"Is that the guy you were talking about?" he said gesturing to Nor-Veer who was floating in the air brandishing the broken and mangled sword. Michael was worried; he'd never seen Angel like this before. Angel was the people's best hero, nothing ever stopped him. But Nor-Veer had thrown him down faster than he had beaten Michael. Nor hovered down slowly and prepared to attack.

"More lambs to the slaughter. If you leave now I will not pursue you; your death will come soon enough."

Angel smiled as he spat some blood out. "You must not know who I am, so let me educate you: I am Angel, one of the greatest superheroes in the world. I have devoted myself to protecting those around me who cannot defend themselves and I will gladly give my life to do it."

Nor sighed softly. "A shame, I had hoped to get through this battle without getting more blood on my hands than was needed." Michael adopted a combat stance and readied himself, but suddenly a blur knocked Nor down to the ground. A figure stood between Michael, Angel and Nor.

"Hey, beware my power," the hero named Bolt said.

Bolt's real name was Andrew Booker. He was five foot eleven and a living embodiment of speed. His hair was shaved thin and he possessed an athletic body. His African American features made his skin look bronze under the sun. Booker's powers enabled him to move at the speed of light. He had been seen breaking the sound barrier just by jogging. In addition he was strong enough to bench press around ten tons. His metabolism burned almost 40 times faster than the average human's. He wore a blue uniform with red lightning bolts on his chest. Unlike Angel's costume, Bolt's was composed of a woven titanium Kevlar skin which protected him from damage. Though he was durable, bullets could hurt him and wound him. However his abilities enabled him to heal incredibly fast. Bolt helped Angel to his feet, who was healing fast. Nor burst out of the rubble.

"Okay let's do this. Attack plan delta five," Angel said.

"Wait what?" Michael asked.

"Just follow our lead," Bolt said. Bolt went first and broke the sound barrier throwing himself into Nor faster than he could react. He quickly pushed himself up and quite literally began running circles around Nor to keep him off balance. Bolt saw his chance and landed an elbow blow into Nor's stomach. Angel leapt into the air and flew as fast as he could and landed a three-punch combo. Angel didn't make the same mistake of trying to disarm Nor this time. He went on the full offensive and began hitting Nor as hard as possible. Nor was still trying to deal with Bolt and wasn't focused on Michael or Angel. Michael supersped forward, he dodged Nor's downward swipe and combined his telekinesis with his fist and smashed Nor down. Nor leapt upward and ignored Bolt and Angel but flew like a torpedo towards Michael sending him flying into the ruins of the Kremlin. Nor pushed Michael with some effort as he held him in place but still didn't utter a sound. Michael desperately tried to break loose. He punched Nor as hard as he could trying to free himself. Michael saw Bolt shoot forward into the ruins breaking the sound barrier. He rushed into Nor punching him at the speed of sound. With their united efforts Michael was able to break free. Using his telekinesis Michael stopped Nor-Veer in his tracks smashing him down to the ground. Bolt and Michael combined their attacks disorientating Nor with their joint speed.

"Get him out here so we can hold him down," Angel yelled. Michael and Bolt nodded and tackled Nor out of the ruins throwing him down on to the ground outside. Angel swooped down at the speed of sound ramming him into the ground. He began throwing his punches at superspeed to try and halt him in his path. Nor threw Angel off him and pushed Bolt back with his telekinesis. Michael rushed Nor grabbing him and smacking him against the ground as hard as he could. Just as they were getting a hold on him Nor made his first sound since he had started the fight.

"ENOUGH!" His voice sounded like thunder and it shattered the glass around the area. He combined his strength with his telekinesis throwing them off him. Michael lifted a chunk of rock from him. Bullets bounced off his back. He turned around and saw a soldier reloading his assault rifle. Michael used his telekinesis to lift him up and throw him at a lump of stone. Angel lifted a tank that was about to fire on Michael and threw it down. Michael nodded at him and Angel nodded back.

"We need a game changer," Angel said as they regrouped.

"What you thinking?" Bolt asked.

"You remember that time in *Sri Lanka* when I had to stop that tsunami? I'm gonna have use it again. See if it will stop him."

"But if you lose control, you'll wreck the area."

"Then I'll I have to be careful. Michael can you focus your telekinesis in to a beam?" Angel asked.

"I've never attempted it before but I can try," Michael said.

"Good. Bolt clear the civilians away from here we'll hold him back," Angel said. Bolt nodded and supersped away. Angel's eyes turned a darker shade of blue. He took a deep breath and suddenly Michael's hearing went crazy. He was sure that his ears were bleeding profusely. The area in front of Angel was being blown apart. Nor fell on the ground his ears bleeding, screaming with pain. Michael focused his telekinesis and a beam of energy shot at Nor. It was working; Nor was on his knees rapidly losing consciousness. Nor looked at Michael and sneered. He began forming a telekinetic shield around him. Both Michael's telekinesis and Angel's shout began to fold around him. Michael concentrated and formed a low level telepathic link with Angel. Michael's telepathy wasn't powerful but he could form links with people for a short time.

"Angel he's formed a shield around him. It's dispelling our powers."

Angel nodded and said, *"Got it, I'll have to increase damage. You do the same thing."* Angel's shout began increasing in power. The shout was making Michael feel sick but he focused and put everything he had into his telekinesis and made sure the beam was at its full power. The shield around Nor began breaking and once again he was thrown to the ground and this time he wasn't getting up. Michael thought they were beating him and began to power down his telekinesis. Suddenly Nor shot up into the air breaking the sound barrier. Angel stopped using his power and Michael fell to his knees and wiped the blood from his ears.

"Never do that again," he said as Angel helped him to his feet.

Bolt supersped toward them. "There's a military checkpoint just outside the city. I dropped the civilians there. They should be good." Michael nodded.

Angel looked up at the sky. "We need to find out who that guy was. I'm going after him." With that Angel flew into the air and broke the sound barrier. Michael and Bolt looked at each other and shrugged.

Angel activated his comm system. "Sarah I need you to track any unidentified objects leaving Russia."

"Did you get to Michael in time? Well obviously you did otherwise you wouldn't be asking me this. Hold on I've got something. Angel I don't know what it is but it's going faster than any plane I've ever seen before, you better kick it into gear. Activate warp speed or hyperdrive." Angel smiled and improved his rate. His wings began rapidly beating as he increased with speed. Angel saw the criminal know as Nor-Veer. He wasn't looking to slow down and he was ascending. Suddenly another boom cracked through the air. Angel realised that Nor was trying to break through the atmosphere. That didn't stop Angel. He broke the atmosphere all the time and what's more he loved to do it. He forced himself to accelerate further.

"Come on, come on," he muttered under his breath. Suddenly they were out of atmosphere. The kinetic energy in Angel's body enabled him to survive without air. He rose into space. No gravity Angel thought, it was amazing. He flew over the International Space Station and had to keep increasing speed. Suddenly Nor blew out of sight. Angel stopped. He looked everywhere but he was gone. He had to have broken the light barrier. Angel winced in pain his abdomen was still bleeding and hadn't fully healed. He flew backwards and then retuned back towards the jewel that was earth.

Nor had successfully evaded the human hero, he changed course and rerouted back to earth landing at a base. He walked through the checkpoints; the soldiers there didn't bother checking who he was. They didn't even bother to look up at him. Nor entered the elevator and selected the last floor. They were almost four miles underground and were completely invisible to any satellite coverage. Walking out he made his way to an office in the furthest part of the base. Knocking twice on the door he waited for the command.

"Enter," a loud voice boomed out. Nor crossed the threshold and stood as straight as he could. The office was lavish with historical items and books. The occupant stood in front of multiple computer screens watching news reports on the events of Russia. The figure was around seven foot tall and had a muscular frame dwarfing Nor. "How did it go?" he asked.

Nor stood straighter still. "It went fine sir. I engaged the child of Vaar; he was strong and I almost believed he could win."

The occupant turned round and said, "Show me how strong he was." Nor pulled his broken and mangled blade from his sheath and showed it to figure. Pulling the sword from his grip, the figure examined it seeing how it had been snapped. "This blade was given to you for the sole purpose of destroying the child. And yet look at this: the blade's material was forged on our planet in the fires below. There is nothing that I have ever seen that can do this."

Nor nodded in agreement. "Yes sir, I know. I first thought the boy would be unable to even think of defeating me but I was taken aback with how much strength he actually possesses."

The figure nodded. "But he didn't show it properly, did he?"

Nor shook his head. "He didn't, which means that your analysis was correct." The figure set the blade down and walked round the table and smiled.

"The boy's father was stupid. The limiters he placed are still there and it looks like he can't even break them; which is extremely good for us."

Nor walked towards the table and said, "Guild Master, send me…" In a flash of movement the figure lifted Nor off the ground and held him in a crushing grip.

"NEVER, EVER call me that here. Until I have earned that title you cannot call me that; until we have left this pathetic planet killing all that oppose us. Do you understand that?" Nor nodded and the figure dropped him to the ground. Coughing, Nor waited to be dismissed. The figure noticed and with a flick of his wrist commanded him to go. "Away from me now and do not return until I command it." Nor nodded and walked out of the office.

Michael arrived at the Russian checkpoint. The death toll had risen to over 3,000 dead and more injured. He watched combat medics, doctors and other medical staff all working together to try and save as many people as they could. Michael saw Charlotte and her family sitting in a medical tent. Charlotte had a gash on her head and the rest of her family had multiple cuts. Michael walked over and hugged Charlotte as hard as could without snapping her in half.

"I want to leave," she said softly.

Michael nodded. "I'll get us out of here." He walked out of the tent and saw Bolt pulling a truck that was full of medical supplies through the camp. Bolt nodded at him. Michael retuned the sentiment. Suddenly out of nowhere Angel landed on his knees and cracked the ground around him. He was obviously still injured. Michael helped him up gently but Angel dismissed him. Angel never liked receiving help; wherever possible it was always him giving the help, not the other way around. Michael thought it was because Angel was a leader. He was always looking out for those around him and never himself.

Angel looked at him and said, "I lost him. Bastard broke light; I couldn't keep up."

"How the hell was he flying? That's what I want know. Anyway, I need to get Charlotte and her family out of here."

Angel raised his eyebrow. "We could use your help in

cleaning up."

Michael sighed. "I told you I want nothing to with The Team. I don't want to be a hero. Please just let me get them out of here." Though they were disheartened at his response they nodded at him and walked further into the camp to lend more help.

Angel and Bolt were two of the five members the group sanctioned by the UN. The Team were sponsored by most of the UN countries meaning that they could intervene in natural disasters and other superhuman affairs. However they couldn't interfere in state matters. This proved to be a major block for The Team; they had to watch atrocities being carried out and wait for a majority vote from the UN before they could be deployed.

Michael quickly put in a call to Sampson Industries so they could be picked up. He sat on the ground and examined the dog tags. The chain was broken but the tags themselves were undamaged. The material was obviously tremendously durable compared to everything else that had been broken and destroyed. Michael sighed heavily and placed his head in his hands. His hands shook as he contemplated what happened. *What I have I done?* he thought as he waited in silence.

Half an hour later the Russian driver pulled up. Michael led Charlotte and her family through the camp and out towards the car. It was the same Russian driver that picked them from the airport. Michael let Charlotte get in the back. He had put a call in to the pilots to have his plane ready for take-off as soon as they got there. The Russian driver opened the front door for Michael. He looked raw with emotion from the attack. Michael empathized with him. In a way he felt responsible, he should have tried harder he thought. Michael sat in the car, the journey was sombre and quiet until Michael broke the silence.

"What's your name?" he asked the Russian.

"Gregory Ivanov."

"Nice to meet you. You seem like you should be working higher up than a driver."

Ivanov smiled. "I was an army engineer. I have always enjoyed engineering. I tried to apply for an engineering job but they said that I was not able because I was from the army." Michael reeled in disgust. His father's company had always been willing to hire new people. How was his father's company being run now?

"I'm sorry about that. Listen, if you ever need anything or you want another job as an engineer then call the company. Tell them to give me a ring and I'll vouch for you." Ivanov smiled and took the card from his hand.

"Thank you sir, I'll think about it."

They reached the airport. The plane's door was open and they awaited Michael's arrival. Michael shook Ivanov's hand and walked Charlotte to the plane. The plane took off shortly after that. It was midnight as the plane rose to a cruising altitude of 52,000 feet.

Michael tucked Charlotte into bed; she looked at him and placed her hand on his chest where the blade had cut through him.

"I've never seen you like that before. I always knew you were strong and I always thought of you as invulnerable, but to see blood pouring from you, it... it scared me Michael. I thought you were going to die. But no matter what they threw at you, you were still there to protect us," she said with tears starting to roll from her eyes.

Michael placed his hand on her face. "There is nothing I wouldn't do for you Charlotte. You're my light, my compass. If I lost you I don't what I would do. Nothing will ever stop me from saving you. Nothing," Michael said softly.

She smiled and began falling asleep. Michael stood up and walked out of the room. He picked up a piece of metal that he'd broken off Nor's sword. He was going to find out what he was and why he had come after him. The metal had some of Michael's blood on it and Michael walked to the back of the plane. There was one last room; a mobile lab he'd had built specifically for the plane. Before he entered the room he used his superhearing. He heard Ryan and Amy talking about Michael. The words hero and awesome were being dropped every few seconds. He smiled. Placing his palm on the palm print reader he walked inside.

"Marcus online," he said. The room lit up.

"Why hello sir. It was a good idea to make my programming roving was it not sir?" a pleasant voice said. Michael smiled. Marcus was an AI Michael had created when he was 12. It was so that Bernard had help in keeping the house in good condition. The house was built with holographic sensors and Michael could create blueprints on the fly when he needed. The lab had several sensors that Michael could use.

"Yes Marcus you were right. Anyway, open a new private file named Russia and analyse this." Michael formed a cradle for the blade.

"Yes sir. I was watching what was happening. I had to redirect three satellites to see it all. This adversary seemed powerful," Marcus said.

"I know, I have to stay on top of this," he replied.

"Sir, analysis complete. The metal is not matching any of the known elements on earth. The only known one is iridium." Michael picked the blade up and looked at it.

"No elements known to man at all?" he asked.

"Yes sir, the blade is almost alien." Michael raised an eyebrow.

"Alien? Interesting. Scan the blood." Blue lights fluttered over the blade and landed on the blood.

"Scan complete. Rendering DNA code." Michael looked at the DNA, there were numerous differences. There were more chromosomes and more strands.

"Show an exploded view of a cell." The DNA zoomed in and showed a cell. It expanded and showed the inside of it. "Wow. Just wow. There are more mitochondria in the cell. It creates energy faster. That must be how my body is enhanced. Add yellow sunlight to it." A yellow light shone on it. The cell's organelles began rapidly multiplying and rejuvenating. "So that is what must be happening when I absorb sunlight. That must mean my body absorbs energy faster than a human. My cells must have had to adapt to do this though. This is unlike any human cell." Michael sat back on his chair watching the holographic projection.

"Sir, there is another trace of blood. It is not yours; rather I believe that it belongs to the hero known as Angel. Should I perform a scan?" Michael stood up.

"Yes perform a deep scan." More blue lights floated over the blood.

"Sir here is a full version of the DNA that is within the blood." Michael stood up. He zoomed in on the DNA.

"Marcus, what do you make of this?" Michael said gesturing towards the extra chromosomes and strands.

"Well sir I believe this is an altered version of human DNA," Marcus stated.

"I agree. Take this away from Angel." The DNA was taken from Angel's code and suddenly the wings began receding from his body. The kinetic energy stopped flowing. "Interesting, once the DNA strand is taken away, Angel loses his powers. In fact without that certain strand there would be no Angel. I believe the same would be the case for Bolt as well. But where

63

does it come from?" Michael said obviously perplexed.

"Sir the average human possesses 23 pairs of chromosomes. Taking that into account would help. But I cannot find any sequence of DNA from any human who has 40 pairs. It is most perplexing," Marcus concluded.

Michael stood. "On a different note, you said you were using the Sampson Industries satellites to monitor what happened in Russia. Were there any unidentified objects seen leaving the area?" Michael asked.

"Now that you mention it sir, Miss Robbie diverted satellite 72A to track an unidentified object. Magnifying now." The image was increased and Michael could tell that it was Nor.

"Speed?"

"Sir the being is breaking hypersonic speeds. It's doing this without any external force." Michael focused on Nor.

"Play recording; I want to see where he was going." The recording started. Michael watched as Angel and Nor flew through the atmosphere. Then suddenly there was flash and Angel stopped. Nor was gone. "Did you scan all regions of space to see where he went?"

"Yes sir the satellites' sensors could not pick anything up. This led me to conclude that he must have broken the light barrier." Michael raised an eyebrow. Nor had evaded Angel by breaking the one thing that was thought impossible. "Sir we are exactly two hours from JFK airport. I believe now would be time to get some sleep," Marcus said. Michael smiled; he wouldn't mind retiring to bed with Charlotte.

"Power down Marcus but help the pilot with weather updates."

"Yes sir." The room's lights switched off and Michael exited and returned to his bedroom. Charlotte appeared to be sleeping. Michael took his shirt off and replaced his torn trousers with a set of shorts. He got into bed slowly taking care not to wake Charlotte. As he rested his arm on his head, Charlotte turned over and looked at him, Michael almost got lost in her deep brown eyes.

"Working late?" she said softly.

Michael smiled. "No rest for the wicked."

She smiled. "Then obviously you shouldn't be working." Michael smiled and kissed her gently on her forehead. She looked at him again. "You found something didn't you?"

Michael's face turned sombre. "I-I may have found what I am and how I have my powers, but I have to check first. It's gonna take me some time but I have to find the answer," he said softly.

She placed her hand on his face. "I'll be there for you Michael; I will always be there," and with that they both fell asleep.

Chapter 4: *Now I'm changing that*

Michael had woken at least half an hour before landing. He went back into the lab and sealed the blade in airtight capsule. He wanted to keep it safe from any impurities in the air. Michael watched as Mary began waking up the children. They rolled out of bed and moaned that they wanted to go back to sleep. Michael didn't have the heart to smile. He walked back into the lab. Michael could still feel the sting of Nor's blade slicing through his skin like paper; he wanted to have a more in-depth look at the wound and how it was healing. Michael took off his shirt.

"Marcus scan my body. I want to see how much damage the blade did to my chest." A blue light centred on his chest and he heard a slight humming noise. Suddenly the light turned red.

"I'm sorry sir but I cannot scan any deeper than skin. Below the skin layer your body begins absorbing the radiation. Odd, it is as if your body is like a lead compound," Marcus noted.

"Shit. What did the skin level scan say?" Michael asked notably infuriated.

"From what I can tell the metal was able stop your healing. You are lucky that you were able to absorb the solar energy otherwise I fear the wound would not have healed as fast as it did," Marcus told him. Michael quickly put his shirt back on. The metal was amazing, Nor had said that it could split atoms. Michael had to find more out about this.

The plane touched down. It rocked Michael but he held on to a side railing. Michael carried the bags from plane to Bernard who was waiting outside with car. He stood to attention and then eased as Michael walked out.

"I trust your flight was easy," he said. Michael looked at Bernard; he had been the closest thing to a father Michael had ever had.

"Bernard something went really bad in Moscow. People died. There were more deaths than in New York. I couldn't stop it I... I was almost killed. Angel was almost killed," Michael said softly.

Bernard looked at him and simply said, "Then you need to know where you came from. It's the only way you will find the answers that you need." Michael looked at Bernard and nodded sombrely. He turned round to Charlotte.

"I need to figure this out. So stay away for a bit." Charlotte looked at him and kissed him gently on the cheek.

"Don't push me away Michael. I meant what I said. I love you more than anything and I need you." Michael nodded. He let Bernard drive Charlotte home. Michael took the scenic route.

Arriving back home in seconds Michael entered the lab. Blue lights shone on Michael confirming his identity.

"Marcus begin reanalysis of the blade. I want to know exactly what it is made of." Michael placed the blade in a cradle. Multiple scans were taken of the blade and surrounded Michael. Flicking through them he read each of them faster than the speed of light. None of the scans were deep enough. "Marcus scan the base of the blade and scan the glyphs." More scans were thrown up again. Michael kept trying to find details.

"Sir I am not able to translate the glyphs into any human language or dialect. It is untranslatable." Michael sighed deeply. He analysed his dog tags and placed them into the cradle.

"Marcus, perform a deep scan on this. Scan for similarities between the blade and the tags."

A blue light flashed on the tags. "Hmm?"

Michael raised an eyebrow at Marcus's exclamation. "What?"

"Well, it seems sir, that the tags and the blade are virtually identical. From surface scans they are similar in nature and possess the same durability. The symbol on the tag also matches up with the blade glyphs."

Michael examined his tags and sighed heavily; there were still no answers and this was getting him nowhere. He placed the tags on another cradle and prepared to issue an order to Marcus.

"Alright, Marcus, repair the chain while I'm examining the blade." Blue lights flashed in compliance with the order. He picked up the blade and inspected it. Michael focused his vision to subatomic looking straight into the heart of the blade. He saw how the blade was made up. Instead of packed particles they moved freely and would then spike back into place as if they were organic. There was a spike of bioelectricity which shocked the particles again. It was incredible and beautiful at the same time. Michael looked at the glyphs. Rather than being written on the blade they were seared as if they belonged to the actual make up of the blade. Michael touched the glyph and suddenly he felt a searing pain in his head. Michael roared in agony as his eyes suddenly went blank.

Marcus watched as his creator fell to his knees in pain. Marcus began diverting subroutines to try and find the solution to Michael's suffering. He began scanning his maker multiple times. No matter where he scanned he couldn't get an accurate reading. Michael's body was throwing up interference through some sort of shield. Was the shield emanating from the blade Marcus wondered? Suddenly there was a shock throughout the house. Diverting subroutines again to find out where it came from, Marcus continued his scan of his creator. Results came back from the scan of the shock. If Marcus had had human features he would have been in awe. The shock was coming from Michael; the blade was somehow charging his powers.

Michael wasn't dead, at least he hoped not. He saw multiple thoughts that were not his. What had the blade done to him? Michael wanted this to end he was scared of what was happening. He saw the blade as it slashed through opponents and cut through material. Michael suddenly understood. The blade was showing him its history. The glyphs must have been charged with some sort of radiation that was shocking Michael's body, but there was no form of radiation on earth that could actually harm Michael. He saw how the different people trained with the blade. How they mastered its different ways of how to kill, maim and destroy any opponent. The blade had been submerged in blood; forged from suffering and placed in the hands of trained warriors. Then Michael saw it; it was Nor. Michael saw a child given the blade. A child who mastered its multiple ways of making enemies suffer. Michael then saw a full-grown and ruthless warrior who would not stop, who would not fail. Michael saw Nor kneeling before a group of people, the figures were dressed in full combat armour with different swords and other weapons. They spoke in a language that Michael could not comprehend. They were on a different planet not earth. It was not as lush or beautiful as earth. The sky was blue but distant lightning storms loomed over the horizon. Michael tried to look closer and as he did he saw that it was not a storm but weapons being fired. Powerful weapons that were all targeted on one specific target that Michael could not see. Nor stood up and bowed before the figures and then set his eyes towards the battlefield and unsheathed the sword. Michael knew that Nor was being sent to fight whatever was there and Michael was almost sure Nor could defeat whatever it was; the bastard was far stronger than Michael and even stronger than Angel. Suddenly the view shifted, Nor lay on the ground wounded. There was no look of fear or dread, it was shame that fell upon his face; he looked as if he was ready for death. Michael saw how he had got the scar that was so prominent on his face. The sword was impaled on the ground next to him and the ground was littered with corpses, the broken and maimed. All of these soldiers were dead or dying. Nor showed no compassion or sorrow, in fact the only emotion he showed was disappointment. Michael saw a figure looming before Nor. It was not any of the leaders that had ordered Nor into battle. It was a force of nature, Michael thought. Michael only saw a shadow but the figure was massive and almost indescribable. The view again shifted. Nor stood before the same figures that looked almost like overlords. One thing Michael had noticed was that they wore the same symbol. It was almost like a family crest and it reminded Michael of the coat of arms on his necklace. Michael still couldn't understand the language but he didn't need to, Nor was being disciplined for not stopping the monster as he could have halted the abomination. In that second Michael almost felt sorry for Nor. He had been put up against incredible odds in fighting the monster. In a way Nor had been sent to die, even if his death was only able to slow down the monster. The wound on his face had fully healed and now made him look more evil. Despite the fact that Nor was within his rights to talk back to these so-called leaders he didn't. Nor remained silent and respectful almost emotionless from the verbal lashing. In that way Nor appeared more menacing like nothing they could say could bring him further down than he already was. After the leaders stopped talking Nor stood up and looked at a holographic projection of earth. The hologram zoomed in and a picture of a baby was presented. Nor's eyes narrowed on the image. The picture again changed to Nor in Moscow within the BTR. Nor sharpened the blade slowly almost like a ritual. The driver caught his attention and showed him a shot on the viewscreen. The picture was of Michael. Suddenly Michael felt sick as his powers were rapidly growing out of control.

Nor looked at Michael, not at the picture but literally at Michael and simply hissed, "I have found you."

Marcus had been diverting power from his main power systems into a sort of taser burst. The exact amount of power came in at around one gigawatt. If that was not enough to shock Michael out of his state, then Marcus would not know what else he could do save his master. Somehow Michael's telekinesis was growing out of control. It was getting more and more powerful and soon there would be insurmountable power that would rip the house apart and maybe even part of the city. Marcus began shutting down some of his unimportant systems. He was ready to hit his creator with the burst.

Michael could not believe what he had seen; alien life and a planet which had been ravaged by war from an unknown force. Michael desperately tried to find logic and more information to formulate a conclusion; but he couldn't.

Worse still Michael's powers were in a flux; he couldn't get a reign on them. He desperately tried but to no avail. Suddenly Michael felt an electronic shock and then everything went blank again.

Michael sat up quickly taking a deep gasp of breath. The lab was slightly damaged but nothing Michael would have any trouble repairing. Lights flickered on and off.

"Sir you are unharmed. Thank goodness. I thought I had killed you," Marcus said.

Michael stood up slowly. "Yeah, whatever you did, it brought me back. What did you do exactly?" The console in the middle of the lab switched on.

"Well sir I redirected power from my power systems and from the reactor in the Sampson Industries building. This gave me a total of one gigawatt of energy which I then used to shock you and bring you out of your coma-like state." Michael picked the blade up and placed it into the console. The holograms became hard light and held the blade in place. He looked over at the tags and saw that the chain had been repaired. He placed it over his neck and walked over towards the other cradle. Michael studied the blade for several minutes until Marcus interrupted him. "Sir what did you see?" Michael didn't speak. He couldn't explain what he saw.

"Marcus ignore all that. Show me all the latest news reports." Several holographic news reports flew around Michael. Apart from a flood in Britain that was being attended to by Angel and Bolt it was a quiet day in the world. Suddenly a breaking news report flew up next to Michael. He pressed a sound function on the report and the reporter's voice cued in.

"*At this time the tornado appears to be heading for this small Kansas town. The tornado is classified as an F-5 and as you can see it is ripping apart the countryside. At a time like this*

only one question can be asked: Where are the superheroes?"
Michael smashed his fist into the wall.

Marcus quickly chimed in, "I can understand your upset sir but if you could stop damaging my areas I would appreciate it."

Michael was in no mood. "If Bernard comes back tell him I'm out."

Marcus flashed a blue light at Michael. "Sir if I may, you have no actual experience in this sort of…"

"I don't care. For too long I've been able to step in and I never have. Now I'm changing that," Michael said and disappeared from the house. Michael didn't need the voice inside his head to tell him what to do; this time he wanted to do it.

Farmer Sam Evans rapidly tried to gather his family. The news had just said that the tornado was going to come through the area. Evans loved the countryside and loved his life, but this was the only downside. Evans' wife had recently died of cancer. Since then Evans had sworn to take care of his seven-year-old daughter.

"Leah, Leah come on. That storm is coming. We need to get into the cellar!" he yelled out. Evans sprinted to the back of his farm. Then he saw it. The tornado was about a mile wide; the winds whipped around the area tearing up the ground. It was too late Evans thought. He wouldn't be able to get back to the cellar now. He suddenly saw that Leah had been playing in the area behind the family barn that was why she couldn't hear him. Evans sprinted towards her as fast as he could against the wind and lifted her up. She looked panicked at her father who was trying to keep her calm.

"I'm sorry Daddy I couldn't find you."

"Oh it's alright baby girl. Hey why don't you close your eyes for a bit, I'm gonna get us back to the shelter." Leah closed her eyes and buried her head in his shoulder. Sam refocused on the tornado approaching him, he couldn't get back to the shelter. If he could just cover Leah then she wouldn't see anything. She wouldn't feel anything. Sam kissed Leah on the head and waited for the inevitable. The tornado got closer and Sam expected to be swept up but suddenly a figure covered them both and kept them sealed to the ground. The figure's frame was twice that of Sam's and held them down as the tornado passed over them. Suddenly they shot out of the storm and appeared behind the tornado. Sam looked everywhere for a sign of the person who had just saved them. *Whatever it was, it was a guardian angel*, Sam thought and kissed his daughter on the forehead.

Michael had just saved the first would-be victims of the tornado. He saw a school bus had been overturned by the wind and Michael shot over to it and lifted the bus straight up. He superleaped into the air with the bus and landed on the ground about six miles away from the tornado. Michael had lots to do, he could hear multiple screams of people. They all yelled for help but Michael knew he couldn't save them all. The closest one was a radio tower that was about fall on a family. Michael ran and leapt into the path of the tower knocking it out of the way. Using superspeed Michael was able to move more people and it enabled him to save them without them seeing him but it wasn't going to stop the inevitable. The tornado was still coming for these people. Michael had only one choice: he would have to stop the tornado himself. Michael began moving towards the tornado until he heard a baby crying. He turned around and sprinted towards where the cries were coming from. Michael saw an overturned vehicle and looked in. There was no sign of parents. Either they had thought that the baby was dead or they had been paralysed with fear of returning to the vehicle. Michael tore the door off its hinges. The baby looked at Michael and stopped crying it placed his hand on his cheek. Slowly Michael ripped the safety belt off the car seat and gently lifted the baby up. Despite the fact that the baby weighed less than a car, he felt nervous carrying him knowing that one squeeze and he could hurt the child. Michael looked around and saw the tornado was getting closer. Michael supersped back toward a civilian rally point. The National Guard were out in force trying to keep people calm. Suddenly a man and a woman ran up to him.

"Oh my god he's alive. Thank you so much for finding him." Michael handed the baby over. He heard a creak of metal. A massive truck was flung into the air and was about to crush a group of people. Michael leapt over and caught the truck with one hand. The people looked up at him not in fear but in gratitude. Michael smiled at the people and turned around to look at the tornado. Michael had to find a way to stop it. He would have to use his strength or something. Suddenly he heard a wrench of metal and saw a bus flying towards him. Time slowed down as Michael scanned the bus; there were still people in it. Michael sprinted towards the bus and surrounded the people in a telekinetic field to protect them from the impact of him hitting the bus. The metal bent around Michael's body. He stopped it instantly and leapt to the door. The door itself was wrenched shut but Michael heaved it off and helped the people out. He smelt gas. He turned around and saw gas leaking from the tanker with his special vision. Michael used his body as a shield and protected the people. That was that. Michael took a short run and leapt towards the tornado.

The winds blistered and tore at Michael skin. Oxygen was sucked out of his lungs but it didn't stop him. Michael tried to stabilise himself using his telekinesis. For some reason his telekinesis was never any good at being able to make Michael fly. There was no doubt that it was powerful enough but it just couldn't give him the lift or speed needed. Michael desperately tried to push himself towards the centre of tornado. He looked around and saw lightning striking out and in different places. A bolt shot directly into Michael, the burst shook him but he quickly overcame it. Michael began forming a telekinetic bubble in his hand. Every ounce of power flowed into it. The air fractured around him with reverberations of Michael's telekinesis. It slowly began building power. Michael then clapped his hands on the bubble and a sound like thunder boomed as Michael destroyed the tornado. The tornado dissipated and the winds calmed. Michael landed on the ground and fell on his knees. The area became unusually calm after the storm abated. Michael heard people crying in joy and for the first time in a long time he generally felt good about himself.

Chapter 5: *I want to find out who I really am; my origins*

Michael made it back to the house in seconds. As he entered he found Bernard stood in the corridor with his arms folded. Bernard had been the closest thing to a parent Michael had ever known. As Michael had got older Bernard had tried to keep Michael close and had tried to make sure Michael could control his powers. Michael knew he was in for a lecture again.

"When you first started using your powers to help, the only thing that stopped me from tying you up with titanium was the fact that you would break out of it." Michael kept silent knowing that talking back would end up with more chiding. "What the bloody hell do you think this is?" he said pointing to the TV.

Michael looked and said, "Damn good television." Bernard slapped him. Bernard knew he couldn't physically hurt Michael but the shock stopped him cold.

"You've no training, no insight and no damned business being a hero. You have never wanted this, never wanted to intervene in anything. Why the sudden change of heart?" Again Michael kept silent. He looked up at Bernard.

"I saw people dying today in Kansas. For the first time I felt fear of not being able to save people. I watched people suffer and all they asked was; where were the heroes. I just wanted to help," he said in a soft voice.

"You self-righteous bastard! The other heroes have trained and laboured for people to trust them and now that people have seen you destroy a tornado by clapping all that fear has returned. Now more than ever the government will want answers and Angel will be practically thrown under a bus because of this," Bernard said.

Michael snarled, "All you've said for the last few years is that I should take responsibility that I have a higher calling. Well now I'm trying to help and you're scolding me. I don't care about politics or shit like that. All I want to do is help."

Bernard sighed. "I've tried to raise you as your father wanted. I've tried to instil in you a sense of right and wrong but now I don't know where I've gone wrong. I'm trying to help you see what the people think. If your father was here h…"

Michael cut him off. "That's all I hear. If my father was here this, if my father was here that. I'm sick and tired of hearing that. If Dad cared so much where is he!" Michael yelled. Bernard was taken aback. "If he cared so much he would be here telling me all this shit. He'd be telling me what the hell I am and how I can do half the stuff I can. I'm fed up!" Michael punched a hole into the wall. Bernard was surprised at Michael's anger but he wasn't scared of him. He thumped Michael in the jaw. Michael's eyes turned red and almost glowed with anger. "You hit me again and I won't roll. You'll fracture your hand against my skin," he growled.

"This is what I mean. You're smart, but you act like a child; a petulant child with the powers of a god." Michael didn't want to hear anything else. He began walking away until he heard a crash on the front lawn. Michael walked outside and saw Angel who was pissed. He had landed hard on the ground causing a depression. Michael walked slowly.

"Angel look I know I should've asked but you were…" Before Michael could finish Angel supersped into him and forced him against the mansion wall. Angel held nothing back and right hooked Michael.

"I've told you so many times," he said while punching Michael. "If you wanna be a hero tell me and The Team first. We can help and train you to show you what we do and how we do it. You don't just stop a tornado without telling me or asking the government whether you are ready. Cause you aren't ready, not yet. I've said it time and time again you're a good guy Michael and you're the most intelligent guy I know, one day you will be the best of us all but until then you do not intervene without our permission." Michael kept silent and stared at the ground. "Michael, you alright?" Angel asked. Suddenly Michael looked up his eyes fully red and his fist clenched. Michael surged forward and hit Angel harder than he had ever hit anything before. Angel smashed into ground and got up slowly. "Damn," Angel muttered as he wiped blood off his jaw.

"I am not a slave to anybody; I am not a person that can be used. I am a person that does not care about politics or anything like that shit. All they do is demand off you and The Team and you give EVERYTHING to them. But I don't care what they think. I could level their cities in seconds. In a week I could reduce their population to nil and that would be the first week," Michael said. Angel didn't know how strong Michael actually was but he didn't want to find out like this.

79

As he began to fly, he suddenly felt a grip around his body. Michael was using his telekinesis and pulled him down. He leapt and punched Angel four times at full strength.

"Don't you get it? I don't want to be a hero. I have the powers of a god and yet I have to help these people. But look at them; they stumble across each other, looking at people because of their physical qualities and not their internal qualities. Their most popular people are vain and shallow because all they value are their looks. They cause wars over petty squabbles then they kill their people because they can. They're no more enlightened than children, hell I've met children with more sense than these people. I-I hate people; doesn't mean I want to hurt them I just want nothing to do with them. They'd never accept me. I mean look at you Angel; do they fully accept you or do they still harbour resentment? They're still trying to kill you because you can rip a tank like paper. Five years ago a petty teenage blogger was able to turn the public against you and The Team. It took you months to prove that the reporter was just trying to make you look bad. Look at what the consequences were. Look what they took from you. That's all it took; one person's word against five of you, just because you have powers. But the real people, those who just want to get along with life are the ones that deserve protection, are the ones that were dying in Kansas. They were the ones that needed our protection and you weren't there. I acted out of instinct if I had thought about it, I probably wouldn't have intervened. Would that have been better?" Michael had said all of that with a hint of sadness in his voice. Angel said nothing. "I will never bow to these so-called politicians who believe in themselves over the people because in the end they will betray us."

Angel got back up and went for a quick punch combo which Michael was able to dodge. There was no doubt that

Angel had more combat experience but Michael still had the same amount of training. His strikes, blocks and counter-attacks were like muscle memory. It kept Angel on guard and reminded him that he didn't know enough about him. Michael used an uppercut to send Angel into the air and superleaped towards him. Michael grabbed him by his neck and used his telekinesis to keep his wings from moving and supporting the two of them in the air.

"I don't know what I am or how I got my powers. I need to find out so I know what I am and what I can fully do. I want nothing to with you or The Team." Michael threw Angel to ground and let himself fall but he wasn't finished he was going to beat Angel until he'd had enough. Suddenly Bernard stood between them. "Out of my way Bernard, unless you want me to throw you into the next country," Michael said.

"Enough Michael! Go for a walk and think carefully about what you do next. Just relax and take it easy." Michael snarled at him but heeded the idea and walked off. Bernard walked towards Angel who was on his knees. "Master Angel, are you hurt?"

Angel looked up and got to his feet. "Nothing but my pride. I've never seen Michael fight like that. Even when we fought Veer in Russia," he said clearly astonished at how easily the 24-year-old had beaten him.

Bernard sighed. "I'm afraid Master Michael will always be stronger; it's what he was built for."

Angel looked quizzically at Bernard. "Built for?"

Bernard dismissed this and said, "A story for another time." Bernard helped Angel up and watched as he ascended into to the air.

Darkness had fallen over New York as Michael kept walking. He was in a rougher part of the city now; somewhere people shouldn't be out at night but Michael didn't care. He saw a small liquor shop and popped in. Choosing a brandy bottle from the shelf he paid for it and walked out. Opening the bottle he took a long drink and kept walking. He couldn't get tired so what was the point he thought. A police car raced past them and Michael took a second to see where it was going and simply shrugged. He walked a couple more blocks and arrived at the alley. Reopening the brandy bottle he took another drink finishing it. Michael tossed the bottle into alley and began to walk away. Out of the darkness three thugs emerged, one brandishing a knife which was aimed at Michael's chest.

"Take a step in here and keep quiet," the thug hissed. Michael sighed but complied with it.

"I don't want trouble," Michael said softly.

"WHAT?" The first thug shouted at him. "I can't hear you."

Michael gritted his teeth and said, "Leave. Me. Alone." The thugs suddenly erupted into laughter. Michael clenched his fist. "No more," he whispered.

The thug walked closer and said, "You give me your wallet and I'll maybe think about letting you go." That was the last straw. Michael lifted the main thug up by his throat and tossed him like a rag doll into the wall.

"WHAT THE FUCK IS WRONG WITH YOU PEOPLE? All I want is to be left alone but you bastards can't leave well enough alone, can you?" he shouted. The thug slowly tried to get up, gasping for breath. Michael kicked him up into the air and caught him, smashing him into the wall. Raising his fist, he smashed the wall next to his head. The thug squealed in fear. "What, you scared of me?" Michael threw another punch and the thug squealed again. "What? I thought you were a big man huh, beating up people, beating up girls? That makes you think you're a big man?" Michael threw another punch inches closer. The thug punched Michael in his chest but his hand simply bent against Michael's skin. He howled in pain screaming for help; Michael threw him away into a wall. The thug behind them had got the idea that he could beat Michael. He threw a sloppy punch at Michael but without missing a beat Michael stopped it. His eyes turned red and he began crushing the thug's fist. "You idiots are a waste of life. There are people here who want to work hard, but because of you jackasses you stop them from moving on." The man screamed as his hand crushed under the pressure of Michael's superhuman strength. The other thug ran off in fear but Michael caught him and brought him back. "Oh no you don't, you don't get to hurt anyone ever again." Michael grabbed the thug and pushed him into the wall.

"JUST LEAVE ME ALONE!" the thug screamed in terror.

Michael's eye twitched. "LEAVE YOU ALONE AND LET YOU DO THIS TO SOMEONE ELSE? No you'll never hurt anyone again," Michael roared. He began squeezing the thug's throat. In reality Michael should've killed him by now but he was still subconsciously holding back. In one mind he was trying so hard not to kill the thug but in another he wanted to break the bastard in half. "DIE YOU BASTARD DIE," Michael shouted. Suddenly out of nowhere a bullet smacked into his shoulder, Michael dismissed it and kept choking the thug. Just as the thug began to give up on life a massive voice erupted into the alley.

"Enough Michael now!" Michael stopped for a second and looked behind him. Bernard stood there with a smoking pistol as the thug gasped for air under Michael's titanic grip.

"HE DESERVES TO DIE FOR WHAT HE'S DONE," Michael shouted.

Bernard walked towards him. "Maybe so but you can't decide this. Just come home with me and I'll talk to you." Michael considered this and dropped the thug who began gulping for air.

Michael walked towards Bernard and simply said, "I just want to be left alone."

Bernard sighed and brought Michael close. "It's alright son, I understand. Come on with you." They both got in the limo and Bernard drove off. Michael rested his head on the side of the car and tried to calm down. He had wiped the blood off his hands and made sure there was no more on him. He had never wanted to kill someone more in his entire life.

"Bernard did you tell Angel I was sorry?"

Bernard nodded and said, "Don't worry about that, Angel will be fine."

Michael sighed. "I didn't mean to hurt anyone. They just wouldn't leave me alone," Michael said, the last sentiment dripping with anger. Bernard could sense it. Michael's depression had got the better of him and had made him into an almost evil being.

"It's alright; I know what you're going through Michael. And I know you just wanted to help those people. I am proud of you that wanted to help but you must learn first how to properly carry out your duties." Michael kept silent. "I know how you feel Michael. You let your anger get the better of you and you acted on impulse. It's alright, it was just a mistake."

Michael exhaled. "I just need to learn who I am. I want to find out who I really am; my origins." They pulled up outside the manor.

"Okay Michael, if you want to truly find out who you are, then you should find your father's lab."

Michael laughed softly. "Either you're going senile old man or you're making a joke. I already found the lab ages ago."

Bernard chuckled and hit him in the head playfully. "No I'm not senile yet boy. Your father has another lab underneath the manor. Use Marcus to deep scan the area. You'll find your answers there."

Michael arrived in the original lab and sat down gently. "Marcus, scan the house's schematics; look for another lab here."

There were a few beeps and then Marcus chimed in, "I find no record of any lab other than this one. I have gone through all the old maps of the house and have done 17 more sensor scans. But there is nothing here sir." Michael looked around and tried to focus. The battle with Angel was wrong; Michael knew that but it felt good. He'd never been able to focus all of his powers like that. Michael switched his vision mode to subatomic looking for any gaps in the actual wall. There was a small, slight chink in one of the titanium walls. Michael dug his fingers into the crack and pulled. The titanium was tough but Michael was able to pull it back. Where the titanium had been there was a new wall. Michael scanned the wall again trying to look through it but he couldn't see anything, the wall was impenetrable to his vision.

Michael stepped forward and said, "Marcus, scan the wall." A light flashed in front of the wall.

"Sir I cannot fully scan the wall. From what I have scanned the wall appears to be made of the same material that the blade you brought back was made of." This took Michael aback. There could be answers. Did his father know of Veer? Did they work together? All these questions Michael thought. Michael punched the wall and suddenly a static shot was sent through his body. Michael quickly removed his fist. Suddenly the wall lifted up and dematerialised. Michael walked through the blinding light that was coming from the room and Marcus lost all trace where his creator had gone.

Michael looked around; the lab was beautiful, the material surrounding him was pure silver in colour with slight blue highlights. Michael was surprised; there was no material like this on earth that Michael knew off. Taking it all in Michael saw that the technology was holographic light and hard light. It was incredible; the light doubled as chairs and tools. Michael had been able to make hard light, but it was nowhere as sophisticated as this. As Michael kept exploring a blue light shot up from the main console. A holographic representation of his father was shown. Michael had only seen his father in one picture from a newspaper. His father looked like a scientist with piercing blue eyes which had tints of red in them. He wore glasses and had normal blond hair but this representation of his father was wearing armour not unlike that of the Veer's superiors. The armour was like battle armour but had an almost organic appearance. The hologram suddenly turned its head and looked at Michael and smiled. The smile was a warm smile that a father gave to his child. The hairs on the back of Michael's head rose slightly. He was surprised to say the least. Then suddenly the hologram began to speak.

"My son, I wish I could actually see you but this is only a recording, which means I cannot answer any of your questions but know this; I am sorry that I have not been there for you. Things were not meant to go this way and I am sorry. I have made sure that you could not see this before your 24th year on this planet. Meaning that you still haven't stopped growing; unlike humans you still have three years left to grow. Your physiology, your powers they will all continue to change as you get older. This is going to be hard to explain without me actually being there to talk to you. You must understand; you are not a human. You have been raised by Bernard as one of them and I am very sure he has done a good job. He is a good man. However humans are flawed. They do not understand what is to coexist in peace; neither can they put aside such petty feelings like jealousy and racism. This being said they have the potential to be better than what they are but they cannot do this themselves because they are ineffective leaders. They need someone who can give them hope and show them a better life. I wished to give them this through you. You are everything they should be. You will help them and you will guide them." Static crackled along the hologram and it cut out for a second but then started back. "This recoding is breaking up; the equipment is damaged so I will be brief there is much I have not told you so you must first find Dr Aaron Dexter, he is a eccentric man but I told him more than I told anyone on earth. He will guide you." The recording faltered and crackled; then disappeared. Michael stood there completely dumbfounded at what he had seen. Was his father really who he said? An alien. Michael racked his brain for memories of his father but there was nothing; no small memory at all of his father or even his mother. Michael didn't forget things that easily but he searched the vault that was his memory for anything. He groaned in annoyance as he grabbed his head. It was as if there was some block in his head that stopped him from accessing anything. When Michael was four he was smarter than the average eleven-year-old. It was one of the reasons Michael didn't have to go college or university. The knowledge he had qualified him as having a doctorate in chemical engineering, medical honours and other doctorates in biology, chemistry, physics and genetics. In short Michael was a genius. Whatever he didn't know he could learn incredibly fast. Michael still didn't even know how he knew some of these things. But for the first time in a long time Michael didn't know what to do nor did he have any clue to find what his father wanted him to find. He had to find Aaron Dexter.

Charlotte walked up the drive to Michael's mansion. The beautiful house had stood there since the sixties and even though it was 54 years old it still looked beautiful though that may have been because Michael did repairs every month or so. That and there was so many new supports added because of the equipment Michael had in his lab. As she passed through the grounds she noticed that there were small craters in the house and a few more in the ground. One of the small stone stands had been broken apart. She had felt a small tremor from her apartment in Times Square but had thought nothing of it. This was the most likely cause. The sun was heavy on her neck as she walked to the door. Just as she was about to knock the door was opened. There stood Michael, whose frame blocked the door. Michael looked tired which was ironic because he didn't get tired. His eyes were heavy and she saw part of his shirt had been ripped. She reached up and kissed him on the cheek.

"What happened?" she asked. Michael sighed as he invited her in to the living room. They sat together on the sofa with Charlotte sitting closely to Michael as if to keep him warm. He recounted the events of the tornado in Kansas. How he had saved the people and in the end stopped the tornado. He then told her about the fight with Angel and how Michael had beaten Angel down faster than he anticipated. Then Michael told her about the lab and what his father had said. Charlotte pursed her lips and said, "I can't imagine what it was like seeing your father and what he told you about who you are. Well it's all a lot to take in. Who is this Aaron Dexter? Have you ever heard of him?"

Michael stared at his hands. "To tell you the truth I've no idea. I've never heard of him but I need to find him and then my father will reveal my full origins."

Charlotte looked at him and held his hand. "Like I told you I'm with you always. I can help you if you'll let me."

Michael looked into her eyes. "Listen, I need you to stay away. This is gonna take me time to fully realise and work out. Once I have my information I will find you." Michael stood up and so did Charlotte. She looked up at him and they held each other tightly. Michael stopped concentrating. Whenever he was with Charlotte he felt at peace. He stopped thinking about his powers or anything that worried him. As they hugged Michael without knowing it began to hover a foot off the ground.

After Charlotte left Michael went to find Bernard who was tidying up the kitchen. He turned around and saw Michael walking inside.

"Master Michael, is there anything I can do for you?" His voice was devoid of emotion but Michael could tell he was angry.

"Bernard I-I I'm sorry for what I said. I didn't mean to say what I said. Everything I said was out of anger and I should have shown more respect," Michael said sheepishly. This caused Bernard to stop for a second and turned around as Michael continued. "You've been the closest thing to a father I've ever had. You had to leave your own family behind so that you could take care of me. I mean what am I? I'm just someone else's son you didn't have to be there for me. I'm not related to you and you have no reason to look after me. But you did. I've really been horrible to people in the last few months and I know I don't have the right to ask anybody for anything. All I want to say is: I am sorry." Michael looked down.

Bernard walked towards him and brought his chin up so that he could look at him. "Michael I never thought I could be a parent to anyone. When your father told me of this plan, I was taken back at the thought that I would have to raise you as my own. But I have tried and I do think of you as my own flesh and blood. I am not angry. Like I keep saying to you... you will be the best of us. You have so much potential all you need is to learn and train yourself. Believe me son you have not unlocked even a small part of your power yet." Bernard gave Michael a fatherly hug and continued in his work. Michael felt better now.

"Bernard one last thing, have you ever heard of a Dr Aaron Dexter?" Michael asked.

"Hmm the name does sound familiar. I believe that he used to work with your father. They are the ones that invented a precursor to holographic projection. They had big plans before your father left." Bernard placed is hand on the wall and pulled a holographic plate out. Michael had designed the holographic technology to run through the entirety of the house, it enabled access to holograms anywhere. Bernard began typing the name into the search engine. Bernard flicked his way through the pages and found a video interview. He threw it over to Michael who enlarged it and placed it on the wall. The video was a news interview from 1983. The caption said "*Dexter and Sampson hold fire from the gods*". Michal enabled sound. Dexter began speaking.

"So Dr Dexter what have you found?" a reporter asked.

"Well recently I and Dr Sampson have found a quite literally fantastic innovation. For ages nanotechnology has been something of science fiction to use but with the help of Dr Sampson we have cemented the ability to create nano machines that can be used for different jobs." Michael studied Dexter. He was around 5ft 10 and was the sort of person who preferred to stay inside. He had long blond hair that was tied as a ponytail. His eyes were a dark green hiding behind thick glasses. He wore a simple lab coat over a shirt and plain trousers. On the other hand his father was a different sort of man. A tall, well built man with piercing blue eyes that had a hint of red. His father was more of a celebrity than a scientist but Michael could tell he preferred his work than making appearances in the public; though he could still put a good smile on for the reporters. Michael assumed that was where he got his red eyes from. He wore a black suit with a red tie and he towered above most of the people.

"Dr Dexter is correct; nanotech is on those things we think we will never discover but we have found it now. It has a wide array of uses. For example, imagine doctors using a nano weave instead of a skin graft for a burn victim. The weave would allow skin to grow underneath it. We could use nano machines to destroy cancerous cells in places that we cannot reach. It is one of the most prestigious innovations and as we unlock more of it through the ages we will find different ways to accomplish things with the use of nanotech." Sampson and Dexter shook hands and awaited question from the crowd of reporters. Michael stopped the video and studied the two scientists. They were both incredibly smart; Michael had thought that he had done well finding new ways to use nanotech but do it when they did was truly something else.

He turned to Bernard and said, "What happened to Dexter?"

Bernard stroked his beard and looked deep in thought. "Well he worked with your father in Sampson Industries. They did a lot of work together and discovered many things but then your father disappeared. Dexter was fired from Sampson Industries for having and I quote "crackpot theories".

Michael raised an eyebrow. "The board did this?" Bernard nodded. "I thought so. When I went to them with some of my theories they shut me down. So where did Dexter go?" Michael asked.

"No one knows but I believe he retired to his laboratory in Montana."

Michael smiled. "Why Montana?"

Bernard shook his head. "I don't know sir. I believe your father said that it gave him clarity of thought." Michael could imagine. Montana was beautiful with its long sweeping plains and picturesque mountains.

"You wouldn't know where it is would you?" Michael asked.

Bernard smiled. "Your father never told me. I believe it was because Dexter wanted to keep it secret." Michael sighed. That would make it harder to find.

He thanked Bernard and walked out of the kitchen down to his lab. As he entered he said, "Marcus get me a scan of Montana. Use satellite 34B." A live picture of the world was shown on a hologram and it began zooming in on Montana.

"Sir why would you want a scan of Montana? It seems a bit low tech for you," Marcus chimed in.

Michael said, "Bernard said that Dr Dexter had a lab there. It gave him clarity of thought." Michael studied the live satellite imagery. There was no trace of a lab on the outside but Michael now knew that Dexter liked his privacy and underground would seem a better place to look. "Marcus, do a thermal and infrared scan of the area." The image changed to a different colour and enhanced. Michael looked at the results desperately trying to find any trace of the lab. He saw a blind spot on the map. "Marcus what do you think that it is?" Michael asked.

"From the measurements that I have just taken I would say it is an underground building. It goes down for another 40 feet and is a mile wide." Michael was taken aback by this. The lab was huge. In fact it was bigger than any lab Michael had ever built.

"Marcus send the coordinates to my watch. I'm gonna go and find this lab." Michael put his watch on checking the coordinates. He walked outside, took a deep breath and supersped away.

The Absaroka Range was a range of mountains that

stretched 150 miles across the Montana Wyoming border which formed the Yellowstone National Park. The correct pronunciation of the area was ab-soar-kah but even the local population mispronounced it. Michael had broken the sound barrier instantly after leaving New York and had got to the mountain range in exactly two minutes. Michael checked his coordinates on his range which was 43° 57' 41" N, 109° 19' 51" W 43.961389, -109.330833. Scanning the area twice he saw no evidence of life. Michael was more surprised at how they had built the lab underneath this area. The air was pure and clean, the region was in a word beautiful. No wonder Dexter liked the area. Switching the watch to the satellite screen Michael could still not see anything that would let him into the lab below. Pressing a holographic button on the map he sent a signal to Marcus.

"Marcus I've arrived at the coordinates and well I've, uh, found nothing. There's no way for me to get into the lab. Any suggestions?" Michael asked.

"Well sir you could try smashing your way through; though I believe if you did Dr Dexter would be a bit upset," Marcus replied.

Michael chuckled softly. "Roger dodger, I'm gonna check out the area. I'll get back to you." Michael switched the hologram off and began walking. Keeping his senses on high alert Michael was ready for anything. Well he thought he was...

Chapter 6: *Not normal*

Michael had only walked ten paces forward when a rocket turret rose up and aimed at Michael.

"You have entered a live fire zone and have exactly six seconds to leave the area," a synthesised voice said. Michael stopped in his tracks and quickly analysed the sound. He quickly deduced that the turret was connected to some kind self-defence artificial intelligence like Marcus.

"Wow, wow! I'm just here to see Dr Dexter. My father was Dr Steven Sampson I just want to meet Dr Dexter. We're friends; well at least I hope we are." Michael didn't know who this guy was so he didn't decide to rip the turret off its platform. He didn't want him knowing about his secret. For a minute the turret looked as if it was going to fire. But it didn't. Michael heard a low rumbling sound from the ground. A portion of the grassland suddenly lifted and moved and a man walked out of the ground. Michael recognised him as Dr Aaron Dexter. Dexter's hair was now a dirty blond and his once white lab coat was now slightly brown in colour. Dexter still wore his thick glasses which hid his dark green eyes. Dexter shielded himself from the sun as he walked towards Michael.

"So you are his son? I could tell; you definitely remind me of him. Well boy what are you waiting for the next eclipse? Come in, come in, I have a fresh pot of tea for you," he said in a clear English accent. Michael was stopped in his tracks. He honestly didn't know what to say but he followed Dexter down the hole.

The lab walls were pristine; despite the fact that Dexter was an absolute mess. Michael looked in awe; he saw equipment that was far more advanced than what Michael had ever seen before. Dexter suddenly stopped and Michael almost walked straight into him.

Turning around on his heel Dexter suddenly said, "Now boy this is going to be a long walk. However if you are anything like your father you can get us to the room down the hall a lot quicker than walking." Michael raised an eyebrow.

"Uh okay I guess. Hold on." Michael put his hand on Dexter's shoulder and supersped to the end of the hall. Dexter took a sharp intake of breath and then a quickly exhaled.

"Ah, you never get used to superspeeding. Such rush."

Michael asked, "You've done this before?"

Dexter looked up at him. "Your father used to use it to get us out of some sticky situation. Like I remember the time when I was being interviewed by the New York Times and I was very angry with the interviewer. I punched him and as I was being restrained your father supersped in and destroyed any evidence of my being interviewed and retuned me to my lab; fun times. Like the other time…" Dexter trailed off. Michael was trying to be polite but he was in awe of the technology in the room that they had entered. This was more advanced than anything on earth. "Nice isn't it?" Dexter said.

Michael turned around. "It's beautiful; I've always tried to make good stuff but this is more advanced than anything I've ever seen or built."

"Yes well of course it is. Your father did build it."

This surprised Michael. "My father built this?"

Dexter nodded. "Yes he said that this was so that I could help you find out more about yourself."

Michael looked at Dexter. "Dad thought about me?"

Dexter was surprised by this. "Your father thought the world of you. He loved you more than anything and wanted so much to stay with you and that's the truth. Now if you'll follow me here I believe you're the only one that can access this console." Michael followed Dexter towards a massive console in the middle of the room. The console lit up as if it sensed Michael coming towards it. Dexter looked in awe at the now lit up console. "You've no idea how long I've wanted to see this work. For the last 12 years I've tried to activate it with no luck but it seems almost sentient," he said. Michael studied the console trying to see any design detail. There were some glyphs on the console itself. They had the same design as on Veer's blade. Michael touched them and he felt a sudden shock in his body. The shock didn't knock Michael out this time or make him feel ill instead it created a hologram of Michael's father. His look this time was different; the armour he wore was almost combat-like this time. His hair was messy and there were a few cuts on his face. His eyes were now a dark red and glowed slightly.

"This recording is the last until you find the base mainly because I don't have time to make more. As I said in the last recording you are not human. However your morals and way of thinking are human. Dr Dexter who I presume is with you will now explain to you what you are. Once you find the base I will take over. I am sorry for this recording being shorter than the last but time is against us." The hologram flickered slightly and then turned into a star chart. Michael tried to make sense of the recording. It was more confusing. What base did he want Michael to find? How would he find it? All these questions and still no answers. Dexter went towards the star chart and began manipulating it.

"Well, now that's happened I will obviously take over. Sit down," Dexter said.

Michael kept standing. "I prefer to stand."

Dexter turned around towards him. "Sit down. It will be easier for me to talk to you." Michael begrudgingly sat down. Dexter said, "Now shall we begin?"

"You are from this giant of a planet here," Dexter said lifting a holographic planet from the star chat. "The planet is called Kord and as you can see it is around three times bigger than Jupiter. So it has a higher gravity than earth's which means a human would die there, a shame as I would love to go. The planet is in a large solar system, accommodating eight other planets. For some unknown reason, the sun there is not running out of energy in fact it is getting stronger. Now the planet has a source of energy within the core. Over the years your people have evolved to absorb the energy enough to the point that they can absorb all types of energy. This means they can survive without food, water and air all because of this ability. Now your telekinesis is natural as are the other abilities such as your incredible strength and speed as well as nigh invulnerability. Kordites can live almost indefinitely because of this. They are generally more powerful on Kord because of this special form of energy which, unfortunately, I never got to learn more about but from what I was able to gather it is primordial in nature; as if it existed before the universe was even fully formed. There are those on your planet that believe it to be slightly sentient."

Michael frowned. "So this energy, it doesn't exist anywhere else?"

Dexter smiled. "Well that's the golden question; and

to be brutally honest I have no idea. But back to Kordite physiology; generally Kordites are naturally stronger and faster than the average human due to their advanced muscular system. In addition Kordites are bigger and have a more muscular physique than that of a human. But that's because of gravity." Michael was astounded, he was an alien. His powers weren't engineered but the result of an incredible alien physique. Dexter looked at him. "Shall I continue?" Michael nodded. "Now the most impressive thing about Kordites is their ability to learn almost anything. Give them an hour and they can learn every language on earth. A day and they can learn every martial art on earth and do it better. You are naturally intuitive. If you were put into school you would have finished by the 6th grade, around 11 or 12. That's why your father taught you everything while you were growing in a vat from age one to three. This is why you can't remember anything from before age four. Your father gave you the knowledge of the earth so you could help people." So this was why no matter how much Michael tried he couldn't remember anything and why he enjoyed learning so much. Dexter started off again. "Now with all these attributes and abilities Kordites are the most advanced species in the cosmos. They developed faster than light travel first and were able to install colonies. Well technically they didn't need FTL as they can fly without it but…"

"Wow wait we can fly!" Michael interjected.

"Yes you can. All Kordites have the ability to defy gravity like gods. You'll probably have to learn first though. Anyway because Kordites were the first they established a Universal Committee where other races could join and consult with the Kordites. The high leaders of Kord are called the Guardians of the Universe. They oversee everything in the galaxy. All universal decisions are made through them. Now the

Guardians are Kordites who have achieved their full powers through continuous training and gaining knowledge. Your father was in line to become Guardian but he declined so that he could further his knowledge of earth. Kordites are good and they are benevolent. However they sometimes have to make choices that to me and the rest of race would seem evil or horrible, but they only do it to protect the universe from damage. In fact your father told of a race of aliens that only knew war. When the Kordites first scouted their planet they tried to warn them that this was the wrong course, but the aliens would not listen to the scout party and attacked them. After the Kordites returned with an army to raise the creatures, resetting them and letting life flourish. From that day on I swore I would never look down on people. Though we may seem bad we are nowhere near that level."

Michael snorted at that. "They're probably almost there."

Dexter scowled. "We may not be totally good but we still try!" Dexter said assertively.

Michael smirked. "Really? Tell that to the guys that blow themselves up because they've been ordered to. Or to the guys who shoot children in schools. If humans show promise, I don't see it."

Dexter scowled at Michael. "Nevertheless earth is becoming more advanced and when a planet gets to the right technological level they are visited by the Kordites. If they have managed to become more peaceful and are not overly violent then the Kordites give them a review and a time limit that will enable them to rise to the right standard. After that the Kordites bestow upon them a gift of some sort; a piece of technology that can further their advancement and then they are invited to join the Universal Committee. From what your father told me the gift we will get is faster than light travel. On the other hand if they show that they are too violent and cannot coexist normally with each other, well then they are destroyed and reset, to give them another chance." Michael raised an eyebrow. To destroy a planet, it sounded almost scary.

"So you're telling me that I'm from a planet that thinks they are gods?"

Dexter frowned at him. "You fool. Your people have been through every trial that could have been thrown at them and they've only come out stronger. There has not been a war there for over a thousand years, maybe more. It is a literal paradise. They are all peaceful but they do not shy away from a fight when they know it is for the right cause. Now this is all your father told me. I assumed the rest he'd tell you, but since he's not here we'll have to find something else to…" Dexter trailed off but Michael noticed something. There was a flashing light within the console that Michael's subatomic vision picked up. Michael went towards it; he shot his fist into the console and pressed the button. Dexter almost jumped out of his skin at the sound of the crack. "What on god's earth are you doing?" he asked as he adjusted his glasses.

"There was a button in the console. It was flashing so I pressed it," Michael said. Dexter suddenly turned his attention towards the star chart. It had shifted its view to earth. But not earth itself but the moon. Dexter manipulated the moon which was flashing. He enlarged and scanned it. The moon opened up and it looked like there was something was within the moon. A few alien glyphs popped up.

"Ah Kord glyphs, it is your language. Your father taught me a bit of it. It says, "Come here". Wait we have go to the moon!" Dexter blurted out. The moon Michael thought. How the hell was he going to get there?

Michael was still pondering the idea of getting to the moon as Dexter lead him to another room. He had learnt that the entire lab had been built into the mountain itself. This room that they were going to was called the "Contemplation room" by Dexter. Dexter motioned for Michael to sit down. Michael rubbed his long black hair and looked out of the window. The vast woodland area stretched as far as the eye could see. He smiled to himself as he contemplated how this lab had been built. From what he had seen, Michael's father had been able to build the lab underground and into the mountain effectively hollowing it out. That explained why he could see the ground in front of him and it also made him realise just how intelligent his father was. But all of this was overshadowed by the big fact that Michael missed Charlotte, he wanted nothing more than to hold her again.

"Tea?" Dexter asked.

"Scotch," Michael said.

Dexter raised his eyebrow. "It's eleven in the morning."

Michael looked at him. "Superhuman metabolism doc, my body burns up the alcohol faster than anything in this world. So I'll have that drink now." Dexter shrugged his shoulders and poured him the drink. Michael took a long sip from it and sighed. "So, any ideas how I can get to the moon?" he asked.

Dexter stroked his chin in thought. "Well as I explained; you do have the ability to fly. Your father used to fly around the world faster than any plane but he never told me how he learnt to do it."

Michael sighed again. "The best I can do is jump or leap. The highest I've leaped is around 22,000 feet. If my maths is right, and it always is, then I'm just around a hundred thousand feet shy of the moon. I could build a shuttle or something but that would take months and after the attack in Russia I don't think we have that long. Do you know who he is?"

Dexter slurped his tea loudly. "Your father told me that on Kord, you have ancestral homes. You and your father belong to the guild of Vaar. Your real name is Ror-Vaar. The guild stands for adventure, justice and protection. Now the one that attacked you belonged to the house of Veer as I'm sure he announced. They stand for war, order and soldiers. Despite the fact that Kordites have experienced peace they still have squabbles. Your family and Veer disagree on how to deal with earth. The guild of Veer prefers to destroy humans because we are violent and cannot get on with each other. While your father and his guild want to give the humans a chance at being better than what they are. Your father never told me that they were all ready here."

Michael took another sip from his Scotch. "So how do I learn to fly? Dear old dad didn't leave any training videos did he? Ah, I'm gonna go home. It was a pleasure meeting you Dexter and thanks for showing me this." Michael stood up and shook Dexter's hand.

"If you need anything just ring, I don't get out much," Dexter said as he shook Michael's hand. Michael nodded at Dexter and made his way to the exit. *The moon*, Michael thought, *nothing can ever be easy*.

As Michael came out of the lab he saw a familiar figure standing outside. Andrew Booker stood with his arms folded waiting for Michael.

"Mike, how you doing?" he said as he shook Michael's hand.

"Fine, wait how did you know where I was going?" Michael asked.

Booker smiled. "Bernard told me about an hour after you went. It's uh, nice out here," he said as he looked at the picturesque scenery.

Michael sighed. "I thought he would. Well you didn't need to I'm fine."

Booker didn't look convinced. "I've known you long enough to know what you're like. Something's definitely up. Tell me," Booker said. Despite the fact that Booker was recognised as the joker of The Team, he knew when to be serious and how to help people. But Michael didn't want to talk. He supersped away. "So that's how you wanna play it?" Booker muttered and followed. Michael was almost home when a blue blur overtook him. Michael could tell it was Booker. Booker was faster than Michael so he was most likely just jogging.

"Booker I said I don't want to talk." Booker slowed up so that he could run parallel with him.

"Mike we need to talk, tell me what Dexter said." They were just crossing over the Atlantic Ocean now. Michael inwardly cursed himself, thanks to him trying to escape Booker he had overshot his home. *No matter*, he thought, *I could use the run*.

"Okay what do you wanna know? Dexter said I'm an alien. My powers aren't the result of some kind of clever engineering but of a highly sophisticated alien biology. He said my people were the most prominent beings in the universe and every decision made by different races is made through them," Michael explained. They had both sped their reflexes up so they could be on the same level; the result was that everything was moving in slow motion. Booker pivoted on his heel and began running backwards with extreme control.

"Well I always said you were special. What are you called then a Martian?" Booker smiled. Michael was getting annoyed; he tackled Booker and carried him to the base of a pyramid. To them, they were running at normal speed but they had already arrived in Egypt. The Egyptian heat sizzled the area. Booker stood up and wiped the dust off his clothes.

"I don't even know where to start with this. Dexter said I'm from a planet called Kord, the people are called Kordites. They're anatomically similar to humans except for that fact that they are bigger and have a better muscular system. They absorb energy meaning that they can survive without air, food and water. Dexter also said that the Kordites are planning to visit earth soon to deem them worthy of either joining a Universal Committee or if they deem them too violent and unruly they will reset the human race. There happy?" Michael said.

Booker sighed and frowned. "Wow that's um, interesting. They're more advanced than us, more powerful and have been ruling over the universe. So when do you think they will be coming?" he asked Michael.

"I think they might already be here. That attack in Russia, I think is a part of a bigger attack. It's just the beginning."

Booker fidgeted as he listened to Michael. "Whatever it is we'll be ready for it. We're good like that. Look Mike I gotta talk to you about something and in fact I may be asking your blessing on this."

Michael raised an eyebrow. "Okay, sure ask me."

For the first time since Michael had met Booker he looked nervous. "Okay, well, and feel free to say no, but I'm kind of dating Sarah. We've been friends for a few years now and we drew closer. I love her and I'd like to stop hiding. Especially, like, from you."

Michael smiled and laughed softly. "Why should you hide from me?"

Booker shrugged slightly. "It's just, well after her parents died; she had no other friends or family. Except for you, you always stayed with her no matter what. She considers you her big brother and I know that you'd protect her with everything you have. That's what makes you so close to her and you can't really deny that you protect her just as much as your own family."

Michael folded his arms. "Yeah it's because she's the closest thing to a sister I ever had. Even though I drew closer to Charlotte I still made a vow to protect her from harm. Maybe I can calm down on that now."

Booker looked up. "What do you mean?"

"It means you, you big dummy," he said as he slapped him on the back. "That you have my blessing and I hope you two are happy forever." Booker started laughing and they embraced in a friendly hug.

"Thanks man, thanks for that. It means a lot," he said.

"But if you break her heart I'll rip your legs off," Michael said turning his eyes red for a second. It looked as the fear of god had been put into Booker. Michael started laughing and shook his hand. "Just joking man, just joking." They continued laughing under the hot Egyptian sun.

Shortly after Michael had explained more Booker had got an alert from The Team so he had had to run off. Michael looked up at sky. It was pure blue and Michael could see the moon. Looking at it made him think back to what the star chart had said. Michael shook his head and supersped back home. Though it was still thousands of miles away it only took him a few seconds. As he walked in to the house he heard talking in the living room and assumed it was Charlotte and Bernard. Charlotte walked out of the room with Amy in tow. She stopped and smiled at Michael when she saw him. She walked to him and planted a kiss on his cheek. Amy turned her face into a look of disgust.

Charlotte smiled and said, "Me and Amy were at home alone so we thought it would be nice to come round and keep Bernard company." Michael smiled. He heard small bangs and looked at a holographic projection of fireworks that Marcus was creating to amuse Amy. She laughed and smiled at the projection.

Michael held Charlotte close, kissed her gently and said, "I'm uh, just going out. You can stop here as long as you want, I'll be back later."

Michael was just about to leave when Charlotte stopped him. "Don't go, don't isolate yourself. Come and have a nice night with us." Michael sighed and followed her into the living room. Michael poured himself another glass of Scotch, a double this time. Charlotte eyed Michael as he drank and listened to Bernard, Marcus and Amy talking. She looked at Michael as he took another drink; he was having a bad day. She knew that his depression was like torture, it ripped apart what little resolve he had left and brought him down faster. Her mother had profiled him and found that he was always covering up the fact that he was depressed. Charlotte had noticed that he drank a lot and if his body didn't burn it up almost forty times faster than the average human; he would be an alcoholic. Normally she could bring him out of it but tonight whatever she did went over his head. A few hours later Mary came to take Amy home. Michael stood with Charlotte and Bernard waving them off and left to go back to his lab. Charlotte went into the kitchen to help Bernard wash up.

"Bernard something's wrong with Michael. Do you know what happened? He did say something about his origins."

Bernard pursed his lips. "I believe he has found out where he has come from and I don't think he likes it." They both suddenly jumped when they heard glass smashing. They both made their way down to the lab.

As they entered they heard more smashing. Charlotte saw scribbles all over the lab saying "not human" and "Alien". Michael was sitting down drinking bottles of Scotch and throwing them at holographic targets that were on the wall. Bernard made Charlotte stand behind her just in case something happened.

"Michael what are you doing?"

Michael looked up at him and smiled. "Doing? I'm not doing anything. Just enjoying some nice Scotch. What are you doing?" Bernard went to grab the bottle from him but Michael simply supersped to the other side of the lab. Though Michael couldn't get drunk he was certainly acting the part. Again Bernard followed him to get the bottle. Michael simply threw the bottle away. "There it's gone, poofed out of existence," he said. Charlotte tried her hardest to fight back tears but they were flowing freely, whatever Michael had been told it was making him feel so bad. Michael's eyes were almost glowing red with anger. Charlotte suddenly ran up to him and grabbed his hand.

She pleaded with him. "Please Michael stop it, just tell us what has happened and we can talk." Seeing Charlotte in tears jolted Michael. His eyes went back to being black and he calmed down. He then proceeded to tell them everything that Dexter had told him. Charlotte wiped her tears away and said, "That's amazing; you are living proof that we are not alone in the universe. It's nothing to be worried about."

Michael smirked. "I'm not worried. But I don't exactly want to be alien. Hell I'd take being a genetically engineered weapon any day of the week rather than this. My race wants to judge earth but some of them want to just destroy us. That's why I thought I'd have a nice drink tonight."

Bernard frowned. "Your father told me much about this, but he left certain parts out, I believe it was because he wanted to tell you."

Michael sighed. "Well this moon base is annoying me. I mean if dear old dad had left some kind of training video then that would have been fine but no. Hell I didn't even know that I could fly". Michael looked down at the floor.

Charlotte chimed in, "Well what about asking Angel? I'm sure he'd want to help."

Michael scowled. "Angel and me aren't exactly on best terms at the moment. I think he'd rather headbutt me than help me."

Charlotte leaned forward and took his hands in hers. She looked into his eyes and said, "Angel doesn't hold grudges, ask him and he will help you."

Michael kissed her on her forehead and said, "Okay I-I I will. So tomorrow I learn how to fly."

Chapter 7: *I can fly*

The next morning Angel came as his alter ego Adam Spence. Adam worked as a forensic investigator and enjoyed his job. Michael had designed a cover which hid his wings from the view of anyone, it made it easier for Adam to enjoy a normal life when he wasn't playing hero. Adam and Michael shook hands and kept silent until Charlotte slapped them both.

"Oh come on you two stop acting like children and say what needs to be said," she announced.

Michael went first. "Um I'm sorry for not telling you. I could have used the backup. Guess I was too proud to say it."

Adam smiled. "Like I keep saying bro if you wanna learn I'm always here. I'm sorry for attacking you. What you did was right and I should've seen that but I didn't. Friends?"

Michael nodded and shook his hand. "Friends."

Adam nodded back. "Alright then let's get to it." Michael agreed and they walked to the back of the mansion. There was plenty of ground were Michael could practice. He used to practice getting his superspeed right here but now he was going to fly. Adam said, "I can fly because of these big feathery things on my back. You, well I don't really know how we're going to turn you into a flying man but we'll get to it. When

I fly I think of just moving a muscle, but when I've seen you superleap it does look like you're flying. I bet you can fly but it must be something that you have to believe. Right, anyway let's have a go. I'll be there all the way with you." Michael nodded. Charlotte and Bernard followed them to the area; Charlotte was waiting in anticipation to see how Michael could fly, she was sure it would be one of the most amazing things she'd ever seen. Michael could hear what Charlotte was thinking and he smiled. He had set up a telepathic link that was stronger than anything he'd ever done with his telepathy. It was a grey morning over New York. There was plenty of cloud cover that Michael would have to break through. Adam disabled the holographic cloak over his wings and readied himself. Charlotte and Bernard stood next to them. Adam turned to them both. "Uh, you guys may wanna take a step back." They took one step back. "No I mean probably a few metres, when Michael superleaps he causes craters and pretty much breaks the sound barrier. That's gonna really hurt if you're not a few more metres back," he explained. They both retreated back to near the mansion and took cover. Adam nodded at Michael signalling him that they were ready. Taking a deep breath Michael crouched down building up force; he left it until the last minute and then shot into the sky. Michael broke through the cloud. He saw Adam fly parallel with him keeping up. Michael thought he was doing it. He rose above the clouds and suddenly began to lose speed. Michael desperately tried to increase speed, but he couldn't and he began to fall. The fall didn't scare Michael it was more the fact that he would be hitting the ground at high speed. He suddenly saw Adam drop down and reach for his hand. Michael grabbed him and they began to slow down.

"You alright, Mike?" Adam asked. They dropped to the ground and Michael kicked the ground in disgust.

"Dammit Dad, why did you have to make things so hard?" Michael said in anger.

Adam patted Michael on the back. "C'mon man, you'll get this you're good at this sort of stuff. I know you'll get it." Adam smiled and helped Michael up.

The rest of the day went exactly the same, except for once when Michael flew slightly upward but then fell back down. It was around 10pm and Charlotte and Michael were sitting outside by the pool. It was just going dark and the lights around the mansion all switched on. The illuminated pool water reflected on to the ground. Michael was drinking water, no more Scotch for a few days at least. Charlotte had a soda. The sky was clear and the stars were out in force.

Charlotte smiled. "Where exactly are you from then?" she asked.

Michael smiled at her. "Well I couldn't draw it on a map for you, but Dexter said it was exactly 17 light years from here. Meaning it's unreachable by any technology on earth. Kind of makes you realise how small we are," Michael said.

"So when you get this flight thing sorted out, do you think you're gonna go there?" she asked.

Michael pursed his lips. "To be honest I don't know what I'm gonna do. First I need to find out what my dad built in the moon for me. Then I will find out whether I want to go to the planet or not."

Charlotte leaned in and kissed him softly. "I love you and I know you'll fix this. You'll be a high-flier like Adam. Anyway you wanna go for a swim?" she said as she took off her clothes and dove in. She rose up for air and leaned on the side. Michael smiled and stripped down to his boxers and dropped in. Michael could see perfectly in the water and saw Charlotte's every move. She had always been a good swimmer. Michael didn't need to hold his breath but he kept his mouth closed. Charlotte swam towards him and pulled him along. They kissed underneath the warm water, for what seemed like hours. Michael let Charlotte breathe through him. He was lost to her and lost completely in thought. He held her tight and stopped thinking. Even though his superhearing went up a bit he was focused on Charlotte. He loved her so much.

The next morning Adam was accompanied by Andrew who wanted to be a spectator. Michael felt a bit more ready today. He stretched out and took a few more deep breaths. He used his superhearing to listen to the various sounds of the New York morning. Before he did anything though, Charlotte came and kissed him deeply.

When they pulled apart Michael asked, "What was that for?"

Charlotte looked at him and winked. She said, "For good luck. Now get out there and fly!"

Michael smiled when Adam interrupted and said, "Come on lovebirds there'll be plenty of time for that later," pushing Michael away from her. Charlotte, Bernard and Andrew took their places and got ready to watch. Michael and Adam walked towards their "take-off" area as they'd come to call it. "Okay Mike we know your take-offs are good, but it's the rest of the flight that you need to worry about. I definitely think you can do it, you just need to concentrate," Adam said. Michael smiled and readied himself. The area distorted as force built up around him and he suddenly shot up into the air. Both Andrew and Charlotte whooped as he shot into the sky. "Damn," Adam muttered and took off to catch up with him.

For the second time in his life Michael was astonished. He shot through the sky, feeling the air rip at him. He heard a boom like thunder and saw Angel coming towards him.

Michael was happy and felt good, until suddenly he started slowing down. No Michael thought he would not lose again. He desperately tried to regain focus but it wasn't working and he began to fall towards the mansion. Angel had shot past and couldn't catch Michael. As he neared the mansion, Michael felt control again and tried to change his fall so he'd land as far away from Charlotte and the others. The air popped around him as he smashed into the ground. Angel crashed down and threw a massive chunk of rock off Michael.

"Yo, Mike you alright? Come on man," Adam said. Suddenly Michael's fist shot through the rock. Adam grabbed him and pulled him out. Michael shook the dust off his head and flexed. He began walking back towards the take-off area. Adam followed. "Look man let's take a breather, we'll try later," he said.

Michael looked at him and smiled. "No I can do this." Michael took another deep breath and then he shot into the air. The world fell away from him as he flew into the air. Michael had full control over everything. He roared with effort as he willed himself to increase speed. Michael broke the sound barrier as he approached the atmosphere. The atmosphere felt warm and Michael closed his eyes until he was in space. Michael was astonished again, space was beautiful. He didn't feel cold and the absence of oxygen didn't feel wrong. He looked at the brilliant ball of fire that burnt in the cosmos that was the sun. The energy was unfiltered and felt amazing, his body was fully restored. Adam shot through the atmosphere and came towards Michael. Adam was wearing a face mask which helped him to communicate. He handed one to Michael who placed it on to his face.

Adam said, "Okay I do a lot of flying, but that was the coolest thing I have ever seen. Anyway you've got a handle on accelerating but we need to work on normal flying; being able to control the speed. Generally I try to keep it under Mach 1 when flying through cities. You can cause massive damage. We're gonna do that and then," Adam said pointing at the moon, "you can find out what's on the moon." Michael stared out into space. His incredible sight enabled him to see further out through the solar system. "Yo Mike you with me?"

Michael looked at Adam and said, "I can fly Adam." Adam smiled and patted Michael on the back. They both shot through the atmosphere and descended back to earth. Michael landed on the ground next to Charlotte, Bernard and Andrew who were still under cover. Michael reached for Charlotte holding her up in the air.

She kissed him deeply and passionately, and then said, "You can fly!"

Michael smiled at her and said, "I can fly."

Michael soared through the dark New York sky. It had been a week since his first flight and he was now making record progress. Adam flew parallel to him high enough that they were not noticeable to the pedestrians below. Adam had been teaching Michael different flight techniques including him being able to land and take off without damaging the area and how to keep his speed under control. Michael was enjoying this. He had made two trips to space and he had enjoyed it more than anything else. Speed wasn't an issue for Michael. He was definitely faster flying than running. Michael hadn't even reached his top speed yet. He'd broken terminal velocity and had gone faster but the one thing Michael wanted to do was to take Charlotte flying. That was something he wanted to do more than anything. A long droning sound cut through Michael's peace when he saw a 747 jet coming straight towards him. Adam grabbed him and ascended above the plane.

Michael shook his head. "Sorry Adam million miles away."

Adam smiled. "S'all right Mike. Thought air traffic was gonna be quiet but guess I was wrong." The both laughed and ended their training.

Adam and Michael landed at the mansion. Adam suited up as Angel to respond to an emergency in Australia. Michael waved him off and turned to look at the city. It was almost three in the morning and pitch black. Michael looked up and ascended up through the cloud. Fresh rain was beginning to fall and it dropped on Michael's face. Michael's thoughts turned to what his father had said about him. "You are everything they should be. You will help them and you will guide them." The words his father had spoken to him didn't describe Michael. But could he be like that? Michael thought. He didn't know. Before Michael knew it, he was in space. Just in geo orbit of the world. Michael closed his eyes and listened. Michael's telepathy enhanced his hearing, meaning that he could hear where there was no sound. There was a wide array of sounds, ranging from gunfire in war-torn countries to casual conversations about work. All these people asking for help begging for a leader that could solve their problems and fix their lives. After Angel and his heroes revealed themselves to the world, people saw them as the second coming. Some even worshiped them as if they were gods. The heroes had strenuously told the people that they were not gods and that they should not be worshipped. Still many saw Angel as an actual angel of god. Michael smiled to himself, he wouldn't want that. He didn't want to be worshipped or thought as a saviour, he just wanted to get on with his life. Compared to New York space was quiet. The peace and serenity was soothing to Michael. He looked at the moon. Underneath there was some sort of base his father had built. What it contained for him Michael did not know but he made his way towards the orbiting satellite. Michael made it there in no time and landed on the surface. The moon was covered in craters from being bombarded by asteroids for millennia. Michael floated over the moon looking for any sign of technology. Switching is vision to microscopic he scanned all the parts of the moon. He switched back to thermal to see if there was any evidence of technology. Michael was about to give up until he saw an object on the surface of the moon. As he scanned it he saw three glyphs on the object. One was exactly the same as he had seen at Dexter's lab. It was a diamond shape with what looked to be two lightning bolts within it. Michael landed and crouched to reach the object. He touched the glyph and suddenly felt a strong tugging sensation. The tugging suddenly became painful like white hot fire. It spread around his legs. He saw a flame licking up towards his body. Michael felt fear and tried to escape the flame. He tried to fly and increase speed but to no avail. Michael suddenly felt immense regret for coming here. He tried to contact Charlotte through his telepathic link but he couldn't. The flame almost covered his entire body and began pulling him apart. Then there was nothingness.

Chapter 8: *Why did you leave me?*

Charlotte woke up at midnight hyperventilating. She desperately tried to get her breath back. She had just felt a terrible pain. Since Michael had set up their telepathic link she'd been able to see into Michael. All of his fears and ambitions; he saw the same with her. It made them closer and able to better connect. She felt the hum of her artificial limbs cycle up. They glowed a light blue which sometimes made her visible in the darkness. She had woken up because she had thought that Michael was in pain. She swore that she had heard him scream. Gazing at the moon, she pondered what Michael had told her; a base on the moon that his father had built for Michael. It was an amazing thought, but should Michael go? What lay there for him? She wished she could be there for him but whatever was there she knew Michael could handle it. He was better than all of them and whatever was up there wouldn't stop him...

Michael had felt pain before but never like this. He was lying on a cold, hard floor. The floor pulsed with a blue light that made it look as if it was alive. Michael got up slowly.

He felt groggy and tired for the first time in his life. There was no energy that Michael could sense meaning he couldn't absorb anything to rejuvenate himself. There was no actual life meaning Michael couldn't see anything. His superhuman vision could barely pierce the darkness. Making his way through the base-like area, he tried to find a wall that he could lean on. Stretching his arm out he made arcs to try and feel for a wall of some sort. Suddenly he felt a cold, hard wall and as Michael touched it an electrical shock startled him out of his tiredness. The area suddenly lit up and ambient light shone through. Michael instantly recognised the technology. It was exactly the same as Dexter's and Michael's father's lab. The computers were almost organic and there were viewscreens feeding images. Michael stopped leaning on the wall and as he did a solid wall opened up. Michael prepared himself for the loss of air and depressurisation but there was nothing. The air stayed still and pure. The brilliant jewel known as the earth floated in the dead of space. Sunlight began pouring through the screen and Michael's body instantly reacted, his veins turned yellow and his eyes red. Energy flowed freely though Michael's body and he took a deep breath. Everything felt better and Michael could take a better look at the area.

There were three pillars. In the pillars there were suits. The first suit was a battle suit with an accompanying helmet. The suit reminded Michael of medieval armour but was twice the size of any armour he had seen before. It didn't look right for Michael. He turned to look at the middle pillar. The suit was more of a skinsuit. The material was white with black fins and a blue symbol. The symbol was exactly the same as what Michael had seen when he had found the object. The bolts were a solid silver colour. On the back was a long and graceful black cape. The last pillar showed a larger armour than the skinsuit but smaller than the combat suit. The suit was a deep red in colour with three silver streaks. Michael deduced that this suit was for exploration; there was some sort of tank on the back but Michael couldn't see the actual contents of the tanks.

Michael took more sights of the lab in until suddenly a deep voice boomed throughout the lab, "Accept your heritage." Michael felt a deep burning sensation on his chest. Desperately he ripped at his shirt trying to see what was burning him. The sensation suddenly stopped and Michael looked at his reflection in the wall; he'd got a tattoo on his chest. Though Michael had never thought of getting one, he also knew that his healing factor would treat the liquid as a threat and purge it. But not this time, it was here to stay. The tattoo sizzled on Michael's skin. It was some kind of symbol; a shield with two crossed lightning bolts and a spear down the middle. Gingerly he felt the seared skin on his chest. There was no pain now and he felt somehow stronger. A barrage of light flooded on to the ground next to him and out of nowhere a console was formed. Michael was stunned; the console had simply materialized out of nothing. He walked towards it and placed his hand on the console. Light flooded to his hand and suddenly another electric shock hit. Michael let out a gasp. It was the same feeling as when he had touched the blade.

It was now midday in New York and the temperature hadn't risen as much as Charlotte wanted it to. She was on a break from college and sat at a cafe. Her thoughts had not left her from what she had felt this morning. She was trying to contact Michael with the telepathic link, but there was no connection as if it had been severed. That scared her more than anything. Michael hadn't always been as refined as he was now. He used to be raw with anger and it took a few years for Charlotte to turn him into what he was now. She still remembered at high school when she was trying out for the cheerleading squad and the girls who had judged her played a prank that was meant as a joke. Charlotte had seen it like this but Michael hadn't. He had been sitting in the stadium seats and she had heard him growl and break off the wooden seats as he stood up. She had had seconds to react and quickly contacted him on their link to stop him. Of course that had led to him falling down the seats. She wanted to ring Adam and ask him to go to the moon and check on him but the television in the cafe showed footage of an earthquake in Los Angeles. As soon as the reporter turned around Angel had flown past rescuing people with Bolt running them out of the area. She gently wiped a tear away. She knew Michael was capable of that but she was scared and somehow she knew he was too.

Michael was scared. He had been in this state before but this time it scared him even more. There was nothingness it was just deep black like death. Michael was on his feet so he tried walking.

A loud voice boomed, "Know your history!" Then there was a blinding light and images smashed into Michael's mind. Michael saw a planet burning then five beings of awesome power shot into view. They battled with beings that looked the same as them. The scene shifted to a cave. Michael was suddenly pulled by two women wearing long white garments like that of a Roman toga. They gently pulled Michael.

The one on the left said, "My Lord, the campaign is progressing well. The four other lords have reported success in quelling the rebellion." Michael was led out of the cave on to a mountaintop. The sky was blue and a yellow sun shone upon him. The mountaintop had a throne. The women sat him down and stood before him.

One of them suddenly said, "Would you like to see how the campaign is progressing?"

No I wouldn't, Michael thought but he stood up and walked towards the edge of the mountain. What he saw scared him. The landscape below was on fire and was being destroyed. Lightning continually shot down at the ground and destroyed parts of it. Four figures shot up from the ground and they stood before Michael and bowed. Each wore a symbol. Michael thrust his hand out unwilling and a symbol was created in the air; the same symbol that was on Michael's chest. The scene shifted. Michael was himself again and was in some sort of place that was floating in the sky. Michael walked through a set of massive doors. There looked to be some sort of celebration going on. Beautiful music drifted through the air and multiple Kordites stood in ceremonial armour. Michael saw the five symbols. His symbol was higher than the others. The five lords walked into the room with their wives. The general hubbub stopped and all gazes were on the immensely powerful beings. All of the other Kordites suddenly shouted, "Hail the Guardians!" repeatedly. The lead one raised his hand and the shouts stopped. Michael got a better look at the leader and what he saw scared Michael. The leader almost looked like his father.

In a loud voice he said, "My fellow citizens. I call you citizens and not subjects because you are what we have fought for. We have finally secured peace on our planet. Now we must look to the stars. We have been given power and now we must see if we can bring peace to the universe. But we will not always be in power. A new era is upon us and that means new Guardians must be chosen. The trials will begin in the next cycle. Peace will reign supreme." When the speech ended thunderous applause rattled the room. Michael felt a sense of pride. The Kordites had endured war but at the end of it true peace had been found. Suddenly the ambient atmosphere was shattered by an explosion that forced the giant doors apart.

A group of rogue Kordites bounded into the room and yelled, "There will be no peace. Death to the Guardians." Kordite guards tried to stop them but these were no ordinary Kordites. They were well trained and extremely powerful. The Guardians didn't convey any emotion. One of them stepped forward. He was different to the others. He did not wear any sort of armour and his tattoos glowed blue over his body. He dispatched the Kordites with such extreme ease that it scared Michael. Suddenly a loud roar was heard and it shook the very building. This time the Guardians conveyed surprise. They walked outside and Michael followed them. A giant being the size of a mountain appeared. It tore structures from their holdings and threw them at the Guardians. They moved with extreme speed and stopped the structure.

"And so another war raged uncontrollably. Rival guilds rose up, though they were not of royal blood, they were powerful and large enough in number to cause the Guardians grief. However they had what they thought would be a secret weapon; the Staari. The Staari were a subspecies of the Kordites; they grew to the size of mountains, taller than those on earth. They were mighty and their power was elemental; their bodies would be covered in fire or storms. The Guardians were hesitant of these mighty beings, not because they feared their power but because the Staari were known to be peaceful. They would never have harmed another living being; thus it was believed that the Staari were being dominated by the telepaths of the guilds. With heavy hearts the Guardians were forced to kill off the entire race. Imagine, millions losing their lives just because of some ignorant fools who wanted nothing but violence. This war lasted another million years. Before we gained peace and before we were properly unified. But the price was high; all animal life on our planet was forced into extinction. Giant beasts that once roamed our planet were killed off and we never saw them ever again. Parts of the planet were left barren for years due to us misusing power in our battles. After that the Guardians stepped down and were replaced by new ones," a voice said.

Michael looked everywhere for the source of the voice until he saw a figure in the distance; Michael couldn't see it properly. A voice suddenly echoed through the darkness.

"My son, you have found me." Michael saw the figure walking towards him. He focused his vision to try and look at the form as he did the figure suddenly appeared in front of him. It was his father. He was wearing some sort of ceremonial garment with the symbol that had been tattooed on Michael's chest.

"Father?" he asked.

"I am your father. Though that may be a lie, I am more of his consciousness, his memories and his feelings. This haven I built for you is a memory or a representation of what you have on your planet. It was built so you could watch over the planet earth," Saar-Vaar said. Michael didn't know how he felt. His father had physically built this place within the moon and it was like a home on his home planet. Saar stepped towards him and looked at the dog tags. "Ah, I see you've been wearing them."

Michael looked at the necklace and looked back at his father. "Yeah, I found them when I was six. Started wearing them and never took them off."

Saar smiled. "They are for you. The tags signify your guild and your rank among us."

"My rank?" Michael asked quizzically.

Saar nodded. "Yes. Since I was to become a Guardian that would make you a prince among our family."

Michael smirked. "A prince? What like royalty?"

Saar nodded again. "Yes, like royalty. Our Guild is one of the royal families meaning that we hold a senior rank."

Michael nodded slowly, processing the information he had just heard. It surprised him; Michael had gone through his life being unpopular and now he was a prince. Michael had more questions to ask his father.

Saar deduced what Michael was thinking as he spoke. "I know what you are thinking my son. I am sure you have many questions. Please ask." Michael was taken aback at this but he quickly collected his thoughts. He looked at his father.

"Why did you leave me?"

The hologram of his father showed real emotion and said, "I did not want to leave you neither did your mother. But to ensure your survival I had to sacrifice myself. I knew that you could thrive without me that you would be safe." Saar-Vaar stepped forward and hugged Michael. The hug was what Michael had always wanted. It made him feel warm inside and as if all his troubles were wiped away.

They pulled away and Michael said, "You mentioned my mother. What happened to her?" An expression of pain formed of his father's face. He held his hand out and a small screen formed. In the screen Michael saw a beautiful woman. She had deep blue eyes with a tint of sliver. She wore a ceremonial dress with the same symbol on her chest. Michael saw that she was around five months pregnant.

She looked into the video and looked behind her. "Is it on? I want to make sure it's on. This will be his only memory of me." She looked back at the camera and smiled. The smile was pure and warm. "Hello Ror-Vaar, I am your mother. My name is Lira-Er-Vaar. I am sorry that I cannot see you but know that I love you. Your name means guardian. You are to be a leader to the people of earth and you will be able to do this. I know. I want to see you, so much. I love you my son."

The video shut down and disappeared.

"I will show you what happened next."

The world went black as Michael awoke in the lab with his father and mother watching over him as a baby. Lira looked at the baby cooing on a small bed; a tear formed in her eye as she watched the child, completely unaware of what was happening. Lira felt a deep pain within her; unlike most Kordites she had a genetic condition causing her to not fully absorb energy. It was time she thought.

"Saar, I cannot hold on any longer," she said as she fell to the ground.

Saar sped towards her and held her steady. "Beloved, not yet please do not go."

Her attention turned to baby Ror. "He'll never see his own mother, hear her call for him or hold him when he is scared." She blinked out tears. "Saar, please do not leave him, he will need you more than ever now. I love you so much Saar." Saar watched as he saw her aura fade slowly.

"No, no please don't leave me. I need you. I still need you." Her form went limp in his arms as the life drifted out of her body. Michael fell on his knees, his ethereal self couldn't do anything to help her. Out of nowhere a giant figure dropped from the air into the peaceful lab. Saar looked up at the figure. "Dar, my son I couldn't save her." Dar sped over and cradled his mother.

"Mother, please you cannot leave me. Please mother not now." Dar realised his mother had passed on. He suddenly turned round to see the newborn baby crying. Rage filled his mind as he lifted his giant arm to crush the child. However before he got the chance a telekinetic shield stopped him. Dar looked at his dead mother who somehow was reaching from beyond the grave to protect her child. The realisation that his mother loved the child did nothing to quell the rage inside. He screamed in anguish and took off towards space. Saar followed him up. As they reached the atmosphere, two knight-like Kordites appeared restraining Dar. They held on to him as hard as they could.

One of them shouted, "Dar-Vaar by order of the Guardians you are to return to Kord."

Dar suddenly shook them off. "LEAVE ME ALONE."

He went to strike the knight but before he did Saar stopped his fist and shouted, "Dar, leave, go into deep space. We will talk soon." Dar shot away and out of view.

A tear formed in Michael's eye. He wiped it away slowly. He looked towards his father.

"That... was my brother and my mother. She... she died. What happened to her, you and my brother?"

His father frowned and said, "The only way is to tell you the reason why you were created." His father stepped forward and placed his hand on his shoulder. "Come my son. I will show you your purpose." A static charge shocked Michael and then everything went black again.

"To tell you about why you came to be is to tell you the story of Kord's history. After the Guardians secured peace, they wanted to set out into the universe to find life. The most important thing about our race is that there are genetic differences between the majorities of Kordites. There are two genetic versions of Kordites: pure bloods and second blooded. A pure blood is a perfect specimen; complete with all of the powers that we can develop. Said powers develop at a faster rate than any of the second blooded Kordites. For the first millennia Kordites were all pure bloods giving us unparalleled force to enforce the vision that we saw fit. However as the years wore on more and more Kordites were being born as second blooded. Though they were strong compared to a pure blood they could never even hope of defeating a pure blood. Even an average pure blood could defeat a highly trained second blooded soldier. In addition second bloods were not as mentally sound; they were more vulnerable to mental disease and they could lose themselves into a rage. In a rage they would become as strong as a pure blood but they would lose all soundness of mind. Because of this they were sometimes denied military service. In addition they were taught a different form of self-defence."

Michael looked quizzically at his father. "What, like, a different form of martial art?"

His father nodded. "Yes; on Kord there are two different types of martial arts the elegant style which focuses on free-flowing moves combined with speed and the brutal style which focuses on strength. Essentially both styles of martial art combine many more into a deadly set of killer attributes. The brutal style is easily the most brutal of fighting approaches; it focuses on strength backed up by telekinetic force. Because of its nature it can only be taught to those of a sound mind. Even some pure bloods were known to become lost to the rage of this martial art. The elegant style focuses on disabling an opponent with speed and accuracy, with a focus on nerve strikes. It takes time to learn and even longer to master. However the brutal form focuses on inflicting the most damage to the opponent. Breaking bones, ripping spinal columns and liquefying organs are all separate moves. Due to the severe mental strain of the brutal style, second blooded Kordites do not usually learn it as it can destroy an individual's mental faculties. Second blooded Kordites were taught a combination of the elegant style and brutal style which enabled them to keep their sanity. Some second bloods, however, were able to learn more of the brutal style without compromising their mentality. In addition to this all Kordites have tattoos marked upon their bodies at adolescence. Unlike human tattoos, these markings show our power and how much is left. If we are hurt the tattoos start to shimmer and fail but as we absorb energy they reform. The tattoo on your chest now marks your guild and power. Bear it well my son. Things, however, could only get worse from there."

Michael looked up at his father and asked, "What happened?" Saar-Vaar motioned to another hologram showing scientists working with the Kordites.

"We got desperate. Genetic enhancement and engineering was introduced to help us find and develop more pure bloods by making them. We decided to play god and we paid for it." Another hologram showed multiple horribly disfigured Kordites fighting others. "Most of the pure bloods had genetic defects which made them unstable both physically and mentally. Those who were physically fine were sent into the military. We needed the bulk to help us fight. But after this genetic enhancement or engineering was outlawed and we continued on where we could. Despite the amount of pure bloods being almost reduced to around ten or twenty per cent of the main population second blooded members were powerful enough to help us win most of the battles that we fought. Our energy absorbing power enabled us to share energy with each other. Military units were able to feed off each other giving us more military fire. So peace reigned over us and the Universal Committee." Saar-Vaar showed Michael pictures of the Guardians beginning to explore space. "They found the first alien race and deemed them peaceful and they were able to contribute to the universe. With that they established a Universal Committee which the Guardians would run and provide support for." Michael watched as the Guardians shook hands with different races of life. "Earth was a new planet. Technologically they have developed slower than any of the other alien races that are in the Committee. A pivotal time in human history known as their World War II was where we saw humanity's destructive nature. Discussions were brought forward. The house of Vaar suggested that humans were to be given a chance to even out. However others suggested that we experiment on the humans. One of these was Vek-Gar. He is what you would call a mad scientist. A lot of his experiments were deemed unnatural. He was one of the main scientists who worked on our pure blood breeding programme. After it was shut down Gar decided to make his own laws. The Guild of Vaar and the Guild of Zaren both wanted to attack and put Gar into prison for his atrocities but he was protected by the Guild of Veer. Secretly Gar went to earth and began his experiments. He posed as the human that you know as Robert *Oppenheimer...*"

"Whoa wait. *The* Robert *Oppenheimer* wasn't human?" His father looked at him and nodded.

"Gar's idea was to see what would happen to humans if they were mutated. When he developed the nuclear bomb he infused it with something called the K gene. It would mutate the humans. At first it killed them but low amounts of the K gene brought out abilities. That is why your friends have powers. The K gene mutated them and gave them their ability. This was wrong. We didn't want this. We wanted to see humans succeeded but this did not happen. After we found out what Gar had done I was sent to find him. I came here in around 1950. My investigations into humanity's history brought up some... alarming events, yes the K gene appeared in a large amount in 1945 but my research showed that some superhumans existed almost a hundred years before the main event. While on earth I didn't make much of an impression. I didn't even build the mansion until 1959; instead I resided here within this observatory. That changed when I wanted to connect better with humans. My intelligence and my increased awareness gave me a leg-up on the humans so to speak. I was able to develop Sampson Industries into a company and built up my identity. I also found that a contingent of Kordites had embedded themselves into human governments. They were lost ones so they aligned themselves with Gar and called themselves the "Followers of Gar". Some of them had risen to high military positions. They had a plan but I never found it out. In fact they hid themselves incredibly well. Gar himself went missing and I never found him. Despite the fact that I was supposed to return back to Kord as quickly as possible, I stayed to observe the humans further than what I had found in my studies. This is when I finally saw that the humans needed a leader. No matter how smart they thought they were they were lost. It was then when I formed a brilliant plan. When I returned to Kord for a review I detailed a plan which would bring humans into line and give them a symbol to follow. Twin leaders would be sent to earth and grow up there. They would eventually reveal themselves to the earth. The planet would be unified under their rule which would bring peace. After around 20 years the Guardians would come to earth to review them. Now this was my idea and I put it into action before I arrived on earth. I had lived among humans for long enough to know that they would not fall easily. I would provide technology and cures for diseases such as cancer and HIV. This would hopefully help the humans better accept the rule. This is what you were made for." Michael looked at his father quizzically and raised an eyebrow.

"Made for?"

Saar-Vaar's holographic features changed as if the projection shifted on his feet. "Yes. You were bred to help people. That's why it's hard for you to stop helping people. I and your mother were pure bloods making you and your brother also pure bloods. Giving you an edge over second blooded Kordites. Unlike other Kordites I placed you within a chamber that would feed pure yellow sunlight into you. Your powers accelerate faster than the average Kordite and you have the potential to be stronger; even stronger than a fully trained pure blood. The plan was to see if two people could change the very outlook of a race and make them better. I begged the Guardians to let me do this but they didn't give permission. They said it was wrong or unethical, but I had to try. Humans showed such a strong notion to learn and conquer every boundary that is why I created both you and your brother." The word brother stopped Michael in his tracks.

"So me and my brother were supposed to be a team. What happened to him?" Michael said softly. Though he was afraid of the truth, he wanted to know what had happened to him. His father's face grew dark.

"As I said you two would be a team. You would be a shield. Your brother was a sword. He would destroy any threat while you would protect them. Your brother's name was Dar-Vaar. It meant destroyer. He was engineered to fight, to kill and to fight any enemy no matter how strong they were. He is also at least 44 years older than you."

Michael looked at his father, he could tell he was trying to dodge the question. "What happened to him?"

Saar-Vaar's expression grew darker still. "He went insane. It took time but your brother began to hate life. It grew worse when your sister died…"

"I had a sister!" Michael blurted out.

His father considered him and said, "Yes Lora-Vaar. She was born normally and wanted to be a scientist but she was born as a second blood making her weaker than me or her mother. However she kept training herself to make herself better than what she should be. On a routine mission to an allied planet she was killed by mistake. There was no yellow sun to save her. She was seven years old. In a rage your brother tore the world's capital apart. This was the start of his madness. When I sent him to earth to live among the humans and see how they showed potential he became worse. He did not see potential. He saw how some humans hate each because of looks and something as simple as skin colour. But the final blow came when your... your mother died." The hologram of his father showed pure emotion. A tear fell from his right eye. Tears sank from Michael's eyes. He had lost his sister and his mother all in the same moment. It was hard.

"What happened to her?" The tears on his father's face stopped.

"As you saw, your mother was born with a genetic condition that stopped her from fully absorbing energy. Though we were technologically advanced we couldn't stop this sort of thing. Despite the fact that she was pure blooded she couldn't heal herself. I had tried to keep her alive with energy supplements. When you were being born she was close to death. She couldn't absorb any of the source energy. She died shortly after seeing you. What came next destroyed all my plans. It is said that your brother heard your mother's last breath from the other side of the galaxy. From that day on he saw life as a mistake. He deemed that life was made by just one stupid mistake. For the next two years he went on a killing spree. The Guardians attempted to stop him but even with their power they could not stop him. I... I had created an unstoppable monster." The area around shifted into a scene. Michael recognised it as a memory. The area was on Kord and it looked like a home. For the first time Michael saw his brother. His brother was at least ten feet tall and was heavily muscled. Bone protrusions lined his arms, but worse were his eyes, they glowed black. Michael saw his father land on the ground next to Michael's brother.

His father held his hands up. "Son stop this now!" His father's voice was full of authority but his brother simply turned around and looked. Saar-Vaar shifted nervously and said, "Son, please the plan…"

Suddenly Dar-Vaar tackled him into the wall. "The plan? Is that honestly all you can think of? Your so-called "plan" is stupid. It makes no sense. I went to see the humans. I tried to see the "good" that you see in them. I couldn't see past their faults because they cannot see past anything. They pick on one another because of looks, because of something as simple as skin colour. They seek something to put faith in but when one finds faith in something that gives them hope, they are mocked and criticised for being blind or stupid." No matter how hard his father pushed he couldn't break out of the hold.

"Please my son, think clearly."

His brother raised an eyebrow. "I am thinking clearly. For the first time in a long time Father and do you know what conclusion I've come to? Life is a mistake. It was a random chain of events that led to it. It has no purpose. Look at the Guardians, no matter how many planets they've found how many of them show promise? But I have found an answer. I am going to destroy each and every planet and every galaxy." Saar's eyes turned a deep blue.

"And after this? You will restart life in your image?"

His brother smirked. "My image? Why would I want life to begin in my image? I'm built to kill and destroy. I am as part of this problem as are the other races. But it takes something very powerful to destroy me, so I have found an antimatter universe. I will go and finally I will be at peace." Michael was scared. His brother was mad. Insane quite literally.

"Please, my son it is not too late. You and your brother can…" Michael's brother increased his grip. His left eye twitched.

"My brother? My brother! I have no brother. He killed my mother. So I will kill him now and you will not have any way of stopping me. I will paint this planet red with yours and his blood." Saar-Vaar's eyes turned blue again and two massive energy beams collided with his brother sending him flying away. The memory ended and everything faded to black.

Michael woke up with a jolt. The lab had lit up and there were multiple holograms. Michael saw his father standing in front of him with the same clothes he was wearing in his mind.

"Ah you look much better now," he said looking at Michael. Looking down Michael saw that he was wearing the skinsuit he had seen in the chamber. He gaped at the suit. Michael looked back at his father.

"How the hell did this get on me?" he asked disgusted by the suit he was wearing.

"It is traditional Kordite wear. It suits you well," his father replied.

Michael gaped. "I do not want to wear this. I look like one of those superheroes."

His father smiled. "That is the idea. You are to be a leader for the humans. I thought this would make them accept you better. I never got the chance to wear them on earth."

Michael looked at his father. "What do you mean "never got the chance"?"

His father walked towards him. "My abilities were already considerable on our home planet. I had been able to help others on various planets, saving citizens from cruel acts of nature. On earth I could do the same thing, I could make a difference. I started saving people secretly. The people started calling me a guardian angel. I never revealed myself because I could not come up with an identity good enough. How I would have loved to reveal myself. But you can save the humans you…"

"Spare me this annoying bullshit. Every damn person keeps saying that people show promise. What promise? From the day I stepped into the real world all I have seen people do is betray each other. If it's not for money it's for power. They start wars over nothing. They threaten each other every day with weapons that can destroy this world. The amount of people I have seen that show promise is finite. Even the heroes that give their lives to protect this world are berated. There is no respect. I don't see any promise. In my opinion the Guardians should start this world again that way people would have a better chance at life."

His father's face grew dark. "You dare speak about them like this? Who is the person you love the most? What about Bernard? Even if there are only three good people on this world it is worth saving. That is what the Guardians do. You are looking at this a stereotypical way. You are what they can be. Better. And one day when they can function better without your help you will leave."

Michael slammed his fist into the console next to him. "Stop this. I don't want to be some saviour. I don't want to help people. I don't want to do anything. I just want to get on with my life. I know you were probably expecting someone different; someone who is proactive with helping people and wants to put his life on the line. But at this time I want nothing to do with them. You want the truth? I'm a depression-struck alcoholic with the powers of a god. In the end I don't want this. I just want a normal life," he snarled.

Saar-Vaar examined his son. He wanted to scold him but that wasn't the answer. "My son I have given you an impossible task. You have to change an entire race's way of thinking. Not because we are better but because it is for their own good; because without guidance they will not survive. You're right, the majority of them are betrayers or materialistic. They want only for their own gain. But there are those that are better. They aspire to be better. That is the reason people deserve to be better. Once you are done you will have accomplished your goal. They will have changed and the Guardians will invite them to join the Universal Committee. There are already others that want to help. Those like the angel, the human lightning bolt and the rest of their team. They were not asked to help but they try. You can give them even more help. And you can be a leader. You say you don't want to be a hero yet I have seen you help people. In Russia when Nor-Veer attacked you fought back. You could have just escaped and let the other heroes fight him. But you joined them. When Charlotte had her accident you helped the people around you. You didn't have to. You could have ignored them. But you didn't .When you were younger you pulled your school bus out of the river. You would have survived and you could have swum away. But did you? No. You helped. You can't stop helping. No matter how hard you try. Even with all the injustice that has been done to you and the atrocities you have seen you can still help them. Why? Because you want to." Michael couldn't reply. He looked down in deep thought.

"Alright maybe I can. But first things first: how do I get this suit off?"

Saar-Vaar smiled. "You must believe that you want it off. It reacts to thought." Michael chuckled to himself. Nothing could be simple he thought.

Chapter 9: *I have to find him*

As Michael walked on to the surface of the moon he gazed at the beautiful sun shining in space. His attempts to get the suit off hadn't worked, so he thought that he would keep it on. His father's words kept coming back to him "Even with all the injustice that has been done to you and the atrocities you have seen you can still help them. Why? Because you want to". The words were burned into Michael's memory. Despite the fact that he didn't want to help he had to admit that he couldn't stop helping people. The voice in the back of his head was always nagging him and this was why. For a second Michael wondered whether his father had tinkered with Michael's brain to make him save people. Michael faced the sun and began absorbing energy. His eyes turned red and his veins glowed yellow. The suit's fabric was lighter than anything on earth. His father said that the suit acted like his body. The membranes could absorb solar energy which would strengthen them to the point of being as durable as Michael's body was. That sounded fun he thought. Michael looked at the earth. It shone in the darkness of space. Looking down he kicked himself off the moon and broke out of its gravity. Gliding down he smiled and put his arms in front of him and began flying. He shot into the atmosphere. The welcome heat felt like a nice warm bath. Michael turned to head off home but he wanted to have some fun. He broke the sound barrier and shot down past supersonic speed and all the way to hypersonic speed. Soaring over the sea the water kicked up after him. Michael found himself smiling with no cares for anything. He could hear and see everything perfectly and welcomed the cool spray of the Atlantic Ocean as he soared across it. He weaved between oil rigs and cruise liners. Michael turned again and went towards Africa. He shot over the African savannah and flew close to the ground. Michael felt the air rush against him, it felt refreshing and soothing. Turning again he flew straight back home. Instead of his normal rough landing Michael gently touched down. He was surprised to see Angel leaning against a pillar.

Michael looked at him and asked, "Am I in trouble again?"

Angel chuckled. "Nah. Satellite picked up an object breaking the hypersonic barrier. Other than another of us no one can do that so I guessed it was you. Dig the suit," he said motioning at the traditional garment.

"Yeah. I uh, I found my father," he said with a hint of sadness.

"Tell me all," Angel said. Michael told Angel everything. He told him about the Kordites that had hidden themselves within the American army. How the K gene granted powers to humans and how the nuclear bomb had given them their powers in the first place. Angel's expression hardened and his eyebrow rose.

"I always wanted to find out where my powers came from. Now that I know, well it doesn't exactly feel good. And the fact that there may be some alien infiltrators inside our military system, well it doesn't make me feel good. I'll need to do some investigation. You on the other hand can look as well."

Michael nodded. "Nor-Veer is still out there. I have to find him. There could be another incident like Russia and more damage and death could be caused. I'll start looking."

Angel's com unit began bleeping. "Ah, well duty calls. See you soon." Angel shot into the air and sonic boomed away.

The suit was still on and Michael wanted it off. As he focused a bicycle chime rang twice. Michael turned around to see Charlotte cycling towards him. She stepped off the bike and looked at Michael then away. Then straight back again.

"What are you wearing?" she said giggling. "You look amazing though."

Michael turned his eyes red as he focused. "I want this thing off now," he roared. The suit slowly responded to his thoughts and dissolved from his skin into a band around his arm. His clothes that he wore to go to the moon were back on and felt normal. "Thank you. Anyway you want a drink?" Michael said to Charlotte. She nodded and they walked back into the house. Charlotte greeted Bernard who made her a cold drink. Michael poured himself a double Scotch. As soon as he did Bernard and Charlotte both eyed him uneasily. "Don't start, I found my father and I've got a lot to tell you. You may want a drink as well…"

Michael told them everything from his purpose to the fact that a splinter group of Kordites had embedded themselves within the US military hierarchy. Charlotte gaped at everything trying to take it all in. Bernard's expression hardened and he poured himself a Scotch.

"Your father never told me of your purpose. He told me of your brother but nothing else. This is a burden that you should not have to bear. Leading an entire species and having to change them?" Bernard shook his head in disbelief.

Charlotte stood up and pursed her lips. "That doesn't worry me as much as it should. What's worse is that the American army and other things have been infiltrated. Who knows how far they could have risen in the ranks?" Michael pushed his hair back. He took a long drink of his Scotch and quickly refilled it. He sat down and focused.

"If this Vek-Gar purposely gave powers to humans, there has to be a reason. My dad said this was part of an experiment. Maybe it so he can destabilise the planet through fear. Bernard, do you know of any major incidents involving beings with certain attributes?" he asked.

Bernard stroked his beard. "There have been a few, some damaging some not so damaging. There was an incident in the first Gulf War. Soldiers claimed to see a local man with the ability to manipulate the weather. Apparently the man was able to cause havoc against the local soldiers on both sides. Another was in the Vietnam War when the Vietcong were in possession of "siêu người lính" translated that means super soldier in Vietnamese. The American soldiers that survived his attacks stated that he possessed extreme inhuman strength and speed. His body could not be pierced by bullets. One report said that he could breathe fire. Some of the commanders stated that this "super soldier" was the reason that the war was lost."

Michael raised an eyebrow. "What happened to this guy?" he asked.

"I do not know. Your father however dug deeper into the story and found that a lone general fought the soldier and killed him. The general was stronger and faster than the super soldier. One report said that he ripped the super soldier in half with his bare hands. Things like that happened regularly at first but then died down. There are still other subjects which are gaining powers every day. You only need to see the amount of them Angel and Bolt have to fight. Anyone with powers thinks that they can rule the world. Others try to keep it hidden." Bernard trailed off. Michael manipulated the holographic images and focused on a small piece of video obtained. The video was a camera phone and showed Bolt fighting a person. Bolt supersped into the person but was blasted away. The being was creating fire blasts with his bare hands. The video finished when the blast sent the phone hurtling away. Michael reviewed other information about the super soldier in the Vietnam War. The K gene must have spread quickly; multiple humans gaining incredible powers. Michael frowned; if the Kordites that were embedded into the military had their powers, why hadn't they destroyed the government or the army? Why wait? Moving holographic reports down, he focused on the Vietnam report. He saw pictures of the general who had taken down the super soldier. He was of a strong build with sharp features. His hair was cut short and he was certainly over six feet tall, however he looked even taller. Michael recognised a tattoo under his battledress uniform. The tattoo was that of a X with a spear going down the middle and a spear going across. It covered the general's chest. Michael pointed at him.

"He's Kordite." Charlotte and Bernard turned to look where Michael pointed. Bernard studied the photo.

"How do you know?" he asked. Michael unbuttoned his shirt and showed them the tattoo of his family's crest. Charlotte blushed slightly and walked towards him. She gently touched his chest.

"When did this happen?" she asked.

"When I was at the moon observatory; it burnt like hell. My father explained that when Kordites reach a certain age they are imprinted. They are shown their family's history and given this tattoo. It identifies their particular family guild and house they belong to. Anyway that general has a family guild. I don't know what it belongs to though," he said.

"I believe this is of some interest," Bernard said looking at a holographic news video. The caption read, "US general assess situation in the Middle East". Michael examined the general. He was a beast of a man with a chest as wide as a redwood tree and hands that could crush a human skull. Either he was steroid using human or a Kordite warrior. A question shot up from the cacophony of voices.

"General Rockwell, what do you think should be done about this new offensive in Afghanistan?" A reporter shouted. The general smiled; a smile that could crack mirrors.

"My friend, this offensive being carried out by the insurgents is a tactical retreat. The insurgents obviously know that they are on their last legs. Though we have sustained some casualties, my soldiers are reporting that most of the militants will be dead within the week. Peace will reign in the region." The general smiled showing his pristine white teeth. Michael sensed something was wrong with the general. It sent shivers down his spine. Multiple reporters popped up enquiring more of the general. Michael switched the video off and slumped down to the ground. Charlotte sat down with him and kissed him gently.

"What's wrong?"

Michael looked at her square in the face and said, "I don't know. All I know is that I need to find them; before they do any more damage." He pulled a hip flask from his pocket and took a long drink letting the alcohol's smooth taste take his mind off the events. Charlotte grabbed the flask and threw it down.

"Why do you drink? The alcohol doesn't affect you but you always turn to it. Why can't you just talk to me or Bernard?"

Michael's eyes turned red. "I don't know. I like it. It can't affect me so what's the point in crying about it!" he said. Michael walked outside and prepared to superspeed away before Charlotte touched his shoulder.

"Michael I know you're stressed now. I know that you feel responsible for this but you can change that now, you can stop all of this and help people," she said softly.

Michael turned round and kissed her gently. "I'm sorry. I... just need time to think," he said staring at his feet.

"Take all the time you need," she replied. Michael smiled and shot into the sky. It took seconds for him to reach orbit. Michael closed his eyes and let his hearing go. He heard all sounds at once and filtered them at the same time. He floated in space until he heard a ticking. Michael's eyes opened and blazed red. The sound was exactly like the bomb he had faced before. He shot towards the sound breaking the sound barrier. Whatever was happening, he would stop it.

Chapter 10: *You can't stop us*

Michael tracked the sound down to an abandoned building in London. He smashed down into ground cracking the concrete around him. He walked towards the increasing ticking, ready to send the bomb into the upper atmosphere. As he entered the building, he scanned the area looking for the bomb. There was nothing, the building was clean.

"Don't bother looking for an explosive device there isn't one," an icy voice said through the darkness. Michael knew the voice it was Nor-Veer's. Michael immediately adopted a combat stance. However Veer simply dropped the rest of his sword to ground and kept standing straight. "Don't bother," he said gesturing towards Michael's stance. "We both know you're not strong enough to fight me. I've come here to talk not to fight."

Michael didn't drop his guard but he relaxed slightly. "What do you want?" he asked, his voice dripping with venom. Nor remained emotionless as if the words dipped in poison didn't even faze him; it made Michael shiver with fear.

"I know you found your father's observatory within the moon. We know he told you about us and that we are within the military," Nor shrugged; the information didn't matter to him. "You may think you have all the information and that you have a chance of stopping us. You do not." Nor supersped towards Michael. "You can't stop us. In fact I've been sent here to convince you to join us."

Michael smirked and pushed Veer back. "Why would I want to join you?"

Nor wiped the dust off of his jacket and sighed. "You are the first example of genetic engineering in over a thousand years of our history. You are one of the strongest Kordites I have ever seen. The only one that surpasses us is your... brother." Nor's voice was made up of contempt; the only thing that mattered was his defeat at the hands of Michael's older brother. "I have fought your brother and lost. But you are young and share our ideals."

Michael shifted on his feet. "What ideals are these?" Nor actually smiled slightly, lifting the emotionless facade for just one second.

"The Guardians are clueless old fools who believe every planet needs saving but earth is a lost cause." Nor threw a small sphere up into the air that began broadcasting different videos of earth's history. "Look at this. They've had millions of years to change and make things better. I looked at their United Nations mandate. They have wanted to wipe away poverty, yet if we are to believe adverts from so-called charities that one's not quite worked out yet, has it? Oh what about this one: nuclear disarmament." He looked up from the list and scoffed. "Last time I looked we may be a bit close to World War 3 for that..."

Michael put his hand up. "Alright, alright what's your point?"

Nor threw the list down. "You share these views do you not? Why don't you join us? Together we can fully take over and raze this planet to ash for the benefit of the humans. Our plan is almost in motion. We have already infiltrated the American military." Nor remained cool and collected. "That was something we excelled at. The last thing is the political parties; all of us will unite the parties into one single government under one single president; a Kordite of course. The United Nations will be last. Once we have full control we will launch a full attack simultaneously on every country. Then when humanity is extinct and we have destroyed every last resistance of humanity we will leave." Veer spread his hands out. "That's all we want do."

Michael looked down at his feet and smiled, his eyes crimson red. "You're right, I can't stand humans. They have such opportunities to change their lives, but instead they argue over ethics and morals. None of them have the will to protect the earth or change it. They are weak. And the plan is foolproof; humanity will not know what hit them. We can finally bring peace and order to this planet." Nor stepped forward to shake Michael's hand, but Michael took his hand away. "But you see that's exactly what makes them unique. At the moment they can't solve any of their problems. But slowly they will find peace. And are we any better? We had to fight a thousand-year-long war to finally emerge with peace." Nor stepped back, his eyes a piercing green. He sighed hard.

"I didn't want to fight you again. You are a brave and noble warrior, but I have to kill you and the rest of humanity will follow." Motioning towards his blade it flew towards his hand. "Including the one you love. How is Charlo..." Nor didn't get a chance to finish her name as Michael tackled him towards a support. His eyes blazed red as the building shook from the impact.

"Never speak her name. I don't care how many of you there are; I will destroy you all. And when I press my boot against you throat, you will know that this world is under my protection." Nor pulled Michael's arm from his throat and pushed him back.

He adjusted his shirt and said, "You've declared war on an army you cannot defeat." He soared into the air and disappeared.

Michael breathed a sigh of relief. He couldn't have chanced a fight with Veer here, the collateral damage would have been too much. He gently lifted off into the air and flew towards the Big Ben clock tower. He landed on the clock face and felt the cool air rush against his face. He needed a new game plan. He searched his mind to see what details he could remember from his encounter with Veer. What was he doing in Britain? The followers of Gar wanted to take over America first; there was no reason to be here. Michael opened himself up to the world. He used his sight and hearing and scanned London for anything of relevance to the Kordites' plan. Nothing, nothing at all. Maybe it was nothing Michael thought as he was about to rise into air and fly home. Suddenly his phone vibrated. He pulled it out of his pocket and checked who it was. Bernard was keeping tabs on him.

"Yes Bernard, what can I do for you?"

"Miss Phoenix is here, she wishes to talk to you and you have an appointment with a board member in the morning." *Great*, Michael thought. He didn't really want anything do with his father's company but he was the owner.

"Got it, Bernard. On my way." Michael kneeled down and removed a flask from a pouch on his pocket. He took a long drink from the flask and sighed. This was the one thing in his life that didn't offer resistance. Subconsciously Michael could feel his eyes turning red. He threw the flask towards the sky and watched it burn in the atmosphere. He rose into the air and flew home.

Michael touched down slowly and walked towards to the door. Before he even got close the door flung open and Charlotte threw herself on to him. She kissed him for what seemed hours. Michael didn't fight it, he loved her too much. His eyes glowed red. Michael carried her inside towards his bedroom. Charlotte began taking her clothes off, Michael followed. He didn't care. His eyes were a piercing red as he threw Charlotte on to the bed. Michael was lost in her beauty but his subconscious screamed at him to stop. He suddenly realised the promise he was breaking. No matter how much they wanted to he couldn't hurt her. The red blaze of his eyes died down to their normal black. He supersped back into the corner and let his head drop into his hands. Running his hands through his black hair Charlotte came over and sat next to him. Sweat ran down her naked body. She sighed softly.

"Michael, I... I'm sorry. I don't know what came over me. I... It's my fault, I should have known better," she said softly. That was the last thing Michael wanted to hear. He scanned her quickly before saying anything. He hadn't broken any of her bones, but she was tired. Her heart raced a million beats a minute. Michael had been relying on instinct, he'd stopped thinking of her as human. H... he had lost control.

"It's not your fault. I didn't exactly try to stop you." He pulled a sly smile that broke her face into a grin. He pulled her close to him. "We can't. Not yet. Not until I find a way to fully control every aspect of my powers. If I ever hurt you, that would kill me. It doesn't matter that no weapon can penetrate my skin. The thought of hurting you pains me. I will never let that happen." They stood up together and Michael helped her put her clothes back on. He followed suit. "Anyway, now that that's happened I have things to tell you…"

Michael told Charlotte about the encounter with Veer; about his plan to destroy humanity and the fact that they were infiltrating almost every part of the American infrastructure. Charlotte pursed her lips and concentrated hard.

"If Veer wants you on their side, then he obviously fears you. The fact that he wants your help means that he realises you are the only thing that stands in his way. But the fact that they want control of the entire political structure…" Charlotte shook her head. "That scares me beyond anything else."

Michael nodded. "I can't let them do this. But I don't know where to start." Michael stood up. "But first I need to work out some stress."

Charlotte smiled. "We could always do something else," she said seductively. Michael smiled and kissed her gently.

It was still late so Michael leaned into her and said, "Why don't we try and get some sleep? It's three in morning." She nodded and they both got back in bed. Michael didn't like sleep but the comfort of knowing he was with Charlotte soothed him.

The nightmare had started the same way that any other did; in a dark room. Michael looked around trying find out where he was. Tentatively, he began walking away from where he was. And then he saw it; New York in flames. Buildings toppling down; the Statue of Liberty decapitated and destroyed. Michael desperately tried to think of something else. He flew into the air and scanned the streets for Charlotte, she could help calm down. Bodies littered the highways and roads. Michael flew towards the only still standing building in the city: the Empire State Building. Michael rose to the top of the building and landed on the roof. He saw a figure sitting on the edge watching the destruction.

"Beautiful, isn't it?" the figure said.

"Who the hell are you?" Michael asked sternly. The figure turned round slowly and Michael almost fell off the building with shock. It was him or just a darker version of him. His hair was messy and his eyes were a burning crimson. His clothes were in tatters and there were burns all over him.

"I'm you, or well the darker version of you; all your hate, your fear and your beautiful, beautiful depression. Look at you: the powers of a god in the mind of broken being. This, this is inevitable isn't it? Oh how I long to get control of your mind and destroy everything around you." Michael felt liked he'd been gut punched. He wanted to rush him off the building and break the thing in half.

"I am better than you. I'm trying to beat you and I will do it," Michael shouted.

"No you can't," his doppelgänger yelled. The whole world began shaking vividly and began breaking apart. Five spires shot up, impaled on each spire were The Team heroes, dead and broken. "You did this, you destroyed these five. Now what else should I kill before I destroy the rest of the world?" Suddenly another spire shot up with Charlotte on it. Michael fell on his knees and roared.

"NOOOOO leave HER alone, take me instead." Michael's doppelgänger let out an unearthly laugh.

"She is the one thing standing in my way of taking you over." The doppelgänger raised a dagger and held it to her throat. She began shouting "Michael" repeatedly as it began slitting her throat. Then the nightmare stopped.

Michael woke up instantly roaring in pain. He shot himself out of the window and flew out of the atmosphere going faster than ever before. No more he yelled he knew that his voice wouldn't carry but he didn't care. He didn't want to wait before his depression took over and he killed her. He flew towards the sun. He could already feel his energy increasing but he knew that the core of the sun burned hotter than anything. It was a chance he could take to die.

Back on earth Bernard ran up to the master bedroom. He found the massive window had been blown out and Charlotte was desperately trying to get Marcus to activate.

"What happened?" he asked urgently.

Charlotte looked in shock at him. "I... I don't know, he was having a bad dream so I was trying wake him up. He was yelling no more and when he woke up he flew out of here."

Bernard thought hard. "We have to stop him now. And there are only two people I know who can stop him." Bernard pressed a button on the wall which instantly communicated with The Team. Rachel Walters, the member of The Team known as Dove, answered.

"Bernard what can I do for you?" she asked.

"Miss Walters, I need you and Master Spence to get into space now. Something has happened to Michael." Rachel nodded and disappeared. Bernard powered down the communicator. He heard Charlotte crying quietly. He sat next to her and comforted. "Don't worry Charlotte they'll get him back."

In space Angel and Dove sped towards the sun. They could both see Michael hurtling towards the sun.

"We've got him. Geez, how fast is he going?" Dove asked.

"I don't know. His powers are sporadic at best, it's almost impossible to map them out. All I know is that he's not in the best frame of mind at the moment and we need to stop him." They were getting closer to the sun. Angel winced at the light.

"You alright, Angel?" Dove asked.

"I don't think I can get too close to the sun, maybe near it but not right by it," he replied.

"I'm light itself I can't feel the sun so I'm gonna power through."

Angel nodded and slowed himself down. "Roger, you go get him Dove."

She didn't reply she knew what she had to do. She increased speed to catch up with him. Michael was hurting really bad she knew that but she had to save him from himself. As she got close to him she grabbed his shoulders and pulled him back with all of her strength. She could feel Michael straining at the force of her. She used every ounce of strength to pull him back but it wasn't enough. Michael kept going. Dove knew she couldn't stop him. *Well this is how it's gonna go*, she thought. All of a sudden a hand grabbed Michael's other shoulder and pulled him back. It was Angel. Even though his suit was burning he forced himself to pull him back. Michael was starting to slow down. Something was holding back, maybe it was Michael's subconscious. Whatever it was it was helping them pull him back.

Atta boy Michael, Angel thought, *fight it with everything you have*. They managed to pull him back to near earth orbit. They put a mask on Michael's face so he could talk. Dove examined him for injuries but there was nothing, no burns at all. But there were tears streaming down his face.

Michael simply said, "No more." Dove and Angel hugged him closely and descended back towards his home.

Angel and Dove didn't stop around for long; they still had a world to protect. Michael walked inside and as soon as he saw Charlotte he hugged her as hard as he could. Bernard held him close as well.

He simply said, "I'm sorry." Charlotte suddenly started crying again. She hugged him and kissed him, holding him close. They walked upstairs where Michael quickly changed his clothes.

"What happened in your dream?" she asked softly. Michael quickly filled her in again. More tears came from her eyes. "You'll never do that. You are stronger Michael than anything and you can beat this. We'll just take it one day at a time." Michael smiled gently.

"I'm sorry Charlotte, I will try," he said softly. They both walked downstairs. Michael leaned into another kiss with Charlotte. Suddenly Bernard cleared his throat. Michael looked around to see Bernard and another man. The other man was African American with a strong build. The man's black hair was greying slightly but he still looked like he could beat Michael up.

"Sir this is Mr David Jones. He is the representative from your company," Bernard said motioning towards the man. Jones stepped forward to shake Michael's hand.

"A pleasure to meet you Mr Sampson, you're the spitting image of your father."

Michael smiled. "Thank you Mr Jones. If you'd excuse me for just one second." He turned to Charlotte and whispered into her ear. "I'll see you later." Charlotte reached up and kissed him on his cheek. She waved to Bernard. Michael clapped his hands together and said, "Shall we begin?" Michael motioned to Jones to sit on the sofa. Jones sat down and opened his briefcase. Pulling out a tablet he began searching for the right documents. "So what would you like to talk to me about?"

Jones looked up and smiled. "When I first met your father I was a wet-behind-the-ears accountant who had no idea what I was doing. Now I'm working at one of the biggest companies in the world. When your father told me about his son, I was ecstatic. Someone who could help me bring your father's ideas to the world. What I wanted to do today was ask you if you want control of the company?"

Michael stared blankly at Jones. "Um... I'm almost speechless. The company is perfect without me. I don't really believe that I'm right for this job."

Jones nodded. "You are young and don't know much about running a multibillion making company. But, son, if you don't take control of the company now the board will. That's something you don't want happening."

This piqued Michael's interest. "Why, what will they do?"

Jones's smile quickly disappeared. "Our R & D section of the company is extremely advanced thanks to your father. Now we make enough money as it is but for the last ten years the board have been pushing military contracts. With the technology we have: genetic enhancement, kinetic energy weapons, and nano weapons," Jones pulled a grim smile, "the thought of it is terrible. You can stop this. With your support the board will back down."

Michael sighed deeply. "I wish I could help you sir, I really do. But I don't know what to do. At the moment I just can't help you. I understand why you want my help. I didn't realise R & D was that advanced. I'm sorry sir. I really am."

Jones nodded and stood up. "Michael, I really do understand your view. But I need your help. If you can't make the decision yet that's fine. But you have two years until your name fails to stop the board. Think seriously about your decision." Michael shook Jones's hand. Jones smiled and walked out. Bernard opened the door. The two nodded at each other.

"Bernard always a pleasure."

"David."

Michael sat down deep in thought. What should he do first? Save the world? Or save his company? No first Michael thought he had to find a big bird and a lightning bolt.

Chapter 11: *Ready to fight?*

Michael hovered over the Atlantic Ocean letting the gentle breeze wash over him. He was over one of the main shipping lanes, waiting for something. He began scanning the area for his target until he felt something beneath him. He looked down and saw an outline of a giant ship. Michael landed on the cloaked object. He knocked gently on the ship. The ship opened up and released two armed drones which both targeted Michael.

An automatic voice suddenly said, "State your business here." Michael froze in place.

"Why is it robots are always try to kill me?" he muttered. "My activation code is, "Seven, alpha, Charlotte"." The drones scanned Michael and suddenly folded their weapons away.

"Greetings Michael Sampson 03." The cloaking device deactivated and the ship appeared. The ship was the size of a cruise liner but faster and possessed more weaponry. It served as a base of operations of the superhero team. Angel had commissioned Michael to build it but had covered it up by saying a private contractor had constructed it. There were no other people aboard the ship as the drones took care of security. Michael heard a boom shoot next to him. Bolt was in his civilian workout clothes and had a towel on his shoulder. Fresh sweat dripped off his brow.

"Hey Mike what's up?" he said wiping his neck.

"Eh, not much Andrew. Just thought I'd come and see how things are going."

Andrew smiled and said, "We're all fine. Actually we're all in the gym training. You're welcome to join us." Michael nodded and they supersped to the gym. The superhero team was simply known as "The Team" and comprised of five members at the moment but there were always others who wanted to join. However the team was forced to keep to a standing number of seven. In the last two years, there had been over 50 candidates that had been deemed too violent or unstable to join. A side effect of being under the jurisdiction of the UN was that they could sign off on members joining. In addition to this all team members were submitted to psychological reviews to make sure they were capable of carrying out their duties. However the team could keep a few secrets regarding information. This was probably why they had never found out about Michael being a founding member. Michael and Booker entered the gym. The gym took up an entire deck of the ship. It had an Olympic-size swimming pool, with other parts of the gym being used for weight training, cardio and even a sauna. Michael saw Angel weight training in a section of the gym. Michael had designed the weights to be handled by superhumans who could lift over five tons. Angel was lifting two 85 ton dumb-bells up steadily. He looked over at Michael and Andrew and smiled.

"Yo, Mike what's up?" he said as he gently put the dumb-bells back into place. As soon as he placed them back into their holders the weight was instantly reduced. Michael designed the place holders with antigravity panels which immediately reduced the gravity around the weights meaning they could be held indefinitely. Angel shook Michael's hand in a firm grip and said. "What drags you out here today?"

Michael shrugged. "Just thought I'd come down to see what's happening on my ship."

"Your ship? I don't think so," a loud voice shouted. Michael turned round to see who had shouted and saw two approaching figures.

Michael recognised them both. The one who had shouted was the superhero known as Tremor aka John Cartwright. Cartwright was a bull of a man standing at well over 6 feet and weighing in at 220 pounds. As his name suggested Tremor had the ability to control earthquakes. This provided him with vast superhuman strength and durability. In addition to this he could literally feel when an earthquake was about to occur. Michael had only seen Tremor helping with natural disasters rather than actually fighting a superhuman. This was mainly because Tremor could hit with the actual force of earthquakes. This could be anything from 1 on a Richter scale to an unknown reading. The other man was The Stranger aka Terrence Masterson. Standing at six feet tall and weighing around 240 pounds he was extremely muscular and possessed a heavy build .Terrence was the only member of The Team that was fine with killing. Other than his name not much was known about him. His abilities enabled him to regenerate his body at amazing rate. In addition to this he could activate his adrenalin to higher levels meaning that he could possess superhuman attributes. At first Terrence was considered to be the weakest of the five; however he had saved The Team multiple times with his incredible ideas. Terrence always carried two six-shooters and used them with devastating accuracy. Michael had built two new models which could fire different slugs, anything from explosive to heavy tungsten rounds. Other than this almost nothing was known of The

ZAC VIRDEE

Stranger. He appeared to be a 32-year-old man in his prime. However there was a rumour that he was over a hundred years old. However both were good friends of Michael's and had always been helpful. Michael smiled at Tremor and shook his friend's hand. He slapped Terrence on the shoulder who simply grunted in approval.

"John how you doing man?" said Michael with a grin on his face.

"Not bad. It's good to see you man. So what can we do for you?"

Michael smiled. "Well, I want to work out some aggression." The four men smiled and turned their attention to the boxing ring. Michael's eyes widened. "What me fighting Angel?" Angel smiled and cracked his knuckles.

Bolt walked towards Michael. "I may not be as strong as you but I bet I can take you down." Bolt raised his hands. "Strength isn't the only way to win a fight," he said.

Michael smiled. "Let's do this then."

Michael and Booker stepped into the ring. They didn't bother wearing gloves because the force their fists made would crush the gloves. Michael had changed into gym wear which was more form-fitting. Terrence was the referee. Wearing his signature fedora, he tipped it up and walked between the two.

"Okay. I haven't done this in a while. No rabbit punches, no below the belt and no breaking the ship apart." Terrence walked back and in a flash shot the bell.

Let's do this, Michael thought. They stood apart and waited. Neither made a move until Michael launched a right jab towards Bolt. Booker waited till the last moment to counter and launched a barrage into Michael's midsection. Each punch smacked into Michael at a thousand miles per hour. Michael felt that. He quickly readjusted and launched his own set of punches. Booker dodged each and responded but Michael was ready this time as he dodged the three punches and blocked the last one. Booker recoiled from the last punch. Though he had incredible durability, hitting Michael at anything below a thousand miles per hour was like punching titanium. Michael didn't let up; he launched another barrage of punches which knocked Booker down.

Terrence tipped his hat up and sauntered over. "Bolt you getting back up?" Bolt shot up and launched himself at Michael. Time slowed down as Michael jabbed Bolt back down to the ground. Michael was still holding back. He didn't want to hurt Booker permanently. Booker bounced off the ground and entered superspeed. He began rapidly hitting Michael and moving faster than Michael could react. But his pattern was predictable. With every blitz he hit Michael with a jab nothing more. Michael's mind entered combat mode as he analysed every pattern that he could see. In the last second he hyper accelerated his reflexes to the same speed that Bolt was travelling and launched a roundhouse kick to Booker's jaw sending down to the ground.

Terrence didn't start counting, he simply said, "I am not even gonna bother counting. He's out." There was some awe from the crowd.

"Mike what did you do to him?" a female voice called out. Michael instantly recognised it. Dove was wearing simple training clothes and walked into the gym. She stood at around 5 feet 11 and had medium build that was pure muscle. She had pure white hair which was akin to snow. She also had pure blue eyes which were like the sea. Walters had extreme powers. She was able to control light and could easily vaporise someone. In addition she could physically move at the speed of light and possessed incredible strength. As with her control of light she could craft weapons of light and had incredible durability. "You knocked him out with one kick. That was pretty epic," she said with a smile on her face.

Michael laughed and said, "I was holding back and he did ask for it." She smiled softly and then concern grew over her face. She walked towards him and held his arm.

"Are you alright now?"

Michael's eyes turned red slightly. "I-I'm fine. It was just a bad dream." She smiled broadly and gave him a big hug.

John moved through the group and said, "Come on man that wasn't a challenging fight for you. Fight me. I'll show you a challenge."

Michael welcomed him and said, "If you think you can take me than let's go." The two men went back into the ring and bumped fists. John's fists were lined with a light blue. They began radiating air rapidly and pure energy could be seen coming from them.

Terrence didn't bother issuing the rules. Instead he simply said, "You know the rules. Just don't break the ship." Michael struck first with all of his strength. John intercepted the punch with his own fist. Michael knew that John was incredibly durable but even he couldn't withstand Michael's punch at full force. The two punches collided with each other and created a shock wave that blew out all the windows. The rest of The Team fell down and the entire ship shook. Michael recoiled backwards, his fist aching from the power of John's punch. Michael suddenly realised that John had lined his punch with his earthquake powers. Lifting his fist back up, Michael could have sworn that he had broken a few bones. John's hand hadn't escaped unscathed. Blood lined his fist and flowed down his hand. Terrence got up off the floor and scooped up his fedora. With a single leap he jumped out of the ring and stood with rest of The Team. Michael repositioned himself as did John. They launched at each other. Moving with blinding speed John launched a barrage of punches hitting with the force of 4.3 earthquake. Michael was winded. John took his chance. He lashed out with a 6.7 quick kick to Michael's temple causing him to fall down on his knees. John prepared to strike the final blow but Michael wasn't finished yet. He grabbed John's legs and pulled them from under him. Michael took his chance and launched more into John's face. Using the force of a 4.7 earthquake, John pushed Michael off him. Landing back perfectly on his feet Michael prepared to re-engage John. Both prepared to strike again until Terrence finished it. Two rounds from his six-shooters clashed into both Michael and John. They both looked at Terrence.

"Enough it's a draw." He pointed to the windows and to the crack in the wall. "I am the one who is gonna fix that not you two. So stop it; it's a draw." Michael looked back and John returned his glare but both broke out into a smile and shook hands.

"I would have won," John said with a smile.

Michael smiled as well. "I know you would have." Whether Michael believed that or not, the two men would never find out.

After a shower and change of clothes, Michael went down to the food deck. Michael had built it with multiple tables and a giant king-sized table where all The Team could eat. In addition to that there was a kitchen which could be used to cook anything that was needed. The deck also served as The Team's rec room. Due to the fact that the ship never berthed anywhere it restored its resources by special supply planes from a company which was a part of Michael's organisation. The ship's size enabled it to house different helicopters and quick response jets; all built by Michael. Booker was cooking a wide array of dishes for them to eat.

Booker was an incredible cook; he had been cooking for years and had tried to teach Michael too. However Michael didn't quite have the touch to be a cook.

Booker had a small cut on his lip that was healing. Michael had offered his apologies but Booker had dismissed him.

"When you step into that ring you have to be ready for any type of beating. You were the just the better fighter," Booker had said. Michael stepped outside and watched the waves kick gently against the ship, though there was nothing to kick against as the cloak hid the boat from any visibility. The sun was gently beginning to sink. Michael exhaled as he felt the sun dip beneath the waves. Michael walked back in and saw the rest of team just taking their seats at the table. Booker began laying the table and dropping glasses on the table. Michael took his seat and waited for Booker to take his seat. Water was poured into their glasses which made Michael laugh.

"Don't you guys have anything stronger?" he shouted to Angel. The Team looked at him like he had sworn.

Terrence suddenly piped up, "No they don't. And believe me I've looked." The rest of The Team suddenly burst out into laughter. As everybody finished laughing, they all dug into the various dishes. Michael enjoyed times like this. The Team viewed each others as brothers and sister. They had made sure they had a good team relationship so that they worked together well in the field. Out of all of them Angel was the one who appeared more in public. He was the one who made the public cheer. Without him The Team would cease to function. Michael helped clear the dishes, though it wasn't needed. Booker had cleared most of it before The Team could react. Michael stood on the balcony. The night air was cool and the gentle ocean spray washed against his face. The pale moonlight glinted off the water and made it look almost pure white. Adam joined Michael outside. He handed Michael a bottle of soda and they both took a long drink.

Adam broke the silence. "Something's up with you Michael. What is it?" Michael looked up. He hadn't realised his eyes were glowing red.

Michael took a long sigh and said, "I don't even know where to begin."

As Michael recounted the events of what happened in London, the rest of The Team had joined them outside. Every so often Adam had to fill John, Terrence and Rachel in with the other details.

After Michael had finished, Terrence chuckled and said, "Shit, I've been alive a lot longer than you lot. I've killed and seen a lot weird things but aliens are a first. Sounds fun." Michael chuckled softly. Out of all The Team, Terrence was the most "unethical". He didn't care about law and order. What mattered to him was right and wrong, nothing else.

"Yeah, well they don't go down easy," Michael said.

"Mike's right, it took me, Michael and Booker to make a dent in one but not without great cost. We have to be ready. If they are invading the political and military sections of the American government we have to be ready," Angel said. The Team nodded in agreement.

John piped up, "Do these guys have any weakness?"

Michael pursed his lips in thought. "I don't really think so. The planet we come from is harsh and unforgiving. Our bodies are capable of unlimited absorption of energy that further enhances our capabilities. Nor took almost everything we had in a fight. Even Angel's cry only wounded him after prolonged exposure. The only thing that punctured my skin was a sword used by Nor made from a material not of earth. It's incredibly strong and is used for engineering weapons on my planet."

Angel nodded. "I remember that." He lifted his shirt and showed the bandaged area of his body that had a glint of blood within it. "This wound still hasn't healed properly. Hell it's one of the few things that can cut me. I've shrugged off tank shells like they were paintballs but that blade. It cut deeper than anything I've ever felt." He turned to Michael and said, "Do you think you can reverse engineer it?"

Michael shrugged. "I haven't got that much of it. It was only a small piece that was lodged in my abdomen. But from what I found out, the metal is stronger than anything on earth. It can literally split atoms. And the strangest part about it is that it records memory, like it's almost organic. I was exposed to it for a small amount of time and I saw decades of history in minutes. But there's no way for me to reverse engineer it. I... I simply don't have enough of it." The Team all looked at the water passing them by.

Terrence suddenly spoke up. "That means we have to kill them." Everyone looked at him as he pulled one of his six-shooters out. "There can be no other option. We've got no way of holding them. From what Michael has said even the prisons we've built for superhumans wouldn't hold 'em. So that means if we're fighting them we have to go for the kill. Hopefully with our combined powers we can put them down." The Team shifted uneasily on their feet.

"Terrence is right," John said. "We can't pull our punches with these guys. Either go for the kill or forget about."

Angel shifted on his feet again. "That isn't how we do things. We have to approach this carefully and with tact. We should approach the UN first, get their support. We can't just start a war without the planet's support." Terrence scoffed and walked away. He lit a cigar and blew the smoke towards the sea.

Michael pondered and then spoke. "We can't do that. We don't know whether the UN would go ahead with our plan or if they're under Kordite control. One thing is for certain; we need to make a decision soon because I doubt they'll give us a head start." Michael finished his soda as The Team thought about what he had said.

Rachel spoke up. "Look, I joined The Team so I can make a difference. So far we've managed to do things well, but this; it's something we could never have imagined. Aliens. People don't trust us fully. They see us doing incredible things but this, this is something we can use to cement their trust. If they see us defending them maybe it will stop the hatred. I don't know. I'm rambling," she said as she hovered in the air.

"She's right," Booker said. "People don't trust us. Maybe this is a way for us to…"

"Enough." Booker was cut short by Angel. He rarely shouted. It was only when he couldn't see what was right. The Team all hushed quite. Even Terrance put out his cigar. "This is their planet. It's their right to ask us or deny our help. This is where the trust comes from. Not putting our point of view across but allowing them to see that we can help them. We will only strike when asked to; nothing more, nothing less. I don't wanna hear any more about this." Angel shot into the air and flew off. Michael resisted the urge to follow. He knew this topic made Angel uneasy.

Rachel leaned on Michael's shoulder and said, "He still feels it; the guilt. Every day, 24/7. That's why he pushes himself harder and harder. Even past his limits. It's not fair." And then it all came rushing back to Michael.

Five years ago a blogger by the name of Alex Denton began spreading rumours that The Team were a hit squad organised by the NSA and the CIA. As the blog was an online production it spread like wildfire. The Team had taken every action they could to show that they were there to help, but it didn't help. Angel had asked Michael if he could trace where the blogger was. Michael remembered that it took him a day of searching and found that Denton lived in Chicago. Angel personally went to Denton to ask politely if he would stop posting the lies. At first it seemed to work; but after three days a headline went live on the blog. It read ""Heroic" Team leader threatens me with death if I don't stop telling the truth". That's when things got worse. Everywhere The Team went to help they were met with protest by other people. Petitions were signed to disband The Team. Mass suicides were threatened. In the end a drastic action was needed. Michael remembered it clearly. Angel came to talk with Michael about his plan.

"There's only one way we can change this. I'm gonna reveal my secret identity." The idea hit Michael like a gut punch. He couldn't believe what Adam wanted to do. At the time Adam was married to a woman named Amy Webb. Michael had met her a few times; she was beautiful. She was around 5 foot 6 and had long brown hair with incredible blue eyes. She had been the main driving force for Adam becoming Angel and bringing together a team. Michael remembered when Angel arranged the press conference. Angel landed in front of the police and the president. He shook the president's hand and gave the smile that calmed everyone down. He took to the podium, confident and ready to reassure everyone. "Good afternoon. The past few months have tested people's faith in my team's ability to protect you." There was a sudden burst of jeers from the protesters who held up banners and signs. But Angel didn't flinch, he just kept smiling. "Ever since these rumours started people have stopped believing in us. I know the last few years have been tough on people. Not being able to trust your own government is something that no one should have to go through. So I wanna tell you something. Everyone has secrets. Our secrets enable us to have a life outside of what we do. But I'm gonna tell you mine and then I'll take any questions you have." Angel took a deep breath and smiled again. "My name is Adam Spence and I've been a forensic investigator for the last ten years. Any questions?" The crowd erupted with questions and flash photography engulfed the area. At first Michael thought this would work and the people would better accept The Team. About a week later Angel had gone home after his day of being on patrol. He'd been helping out with clean-up effort after an earthquake in China. Michael had tried to convince both Angel and Amy to live on the ship but they had denied his request. They both wanted to keep a normal life. Angel had landed in the backyard to avoid any unnecessary attention. He approached the back door but found that it was ajar. He didn't find it strange, Amy never minded a bit of cold air. Adam stepped into the house and placed his radio on the table and then suddenly noticed a few spots of blood. Adam followed the blood trail into the main room and that's when he saw it; Amy's blood-soaked body lay on the floor. Adam immediately carried out an evaluation on her. She'd been stabbed multiple times and worst of all she'd been gang raped. Angel noticed that "freak" had been written multiple times in Amy's blood. The next few days were awash with in media coverage of Amy's death. Angel decided to give a statement to reassure the people that he was coping with her death. Again he approached the podium except this time he was fighting back tears.

"Good evening. My wife, Amy was a kind, loving and warm woman. She loved everybody. No matter their race, looks, religion or anything else. I have received news that she was at the time carrying my child." Adam stopped for a second as his bottom lip quivered. Dove had been there and she gently rested her hand on his shoulder. Angel continued.

"I know that, that child would have been in wonderful care with Amy. She was a shining example of what we should be and act like. I will not be pursuing the people who did this. We have other matters to attend to and I would like to focus on that first. To the people that have committed this attack I say this: do not be afraid of me. Please give yourselves up so justice can be carried out. Thank you." Michael knew that it took a strong man not to react to what Adam had seen but Adam continued strong. There were only a few times when Adam broke down from the pressure but he continued being the team leader that was needed. The group that murdered Amy was never found.

Michael refocused back on where he was. He blinked a tear from his eye. Thinking about Amy always made him feel sad; another life stolen.

"He's probably gonna be fine but I need to go and talk to him."

Rachel nodded. "It hurts him more than anything. Please Michael he needs you." Michael nodded. He gently ascended into the air and quickly gained speed. Using his superhuman vision he saw Adam hovering in the upper atmosphere. His giant white wings twitched gently. Like Michael, Adam could go a long time without breathing though he was wearing a small breather apparatus which enabled him to breathe and talk in areas without oxygen. Michael approached Adam. Adam acknowledged him by offering him a mask. Michael took the mask and clipped it to his face. They both hovered there in silence for what seemed like hours.

Angel broke the silence. "You know I hate having this hearing. I remember when I was helping you get a handle on it. With you it got worse with age. Bernard had tried to teach you but you needed someone with experience. You said to said to me "How do you handle it? Hearing everyone's cries at once?" And I couldn't answer you. Because I don't know how I handle it. When we avert a crisis or stop a superhuman from killing someone, I hear people talking about us, criticising us for doing our job and trying our hardest to save lives. Sometimes I read what people write about us. Some of them are kids and they think they can do my job better. It's heartbreaking that even after everything we've done, after everyone we've saved they still can't find it in their hearts to trust us. That's why we have to do it their way, play by their rules." Michael kept quiet. Adam continued. "When I revealed myself to the world I thought I could protect everyone. I was arrogant enough to believe that with my power I could save every last man, woman and child. Then when I lost... Amy I was powerless. In a single second I lost the one person that never looked at me with indifference. The one person I loved more than anyone on this planet."

Michael finally spoke up. "I understand Adam."

Adam looked at him. "When I was ten I tried to cut my wings off. I took the biggest knife I could find and tried to hack the wings off. Someone at school had torn my coat off. I was stronger than everyone but I never laid a finger on anyone there. But anyway the guy ripped my coat off and there they were; twin, massive, white, wings. Then everybody started jeering at me. So I rushed home. My parents were never in so I was at home alone. I still remembered staring at my reflection with my wings. But nothing happened, the blade snapped against them so I never tried again and that's when I started helping people. Look Mike I understand why you don't wanna do what we do. I don't blame you. But please let us gather more proof. And then we'll do something."

Michael thought hard. "Adam, let me look into this. It's my play, my planet, I need to do this. Please. Let my life mean something other than causing the destruction of the planet."

Angel smiled. "Mike you're a good guy. And I know we need to investigate this further. Just don't do anything stupid." They both chuckled and both of them suddenly picked up a woman screaming. Adam immediately focused on the scream and he looked at Michael. "Duty calls. Take it easy." Adam's wings suddenly sprang into action as he shot back towards the planet. Michael smiled; he didn't want to go back yet. He let himself float upwards further into orbit. He was just about in the same orbit as the International Space Station. Michael looked across the earth and saw the ISS continuing its orbit of the earth. Michael's father's company had poured funding into the ISS project. In the last five years upgrades to their oxygen and new docks for escape pods and shuttles had been implanted by Sampson Industries. Michael's father had had an interest in the ISS and it being built. Ever since Michael had developed his eyesight powers he'd made it a goal to track the station. Michael suddenly refocused on what he needed to do. It was time to revisit his father's observatory.

Chapter 12: *Look and see your target*

Michael approached the moon and landed gently on its surface exactly where he had been the first time round. A blue light covered him briefly obviously making sure that Michael was who said he was. Suddenly blue fire covered his legs and travelled up his body but Michael wasn't scared. He knew what was happening this time. Seconds later he appeared within the observatory. It exploded with holograms which buzzed around him. Michael clapped them away and moved towards the observation window. Michael hadn't really learnt how to use the observatory's systems but he was a fast learner. Michael quickly deduced that the window served as a way to pull apart the planet in holographic form. The holographs were an advanced version of what Michael used back at the house but they worked the same. He began "pulling" countries off the planet and manipulating them to search for clues. He looked at countries that had an "alien"-like national landmark such as the Pyramids or even Britain's Stonehenge.

"Isn't that too obvious my son?" said his father thoughtfully while looking out of the observatory window.

His voice echoed throughout the observatory.

Michael smiled. "Took you long enough; so where would you look?" Saar-Vaar moved towards the observation window and pressed a holographic button and the whole screen blacked out. Michael looked quizzically at his father's almost ethereal appearance. His face almost showed a "wait for it" look. The observation window suddenly showed the countries in a red colour.

"Here, I have converted the map to pick up any Kordite technology that appears on the planet. Look and see your target for what it really is." Michael walked towards the window and began manipulating the planet to try and find the biggest source of Kordite technology. Michael analysed every country in superspeed, his brain working faster than any other computer on earth. A pattern suddenly emerged; the largest amount of Kordite technology was focusing in on Britain, specifically London the capital. Michael had a target; now it was time for him to investigate. He approached the wall and summoned a holograph which was a teleporter to take him outside the observatory. Within seconds he appeared outside on the moon's surface. Michael ran and jumped off into space. He flew into the atmosphere and welcomed the warm embrace of the flame across his body.

Michael changed direction as got down to a lower altitude and flew towards London. Michael raised himself up on to the so-called "Gherkin" building. It was around nine at night and the moon hung in the night's sky. Before Michael had left he had picked up a scanner that could locate traces of Kordite technology. Michael suddenly heard a bang next to him. He turned round to see Tremor and The Stranger standing behind him. Tremor had changed his into his uniform; it was blue with a white crescent moon in the centre. Michael wasn't surprised that they were there but he was intrigued.

172

"How did you two find me?" he asked.

Before Tremor could answer Terrence piped up. "You leave quite a trail," he said referring to Michael's flight patterns. Terrence didn't quite have a uniform in the normal sense. It was more of a set of clothes that Michael had woven with titanium and Kevlar. Terrence also wore a brown trench coat and his boots were actually jet thrusters capable of slowing falls and aiding him in jumping but they were not capable of sustained flight. John knocked Terrence's fedora hat off making Terrence scowl as he bent down to pick it up.

"Technically he's right satellites picked you up as soon as you entered the atmosphere. That and we are on patrol here. So I guess the question is what are you doing here?" Michael filled them in on what he had found in his father's observatory. Tremor pursed his lips. "If that's true then we need to intercept them now." Michael and Terrence nodded in agreement. Terrence pulled out one of his six-shooters and began twirling it around in the air. "Do you think a Kordite will be with the tech?"

Michael shrugged. "To be honest I don't know but if one is there then we'll have to be quick and try to immobilise them."

Terrence smiled. "Sounds like a plan."

Michael walked towards the edge of the building and activated his scanner. "This could take some time, why don't you two go ground side while I stay up here?" Before Tremor went he handed Michael a communication device. Michael placed it in his ear and motioned for them to go. They nodded and both jumped off the building. Tremor landed and caused a crack around the area. People gasped at the sight of Tremor but then started pulling out phones to take pictures.

The Stranger engaged his jets to slow him down and landed with precision, he didn't indulge the people around. He simply tipped his hat to a group of women and said, "Ladies."

173

Michael ascended into the air and held his altitude, scanning for any remnant of Kordite technology. Suddenly a tone went off on the scanner. Michael quickly began scanning the area. He moved around trying to get sight of where the tech was.

"Tremor I've got something," he said over the com.

"Roger, do you know where yet?" he replied. Michael frowned as he desperately tried to scan through the area. And then he saw it. A black truck eased its way through the centre. Michael switched his vision to thermal and scanned the truck. There were three heat signatures and one block of heat. Michael moved towards the truck and the scanner started beeping again.

"Tremor I've pinpointed it; a black truck in the city centre. I'm picking up a signal. Go for it!" he said.

"Roger Mike I'm going." Tremor turned to The Stranger and said, "City centre, let's go." Tremor sprinted off and accelerated to a speed of 50 miles per hour. Terrence looked around and saw a crowd surrounding a guy on a motorcycle. He walked up to the bike and tipped off his hat.

"Hi there, official Team business I need the bike. I'll return it later or you'll be reimbursed," he said politely.

The frat boy on the bike turned round and sneered at him. "Screw off you American prick. Don't swagger 'round here like you're a big shot!" he said while pushing Terrence back. Terrence sighed and then launched a straight jab at the frat boy knocking him out. He turned to the girl trying to wake him up.

"Tell him not raise his voice to his elders when he wakes up. Oh and he'll probably want a painkiller for his headache." Terrence revved the motorcycle up and roared off down the street. Up front Tremor kept up his pace, vaulting over cars and trying to bypass people on the street. He saw the truck in front of the next column of cars and stopped in his tracks. He heard a motorcycle engine approach him and saw Terrence get off.

"That's the truck we want," he said pointing at the black truck.

Terrence nodded. "Put on a show superstar." Tremor harnessed his power and shot hit at the back of the truck, almost shoving it off the road, but it recovered and sped up, ramming cars off the road. The rear doors swung back to reveal three K humans jumping out.

Tremor clenched his fist. "Michael we've got resistance. Go after the truck. Now!"

"On it," Michael replied. Tremor almost took a punch to the jaw. He ducked and countered with a vicious three-punch combo and then ended with an earthquake blast sending the K human into a parked car. In a flash Terrence pulled both his six-shooters and shot twice at both the remaining K humans dropping them instantly. He still had sight of the truck. Switching the revolvers' ammo to tungsten he aimed the shot at the tyre. Suddenly a flash appeared into the bullet. Terrence looked at the figure in front of him. She was around 5 foot 11 and was dressed head to toe in black armour. She was a Kordite.

Terrence smiled grimly and said, "I'm not afraid to hit a girl." Terrence could imagine that underneath her helmet she was smirking as she walked towards him. Terrence fired as many times as he could but she simply dodged the bullets. She continued walking towards him and simply palmed him into a bar nearby. Terrence stirred gradually looking around at the scared patrons. He looked at his chest and pulled a measure of glass out of his abdomen. He got up slowly and exhaled. "Damn she's strong." Terrence suddenly focused and began raising his adrenalin levels giving him his strength back. Terrence rushed out and delivered a barrage of blows. He finished with a right hook to her jaw. But nothing happened. She smacked him down and lifted him up and then hurled him into a building. Michael shot down just as she did. He knew that Terrence could survive the fall. Michael threw a right hook sending her down to the ground and lifted her back and used an uppercut to send her up into the air. Michael could hear Terrence cursing as he got up. Tremor sprinted back. Michael threw his hands up in the air in frustration.

"Where the hell did you go!" Michael yelled.

Tremor yelled back. "Crowd control." Michael cursed under his breath. He looked up and saw that the Kordite solider was already recovering from Michael's massive punch.

"She's a Kordite. I gotta deal with her. You get The Stranger and go after the truck." Tremor nodded. Michael shot up into air and re-engaged the solider. He landed three more blows but the rest were blocked and reversed. She got the upper hand and knocked Michael down. She appeared behind him and smashed him back down. Michael stopped himself and countered her next blow. He grabbed her and swung her by her leg into the Gherkin building.

"Mike watch for the buildings. You gotta get her out of here," Tremor said over the com unit. Michael agreed. He couldn't let this turn into Russia all over again. Michael swopped down and grabbed her while she was still recovering. He used his incredible eyesight and saw that Mount Snowdon wasn't too far from where they were. Michael increased speed and flew her towards the mountain. Pinning her against the mountainside he entered superspeed and began punching her as fast as he could. The mountain groaned under the force of Michael's punches. He landed more blows and lifted her back up. Summoning all of his telekinetic power he shot her away towards the atmosphere. Michael took a deep breath and flew back to London as fast as he could. Appearing over the city centre of London, Michael desperately searched for Tremor and The Stranger. He suddenly heard Tremor grunt over the com unit and quickly tried to make contact.

"John where are you?"

Tremor's voice sounded frantic over the com unit. "Mike, I've got the truck but there are multiple K humans. We need to finish this now. What about the Kordite; where is she?"

Michael flew down further and responded. "I managed to get her out of the country. Where are you now?"

"We're coming up to London Bridge along the Thames river." Michael increased speed and shot down to ground level.

Tremor shrugged off bullets from the truck. The soldiers were trying to stop him and Terrence from getting anywhere near the truck. A soldier suddenly armed a rocket launcher and prepared to fire at Terrence. Tremor reacted as fast as he could. The rocket launcher was an AT4 light anti-armour weapon. The rocket travelled at exactly 290 metres per second; meaning that Tremor had to be faster. He leapt in front of the rocket and formed a shield out of earthquake energy blocking the missile down into the ground. The explosion's force sent Tremor into a car. Recovering quickly Tremor continued running desperately trying to catch the truck. The Stranger urgently tried to accelerate on the bike he was driving. Using his six-shooters he shot down multiple K humans who were trying to stop him. Tremor leapt over a car causing a small depression on the ground. He got a good look at the truck and realised he could get there. But then he saw it. A K human armed another AT4 rocket and fired at a car. Civilians scrambled to get away from the car before the rocket fired. The woman and her daughter desperately tried to get to safety. Tremor wasn't the fastest member of The Team, but he was no slouch. He double timed it over to the civilians and lifted them up. As the rocket hit the car Tremor leapt with the civilians towards the bridge. He arched his back and used it as safety shield to crash into an empty car. Tremor checked the two were all right and sprinted off towards the truck. Michael soared through the sky focusing on Tremor and The Stranger. He increased speed trying to get a visual on were the truck was going.

"Tremor, what's life like on the ground?" he said.

"Not good. Multiple K humans are engaging us. We need to find out where their destination is," Tremor yelled. Michael didn't reply. He focused back on where the truck was headed. He accelerated and tried to think where the truck would go. He focused his superhearing and listened to the driver. He suddenly heard what he wanted to. They were headed for Heathrow Airport. Michael quickly accessed Tremor and The Stranger.

"Guys they're headed for Heathrow Airport. They must have some sort of transport getting them out of there." Michael knew they wouldn't reply to him. They both knew where they were headed.

Heathrow Airport was one of the biggest airports in the world and one of the busiest. On a daily basis there were around 1,288 air transport movements meaning that it was always busy. Michael flew under the radar, not wanting to be picked up by the police or any other monitor. He landed on the ground and slipped into cover. He saw four soldiers tending to a C-17 Globemaster III. The massive plane was being fuelled. This was obviously the plane that the truck was headed for. It had military markings all over it. Michael suddenly heard an explosion rip through the terminal. Michael saw the truck power through the building towards the plane. Tremor leapt through the wreckage and The Stranger performed a wheelie jump trying to reach the truck. Multiple K humans followed. Michael sped over to the soldiers and engaged them. They were all strong but nothing compared to Michael. One by one they went down but then Michael realised something. The K humans were just stalling the three of them. Michael turned round to see the C-17 preparing for take-off. He whistled to get Tremor and The Stranger's attention. They both turned to look at the plane beginning its take-off. Michael analysed the plane and quickly realised that stopping it in the air would cause civilian casualties.

"Terrence I need your guns now!" Michael yelled. Terrence complied and threw him the guns. He aimed and switched to grapple mode. The bullets moulded and gained two sharp ends. He fired two shots; one into one of the two engines on one side and one on the other side. The plane accelerated down the runway and began to take off.

"Can you do this, Michael?" Tremor asked.

Michael nodded and smiled. "Child's play." Michael waited until the steel ropes went taut and held strong. His feet dug into the ground causing them to drag slightly. But he held fast and then pulled back on the ropes snapping the wings off. The plane dove into the ground crashing into a burning inferno. Tremor and The Stranger high-fived while Michael went to investigate the wreckage. He moved through flames and lifted part of the structure away. He pulled out a box and began searching for clues. Michael saw a few symbols on the edge of the crate. Michael recognised them as Kordite.

"Found something?" Tremor asked.

Michael nodded. "Kord symbols. This is probably the tech they were trying to escort. I'm gonna see what's in there."

Michael pressed one of the holograms. When his father had subjected him to the knowledge of Kordites, he had learnt how to properly access a holographic presentation. The hologram floated up and began showcasing Michael multiple pictures.

"What is that stuff?" Terrence asked.

Michael didn't take his eyes off the hologram but answered him. "It's a holographic presentation of what's within the case. From what I've pieced together it's some kind of dirty bomb." They were all interrupted by a smash behind them. They turned round to see the female Kordite soldier had recovered from Michael's assault. She removed her helmet and revealed long black hair that fell down around her shoulders. Michael was stunned; he had expected her to be like Nor but she was dazzlingly beautiful. Her eyes were sharp silver and glowed with anger.

"They had warned me that you were strong. From what I have seen I am disappointed," she said softly. She suddenly rushed the trio at full speed. Michael prepared for her assault but she smashed into Tremor first knocking him down and then kicking him into the air traffic control tower. She then rushed over to The Stranger. Terrence desperately tried to shoot off a few explosive rounds but she danced around the shots almost majestically and then wrenched Terrence's arm out of his socket and threw him into the remains of the broken terminal. Michael prepared for the next assault. She rushed him into a wall and held him. "They said you have a warrior's heart." She put her hand on his chest feeling his heart beat. "They were right. I am Kor-Veer, Nor's sister." She suddenly kissed Michael and lingered. Michael wanted to spit in disgust but she stopped him. "You could be with us Ror. Take your rightful place. We could be together." As she finished talking, a punch connected with her jaw sending her flying back. Tremor's body was bloodied but he could take it.

He rushed Kor and unleashed a barrage of blows connecting with his earthquake powers causing her to fly back. The next punch sent her into a vacant plane docked at a nearby terminal. Kor shot back at Tremor, but he was ready and punched her down into the ground. He raised both his fists into the air and smashed her down. The whole ground shook with his power. Michael quickly re-engaged Kor. He lifted her up and threw her down then smashed her again. Michael got the upper hand and held her down. As he did her eyes turned a sharp silver again but this time they glowed with power. Twin cylindrical beams shot into Michael sending him flying back. She shot at Tremor who tried to block it but was rushed down. Michael felt his chest where he had been hit. His skin was darkened and felt warm. Before he could react Kor pinned him to the ground. She put her boots over his wrist and held his throat down.

"You could have the whole universe and everyone bowing before you. Yet you continue to protect this human filth. For that you must die." Michael could feel his eyes heating up. They began glowing red and shining. The heat irritated Michael, he roared with anger and then two red cylindrical beams shot straight at her sending her flying up into the air. Michael stood up and then fell on his knees. He felt weak, like all of his energy had just left him. He suddenly felt a hand on his shoulder. Kor helped him up gently and placed her hand on his cheek. "The humans never properly taught you how to use your powers. Your energy vision is finally manifesting. It fuels from your solar energy reserves. I could teach you, my love. You could finally learn the full extent of your powers," she said softly. Michael pushed her hands away and superpushed her back a bit. He stood up again and adopted a fighting stance. Kor sighed softly as if she didn't want to fight Michael. He readied himself until two explosions smacked into her. Terrence had pulled himself out of the terminal and had fired on her with his two six-shooters.

"Ain't leaving you to fight her alone Mike." Michael smiled and summoned all of his powers back. Kor's eyes turned silver again and she fired her energy vision at Terrence. Michael quickly met her blast with his own and the two energy beams collided and then shorted out causing a small explosion which pushed Kor back. Michael rushed her and unleashed a barrage of blows pushing her further back. She fell on her knees. Michael had got her where he wanted her and he prepared to deliver another final blow. As he winded up his punch he was hit by a green blast. Michael pulled himself up and saw Nor-Veer land in front of them all. He helped his sister up.

"Sister, are you hurt?" She looked irritated as Nor stepped in front of her.

"No Nor, I am fine. The son of Vaar is strong. But he has not got full control of his powers yet." Nor barely registered her existence as he walked towards the trio of heroes.

"Go sister, the master needs you back at the base." Kor shot up into the air and sonic boomed away. Tremor suddenly rushed back and tried to throw a punch at Nor but Michael stopped him. Tremor turned round and tried to wrench his arm off him.

"Tremor we can't fight him. This was the one Angel and Bolt barely stopped." Tremor stopped and calmed down. Nor remained emotionless and ascended into the air, his eyes turned a dark green and shot three times at different targets around the airport.

"That should keep you busy," he said as he flew away. Nor had shot at the air traffic control tower, a terminal and a plane. Michael shot over towards the top of the air traffic control centre. He held up the top of the building and surrounded the people inside with a telekinetic shield. He gently laid it on the ground. Tremor was holding the plane up while emergency services attended to the stricken plane. The Stranger was helping others up in the broken terminal. They all met up where Kor had left a crater in the ground.

Michael turned to Tremor. "Do you need my help here?" he asked softly.

Tremor put a hand on Michael's shoulder. "No, it's best you get yourself out of here. The British prime minister will want a full report. Angel should be here soon." Michael nodded and shook both of their hands. He took off into the air and disappeared into the sky.

Michael didn't go that far, he landed on nearby building and ripped what remained of his shirt off. Michael saw a shop nearby and dropped down. Before he entered the shop he supersped back to his house to pick his wallet up. Michael walked into the shop and picked a bottle of brandy from the shelf. He walked towards the young girl cashier who gaped at Michael.

He smiled and simply said, "Wild night." Paying for the brandy he exited the store to an alleyway. Michael made sure no one was looking and ascended into the air. He took a long drink from the bottle letting the liquid refresh him. Michael downed half the bottle in one single gulp. He looked over at Heathrow Airport. He used his superhearing and listened to people's conversations. He heard cries and people sobbing. Michael's eyes turned red as he finished the rest of his brandy and shot into the air. He rose out of the atmosphere and flew towards Mercury. Landing on its cratered, volcanic surface he began absorbing sunlight. He felt rejuvenated and reflected on the fight. Michael had made sure the weapon had been destroyed. His thoughts dwelled upon Kor. The kiss had shaken him up; it had generally seemed like she didn't want to fight Michael but wanted to help him. He shook his head trying to get the thoughts out of his head. He wanted to go home and be with Charlotte. He leapt into the air and flew back to earth. He entered the atmosphere and landed at home. All of a sudden Michael felt tired as if all of his energy had left him. He landed outside the mansion on his knees causing a crater on the ground. Woken by the sound Bernard sprinted out armed with a shotgun and a torch. He shone the light on Michael and stepped back in surprise.

"Master Michael, are you all right?" he said in worried voice. He helped Michael up who stood uneasily.

"I've got a lot to tell you. Let's go inside."

Bernard helped Michael into the living room, who dropped on to the couch, while Bernard entered the kitchen. He took a deep breath as soon as he focused, he felt his strength return. Bernard brought a tray in with two black coffees. Michael added three sugars to his coffee and took a sip. They sat quietly for a few minutes before Bernard broke the silence.

"So what happened?" Michael filled him in on the trip to The Team's headquarters then back to his father's observatory where he found evidence of the technology and finally he went over the fight in London. Bernard looked grimly at his coffee. "Looks like things aren't going well for you son. What weapon did you find?"

Michael sipped his coffee. "It was the Kordite equivalent of a dirty bomb. Strong enough to level a city, but it was destroyed in the crash. What surprised me was the amount of military personnel that were present. They were all K humans and all were highly trained. Looks like the Kordites are more embedded than we thought."

Bernard placed his coffee cup on the table. "What about Heathrow? Was it wrecked beyond repair?"

Michael shrugged. "The air traffic control building was destroyed. One of the terminals was wrecked to the point that it was falling down. A 737 was damaged as well. The runway will need to be tarmacked again. So it will take some time before it's fully functional again. I tried to limit civilian casualties but it was tough and it didn't help that we were engaged by the Kordite soldier. And that one of my new powers developed. I need to go and figure this out." Michael stood and turned to walk out of the door. Before he did Bernard embraced him like a father embracing his son.

"Son, you know I'm here for you if you need to talk, know that I am here for you." Michael nodded. He walked out of the house and flew towards Times Square. Michael kept his speed low but fast enough not to be seen. Michael hovered outside Charlotte's apartment window and gently tapped on the glass. Charlotte woke up and walked towards the window smiling at him. She opened the window letting Michael in. He gently dropped on to her floor. She hugged him and held him for what seemed like hours.

"You look like hell," she said, whispering.

"I feel like it. You wanna go for ride?"

She looked up at him and smiled. "You promised to take me once you got it handled. Do you?" Michael smiled and suddenly they were out of the window. She didn't even realise that they'd been floating all the time. Michael flew upwards towards the Empire State Building and landed gently on the top deck. She exhaled quickly and inhaled again. "That was very cool," she said with glee.

"You should see the world from up there," he said pointing towards the sky. "It's amazing, every light sparkles and it's even better above. I wish I could show you it all." Michael looked away from her face as he felt his eyes turn red.

Charlotte moved in front of him. "What's wrong? There's something you're hiding from me."

Michael smiled softly. "Am I that easy to read?" he asked.

She placed her palm on his face. "I've known you for years, so I should be able to read you." Michael sighed and recounted the events of London to her. He skipped over some of the parts, specifically about Kor. Charlotte didn't get jealous but he didn't want to upset her. She focused intently on Michael; he recognised the look. It was the same one her mother had when she had therapy session with Michael. She stood thoughtfully and said, "Do you think they are rearming militaries with Kordite weapons?"

Michael shrugged. "I don't know. I'm sure the weapon was going to be used in their takeover but from what I've learned the takeover is supposed to be quiet. To be honest I don't know. In fact there are a lot of things I don't know," he said softly.

"You'll find it out." She playfully knocked on his head. "There's a big wonderful brain in there. What I'm more surprised about is your new power."

Michael chuckled softly. "I know; so am I. I think I need to learn how to control it properly before I use it again."

She smiled at Michael and leaned in to kiss him again. She lifted her leg up playfully. "Can we spend tonight here? It's always nice here."

Michael nodded. *For you anything*, he thought.

Chapter 13: *They cannot stop us*

Kor and Nor walked through the army base. They were dressed in primitive human clothing that bore symbols of the US army. The human guards were nothing more than humans but they were loyal to a point. Kor felt distant she lingered back to Ror; he was every bit the soldier that he had been designed to be. But he felt... broken. One of her focus points in her studies was her telepathy. She had peered into Ror's thoughts during the fight. While most of them were focused on anger, she saw the pain of him not knowing who he truly was. She saw how life had rewarded him, how the humans had treated him. It was unfair. She wanted to help him. But at the focal point of his thoughts she saw the woman he loved; Charlotte. The human female had moulded him back from what he once was. She had kept him together. Kor sneered in disgust so much that her brother noticed.

"What is troubling you, dear sister?"

Kor stopped walking and looked at her brother. "The son of Vaar; must he be killed?"

In a flash Nor rushed her back into the wall. "Yes little sister he must be destroyed. He is a freak, an aberration of what we truly are. All humans will share his fate." Nor let her down gently. "Now sister I hope you never bring this up again, especially in front of the master. You remember what happened last time? They cannot stop us. More importantly he cannot stop us. Now no more arguing and follow me sister," he said walking off. Kor looked at the dent on the wall and followed her brother, but her thoughts turned back to Ror. Did she want to kill him? She searched her heart for the answer but could not find it.

Entering the main compound Kor and Nor were saluted by two other low-ranking Kordite soldiers. Though they were needed Kordites could not be spared neither could the lack of them catch the attention of the Guardians. Sitting on a seat in front of a dozen computer screens, General Rockwell observed the multiple news reports about the events in London.

Without turning around, he said, "What happened down there?" Kor went to answer but Nor stopped her.

"The child of Vaar intervened; he destroyed the shipment and killed multiple soldiers. If not for my sister then we would have been completely at a loss…"

Rockwell's hand shot up. "I did not ask you." His voice was still but the malice could be felt within it.

Kor stepped forward. "I intervened when the human heroes tried to destroy the truck. They were easy enough to beat but…" she lingered for several seconds before Rockwell broke the silence.

"But what!" he shouted.

Kor straightened up. "Ror-Vaar engaged me. He flew me into a mountain and threw me out to sea. When I recovered my strength it was too late. But I re-engaged and…"

"And you were defeated." Rockwell finished. Kor nodded. Rockwell rose from his seat and stood at a height of seven foot dwarfing the two siblings. He was not wearing make-up like he did in front of the humans so all of his scars could be seen. "*The supreme art of war is to subdue the enemy without fighting,*" Rockwell smiled at Kor. "Sun Tzu, a human philosopher and general said this. His theories of warfare are most... interesting, I must confess that I would've like to meet him. I must say humans have an... interesting history, full of warlords who thought that they could conquer this world. Yet all of them fell short, every single time." Rockwell moved in a flash and grabbed Kor by her throat. He lifted her two feet off the ground. "Alexander, Genghis Khan and others like him did this; humans did this. We are better than they are, we have been trained for longer than them but do you want to know what the difference between them and us truly is?" Kor didn't answer she knew it was rhetorical. "These men had armies of soldiers and not excuses. They led fully trained soldiers into combat to win their battles. And what am I left with? You and your pathetic excuses." Rockwell squeezed harder; though she was invulnerable to basic harm she knew that he could break her neck with just a bit more pressure. "This operation has been in planning for more than 70 human years. We have corrected the course of human history, influenced it for the better and made them what they are now. In other words the humans have been mere playthings for us. The end of our plan is almost ready for its execution and I will not let you RUIN it. For I am the leader of our guild, High Father Zor-Veer and you will do your duty." Kor looked pleadingly at her brother for aid but he kept looking forward. "Your brother is a true soldier; even when he sees family being threatened he does not scare from his duty. That is what you must become." He dropped her and turned away. "Now, get out of my sight." Kor made a hasty retreat. "Nor, where does this boy live? I believe it is time for me to visit him."

Michael once again entered his father's company building. Sampson Industries was one of the tallest buildings in New York making it an almost shining beacon of the city. Michael entered the elevator and tolerated the cheesy muzak and stopped at the 22nd floor. But then he reconsidered; he set the elevator to take him to the top floor where his father's office was. The office of Dr Steven Sampson had not been disturbed since his death. Some would say it was out of respect but it was specifically stated in his will. The will also stated that only one person could open the door: his son. Michael entered the floor and walked towards the office door which was just a metal slab. Michael looked quizzically at the metal and examined it with his different spectra of vision. Nothing he thought. Michael placed his hand on the metal and felt a light buzzing as a blue light surrounded it. His father had taken a huge chance in using Kordite technology; hopefully people would have thought it was just a safety measure. The metal slab lifted ominously making Michael feel anxious. His right hand started shaking. Michael lifted it up and held himself together as he entered. Clinical depression and anxiety were harsh things. It was like having a loaded gun pressed to his head for most of the day. He gritted his teeth. When he had first been diagnosed with depression, Bernard had tried to get Michael to use antidepressants. But Michael had declined, he had thought that he could power through it. Now he knew that that was a mistake. He should have tried but in the back of his mind he was always worried that the medication wouldn't work; that his physiology would repel the drugs and he'd be stuck were he already was or deeper. But there was nothing he could do now; hopefully the therapy with Charlotte's mother was paying off. Michael entered the office which was in complete darkness. As soon as he set foot into the room, the entire office lit up.

"It's nice isn't it?" an ominous voice said. Michael almost jumped out of the window. "Sorry that was a bit ominous wasn't it? Anyway, I know I'm speaking to you son because, well no one can get in here, which is good because 90 per cent of the office is Kordite technology. Just a few comforts from home that I could use and which would benefit me personally. Don't bother talking to me I'm not the observatory." The recording paused for a second. The office was beautiful. There was an eight-track record player and a pile of golf clubs. "Now either you've decided to take control of the office or you've just come here out of curiosity after you found the observatory. Whichever it is I need to tell you this. When I first started this company I wanted it to be clean. No underhand deals or corruption. I wanted to be an ideal businessman. Don't take my words wrongly this was incredibly hard. There were many people who wanted to take the company in different ways. Some were good but most were wrong. I'm telling you all of this because you need to be wary of the people on your board and keep them in check. I know you can do it my son. Oh and don't let anyone except for David up here or maybe your significant other." The recording finished leaving Michael at a loss. He walked towards the record player and played the first track he found; a personal favourite of Michael and his father's; *Piano Sonata no14 in C sharp minor* or *Moonlight Sonata* by Beethoven. The music started playing gently soothing Michael as he sat on the big office chair. In his mind's eye Michael could imagine his father being a businessman then trying to sort out Kordite affairs and then being a father. It must have been hard he thought. Michael closed his eyes and let his thoughts wander and then refocused on the events of London. He replayed everything back, from the time he landed there to the time he flew away. There was nothing there that he could pick back up on. Michael looked along table and saw two Kordite symbols. He pressed them both and holograms began fluttering around him. Michael looked through them and found a world news hologram. He pressed the play button and watched the reports on the events in London. Michael keyed the sound.

"*After last night's events in London all the members of the superhero Team have responded to begin the clean up. Eyewitness reports state that that two members from the superhero Team, known as Tremor and The Stranger, as well as a unknown superhuman engaging multiple other superhumans. Damage to Heathrow Airport is said to be in the millions already. In addition the superheroes known as Angel and Dove have responded to an ecological disaster in the north of Wales. The famous Mount Snowdon is said to be damaged in the event of last night's battle. Members of The Team were unavailable for comment.*"

Michael switched off the sound and slammed his fist on to the table; it didn't even leave a mark. *Idiot*, he thought. Michael pulled his phone out and rang Sarah whose office/ secret base was ten floors down.

"Sarah come to top floor, I'll explain when you get here," he said softly. Sarah complied and within minutes arrived on the top floor. She gingerly walked through into the office and stared in awe at the architecture.

"So I suppose you bit the bullet and opened the office? It's nice," she said gently. Michael nodded nonchalantly. "I saw what happened in London last night." Michael looked up and nodded in no fashion meaning that he didn't want to argue with her. Sarah was committed to The Team's methods and goals meaning that she obeyed them completely. Sometimes she and Michael argued but they always ended up friends again. "No I'm not gonna shout at you. I'm proud." Michael looked up at her and smiled gently. "You didn't take liberties like in Russia. You tried to protect people and you tried to get the fight out of the area."

Michael stood up and turned his eyes red. "Who are you and what have you done with Sarah Robbie?"

Sarah smiled and said, "Don't be a jackass, I mean it."

Michael smiled softly. "Have you spoken with Angel yet?"

She nodded. "Yeah, you're not in trouble. Him and Dove sealed up the cracks in the mountain. Other than that they're actually praising you. You pretty much saved them all. So stop beating yourself up and believe in yourself. Oh and Angel filled me in on the whole alien thing. And I'm gonna do this as the biggest nerd ever." She ran up and gave him a big hug. "Oh my god! I just hugged an alien," she squealed.

Michael chuckled. "Well enjoy the office, have a look round and get a feel for it. It's yours until I take over." She gaped at him and hugged him again. Michael smiled and walked towards the window. "I'm gonna need to go to the moon now. I'll see you later." He pressed a button and the window opened. Before he did anything Michael pulled out his phone and rang Charlotte. She answered in her normal beautiful voice. "Hey, I need a favour from you."

"What is it?" she asked softly.

"I need you to go to the manor for a few days. I'm going off planet so I won't be close. Just please stay there; it will make me feel better if I know you're safe," he said.

"That's fine I'll be there. What are you going to do?" she asked softly.

Michael pondered the question; he didn't exactly know what he was going to do. "I'm going to see my father about the fight that happened in London."

"Okay that's fine. I hope it goes well for you." They said their goodbyes and Michael hung up. Michael launched himself into the air and flew towards the moon. He exited the atmosphere and directed himself to the moon in two fluid motions. Landing he walked towards the teleporter site.

Kor moved around her apartment. She hated being closed in for so long but Nor had made it clear that she was to lay low. She'd been on earth for around five years and had grown accustomed to the drink coffee. It had a smooth flavour and taste. She was on the top floor of the building so she could see a lot from the roof. She walked into the hot sun and began absorbing the sunlight. Her veins turned a bright yellow and her eyes deep silver. She exhaled gently and dove into the pool. She went all the way to the bottom and kicked off the wall flying towards the other side and back again. She enjoyed the water, it was cool and crisp; a complete difference to the weather above. She was trying to focus on her form but her thoughts had gone back to Ror again. She couldn't get him out of her head. It made her sad thinking about his lonely existence on earth. Kordites' innate ability of telepathy meant that they could share dreams. They could feel each other's feelings but he had never felt that. During the fight she had purposely formed a telepathic link between him and her. She could now feel his emotions but he couldn't feel her. She stopped her swimming and sank towards the bottom listening to his heartbeat.

Michael reappeared in the observatory. He walked towards the window and began activating holograms. He was searching for more clues about stores of technology, as he did he felt his father appeared behind him. Michael still wasn't used to sharing a room with a ghost but he was beginning to get used to it.

"I found your office; it's not mine yet but it is nice," he said softly.

"I remember the office like I was in the chair yesterday. Signing business deals, changing the world with new technology; everything was easier back then. I brought your mother to earth and she agreed that the planet was beautiful. She wanted to live here." His father moved next to him and watched his son manipulate holograms. "I saw what happened in London last night. The Kordite soldier Kor-Veer is the same age as you. She was born after your brother fought the Guardians. Unlike the other members of the Veer guild she pursued science and the proper use of her telepathic powers. But her father wished her to use it for torture. Our telepathy is one of our most vicious powers. We can delve into a subject's mind to repair it or tear it down."

Michael turned round to confront his father. "I've only used my telepathy to set up a link with Charlotte so we can share our feelings more intimately. I never tried to poke into someone's mind it's not right."

His father nodded. "I understand my son. On Kord, guild members establish links. Family members within them used to share dreams and protect each other. Your brother set up one with your sister so she would never be scared. I remember she once had a nightmare. Your brother was half a galaxy away and he felt her pain causing him to fly back and stay with her." Michael was listening but tried to focus on his work. His father suddenly gasped. Michael turned around immediately. His father looked in shock at the footage captured during the fight in London. "You did not defeat her. How could you not defeat her!"

Michael was surprised. He replied, "We did beat her, I almost landed a final blow on her."

Saar-Vaar began muttering under his breath phrases like "limiters", "not ready" and "foolish".

"Dad what's wrong?"

His father looked at him. "I am sorry my son, I sent you into this fight too early. The limiters have not been overcome. With them you will not defeat the followers of Vek-Gar. I am sorry my son." Water began flowing around Michael, the air supercooled freezing him down to his bones. Ice began building up around Michael.

"Father what are you doing to me!" he yelled over the rushing wind.

"I am sorry my son you must learn more about your powers and learn to overcome your limits." His voice faded out as other voices entered his head. Michael yelled in pain, but his yells could only be heard by one.

Kor suddenly began shaking in the water. Her telepathic link with Ror was screaming out to her. Something was happening to him, he was in pain. A tear rolled down her cheek as she flew to the surface and rose above. She focused her telepathy trying to overcome his screams. She fell on her knees as she tried to find his thoughts. She engaged her hearing to try and hear his heartbeat but she couldn't. Was he dead? As she kept pondering she heard a sonic boom approach her. She saw Nor land before her; she desperately tried to hide her pain from her brother.

He caused a depression on the ground and addressed her. "Sister, enough resting; we have been summoned by the high father. We have found the child of Vaar's home." Kor stood up and nodded. She rushed into her apartment and picked her bracelet up from the desk. She activated it and armour flowed over her. The telepathic link was still fuzzy and she could still feel the pain. But she had to focus now.

Chapter 14: *We want the boy*

Bernard carefully cleaned the kitchen making sure that every area was spotless from any dust. He heard a giggling from behind. Bernard smiled. Charlotte and her family were stopping over while Michael was investigating; though Bernard had a harsh history in the military he was still able to make children laugh.

"I wonder what that sound is. Wherever could it be?" he said in his most posh accent. From behind a table Charlotte's little brother Ryan ran towards him. He lifted him up and held him high rubbing his little head.

"Ryan, are you annoying Mr Bernard again?" Mary said in sing-song tone.

"No, no Bernard is the dragon. I'm trying to free the princess," he replied back in a childish voice.

Mary smiled and addressed Bernard. "Are you sure you need to be doing this Bernard? I can do it if you want?"

Bernard dismissed her. "Not if hell had frozen over would I let a guest do this work, Miss Mary." Mary smiled and took Ryan from his arms and put him down.

"How's Michael doing?" she asked softly.

Bernard closed the door and turned round to talk to her. "To be honest I don't really know. Michael is closed off to me at the moment. I've accepted that his depression has broken him and it's hard for him to convey emotions. I've seen it in soldiers who have PTSD. If Michael was any less of the man he was now, he would have failed. But don't mistake me, he wants to die. He's tried. It scares him the amount of power that he possesses."

"The revelation that he is an alien has hurt him even more. He drinks more and more every night and though he can't get drunk he is dependent on it. The only thing he views as important to him is Charlotte. It's like she cast some sort of aura around him which makes him forget the depression. He would never hurt her, in fact he would die before he hurt her. I remember a few days ago when he had a nightmare. He dreamt that he hurt Charlotte and that forced him to try and destroy himself. He flew straight towards the sun to kill himself. That was just a dream and look how he took it, it almost drove him to death."

Mary sighed softly. "I know, I've seen it in his eyes. But there will come a time when he won't be able to stop something from happening to her. How do you think he will take it?"

Bernard looked at her. "I don't know. He's a strong lad but that might be the straw that broke the camel's back. She's the only thing that's keeping him alive. I wish his father had stayed here. Lord knows he would have made sure that he didn't end up like this."

Mary put her hand on his arm. "Don't say that Bernard. You've done everything possible to raise him correctly and it has paid off. Yes Michael is broken slightly but he is a terrific person and one day he is going to be the best person here."

Bernard smiled. He continued dusting till he heard a knock at the door. "Are you expecting anyone, Bernard?" Mary asked. Bernard's survival instincts pinged on, he knew that there was nobody coming today and that Michael was busy.

He pressed his hand on the wall and holograms floated up. "How may I be of service Mr Smith?" Marcus asked.

"Good afternoon Marcus, please perform a perimeter scan and give me the read-outs." There was a series of beeps as the scan was conducted.

"It is done, formulating the scans now." Bernard picked one of the holograms and looked at the scans. There were four hostiles surrounding the house, all were dressed in black armour. Bernard went wide-eyed and realised who they were.

"Charlotte, get in here now!" he shouted. Charlotte walked in with Ryan in her arms. "Get your family into the new lab and seal the door, only open it if Michael or I ask you to." Charlotte nodded and grabbed Mary's arm to take her into the lab. "Marcus set your defences to maximum and protect them with everything you have. Send a distress call out to The Team, priority 1; get them here as fast as possible. Begin defence systems "open the hushed casket.""

Kor was getting annoyed, she hated waiting round. All of the Kordites were wearing full amour and were standing to attention. There were four in the area, herself, Nor-Veer, the high father and his brother Zar-Veer. Zar-Veer stood around ten foot and was dressed in full armour. He didn't talk much and though he was her uncle, they didn't act as family but that was how it was; military before family, soldiering before blood. The high father had warned them that they had to take Ror down as fast as possible otherwise things would get messy. Zor had knocked on the door multiple times. Nor was getting impatient, he reached for his blade but Zar stopped him and pushed him back. The door wasn't going to open, Nor thought the child was scared. But then it opened.

Bernard opened the door and looked at the seven foot giant in front of him. Bernard remained calm. "How may I help you, sir?"

The Kordite slowly removed his helmet and smiled. "Why good afternoon, I would like to see Ror-Vaar." Bernard had to stall, the defences were almost cycled up and The Team were almost here.

"While I have met a wide array of people from all over the world with special names that is not a name I have ever heard."

The Kordite's face turned from a smile to a scowl. "Do not play dumb with me, I know he lives here. I will not harm you neither will I destroy this beautiful home if you give the boy to me. If you do not produce the boy I will kill you slowly and in more pain than anything you have ever experienced." Bernard realised that there was no more stalling and that the Kordite was ready to kill him. No matter, he thought. Bernard smiled as if he was not fearful of the giant in front of him.

"Did you know that when the master first came here and entrusted me with his son's life he told me to expect this. Do not think me unprepared for a fight." In a flash of movement Bernard pulled a Kordite rifle from the cupboard. He yelled quickly, "Marcus now!" Twin turrets popped up from the ground and began fighting the Kordites. Bernard activated the rifle and fired a single powerful shot at the Kordite soldier in front of him sending him flying back. The rifle was built using advanced Kordite technology which siphoned energy from the target. The Kordites were already recovering from the surprise attack. Another giant Kordite dwarfing Bernard rushed towards him. The rifle needed to recharge again meaning that Bernard was in danger of being crushed. Bernard prepared for his death, he had done everything he could to protect Michael and he wasn't getting any younger. He smiled with contentment. But suddenly a blur smacked into the giant sending him flying back. Bernard smiled with relief. If there was a god he had just sent his angel.

Angel flew towards the giant Kordite again ready to strike. Before he could do anything another blur shot into him, blowing the wind out of his lungs. Angel recognised the Kordite, Nor-Veer. Nor remained emotionless and almost melancholic at Angel who smiled back at him.

"Ready for round two?" Angel said.

"I will tear the wings from your back, human filth," he said in an emotionless tone.

Angel was nerved by the remark but smiled again. "I'm not alone." Out of the blue, the rest of The Team members descended down.

Bernard had recovered and picked his rifle up. He said, "Let's kick these bastards off my property!" The Stranger sprinted into the battle wielding his two six-shooters and chose the first target in view, which also happened to be the biggest guy there. Terrence changed his six-shooters to explosive and began firing at the target. The rounds exploded on impact but didn't cause any long-lasting damage.

Terrence looked back up at him. "Er, guys need a little help over here," he yelled. The Kordite wound up his punch and was ready to deal the final blow. Before anything happened Tremor shot into the Kordite, pushing him back with all of his strength. Tremor went all out; he lined both fists with earthquake energy and began landing multiple punches. They ranged from 3.4 to 7.8 on the Richter scale but the Kordite was almost unfazed and got up. The Kordite growled and rushed him. Tremor rolled and pushed the Kordite off him. Standing up slowly, he winced and felt his chest. Damn, cracked rib he thought as he readied himself for another fight. Angel was hurtling around Nor desperately trying to not get close to him. He couldn't use his angel cry yet because he could damage the city. Angel flew back into Nor pinning him into the ground and kicking up dirt around him. Nor pulled his blade and swung at him multiple times. Angel dodged and countered with more blows and punches.

"Dove, where's Bolt? We need him now," he yelled through his com unit.

"He'll be here anytime now." Three sonic booms blew out everyone's ears around the area. Bolt rushed into Zor pushing him back towards a wall.

"Sorry I was late, responded to a distress in Bolivia. What'd I miss?" he yelled.

"Eh, messed up, about to die. You know the normal," Terrence replied sarcastically.

"Cut the chatter now. Attack these guys like a team. We can't miss a beat." The Team reformed back into a fighting unit.

The four Kordites barely made a sound as The Team began fighting them. That was the weirdest thing for Angel, normally when he fought most superhumans they were always complaining about how the world had treated them badly and how the government didn't help them enough. But the Kordites were quiet; Michael had told them that it was because they were soldiers meaning that they weren't in the mood to make jokes. The silence was almost eerie; but it meant they had to hold nothing back. He directed himself at Nor and readied himself for the fight. Angel held Nor tight as he flew him through a wall. Nor quickly recovered and tried to land more blows on Angel. Using superspeed Angel dodged most of the blows, but he had to admit this was gonna be a hard fight. Angel kicked Nor down and landed a superhuman punch rupturing the ground beneath them. Leaping back Nor attacked with superhuman efficiency and almost landed a blow from the mangled sword. Angel knew to avoid it, that sword wound in his gut still hurt even though it had been weeks since the fight. Quickly stopping his blade hand, Angel headbutted Nor pushing him back. Taking a quick look around Angel saw that The Team were being beaten back. The fight was taking a lot out of them. Angel noticed that the lead fighter or commander of the group was fighting off multiple heroes by himself. That was Angel's main target. Summoning his angel cry he roared at Nor sending him hurtling towards space. He tackled the leader into a nearby vacant car, but was swatted away. Angel recovered but not fast enough it seemed as the leader rushed Angel through a building. Angel shook off the dirt and rocks as he stood up. The leader engaged in combat with Angel, outclassing him in almost every way. The final blow sent him down into the ground.

"So, you are the infamous Angel or is it Adam?" the leader said. Angel replied not with words but with fists pushing him back. "Nice, but it appears that your defeat has almost been assured. Give me the boy and we can stop this fight."

Now was the time for Angel to speak. "Michael is as much as a child of earth now and he belongs here. And by god I will protect him with everything I have!" Angel shouted.

The leader smiled. "I guess I should have anticipated this. But I, High Father Zor-Veer, will take him after I have ripped you apart." Zor tackled Angel through a wall and landed a barrage of punches making Angel bleed. Standing up uneasily, he prepared for another round. "You do have potential, don't you? Would you like to know the truth behind Amy's death?" Zor said menacingly. Angel sped into Zor rushing him through another building.

"What the hell do you know of her?" Angel shouted. Zor smiled and pushed Angel back.

"Well, back when your team had first been set up your government wanted to test you, to see if you would ever turn from the people's interest. We let that blogger spew lies about you but you resisted and maintained your strength. And then we took your wife." The revelation made Angel fall on his knees. "Yes, the disclosure of your identity made it just that bit easier; we released four of the most evil people I have seen in all of my travels and set them upon your wife. I believe they even videoed it, I sure if you looked hard enough you'd find it on the Internet," Zor said chuckling.

Tears formed in Angel's eyes. "You... mean-"

"Yes, if you hadn't have revealed your identity to the people your wife would still be alive. Her death is on your hands; her blood is smeared all over you, as is the blood of those you failed to save. I am told that her last words were "Adam save me". Fitting is it not?" Angel slammed his fist on the ground repeatedly. Zor had done what he wanted; he had broken their leader. Now he would break The Team.

Kor moved stealthily into the mansion. She had bypassed the fight, not wanting to be engaged by the human heroes. As she moved into the house, a light shot into her throwing her through the mansion and back towards the field. Stopping herself and somersaulting back into the air the human hero Dove shot down. Her uniform was yellow with a white cape and a white star on her chest.

"You are not getting inside," she said. Kor smiled and shot towards her smacking her down to ground. Before she could land another blow a light blast sent her flying upwards. Damn she thought that actually hurt. Kor doubled her speed and tackled Dove into another part of the mansion. Dove spat blood out, she got back up and began landing blows on the Kordite. Kor dodged and countered most of the blows but she had to admit; the human was good. She reached into her mind with her telepathy and began entering her deepest thoughts. The human screamed in pain as her thoughts ripped her apart.

Angel couldn't stop the tears; he had killed his wife. The government had sanctioned this; they didn't care about anyone only themselves. Angel repeatedly hit the ground with his fist almost breaking it down. He roared with anger almost giving in to using his angel scream. He suddenly heard a girl whimper. Angel looked at her crying over a dead body; her mother. Part of the building was about to collapse. Angel shot over and stopped it with one hand pushing it back. He picked the little girl up and landed outside with her. She smiled at him and swiped a tear away from his eye. Angel smiled and then heard a sonic boom overhead. Nor was returning, Angel had to cut him off now. He flew as fast as he could tackling Nor upwards and their bloody battle started all over again.

Terrence wasn't doing too good, he had multiple wounds over his torso which were all healing. He suddenly heard Dove screaming; Terrence double timed it over to her position and saw her on her knees. The Kordite female was the one from London. Terrence fired four times with electric rounds to try and stun her.

He yelled out, "Round two sweet cheeks!" The Kordite rushed him, slamming him into a vacant car. Terrence tasted blood in his mouth, he quickly had an idea. He spat the blood over the Kordite's face, she reeled back in disgust. "Damn, you didn't even wait until the third date darling!" he yelled. He hoped the taunts were working. She rushed him again trying to tackle him yet again. Terrence dodged her, firing two incendiary rounds at her. The napalm set her on fire making her rush away. Tremor was still trying to take on the big Kordite. He was incredibly strong and Tremor was in danger of being overpowered. The Kordite lifted both of his arms and smashed downwards. Tremor held firm and managed to halt them. The force was incredible and Tremor was losing ground. He roared with effort desperately trying to hold his arms up. Tremor began to rely on his earthquake powers to give him an edge, but it wasn't working. He had to make a judgement call, he let go and pushed himself back. He rushed to the side and stopped holding back. He slammed his fist into the Kordite with his entire earthquake strength going above any known earthquake that had struck the earth in all of its existence. Tremor felt the entire eastern seaboard shake but he regulated the damage so it all fell on the giant Kordite. The force sent the Kordite soldier flying through the city until it crashed into a skyscraper. Tremor fell on his knees gasping for air trying to stop a nosebleed. That had taken almost all of his energy; it felt like he had been repeatedly kicked in his stomach. Before he had a chance to gather his energy back Terrence flew into him.

"Damn man, watch where you're going!" Tremor yelled. Terrence gave him the finger and sprinted back into the fight. Bolt rushed back into the fight and threw himself into the female Kordite. He unleashed a barrage of blows into her abdomen. He then lifted her up and smashed her down on to his knee. It didn't break her back but it stunned her momentarily. He kicked her in the ribs as she tried to get back up. Before he had the chance to land another blow on her, she pushed him back with her palm sending him flying into the ground's massive walls. Bolt forced himself back up and dodged her rush. Tremor had rejoined the battle and had been attacking the main Kordite. From his analysis the guy was the equivalent of a ground commander, meaning that if he took him it might make them retreat. Tremor rushed him back and landed three 4.5 earthquake blows.

The Kordite was barely stunned and landed a sharp kick into Tremor's gut. That blew the wind out of his lungs and released him of his energy. That's it Tremor thought, he was done for he needed a breather to regain his strength but these guys weren't making it easy. The giant Kordite had jumped back from the skyscraper and lifted Tremor up by his throat. With his last ounce of energy Tremor launched two defiant punches but they were shaken off and he prepared for the worst. As he awaited the last blow a light blast shot into the giant sending him hurtling away. Dove had switched herself into a light form, she blitzed around smashing into the different Kordites. Terrence rushed towards Tremor with a hypodermic needle filled with adrenalin. Terrence stabbed it into Tremor's shoulder giving him back some of his much needed energy. The four members stood back up gingerly and readied themselves before the three powerhouses.

Angel pushed Nor back into a rooftop trying to get away from the civilians below. He had been listening in to the fight by Michael's house and it wasn't going well. They needed Michael but he hadn't got here yet. Where was he Angel thought as blocked another punch from Nor. It was time to use his angel's cry. He took a deep breath and screamed at Nor sending him hurtling and causing damage around him. Angel knew that the damage couldn't be helped; they couldn't change the fighting area. Nor tried to recover and fly back at him but Angel was ready. He intercepted Nor and tackled him down to the ground sending massive punches into his chest. Angel pushed Nor's head into the concrete repeatedly, trying to get leverage over him. Nor stopped Angel's fist and kicked him upwards. Angel quickly recovered but was smacked in his head and then shot up from the ground into the sky. Stopping himself above the building he looked down at Nor. Nor smiled and shot up towards him, Angel had no choice but to fly down to meet his blows. The collision of the two beings at the speed they were travelling created a shock wave which erupted blowing part of a building away. Angel wanted to break off and try and stop the destruction but Veer wouldn't stop; he had to continue. Speeding back over towards Nor Angel prepared to land another blow but he was cut off. A green blast of energy shot into his chest sending him hurtling back. Angel gasped as he felt the burnt part of his chest; that hurt he thought. Nor's eyes had turned bight green and he began to fire, Angel countered with his scream. The scream overpowered the energy vision and caused a small detonation dazing Nor. Taking the initiative Angel lifted up Nor and flew him back towards Michael's mansion. As he arrived he saw The Team in a stand-off against the other three Kordites. He didn't wait for either to launch an attack at each other; he screamed and sent them flying back. The scream vaporised parts of the lawn and multiple pieces of rock.

"Guys no more holding back; we have to kill these guys now!" he yelled. All members of The Team nodded and began a second attack. Tremor re-engaged the female Kordite, Bolt went after the commander, Dove and The Stranger went for Nor and Angel changed targets for the giant Kordite. "Lucky me," Angel muttered under his breath. He sped forwards and pushed the giant away. It wasn't an attack rather a diversion to try and gather a footing in the fight. Angel sped towards the giant and dodged his huge fist, gut punching him as hard as he could. The giant reeled but Angel didn't let up he landed two more hooks and then kicked the giant as hard as he could in the knee. Angel summoned his scream and roared at the giant causing the area around them to crater. Angel was about to land another punch before the giant caught his fist. Stunned Angel launched more blows at his arm trying to get out of the lock but it was to no avail. The giant stood up, dwarfing his height and roared at him. He lifted Angel up and leapt towards a building using Angel as a battering ram. Angel desperately tried to land more punches on him but it had no effect. Angel had one last weapon he could use; his wings. He commanded his wings to beat as hard as they could. The force lifted them both into the air and they ascended above the city. The giant grabbed at his wings trying to keep them still. He then began to pull; Angel realised what he was doing.

"Oh no, you are not taking my wings," Angel yelled. He didn't want to use the cry above the city, the damage would be immense. But he had to, otherwise he wouldn't survive this. Angel roared at the giant, the air began rippling with power dissipating the clouds and the area beneath them. The highest building's glass smashed and began raining down on the people below. The building's supports began buckling under the power of his cry. The giant finally let go of Angel's wings and fell to earth. Breathing a sigh of relief, he flew back down; he couldn't let the thing be alone with civilians.

He activated his com unit. "Any station, any station this Angel 01. I and the superhero team are currently engaged with four category ten superhumans. I need emergency evacuation protocols and air support. Bring the rain." Static crackled over the com unit.

"Roger Angel, this is *USS Enterprise* aircraft carrier docked in New York harbour. Beginning launch procedures for our squad and sending the alert for evacuation. Bringing the rain." Angel smiled; at least they were getting back up. He returned to ground level and looked for the giant. Where the hell was he, he thought? Angel heard a massive roar and he felt a sharp pain in the side of his stomach. He looked at the dagger within him and gasped. He headbutted the Kordite behind him sending him flying back. Reaching back he yanked the dagger out dropping the blade on the ground.

"Please help me," a civilian yelled out. The giant had lifted a man off the ground and was prepared to crush the man's head. Angel had to do something, he stepped on a manhole cover flipping it up. Aiming it at the middle of the Kordite's arm he tossed it as hard as he could. The Kordite dropped the man and stepped back in pain. Angel sped over and caught the man; making sure he was okay. A voice suddenly crackled over his com unit.

"Angel this is *USS Enterprise* control tower, we've dispatched Black Hawk helicopters to evacuate civilians. Flight squad Echo Bravo is on route to give you a hand."

"Roger thanks for the assist *Enterprise*." Angel switched his com unit to the squad link. "Flight Echo Bravo, this is Angel I need you to put down everything you've got on my position. This will be "danger close.""

The pilot's voice crackled over the com. "Understood Angel, "danger close", good luck."

Angel turned to the civilians and yelled, "Clear the area, go now!" Speeding over towards the giant Kordite he grabbed him in a lock and held him tight. He heard the F-35 engines coming towards him preparing to fire on Angel's position. Missiles began to rain down on the Kordite, the heat was amazing but Angel had been through worse. The force sent them back and the F-35's roared over them. The Kordite got up slowly, dazed but unharmed. Angel saw multiple Black Hawks flying towards the city to pick more civilians up. The National Guard had also rolled up ready to close off the area. That was good, at least people would be safe. Before he could do anything the giant soldier smashed Angel's head down and threw him back towards Michael's mansion. Angel crashed down, a he spat some blood out and got back up slowly. Most of The Team were down and unconscious; The

Stranger was fighting both Nor-Veer and the female but he was outgunned and thrown to the ground. Bernard held his rifle high and tried to fire but it was knocked out of the way. Angel tried to get up but a massive foot collided with his head. That was the only thing he remembered.

Kor relaxed herself, the fight had been hard but eventually The Team had been brought down. She walked into the remains of the mansion and inspected the area. The architecture was beautiful but it had been ruined from the fight. She detected a pinging sound with her superhearing. She recognised the sound as a generator. She placed her hand on the wall and an electric blast pushed her back.

"You are not authorised to be in this house, leave now or I will take defensive measures," an ethereal voice said. Kor smiled it was an artificial intelligence.

"Construct, you are an artificial intelligence with no roving program. There is nothing you can do to stop me," she announced.

"That is where you are wrong. My creator told me to protect human life especially those within this house. Though I cannot feel emotions I can mimic them and I know that I will fight you with all I that I have," the intelligence retorted. Kor was surprised; the intelligence was ready die for whoever was in this house. Three generators popped out and shot at her. The electricity was extraordinary and she could feel its burn. She stood back up and walked defiantly forward. More generators fired on her but she remained undaunted. Whoever was here meant a lot to Ror. She searched the house with her superhearing for any heartbeat. Then she found it, four heartbeats coming from beneath her. She could force her way in from the top, but that would be too easy. She walked towards a wall and found that it false. Ripping it away from its bonds she threw it away. The wall behind it was made of Kordite material; finally a challenge. She punched the wall and then she punched it again.

Charlotte gasped at the sound of the thud. She quickly activated Marcus.

"Marcus, what the hell is happening?"

Marcus responded back but his voice sounded hazy. "Forgive me, Miss Charlotte but my systems are running on backup energy and are barely holding. I can't keep the systems up for much longer. A Kordite is trying to rip the doors down. Forgive me Miss Charlotte I can no longer protect you," he said. Charlotte heard a whimper as Amy grabbed her leg.

"Charlotte, I'm scared. Where's Michael?"

She held her tightly and hushed her gently. "Don't worry, he'll be here soon." Suddenly the wall broke down. Charlotte screamed, "Michael!"

Michael struggled under the pressure of the knowledge of his race. More knowledge was being fed into him, information about his powers and other topics. Multiple voices bombarded him but Michael heard something. Over and over again, his name was being repeated. Michael focused on this sound and tried to clear it up. He suddenly recognised the voice: Charlotte. Anger surged through him; his eyes turned red burning with rage. He began vaporising the ice. He broke free and launched himself up.

"My son, no don't go!" his father shouted. Michael didn't hear him. All that mattered was Charlotte was in danger.

Bernard used the gun to steady himself, his leg was broken and his weapon was out of ammo. The superhero team had been incapacitated, the only one who was remotely conscious was Angel but he was in no condition to fight.

The Kordite leader picked Bernard up by his neck and held him high. "Your team have been disabled and you cannot fight us. Now tell me where the boy is," he asked, his voice dripping with malice.

Bernard spat blood out to the ground said through gritted teeth, "Go to hell."

The leader smiled and hissed, "I will enjoy this." Before anyone could do anything a sonic boom smashed into the leader pushing him through New York. Michael had realised what had happen as he entered the atmosphere. He had seen what was happening and made his entrance. Michael held the Kordite down and landed multiple blows.

"You think you can threaten my friends!" Michael roared. "And my family! DIE!" As they flew over the area a squad of F-35's rolled up behind them and began to fire. Zor kneed Michael in the chest but Michael held on. He slammed him into the ground and blasted him with his energy vision. They stopped on the other side of Manhattan Island. Michael pulled himself up. Michael noticed multiple helicopters preparing to land and pick up civilians. Michael turned his attention back to Zor.

The Kordite stood up and emitted an earth-shattering laugh. "Wow that was a rush! It's been years since I felt pain. I must admit you are an impressive specimen. I had thought my son's reports were an exaggeration. But it seems they were not." Michael was ready to fight, but he felt a pain in his ribs. "Ah, yes that was one kick to your abdomen. I think I cracked a rib." Michael wanted to kill him, no more holding back. "Ah, I can tell you want to fight me and then kill me, but look," he said pointing towards one of the buildings behind them. Michael looked and focused on the building and watched as an elevator rope was about to snap. "So what's it gonna be child, fight me or save them?" Michael gritted his teeth. He used a telekinetic blast to send the Kordite hurtling away. Michael turned around and watched as the elevator dropped. Michael waited as time slowed down. He counted to three and then leapt towards the elevator. His timing had been perfect; he had caught the elevator in time. Michael landed on the next building and placed the elevator down. He ripped the elevator doors off and threw them back off the building and quickly supersped away. Landing back at the mansion, he checked around. Nor and his sister were gone as well as the giant Kordite. Michael picked up Bernard and carried him inside, placing him on the sofa he brought up a hologram of his medical status. Rushing outside he helped Dove up and they both checked on the rest of The Team. Angel groaned but lifted himself up.

"Mike things have just got worse. We need to finish this," Angel said through gritted teeth. Mike went back inside and activated Marcus.

"Marcus, where's Charlotte?"

"Sir I... c. Total systems failure." Marcus sounded like he was broken; Michael made a mental note to fix Marcus later. He made sure Bernard was comfortable and went to check on the lab. The door had been broken down and the computer systems were all destroyed. Michael lifted the wreckage and threw it away; and then he realised Charlotte was gone and so was her family.

Chapter 15: Project: *Soaring Eagle*

Michael hovered above New York. The city had been damaged in multiple places and a massive evacuation was underway. Aftershocks were being felt all over the eastern seaboard after the massive blow that Tremor had dealt on the giant Kordite. The *USS Enterprise* was taking people to New Jersey and other places where they could be safe. Michael didn't care, the city could fall down for all he cared nothing mattered any more. Using his superhearing he scanned the planet for Charlotte's heartbeat; but he couldn't hear her. A tear formed at the corner of his eye but it didn't have the chance to fall. Michael used his energy vision to burn it away; no more tears Michael thought. While he had been trapped in the observatory he had seen how energy vision worked and how it could be used. At least something good came from being trapped. But then it returned; the sheer anger that Michael felt at his father for holding him within the observatory. Rage flowed through Michael's veins again making him want to break something, kill somebody, throw the moon out of orbit or even kill himself. He needed Charlotte back; she was the only one who could help him. He didn't bother opening his eyes; he knew they were red anyway. A news helicopter came in the vicinity of Michael.

"Get back," Michael said softly. The helicopter didn't move; Michael opened his eyes and aimed a warning shot of energy vision above the helicopter. The helicopter quickly retreated away from Michael.

"Whoa Mike cease fire now!" Angel shouted. Angel slowly approached Michael, his stomach was bandaged from the dagger wound and he had a small cut above his eyebrow.

Michael looked at Angel. "Get away from me Angel," he said softly. But Angel approached gently.

"Mike, I know you're hurting but I need you focused. I can't have you hurting civilians." Michael turned to Angel his eyes blazing red.

"THEN TELL THEM TO LEAVE ME ALONE!" he roared. His voice almost shattered some windows below. Angel descended gently towards Michael. He had to be wary of Michael; he was in a state of emotional turmoil and if it had to happen, Angel would have to physically pull Michael down.

"Look Michael, they're just scared. I know you're upset. I can feel your pain." Angel came close and held Michael steady.

Michael kept repeating, "No more." They descended to the top of the nearest building. Michael walked towards the edge and looked at the people running towards the nearest makeshift aid centres. They were scared; the followers of Gar had almost killed The Team in a fight and now the people's faith had been shaken in them. Maybe this was their plan all along Michael thought, to first show that they couldn't protect them and then to take over planet.

Michael sighed and sat down. "I'm sorry Angel I don't want to hurt them. I just need her back. She's the only thing that's kept me alive these past years. I tried to listen for her heartbeat but I couldn't hear it," he said softly.

"Mike it doesn't mean that she's dead. They may just be shielding her from you. Who knows what they can do?" Angel replied.

Michael looked at Angel and said, "How's The Team?"

Angel's face grew dark. "Terrence is being treated for injuries but you know him; he's probably healed already. John's resting; he almost brought down the entire eastern seaboard with his attack. Dove's receiving some dressings but she may need some psychiatric help; that woman did a number on her mentally." Michael gritted his teeth. This was all his fault; if Michael had given himself up then he could have saved everyone. It seemed that Angel knew that what he was thinking. "It's not your fault Mike. You've no idea what would have happened if you had been there."

Michael shook his head in denial; he stood up and flexed his muscles. "I've got to check on Bernard. I'll talk to you if I find something," he said as he lifted off into the air. Angel nodded at him and flew off. Michael increased speed as he soared towards his mansion. As Michael approached the mansion, he heard a girl crying. Using his superhearing he focused in on the cry trying to locate the girl. At first Michael wanted to leave it, he had done enough and now he wanted to go home. But there it was again; that little voice in his head nagging him to see what was happening. Turning round he focused on the crying and saw a woman, about 18 crying on a window ledge. Michael flew and shot towards the girl. He appeared in a blur not even alerting the girl to his presence. She had long black hair and her blue eyes were red raw from crying.

"Uh, hello?" Michael said softly. The girl almost jumped out of her skin; she practically hugged the wall.

"Get the hell away from me. Just... just leave me alone," she said in tears.

Michael held his hands up and backed away slowly. "Whoa, whoa I just wanna talk. Not gonna pull you down from there. Just want to talk!" Michael replied.

"Well, I know what you can do. You're like one of those superheroes and you can force me down but if you come any closer I swear to god I will jump!" she shouted her voice breaking.

Michael smirked. "Do I really look like a superhero?" She examined him in his tattered shirt and black jeans. She kept silent. "Now really, why are you up here?" Michael asked softly.

She didn't say anything at first but then she began to talk. "My life just isn't worth living any more. My mom hates me, my dad hates me. Hell my entire family hates me," she replied softly. Michael kept silent and didn't interrupt. "I just wanna sleep forever and not have to worry about pretending to everyone that my life is good."

Michael nodded and said, "I know what it feels like. Trust me I do."

She smirked at him and said, "How can you possibly now what it feels like?"

Michael pursed his lips and said, "You wake up every morning regretting even waking up and just wanting to sleep. You have to pretend that you feel when in reality you're dead inside like a zombie. Some days you barely can put on your own clothes or brush your teeth. You alienate everyone around you wanting to protect them but in the end they just think you're a jerk. And in the end you just want to die." She looked at him in awe as if he had just described her entire life to her. "Do you have the same thing?" She nodded. "Before we go anywhere else, tell me your name."

She looked at him and said, "Kelly," almost whispering the name.

"My name is Michael. It's nice to meet you." She nodded at him.

"Have you ever tried to kill yourself?" she said softly.

Michael nodded gently. "Yeah I have; trust me there's not a day goes by where I wish I wasn't alive. Or that I couldn't do what I can do," he said. "But unfortunately I can't die."

She looked up at him quizzically. "You're a superhero?" she asked softly.

Michael shook his head. "I'm no superhero but I do have superpowers, as you can see. What do think of superheroes?" he said.

She lit up gently. "I really like them; they're one of the few things I like. I wish I could be one," she said enthusiastically.

Michael smiled. "It's harder than it looks," Michael said grimly.

"Why don't you become a superhero?" she asked gently.

Michael pointed at his head. "Got too many problems up here; need to fix my head first. Same thing you have to do as well." She looked up at him. "You need to talk to somebody maybe even a professional or if you have a specific family member. Tell them how you're feeling and how much you want to do this."

She nodded gently. "I can talk to my aunt; she's pretty much like my mom."

Michael smiled. "Then go back inside; or I can give you a lift down."

Her face lit up. "You'd do that?" Michael smiled and held out his hand. She got up gingerly and stepped towards Michael. She reached for his outstretched hand and grabbed it.

Michael pulled her close as she sobbed into his chest. He whispered, "It's alright, I've got you." He gently descended to the ground. After making sure Kelly was alright Michael shot back up into the air and flew towards his mansion. Landing gently, he walked through the gaping hole in the house and went down to the lab. Bernard was sitting on a gurney with his leg in a cast and a bandage on his arm. Holding a class of brandy in his hand he took steady sips as he moved different holograms around. As Michael entered Bernard smiled and tried to stand but Michael supersped over and gently pushed him back down.

"No need for that Bernard, you need to rest," Michael said.

Bernard was defiant. "What I need to do is get up and help you find Charlotte and her family."

Michael pushed him back down again. "No what you need to do is rest; I need to try and fix Marcus before we do anything." Michael pressed his hand against the wall, summoning multiple different holograms. He activated the diagnostic systems trying to see how much damage Marcus had endured. Marcus had exhausted his energy trying to defend Charlotte. "Marcus, come on buddy, wake up." Blue lights flickered gently.

"Sir, I am trying to run a self-diagnostic but I cannot fix myself. I may need your help," Marcus said in a broken voice.

"It's alright buddy I'm gonna fix you up first." Michael pulled his jacket off and began his work.

The White House was abuzz with activity after the attack on New York. Kor made her way with the high father and Nor towards the Oval Office, though their names were different in front of humans. The high father was known as General Sam Rockwell, Nor was known as Lieutenant Colonel Nathan Simmons, and Kor was known as Captain Katherine Myers. The three walked carefully towards the Oval Office. The high father knocked once and a Secret Service officer opened the door.

"General Rockwell to see the president," he announced. The Secret Service officer closed the door quickly and then reopened it ushering them in. The trio walked in and patiently waited for the president to stop what he was doing. The president had black hair and green eyes. He had a thick bushy beard and stood around 5 foot 10. James Navarro was the 44th president of the United States though in reality he was the 43rd since President Grover Cleveland was voted for twice as the 22nd and 24th president. Navarro had been in office for around three years and was a lifelong campaigner against superhumans. He was the main critic of the superhero team and was the main voice behind strict rules enforced on The Team's missions.

He took his reading glasses off and looked over at the General. "So, Sam what the hell happened in New York?" he asked in a sharp voice.

The high father stood up straight. "Sir it seems a group of superhumans were threatening an area outside of New York. The superhero team engaged the four but were defeated quite profoundly." Kor wanted to smile; the superhero team had gone down a lot easier than they thought they would. Navarro poured himself a small glass of water and took a long sip.

"How the hell did this happen; on American soil no less?"

Zor spread his hands. "Honestly, Mr President I don't know. The *USS Enterprise* is on station and did intervene but even then there was a large number of casualties. Parts of New York will need immediate rebuilding and new supports."

James walked around his desk placing his hands on the top. "I don't like this; you need to step up the amount of soldiers you deploy to New York. We need to be ready for another attack. We can't let this country be ravaged by these freaks of nature."

Zor clenched his fists behind his back. *How was it that the human could be so arrogant about his position?* he thought. If he ever saw the wonders of Kord he would die from the greatness. Zor bowed gently. "We will do our best to find these "freaks". In the meantime I'm asking you again for permission to begin Project: Soaring Eagle. It may be our only way to protect ourselves from these attacks."

Navarro nodded in agreement. "Yes, it may be our only source of salvation. Begin the activation." With a courteous nod the president dismissed them. Zor smiled gently as he walked out. Project: Soaring Eagle had been created to appeal to the president's idea of patriotism. The project's real idea was to implement Kordite technology into to the military; an easier way of starting the takeover. The trio walked out of the Oval Office and began their walk through the White House.

Kor got close to Zor and whispered, "High father when..." In a flash of movement Zor grabbed her by the throat and smashed her into the wall not hard enough to leave a mark.

"Never call me that in front of the humans," he hissed. Kor desperately tried to push the high father away as he tightened his grasp. "Nathan you will do well to teach your sister how to be a soldier or so help me I will make you split her skull." Zor dropped her and walked away. Kor grasped at Nor's hand to help herself up, but he swatted her away.

"Learn to control yourself sister and stand on your own two feet or as father commanded I will kill you." Nor walked off as Kor stood up gently, she scowled at them.

Her thoughts once again dwelled upon Ror; his telepathic link had almost gone cold as if he had closed himself off to everyone. *Strange?* she thought. The abduction of the woman had taken more of toll than she could have imagined. The revelation made her seethe with hatred; what could she give him that Kor couldn't?

Michael wiped some dirt of his face. After almost four hours of tinkering Michael had got Marcus up to 50 per cent power and rising; Marcus was currently repeating *HMS Pinafore* in multiple languages. Michael had heard that his father was fascinated by the musical and enjoyed it. Michael had thought that it would be a way to honour him though now he regretted it and mostly he wished to god that he would shut up.

"Marcus I'm pretty sure your speaking capabilities are back online!" he yelled over the racket. Blue lights bleeped rapidly.

"I'm sorry sir I was simply trying to gage whether I was my usual annoying self," the artificial intelligence retorted in an almost sarcastic tone. Michael chuckled as he finished repairing Marcus's systems. Michael pulled himself up and began manipulating hologram diagnostics. Marcus wouldn't be able to reactivate the house's defences but he could provide logistical backup; good enough Michael thought. Bernard had fallen asleep while Michael had been fixing Marcus. He was slowly rousing.

"Master Michael, how long have I slept?" he asked groggily.

Michael responded immediately. "Four hours."

Bernard looked at him and almost jumped off the bed. "Impossible I was only trying to rest my eyes for a bit not for four hours. I have things to do, and I have to start remodelling the manor."

Michael held his hand up to signal him to stop. "I'm gonna do that in a minute." Michael directed his attention to Marcus. "Marcus you up for little remodelling?" he asked.

Blue lights flashed. "Yes sir, what would you have me do?"

Michael smiled. "Initiate bunker!" A single blue light flashed showing that Marcus was activating the bunker mode. One night when Michael was 14 he was bored; so he began drawing up designs for a safety mode if the manor was ever attacked. The bunker mode used titanium reinforced walls to form over the damaged parts of the manor. Walking upstairs Michael watched as the titanium spread over the wounds on the house and began sealing shut. The door was now a metre thick of steel which could only be opened by Michael or Bernard.

Bernard hobbled up the stairs on a crutch and looked at the sheets of titanium. "I hope this isn't permanent," he shouted out.

Michael shook his head. "I'm gonna fix it up, but I need to find someone first." A twinge of pain attacked Michael. He still really couldn't believe it; Charlotte was gone and there was nothing Michael could do. He racked his brain trying to find a way to trace the Kordites. Michael pulled a hologram off the wall and manipulated it selecting the cameras that Michael had placed around the manor grounds. Most of them had been destroyed but the footage was all captured and saved. The footage was mostly blurs from the fight and a few stills were of Terrence fighting but there wasn't much to use. The only camera that had survived was the one in the bushes. Michael pulled the camera footage up and began to play it through. Michael grimaced at the fight; The Team had been beaten quite comprehensively. They had needed Michael's help but he wasn't there; he was busy being kept prisoner by his own damn father. Michael recognised Nor and Kor but the other two were different; more powerful and infinitely more lethal. Analysing the leader he had tackled over the city he recognised the symbols over the armour. Michael didn't want to admit it but he had to use the Kordite lab downstairs. Bernard sat down on what was left of the sofa and rested his leg. He looked at the projections on the walls. On the layers of the titanium were small cameras which were relaying images back over the inside.

"Not quite a window but it'll do," Bernard muttered to himself.

Michael still didn't like the idea of using the lab. After the events in the observatory Michael didn't trust the Kordite technology; but if it was the only way he could find a lead to the Kordites then he was going to use it. Blue lights lit up the lab. The computers weren't dignified by any buttons or other objects rather they had a smooth surface which could be used to literally make holograms. Michael had learnt how to properly use the technology while in the observatory. He uploaded a picture of the leader to the computer and filed it in the directory of Kordites. After a few seconds a single match was found. Michael pulled it out and began scanning through the document. The leader was "High Father" rank or "General" and his name was Zor-Veer. An ambitious soldier he trained from birth to be the best and fight better than all. Michael noticed that over time Zor began to exhibit sociopathic and narcissistic tendencies. Over time he began to distance himself from the Guild Master and led his troops to believe he was the rightful guild master. Zor wanted to eventually stage a coup d'état over the guild and lead it instead of the main Guild Master. Michael noticed that he and his father had had multiple run-ins. They didn't agree over anything, specifically over what to do with earth. Michael scanned his family records and found something intriguing. Kor and Nor were his children. Nor was the oldest by a hundred years or so and was the more favoured. Kor on the other hand was more of a scientist. At the very start of her education she was intrigued about science more than warfare making her a pariah in the Guild of Veer. She was shunned by her father but was taken in by members of the Guild of Vaar specifically Michael's cousin. Strange Michael thought as he viewed the documents. Switching back to Zor he found that at an early age he was fascinated by Gar. When Vek-Gar went to earth and began his work, a sect within the Guild of Veer known as the Followers of Gar travelled to earth to assimilate the populace and began killing them off. This matched up with what Michael knew so far but what was strange was that Zor threw himself into the military rising through the ranks rapidly and earning himself medals. This was strange not only did Zor thrive in the military; he enjoyed it. Michael moved the directory away and formed a chair made of hard light holograms. He sat down and thought it over. Zor was almost religiously driven to fight for Gar. It almost resembled a fanatic's belief, but the worst was that Zor was a soldier through and through. The directory mentioned that he was a barbaric. He had participated in a few Kordite campaigns and had a thing for dismembering his victims. Though the Guild of Veer were soldiers and lived for the fight they reprimanded Zor severely even threatening to throw him out of the guild and submitting to him to same amount of pain that he submitted his victims. Michael switched the directory off. He suddenly had an idea; he wanted to see if the computers were linked up to Kord in the present. He searched for some kind of newsfeed; and he found it. Michael manipulated the news and read about different events. Michael searched for the latest event and saw that the Kordites were at war, almost gaping at the fact that someone was even dumb enough to fight against the most powerful race in the universe. Michael read more and found that the race they were fighting was called the "Ziborian Empire". Native to a planet called Zibor they were almost destroyed by the Guardians almost a thousand years ago. The Guardians almost drove them to extinction because of their violent and decadent ways. The worst problem about them was that they possessed immense superhuman physiques. Michael opened a report on them and it showed Michael how strong they actually were; they could even fly under their own power. They posed a direct threat to everyone in the area. Their powers weren't dependent on energy and they had the ability to turn their skin into a diamond-like crystal substance; despite this very slight advantage they still couldn't match a pure blooded Kordite in strength but they were equal to a second blooded Kordite. In addition to this their ability to turn their skin into crystal helped them deal incredible damage. The nearby planets had begged the Guardians to intervene and intervene they did. Michael read the reports and there was video evidence of how the Guardians fought them. It was bloody and the Ziborians almost overwhelmed the Guardians. After a month of fighting the Guardians destroyed most of them. However they left a few survivors thinking they could change the outlook on their ways. But the opposite occurred; the new Ziborians trained themselves into a warrior race. Over thousands of years they became better and fifty years ago they restarted the war. Michael kept reading and found that none of the races in the Universal Committee were lending their aid; out of fear. Michael put his head in his hands and sighed over what he had read. The Ziborians were horrible but they weren't Michael's problem; hopefully the Kordites could stop them before they got close to earth. Michael had to deal with Zor and rescue Charlotte. He pulled out the directory and quickly pulled up Zor's physical aspects; anything that could help Michael identify him. Michael activated the face recognition software with Marcus and pulled Zor's face from the Kordite computer and sent it to Marcus.

227

"I need a favour from you Marcus. Hack into the military files and pull all their personnel from the army. Match it with the picture that I just gave you."

A single blue light activated. "Sir, you do realise that hacking into military personnel is illegal?"

Michael shrugged. "Then make sure you don't get found out."

Blue lights fluttered. "Very well sir, here I go."

Chapter 16: *I have found them*

Michael hadn't wanted to but he had fallen asleep. From the start of the nightmare he knew what was going to happen. Michael didn't bother checking his surrounding he just walked out of the black room. New York was again in flames, in fact it almost resembled the city in its state after the fight with the Kordites. Michael shot towards the Empire State Building and landed on the top deck. Michael's doppelgänger or "Evil Michael" sat on the edge watching the flames and destruction.

"I hear Charlotte's been taken," he hissed and then turned round revealing a new scar on his face. "Lucky for me, now I can fully control you."

Michael gritted his teeth and said, "I will not let you take control from me. I am stronger than you."

The doppelgänger smiled. "Stronger than me? You don't even know when someone is watching you." Michael looked quizzically at the doppelgänger. "You don't know do you? Look inside your head Mickey, can't you feel that icy claw at the back of your head?" Michael concentrated and looked inside his head. Spreading out with his telepathy he found what could only be described as a hole in his head. Delving into the hole he found who was watching him: Kor the female Kordite. "Yeah, it happened during your fight with in London. She found her way into your big ole' brain and she's been watching you ever since." Michael wanted to tackle him off the building but he was frozen in place. Out of the flames Charlotte and Kor shot up and were strung up beside each other. Chuckling, the doppelgänger stood up and walked between the two. "Look at these two; probably the only two women that actually care for you. Now I'm gonna ask if you can choose between them." Michael wanted to pick Charlotte but he was unsure. "Not as easy as you would think is it?" For some reason Michael almost felt affection for Kor as if they were in love. "You feel it don't you now. It's almost like you love each other. Now why is that? Well I was trying to find the answer to that and I couldn't believe I was so STUPID!" the doppelgänger shouted causing further damage to the building. "It's because you're the same. The attraction is normal between you; you're almost the same and that's why you feel that love." Michael fell on his knees. Was it true? Did he really love her or was this just another evil trick by his brain to break him? The doppelgänger walked back towards the edge and laughed again. "No matter you'll still kill them both."

Michael suddenly looked back at him. "No I won't, I will never hurt her."

The doppelgänger tackled him into the ground. "YES YOU WILL. I will make you split her skull and throw her body into the sun." Michael wanted to wake up, he couldn't take it any more. He just wanted to wake up.

Kor suddenly woke up from her sleep. Her telepathic link with Ror had been found. She focused in on the link and felt Ror's pain. He was having a nightmare; his broken mind was taunting him again and she could feel his pain. A tear leaked from her eye as she looked at what he was going through. Kor sat up and tried to soothe his thoughts with her telepathy but he was fighting it. He was mentally worn out and she couldn't help him. Kor tried to go back sleep but she suddenly heard a scream. Rising out of her bed she floated towards the balcony and saw the source of the scream. A young human girl had swum out into the ocean and now she was screaming for someone to help. Kor almost scowled at the event. Humans did not even care for their children she thought as she went back inside, but the screaming kept on going. Kor wanted to fall asleep trying to ignore the cries of the girl; but then she decided. Moving fast enough to be a blur she appeared over the ocean and fell into the sea. She grabbed the little girl's arm and gently pulled her out. Speeding towards the beach she carried the girl and placed her gently on the ground. The parents ran up to her and began shouting praise at her. At first she wanted to scold the parents for being so far from the child but she didn't. What scared her most was that she enjoyed it. The little girl beamed at her smiling and gave her a small toy. Kor smiled and began walking away. Before anyone around her asked any question she disappeared and reappeared at her apartment. She walked inside and poured herself a cup of coffee. She sat down and pondered what had just happened and what happened with Ror's telepathic link.

"I have found them sir," Marcus announced in a loud voice. Michael shot up almost flying through the wall. He took two deep breaths and concentrated his thoughts. "Sir, your brainwaves are through the roof."

Michael stood and exhaled shakily. "I'm fine, just bad dreams. What have you found?"

A few blue lights fluttered. "Sir I have found a match for the Kordite. There are some variations but the match is 99.5%

the same." A holographic picture appeared and Michael recognised the picture. General Sam Rockwell; the general Michael had seen on the news. Michael studied the picture; Marcus was right, there were a few differences but they were cosmetic. The general's face had been cleaned up covering the scars around his face. Michael had another hunch; he sent the two pictures of Kor and Nor to Marcus.

"Run these two pictures through the database. Check for relevant matches." Blue lights fluttered as Marcus began checking again. Michael knew it would take a few minutes so he walked upstairs to find a drink. He made his way upstairs and found his liquor cabinet. Surprisingly it was the only thing had that survived in this room.

"You don't need that," Bernard said from behind him.

Michael sighed deeply. "I just want one drink, please it'll help."

Bernard limped towards him and said, "No, you don't need it son. You're strong enough to go without it; fight it boy fight it." Michael gritted his teeth and reached for the small glass and began to pour it. Bernard grabbed his arm. "Son, please! You don't need it. The drink only makes it worse."

Michael began shaking. "Please Bernard, I just need one drink." A tear exited Michael's eye as he gently put the glass down.

Bernard put his hand on his shoulder. "You've made the right choice son. It's always hardest the first time." Michael gritted his teeth, he just wanted a drink. Just one he thought; but he knew Bernard was right. He was about to say the one thing that scared him more than anything.

"Bernard, I'm an alcoholic."

Bernard put an arm around Michael and held him steady. "It's alright, son, it's alright. You've made the right choice and it will get better from here on out."

Michael's eyes blazed red. "I've read about the withdrawals, I don't know if I'll be immune to it but I'm scared Bernard."

Bernard pulled Michael close. "I know son, I know but you can get through this."

Michael's hand started shaking as he looked at the liquor; he could picture the warm brown liquid pouring into a shot glass and the peace that it brought him. Michael let his eyes turn into full dark red as he powered his energy vision up. Twin streams of red did away with the cabinet and over $100 of alcohol. Bernard smiled and he quickly retreated out of the room to get a fire extinguisher.

"Best use this before you burn the house down," he said sarcastically as he doused the small flame. Blue lights flashed just as Bernard walked out of the room.

"Sir I have found the other two military personnel. Both are matches." Two holograms flew up. Michael checked them against his personal memories. Kor looked like Captain Katherine Myers and Nor looked like Lieutenant Colonel Nathan Simmons. They both had affiliations with the general. Interestingly they had both served in campaigns of the US military.

"Marcus, is this all you found?" Michael asked. Blue lights fluttered.

"Nothing specific sir, all three had ties to different projects within the military."

Michael frowned. "Look for something classified, go deeper into their history." A single blue light flashed as Marcus began working on it. Michael looked at the ruined drinks cabinet and sighed softly. He moved to his beside table and opened the drawer. There were multiple items including pens, a flask and a bottle of soda. For a split second Michael wanted to pick the flask up but opted for the bottle of soda.

He downed the soda in a single gulp; not quite as good as the brandy or Scotch but it would do.

Blue lights fluttered again. "Sir, I have found something and I think you are going to like it."

Michael nodded. "Tell me."

Blue lights fluttered. "Sir, in both files I have found classified files categorised in level six or higher meaning they are only seen by the president and his highest officials. The file makes reference to a Project: Soaring Eagle."

Michael raised an eyebrow. "What is it?" Michael took a seat as Marcus began explaining.

"Project: Soaring Eagle refers to bringing in experimental technology to military arms. There was defiance to it by a few of the president's advisors but he has since enabled it."

Michael looked at the hologram. "Why?"

"It is because of the events of New York. The project enables the military to take a stronger stance against superhumans. From what I have found out the weapons involved could put The Team out of business. Some of the weapons are coming from Sampson Industries."

Michael stood up. "What? What kind of weapons?"

Marcus began speaking again. "Sir, Sampson Industries are providing high energy weapons such as cutting lasers." Michael paced the room. Sampson Industries' proprietary X-5 laser cutter was being used for mining purposes at this specific time. Michael had designed it when he was younger and intended it for asteroid defence and mining hard rock deposits.

"Marcus, are there any designs for the weapons?" Blue lights fluttered and three holograms appeared in front of him. Michael began manipulating them checking for differences; maybe there was something within the designs showing they weren't Michael's designs. But they were exact copies right down to the last iota of detail. "Who from the military signed off on these designs?" Michael kept playing with the designs before Marcus spoke up.

"Sir, it appears that General Rockwell signed off the designs after several meetings with board members. The project cost around seven billion dollars." Michael pondered this for a bit; if the business had been done in Sampson Industries then maybe there were recordings of it. Michael had to go back to Sampson Industries.

Michael stood outside the entrance of Sampson Industries. The inside was slightly lit because of a few security guards inside but other than that there was no one else. Michael looked towards his father's office on the top level and shot up towards it. The walls were blacked out which was normal because it had never been used. Michael hoped his father had the same idea of entering a place. Scanning the area, Michael found a small lump on the window. Pressing it down, there was a hiss and a flash of blue as light began scanning him. There was a series of chimes as the window retracted and Michael entered the room. Activating the lights he switched the eight-track player on and sat down at the desk. Michael pulled a USB stick out of his pocket and placed it on the desk. Blue lights flashed around it and the data appeared before him in holographic form. Selecting Marcus's program, he began uploading the system with his father's systems. There was a series of chimes.

"Sir I am fully uploaded into the office's systems. I have full access; where do you think I should start sir?" Michael placed his hand on the desk and pulled holographic material up. The office's systems were linked with Kordite technology making it easy for Michael to transfer files from the lab at home to this one. He swiped through data and pulled out the deal with Sampson Industries and the military.

"Marcus, check through video files in the boardroom."

Multiple lights flashed and video data flew up. "Sir, if the deals have been done under the table, there might not be any record of them." Michael considered that as he began searching the records for the deal; but there was nothing there.

"Marcus, I have an idea."

A single light flashed. "What is it, sir?"

Michael began searching through other databases in the systems to find another video system. "Search the building, specifically the boardroom, for any other recording devices to do with Kordite technology." Blue lights began flashing around as Marcus began searching. Michael stood up and looked at the city. No wonder his father liked the office, it had a beautiful view.

"Sir I've found something, a secondary video system unknown to anyone here." Michael smiled; his father was a paranoid man and knew that he didn't trust any of the board members as far as he could throw them. A hologram of video files flew up around Michael. The files went as far back as the early seventies. Michael focused on the latest ones and began filtering through them. One of them was very familiar; the picture was of Rockwell.

"Marcus begin playing these videos."

The video started off with Rockwell and a board member entering the room. The board member motioned for Rockwell to sit down but the general did not.

"General I heard you didn't like the other board member so I had him fired. Don't want to jeopardise our working relationship. Frank Armstrong is the name, what can I do for you?"

Rockwell folded his arms. "The last board member I spoke to was an imbecile and deserved to be fired. I trust you are more... open to negotiation."

Armstrong smiled a sly smile as he picked up a small glass of brandy and took a sip. "Well I don't like to brag but I prefer doing business like this, more incognito than anything else. So again I ask you, what can I do for you?"

Rockwell smiled again and finally sat down. "I'm here for a high energy weapons system. Something, like a mining laser."

Armstrong smiled and walked over to a computer on the wall. He activated a file called "special projects" and showed it to the general. "R & D has done quite a few projects with some of our innovations, but I haven't seen anything about a mining laser."

Zor pulled a horrible grin. "It's a prototype called the X-5 laser cutter used for mining in harsh conditions. I believe a wonder child designed it at the age of 17; quite amazing."

The board member grinned. "You mean the heir to the company? He's a smart kid but he's not getting anywhere near this company. However we do have a few deep black operations involving the X-5."

The general stood. "Interesting. Can we start pricing?" Armstrong poured a glass of brandy and handed it to the general.

"How does nine billion sound?" The general clinked glasses with Armstrong.

"It sounds reasonable. What else do you have for me?" The board member took a small drink and handed him a tablet.

"There are a few R & D projects utilising nanorobots as bomb coverings. Also got something to do with new fighter jet engines enabling them to go faster than ever."

The general smiled. "We've got some business to do then. Let's get started and make sure this stays off books."

Frank Armstrong let a horrible grin loose as he walked towards the general. "General I always do business off the books." Michael switched the recording off.

Michael's eyes glowed red as anger flowed through him. Jones had been right, Michael needed to take control of his company to stop these underhanded deals.

"Marcus, send all these files back home and close down the systems. We're going home." Blue lights flashed and Michael took the USB stick home with him. Exiting the window he made his way towards the mansion. Michael landed back at the manor and sped into his lab. Looking around he found the X-5 on the worktop and lifted it up. Examining it closer he realised why the Kordites were so into the idea of using the X-5. It used a specific kind of radiation, specifically uranium-235 weapons-grade. A stronger strength made it better for cutting through materials. Michael had created a nano shield to cover the uranium giving it the ability to never leak radiation. It was the same one he used for Charlotte's hydrogen cell. Michael pressed a few buttons on the X-5 as it began powering up. He wanted an idea of how powerful the weapon was and he could feel it. No wonder Zor wanted it he thought as he switched it back to its dormant mode. Michael began reading through files again to get a better scope on the three Kordites who had been in the military.

Chapter 17: *Return to me*

Nor sat in his office going through different files. There was nothing to do and these files were boring at best. A knock came at the door. Nor looked up.

"Come in."

A human soldier walked through and saluted. "Sir, I was wondering what you wanted me to do with the family that we detained?" Nor almost snapped the human's neck with his telekinesis.

"Do not touch them until the order is given, understood?" The soldier nodded and walked out. Nor put the paper down and decided he was not going to let his brain fall apart. He floated upwards gently and folded his legs, closed his eyes and went into a deep trance focusing on everything around him, from the sound of water rushing through a filter to a bug flying around in the other room. The silence was golden; until a knock came at the door. Nor opened his eyes which were shining a brilliant green as anger flowed through him.

"What is it?" he said not bothering to show the anger in his voice. Expecting a human soldier he was surprised to see a Kordite soldier enter and kneel before him.

"Knight Warrior, I have news of your sister." Nor moved towards him. He had almost forgotten what his Kordite rank was; the knight warrior rank was the same as the human rank he was used to hearing.

"Very well, show me," he said. The soldier handed him a hologram of a video showing him his sister save a human infant from drowning. Nor's face reeled in disgust; what was his sister thinking? He dismissed the soldier who stopped for one second before leaving.

"You also have a communiqué from Kord." Nor looked up at him: a call from Kord must be important.

"Put it through." The soldier nodded and let the hologram play out. Nor knew who it was; on instinct he fell on one knee and placed his fist on the ground saluting the figure in the hologram. The figure had multiple scars over his armour which was crimson red. He stood at around 8 feet tall and could easily intimidate Nor.

"It seems respect is still in your nature despite what you are currently doing," the figure said in an authoritarian voice.

Nor did not look up. "I still understand respect, Guild Master Veer." The Guild Master was leader of the guild and the highest rank in the guild just below the Guardian.

"But you do not understand orders, do you?" the Guild Master boomed.

"I am following my own orders now not those of a weak indecisive leader," Nor retorted to him.

The Guild Master's eyes flared a bright blue. "You dare…"

Nor stood up in defiance. "I dare! You are not a leader; you are just a weak dog to be ordered and commanded whenever they want you to. You destroyed my family because they wanted to adhere to a value that the Guardians themselves stood by."

The Guild Master didn't get angry, he simply sighed with sadness. "I trained you boy, watched you become the soldier that you are now. You think the Guardians would stand by this madness they tried twice to stop? Once it cost you most of your family because of a fanatic belief that you father holds."

Nor wanted to hurl the table through the hologram but he didn't. "Ideals that we should all stand by; the humans of earth are a weak and feeble race. They need to be destroyed now."

The Guild Master stood straighter. "Then let the Guardians judge them it is not their time yet." There was silence between the two until the Guild Master continued. "When you joined the military you swore an oath to safeguard Kord and all the Universal Committee planets. Earth will soon be able to join us if they pass. Remember the forefront of our principles is that there is the potential of good in every being. If there are only seven good humans the Guardians will spare them. We may have protected Gar when his experiments helped us but we ousted him when he went over the top. Your father is failing you."

Nor didn't say anything for a bit but then he replied, "But... what about the child of Vaar?"

The Guild Master sighed. "He is not of your concern; the Guild of Vaar is now one of our allies. We have never been stronger with their cooperation than without it. In fact we have been trying to locate the child as well so we can bring him back to Kord." Nor kept quiet. "Nor, son, the child of Vaar is there to help the peace process not to endanger it. I too remember what his brother did to the galaxy; I was there with you as he wiped out cities and planets because of a mistake. But this boy is different."

Nor looked up. "How do you know?"

The Guild Master smiled. "His father assured me that history would not repeat itself and I trust him." The silence was eerie. "Nor I watched you fight for Kord when peace was under threat and now you must return. You haven't seen the news files on Kord for a long time, have you?" Nor shook his head. "The Ziborian threat has returned and we need to act. The war is taking its toll on the universe and we need to stem the tide of causalities now. Otherwise the Ziborians will beat us back and we won't be able to defend the others. Imagine it child: trillions of casualties because we, the strongest race, in the universe were fighting amongst ourselves. Can you live with that?" Nor looked down at his feet. Was the Guild Master correct? Was it worth continuing this worthless crusade with the threat of trillions of deaths? Nor looked at the Guild Master.

"I... I thought we were doing the right thing, my liege. I thought I was safeguarding Kord from another event like the last." Nor fell on his knees with the recollection of the human lives he had taken. A tear slowly sank from his left eye. "I have done so many horrible things, committed atrocities that will never be forgiven by anyone. Forgive me Guild Master for what I have done."

The Guild Master looked at Nor like a father looked at his son. "You can be forgiven. How can anyone blame you for what you have known ever since you were a young boy? You were indoctrinated to believe a certain thing and you didn't know any different. Your sister tried to escape and look what happened to her." Nor remembered how his father beat his sister to almost a bloody pulp because she wanted to be a scientist. "Come back to us. I will leave an operative on the moon who will teleport you back here."

Nor shook his head no. "I cannot. Not yet Guild Master."

The Guild Master looked quizzically at him. "Why not?"

Nor looked at him. "If I leave now my father will accelerate his progress and destroy the planet. The child of Vaar will not be able to stop father and his second in command."

The Guild Master nodded in agreement. "I understand child. Zar is one of the most prolific soldiers I have ever seen and he is one of the biggest threats to the child. I am happy that you have seen the error of your ways. I await your return child." The hologram switched off. Nor breathed a sigh of relief; it felt like a weight had been taken off his shoulders. Nor could return to Kord and fight the Ziborian threat. Hopefully he could make his sister see sense and return to Kord with him.

Michael had spent the last few hours working to find clues or anything on Charlotte's location. The military documents Marcus had found had showed him how far the Kordites had gone to blend with the human population even going as far as to give false birth dates and other data. Michael had scoured every file he had to find a trace on Soaring Eagle and where it was being transported to and from. This item was hidden from all eyes even satellites. Michael sighed softly. Blue lights flashed.

"Sir, don't you think it would be easier if we contacted The Team for help?" Michael sighed again. He wouldn't mind asking The Team for help but what condition were they in and would they be ready to help him?

"Marcus, give me satellite coverage of the Atlantic Ocean." A holographic screen popped up and gave him coverage of 106,400,000 square kilometres. The vast expanse of water covered 20 per cent of the earth's surface and was home to many different species of marine biology. Maybe it was time for him to pay his visit to the ship. Michael pulled on a spare coat and sped into the air flying towards the atmosphere. Using his thermal vision he began scanning every square foot of the Atlantic trying to find the ship. He picked up a big image and smiled; there it was. Shooting down towards the heat source he landed on top of the ship. Two turrets came up and aimed at him.

"Identify yourself or lethal force will be used," a robotic voice said.

"That's it. Robots really hate me," Michael said. The turrets moved closer towards him.

"Lethal force is now going to be used."

Michael raised his hands and said, "Seven, alpha, Charlotte." The turrets stopped spinning up.

"Greetings Michael Sampson 03." The area opened up. Michael descended on to the deck. The whole area was blacked out meaning that The Team were all in the med bay.

"Marcus, you online?"

"I am sir; my systems are always on loan to The Team."

Michael smiled. "Good. Where are they?" A blue light began flashing.

"They are all in the med bay." Michael smiled and sped down. He stopped smiling as soon as he entered. Terrence was lying on a bed with multiple bandages despite the fact he was already healed but he was tired. John had a broken arm and was sitting up but looked incredibly pale. Dove was asleep and looked peaceful with Angel sitting by her side. Bolt had his leg in a cast and was resting. Michael walked solemnly in and sat with Angel. Angel's eyes were red raw. Michael could understand: The Team were like a family and Angel was always at the head leading them. The fact that they could have been beaten as badly as they were Michael could already imagine what was happening; people around the world showing their disbelief in what had happened with The Team, teenagers who had recorded the fight on their phones complaining on forums how they should do better and politicians begging for a reform change. All part of the Kordite plan Michael thought, destabilise the public and make them embrace chance.

Adam turned round and said, "Hey Mike." He cleared his throat. "What can I do for you?"

Michael shook his head. "Nothing Adam, I'm here to check up on you. What's happening?"

Adam brushed his hand through his hair. "I don't know where to start. Terrence is a fast healer, he's just being lazy."

Terrence suddenly shouted, "I heard that."

Adam chuckled. "John's having a rest, he almost destabilised the entire eastern seaboard. It took a lot out of him so he's getting some much earned sleep. Rachel's tired; she's taken a lot out of herself but I think the damage is almost psychological. That Kordite did a number on her with her telepathy; pretty much almost knocked her out. Booker has seen better days; one of them broke his leg so he needs that healed now. Fortunately we've got some of the most advanced medical systems known to man so we've got that leg set and it should heal soon."

Michael sighed. "I'm sorry; Adam I'm so sorry man. I did all of this. I hurt so many people."

Adam put his hand up. "Don't; none of this is your fault. They started this fight and we fought back; simple as." They both kept silent until Adam spoke up. "You look like crap. What's wrong?"

Michael sighed deeply. "Get comfortable."

Michael told Adam everything from the X-5 and other military records that the Kordites did. As he did Terrence and John hobbled over and sat with them. Michael kept his voice down to let Booker and Rachel sleep. The members of The Team were quiet when Michael finished until Terrence broke the silence.

He placed his fedora on his head and said, "You mean to tell me that these bastards have served with the military and are actually close with the president and you built them a weapon."

Michael held up his hand. "Okay first of all: I didn't build a weapon I built a drill capable of cutting through most materials. Second of all: yes the general is friends with the president and he considers him a close one at that. Plus the "weapon" has to have had its systems completely reversed to act like a weapon."

John piped up. "Who can reverse it like that?"

Michael shrugged. "I designed that thing when was I was bored meaning I should be the only one who can actually do that." The three members looked at him. "Stop, don't be stupid I wouldn't do that. If I didn't do it then there's probably only one other who could." They looked at him again.

Adam asked. "Who?"

Michael rubbed his face and said, "Kor; she's a scientist as well as a soldier."

Terrence piped up again. "The bitch that almost broke Rachel? Good I get to kill her."

Michael understood his anger but before he could speak Adam started talking. "I don't think we can beat them." They all looked at him in dismay. Angel sighed heavily. "Look what they did to us when they were bored. Put all of us in the hospital and we barely made a dent in any of them." Angel looked at Michael. "I can't speak for the rest of us but I wasn't holding back on that giant bastard and I couldn't take him down."

Michael considered this. "You didn't use your scream at max power though, did you?"

Angel shook his head in disagreement. "Couldn't have done that in a city, but if they were in a space without civilians then I could go full power. I don't even know what full power is on my angel cry." Michael looked at him. "Yeah I know it sounds weird but it's way too unpredictable. I used it as hard as I could on Pluto and left a divot in the crust. I split a meteor in half as well. Maybe at full power I could cause some damage to these bastards."

John sighed. "I hit that guy with an earthquake which could have levelled a continent and he barely flinched. Whether I could go any higher I don't really know."

Terrence rubbed his hands together. "I hit them with all of my gun power but nothing happened. Maybe one of those thingamajigs could help."

Michael smiled grimly. "Thingamajig really? Anyway we may have to be careful with these guys."

Terrence asked, "Why?"

Michael focused. "I found some documents of them from Kord. Turns out Kor and Nor were indoctrinated into their father's ordeals. When Kor tried to runaway and join my guild she was beaten by her father to a bloody pulp."

John looked at Michael quizzically. "So? You're telling us to feel sorry for these two? After what they did to Dove, Russia, New York?" John looked up at him. "Charlotte?"

Michael's eyes turned red. "Don't even think about mentioning her name. I left her there so you could protect her and look how that worked out."

John snarled, "Really? You're blaming us? If I remember correctly you're the one they're after; you. If you hadn't come to earth then none of this would have ever happened."

Michael stood up. "You wanna play that card? I never asked to be born and I wish to god that I could find some sort of way to die. So, next time you play the whole "alien threat" factor, remember that."

Tremor stood up and sized up Michael. "Yeah, you keep telling yourself that. But Angel told us about Amy's murder and said that your race murdered her. So in actual fact: EVERYTHING IS YOUR FAULT"!

Michael lost it. In a flash of motion Michael grabbed John by his throat before he could do anything. He lifted him and let his eyes glow a bright red. "DON'T YOU THINK

I KNOW THAT, YOU ASSHOLE? Everything that has happened to her is MY DAMN fault." Michael was working on instinct he began squeezing the life out of John's throat. "No more," he whispered. Adam grabbed Michael in a neck hold trying to pull him back but Michael wouldn't move. Adam hoped that he had the same weak points and used a knee to hit the back of his knee and pulled him back. Michael suddenly stopped doing anything as Angel pushed him and John back.

"Enough both of you!" He pointed at John. "I ever catch you talking to him like that again I swear to god I'll fly you into space and let you die. Michael's done everything he can do to help us and you think you can make him the bad guy? I don't think so. In case you've forgotten Michael built all of this for this. So take a walk and think real hard about what you're gonna do next!" John took a deep breath and walked out. Adam was almost shaking from anger; Michael didn't see him get angry that much and he rarely threatened any of The Team but this was different. John had crossed a line and Adam had to remind them who they were. Michael pulled himself up and let his eyes go back to black. He stood back up and sighed deeply. He couldn't blame John; he knew he was right.

"Adam, he's right; this is my entire fault. I brought this upon you all, I should have never told you anything and just dealt with it myself." Adam shook his head no, so did Terrence.

"This ain't your fault, Mike we still would have helped it's what we're here for," Terrence said patting Michael on his shoulder.

Adam spoke up. "John's a tough bastard but what happened to us has never happened before. We've been outnumbered and outgunned but in the end we've always found something to help us even out the numbers. But not this time; this time these guys are gunning for us and aren't giving us any time to prep for it. But right now Mike we've got to find these weapons systems. If they get out of hand then we could be looking at a war on all superhumans even the ones that are trying to get on with their lives." Michael nodded and stood up. He was about to walk out before Adam called him back. "Mike, can you help her?" He said while looking at Rachel. Michael didn't say anything; his telepathy was largely unknown to him as he'd never used it properly except for setting up a link with people. Angel looked back at him. "Please, Mike can't you try at least?" Michael looked at her Rachel. She wasn't reacting to anything; no outside stimuli.

Michael sighed softly. "I can try." Adam nodded as Michael sat down next Rachel. Adam held her hand gently keeping it steady as Michael focused. He reached with his thoughts and directed them into Rachel's head; and then everything went black.

Michael stood up in a dark place searching for Rachel. Scanning the area he quickly deduced that he was in Rachel's representation of her mind. *What had Kor done to her?* Michael thought as he walked forward. The mental torture that had been carried out on Rachel had put her into a catatonic state and Michael had to find a way to help. He called her name.

"Rachel, Rachel it's me, Mike I'm here to help you." His words echoed into the dark but no reply came back. Out of the black a light shot towards Michael. Time slowed down as Michael dodged out of the way. It was Rachel and she was running from something. Michael looked back scanning further into the dark to see what she was running from. Michael gently floated into the air and followed Rachel. Increasing speed he caught up with and grabbed her arm pulling her down. Rachel was incredibly strong but Michael held her down as she struggled. "It's me Rachel, Mike, I'm trying to help you." Her eyes were red raw from tears and she was still crying.

"She showed me the truth Mike. She showed me how we hurt each other; all the death and destruction that we've caused. We need to be destroyed. I NEED TO DIE." Michael understood now. Kor had poured the entirety of earth's history into Rachel's mind and had showed her every bloody part of it.

"Rachel, I know what she showed you but none of that is your fault. You need to realise that there's no guilt. The Kordite was trying to break you and she will only succeed if you give in."

Rachel cried into Mike's shoulders. "I... I can't Mike. I have no power here. She took it from me."

Michael looked into her blue eyes. "Rachel you were flying, you almost broke my grip. You have all of the power you need." Rachel kept crying. "Rachel, look at me and just focus." She looked at Michael and kept looking at him. Michael was going to play a hunch. Using his telepathy Michael reached out into their thoughts and found her powers within her. Using his telepathy he pushed her thoughts of her powers forward and reshaped the area so that he could absorb Rachel's light. Michael's veins glowed yellow and shone in the dark; his eyes turned a full red and began shinning. Rachel looked at him in awe.

"You're stronger than what you think and you are stronger than her." Rachel smiled softly. Michael felt her mind opening again as the area shone yellow and they returned to consciousness.

Michael fell on his knees as Rachel stirred in her sleep. He felt tired, incredibly tired; the telepathic event had taken almost everything Michael had. Rachel suddenly woke up and hugged Adam holding him tight. Michael stood and saw Terrence smiling wildly.

"Damn son you brought her back. Good kid." Michael smiled. John suddenly walked in and saw Rachel awake. He face softened into a smile as he clapped Michael on the shoulder.

"Mike, you brought her back. I'm sorry about what I said. It was out of fear. Thanks for saving Rachel."

Michael smiled softly. "I try my best," he said gently. The four members laughed gently. Rachel stood up and slowly walked towards Michael. She hugged him and kissed him gently on his cheek.

"I am stronger than them aren't I?"

Michael nodded. "You are and you can beat them." She smiled and hugged him again. Michael let them celebrate as he walked out. The moon shone over the sea as Michael watched the waves gently lap against the ship's hull. Adam walked towards him and leant on the railing.

"Mike, I've been thinking; there's someone we can see. He's an old friend named General Robert Norton, he was in charge of the army's main division until Rockwell or Zor took it over. He may know something about Project: Soaring Eagle. When you're ready meet me over Alaska. We'll go see him."

Michael nodded. "Yeah I'm gonna go check in on Bernard then I'll meet you there." Michael rose into the air and waved bye to Adam. As Michael flew above the ship he shot into the sky breaking the sound barrier and flying through the atmosphere. Looking at the sun he absorbed energy lighting up his veins. He almost glowed like a beacon above the atmosphere lighting up the darkness. Feeling refreshed he re-entered the atmosphere and dove towards his home. Michael landed gently in front of the titanium fortress. Placing his hand on the surface a small entrance revealed itself and opened gently. Michael stepped in and saw Bernard sitting on what was left of the leather sofa. He smiled as Michael walked towards him.

"Alright, son, how is The Team doing?"

Michael shrugged gently. "Superficial injuries but they'll be fine. They're a bit down though; they didn't expect to beaten so easily."

Bernard pursed his lips. "I wouldn't tell them this but I was surprised to see how long they lasted. The Kordites must've been going easy on 'em." Michael wanted to be surprised by Bernard's admission but the truth was: The Team was lucky. All of the Kordites especially Zor must have held back otherwise the fight wouldn't have lasted as long as it did. Michael rubbed his face as he turned to Bernard.

"If that's the case I don't know how long I will last in a fight. Zor almost broke one of my ribs my kneeing me in the chest. How the hell am I supposed to last in an outright fight?" Michael asked with uncertainty in his voice.

Bernard smiled softly. "It's different with you son. You are the strongest of us and this is why Zor wants you to be unleashed. Without your mental limits you will be able to defeat him."

Michael shook his head in a no fashion. "But how do I overcome them?"

Bernard shrugged. "You need to expose yourself in a fight where you need to win. With Charlotte's life in the balance you'll do anything to save her and her family, won't you?" Michael nodded. He would die before any harm came to Charlotte. Maybe that's what it would take? Michael thought. Putting myself in a situation where I have to win.

Michael stood up. "I have to go now Bernard. Me, and Angel are tracking down a lead he thinks that'll help us."

Bernard nodded. "Be careful son, the Kordites won't hold back when you find them. You will have to kill them." Michael nodded and set off.

Chapter 18: *Knew there was something fishy about those bastards*

Michael hovered over the Alaskan city of Anchorage. Home to 298,610 residents it had the largest number of residents in all of Alaska. The cold air whipped around Michael's skin but he barely felt it. It was more of a relief. Michael preferred the cold, it felt refreshing compared to the heat. Bringing his wrist up, he activated his watch's connection to Marcus and issued an order.

"Marcus, search for a General Robert Norton in the general area of Anchorage." There were a few bleeps as Marcus began searching through the database.

"Sir, there appears to be no match for Robert Norton in the area." Michael raised an eyebrow. A gust of wind whipped his hair up as Adam came towards him. Adam wasn't wearing his superhero costume opting instead for a normal outfit.

"That's because officially he doesn't live here. Officially he's a resident of Los Angeles. He's got a mountain cabin that he calls his home away from home."

Michael rolled his eyes. "Where exactly is this cabin?"

Angel smiled. "Follow me." Angel shot down towards the woods outside the city. Michael followed suit and they both landed in the woods together. The area was quiet and peaceful as they hovered through the trees. Adam looked around and signalled Michael to follow him. Before them both was a small utilities shed smaller than a cottage but large enough to house at least one person. Landing on the ground a series of turrets popped up from the ground.

Adam turned and looked at Michael smiling. "Michael, what did you do?"

Michael looked round at his surroundings. "I didn't do anything; robots just hate me even though I build them," he muttered.

Adam smiled and walked towards the turret. "General it's Angel, tell your attack dogs to stand down." Silence struck as they waited. The turrets refocused and then suddenly sank to the ground. They both walked towards the shed; Michael let Adam open the door first. Michael walked inside and was astounded at what was inside. Though the outer layer was wood the inside was made completely of metal and reminded Michael of an elevator car. Adam pressed the only button on the wall and they descended. It was about a minute before the lift reopened again. The complex underneath resembled that of Dexter's lab on a much smaller scale. It wasn't as advanced leading Michael to conclude that it was man-made. There was no one in sight at first until a whirl of movement caught Michael's eye. The man walking towards them was around six foot tall with snow white hair and deep blue eyes. He walked past Michael and went straight towards Adam.

"What the hell are you doing here son, this is the only place where I get some peace and quiet. And I sure-as-shit do not need you brining any unknowns down here. So, you've got 13.2 seconds to explain what the hell you're doing here."

Adam smiled. "Good to see you too Robert. This is…"

Michael cut him off. "Michael Sampson, pleased to meet you."

Norton raised an eyebrow. "Are you yanking my chain? Is this THE Michael Sampson as in the prodigal son? That still doesn't explain what the hell you are doing here."

Adam sighed deeply. "You may wanna pour yourself a drink, this is gonna take a while."

Adam filled Norton in on everything they'd found out. On occasion Michael had to add some detail. The trio were sitting in three different recliners. Norton had poured himself a Scotch but as soon as they began adding more detail he made it a double.

"Always knew there was something frosty about that Rockwell bastard, but an alien, now that's something new. Knew there was something fishy about those bastards. They creep me the hell out especially the ice queen."

Adam looked at Norton. "Who's the ice queen?"

Norton looked at him and said, "You understand English, the woman that was always with him."

Michael smiled. "He means Kor." Adam nodded.

"But still I shouldn't be surprised; I've seen some crazy things with this bastard," he said pointing at Adam. Michael nodded but kept quiet, he eyed the Scotch uneasily. Michael clenched and unclenched his fist repeatedly. Norton noticed. "You're an alcoholic, aren't you son?"

Michael looked up at him. "I…I've suffered from it for a few years now. I recently stopped myself from having a drink for the first time."

Norton nodded. "It's alright son. My son went through it as well. The first time is always the worst. You may be a "superman" but psychologically you can still get the withdrawal effects." Standing up Norton threw the Scotch down the sink and poured him and Michael a glass of water. "My mistake son, don't worry about it." Michael nodded.

"Did you know my father?"

Norton nodded. "Indeed I did. A nice guy and ambitious as anyone around here, but not for hurting people but trying to help them. He was a nice guy. A helluva a nicer person than the bastards that are running your company now. Anyway what is it you want to ask me about?" Michael pursed his lips and looked at Adam. He smiled and nodded for Michael to go on.

"Before you were fired from your job did Rockwell have any secret operations like unknown from the president?"

Norton let out a deep chuckle. "There are a lot of things we keep from the president for plausible deniability. But Rockwell played his cards close to his chest like he was already being watched by the buzzards. But before I left I did some digging on him. Turns out he had quite a few projects not sponsored by the White House. Like he had outside resources, which isn't weird. Sometimes we use private contractors but I couldn't find any contractors funding him."

Michael looked quizzically at Norton. "What kind of contracts?"

Norton shrugged. "Couldn't find out what they were. I had a private analyst do some digging. And he said that the contracts were protected by some of the most sophisticated software he'd ever seen. He couldn't even break through it."

Michael looked deep in thought. "Not to be pushy, but what are you doing now?" he wondered aloud.

Norton chuckled. "Not pushy at all. After I was fired I set up a private military company or PMC called "Black Arrow"; it was small at first but now it's one of the largest in America. I started recruiting rangers and marines all good men. We don't take contracts from the Pentagon but rather we do missions in Third World countries. They might not pay as much but they feel good."

Michael nodded. "What sort of equipment do you have?"

Norton shrugged. "Standard and all up to date. We recently switched out Black Hawks for Boeing Ospreys. Good machine I'll tell you that much. For close air support we use MH-6 Little Birds good for fire support." Michael nodded. With that sort of equipment Michael was sure he could use it in case of a small war.

"General, are you sure you didn't find anything else?"

Norton shrugged again. "I wish I could help you son, the only thing we found was about a small carrier group. For some reason it never birthed anywhere and was always moving but no one in the navy knew anything about it." Michael raised his eyebrow. A carrier group that never birthed and had no record within the navy seemed like something that Michael should investigate.

"Norton, the files that you had your analyst try to break into to, do you still have them?"

Norton nodded and stood up. He walked over towards a small desk and opened a drawer taking out a small USB stick. "Here you go son, I hope you have better luck than we did." Michael nodded. Adam had actually nodded off during the conversation between Michael and Norton. Norton smiled. The smile was almost fatherly. "He's a busy kid and a smart one, but he never stops to think about himself but I'm sure that's what makes him a better leader." He turned towards Michael. "Listen son, you ever need us in action just give me a ring, free of charge." Michael smiled and shook his hand. He then clapped Adam on the shoulder waking him up.

"What'd I miss?" he said groggily.

"Nothing that can't be caught up on," Michael said. On the lift up to the surface Michael told Adam about the carrier group.

"I suppose that merits looking at. If you find something call us, we'll be ready to move." As the stepped out of the elevator they shook hands. Angel readied himself and shot into the air. Michael lifted up gently and watched the ground fall away as he flew into the atmosphere.

Nor walked through downtown Los Angeles, the sun shone down on him and made him feel content. Looking towards the large apartment building he increased speed arriving in the lobby. The lobby worker smiled at Nor as he walked in. Normally Nor tried to avoid contact with him but he actually wanted to talk to him.

"Hi Nathan, here to see your sister?" he asked with a beaming smiled.

Nor actually smiled gently. "Yes, is she here?" The attendant nodded. Nor smiled back and walked towards the elevator. He pressed the button and waited for the elevator to arrive. Stepping into the elevator he pressed the penthouse button and waited for the high-speed elevator to arrive. Stepping out he walked towards the penthouse door. Knocking on the door once he opened the open door and walked in. The door was never locked; for some reason Kor never had the door locked. Just how she was thought Nor as he walked through the apartment. The entire area was immaculate, not a single thing was misplaced. Kor was always incredibly neat and it spread to how she took care of herself. Nor walked out towards the balcony and found Kor in the pool. She was completely submerged at the bottom of the pool and her eyes were closed. Nor would normally pull her out but for her it was the only time she could feel peace. Nor sighed heavily as he sat down on the deckchair and thought back to when Kor was younger. The Guild of Vaar was much more forgiving and peaceful than Veer. At an early age Kor demonstrated an incredible amount of knowledge and loved science but not war. From then on she devoted her time to her studies rather than training.

"A mistake that is what she is," his father told his mother. "She must be killed." Nor remembered his mother slapping his father as hard as possible. The shock wave almost broke the very place down. Back then Nor was loyal to the cause; he despised his sister with a heated passion. Kor realised this and tried to run off and join the Guild of Vaar. She would have been safe if her father had not of found out. The Guild of Vaar demanded that Zor be punished for even thinking of punishing her but at that time the Guild Master of Veer decided to side with Zor. The punishment that faced Kor was 15 mini-cycles or 15 days in a white room. A white room was an area outside of space time, a place where there was no energy for a Kordite to absorb energy. It was literal torture for a Kordite to endure. If they were not strong enough mentally the subject could literally go insane. The court where Kor was on trial was full of citizens of the Guild of Veer. Ten honour guards surrounded the Guild Master and Kor. The Guild Master paced around her hurling insults and telling her of the horror that lay before her. Nor and his father were sitting behind the Guild Master and watched the trial. Kor looked at Nor with pleading eyes begging him to save her. Looking back on it Nor should of intervened and fought back against their father. At the trial Zor approached the Guild Master.

"Guild Master, let us not worry ourselves with this as a public punishment. Let our family take her for punishment. Besides the sentential is not true terror." Zor faced Kor. "I will show her pure terror." Back at the family palace Zor approached Nor. Kor was in binds that were designed to siphon off energy from her. "So I want you do something for me."

Nor kneeled before him. "Anything High Father."

Zor smiled at him. "Beat your sister to within a nano-cycle of her life."

Nor looked at him dumbfounded at the request. "S... Sire."

Zor tilted his head gently. "Are you deaf child, I want you to beat your sister as physically hard as you can and do not hold back," Zor reiterated. Nor looked at his sister; she was practically pleading with him not to.

Nor looked back at his father. "I will comply." He walked towards his sister and raised his fist.

Nor had desperately tried to repress that memory; though he was loyal to the cause, every punch, every sound she made haunted him. His mother had practically disowned him for what he had done. Nor couldn't blame her though she was right; he should have shown some backbone against his father. But it was all in the past now. Nor had been in thought for so long that he hadn't realised that Kor had floated up to the surface and was almost standing on the water's surface. He looked up and smiled at her. She almost beamed back.

"Brother, since when do you smile?" she said.

Nor smiled more and floated towards her. "Sister, I have to tell you something. It is very important." She nodded gently and sat down next to him. Nor told her everything about the Guild Master's call and how the Ziborians were killing everyone around them. He told her that the Guild Master had called them home and they would not be charged with any crimes. He also told her about the peace agreement between the Guilds of Vaar and Veer. She looked at the water and didn't take her eyes off it.

"I... I don't know what to say." Nor could emphasise with her; the beating she had taken had taught her to never question what her father was telling her.

"Kor... Sister, we do not have to listen to him any more but we must keep our cover. The child of Vaar is sure to make a move against our father soon."

She nodded in agreement. "The first time I fought him I could feel how different he was; the way he threw himself in front of the humans to help them. But I could feel that he was broken inside. He has been away from his family for too long. He needs their comfort."

Nor looked away. "When I fought him in Moscow I used rage to push him down but he still fought back at me. Though my telepathy isn't as strong as yours I felt it too. Though he wanted to keep fighting there was something within his mind that almost, I don't know, made him want to lose and want me to kill him."

Kor nodded. "He is suffering. His psyche is completely fractured and there is only one thing that has held him together." Nor looked up at her. "Charlotte: the human we took from his mansion. From what I've pieced together she is the only thing that has held him to this life. Without her he is breaking apart slowly; meaning that when he finds her he will come with everything he has. And fight to his last breath to save her."

Nor stood up and paced back and forth. "We have to find a way to show him that we are not helping our father. Can you warn him with your telepathic link?"

Kor shook her head. "I... I can't. The link was shattered recently, as if his very psyche was fighting it off. There's no way we can warn him. We'll have to do it when he comes for us."

Nor hovered a foot off the ground. "Yes we must find a way especially without alerting father. The shipment should arrive within the week with the weapons. We cannot intervene." Kor begrudgingly nodded. Nor floated off the edge of the building and prepared to fly off. Before he did he looked back at his sister. "You must be careful sister. If you want to save humans be quick about it. I found out and if you are not careful, father will as well. Though the humans may be joining the Universal Committee and it will soon be our sworn duty to protect them, father, will have them destroyed before we are able to do anything for them." Kor nodded in agreement. Nor looked forth and shot out of view.

Michael lay on his bed. Ironically it was his most hated room but it had survived the attack.

"Surprise, surprise," he muttered. He was practically bored so he was trying to get some sleep. But he couldn't; he simply lay awake on his bed looking at the ceiling. Michael had tried searching for the small carrier group but he hadn't found anything unusual. So he had commissioned Marcus to scan every square inch of the oceans using satellites. Stretching out he tried to find something interesting on the ceiling to concentrate on. But the ceiling was barren. Michael made a mental note "Put a puzzle on the ceiling". Rising off the bed gently he floated closer to the ceiling. Out of the corner of his eye blue lights flashed around.

"Sir believe it or not I have found something."

Michael dropped to the ground. "What is it?"

A single blue light flashed. "On a hunch I decided to use buoys to detect strange wave movements while the satellites moved into position. Normally ships can make a movement, the bigger the ship the bigger the vibration. I tracked a certain type of wave disruption and found one big enough to be a carrier." Michael looked at the wall and placed his hand on it. Pulling out the holographic data that Marcus was referring to do, he began manipulating the map. Michael tracked the data and expanded the map. The main disturbance had been tracked to the Pacific Ocean; around 800 miles off the coast of San Francisco.

Michael shrugged. "Seems like a place to look."

Marcus flashed three times. "I am almost sure there is a carrier and maybe more ships there. I have been researching carrier groups and after looking at how the navy uses them they are normally protected by a variety of other ships such as destroyers and cruisers. If that is correct then I suggest taking someone with you specifically the heavy hitters of The Team such as Angel and Dove."

Michael nodded. "Duly noted. Look after Bernard for me," he said as he jumped out of the bedroom window. Michael stopped himself in mid-air and flew straight up towards space. He arrived in orbit and looked down at the Atlantic Ocean. Scanning it with his superhuman vision he found The Team's headquarters. Preparing himself he shot down towards the ship. As he arrived he didn't bother going the usual way opting for the balcony. Normally the crew member around would alert the alarms but the only member down there was The Stranger. He had a strong habit of smoking cigars and the only place he was allowed to smoke was on the balcony.

He nodded at Michael as he landed. "Howdy, Mike, can I help you?"

Michael shook his hand. "Where is the bird?"

Terrence took another drag of his cigar. "He's in the CIC." Michael thanked him and made his way there. The CIC or command information centre was where Angel and The Team measured reports from the world and ordered them in priority of how they could assist. Additionally the ship's weapons systems were all there and able to be fired by a touch of a button. Angel was sitting in the main chair watching different screens. Michael placed his hand on Adam's shoulder. He looked round.

"Adam, I found them."

Chapter 19: *All this for one weapon*

After Michael had told Adam about the presumed location of the carrier group, Adam had assembled The Team. However it didn't look good; Tremor and Bolt were out because of their injuries and needed more time to heal meaning that there would only be Angel, The Stranger and Dove. But Terrence would have to stay behind and take care of Tremor and Bolt. Still that would have to be enough. The trio hovered at around 3,000 feet above the sea. They had been continually searching the area for the carrier group.

"Mike, are you sure they're not using a cloaking device or something like that?" Dove asked.

Michael shrugged. "Normally I'd say no. Stealth today means radar stealth not visible eye stealth. But since they were able to repurpose my drilling laser, they might be able to build something like that." Angel had momentarily disappeared from view, when he returned he shook his head no.

"I haven't seen anything. Are you sure the group is here?" Michael activated his watch and brought up Marcus's findings.

"Marcus used buoys to search different wave vibrations to calculate the size of a ship. His best efforts had put them around this area. But…"

Angel looked at him. "But what?"

Michael looked down again. "Honestly, it's a big ass ocean to cover. The satellite would better be able locate something than buoys. We may just have to work with what we have."

Dove suddenly floated forward. "Maybe not."

Michael looked at her. "What are you thinking of?"

Dove lit up gently. "Well your cloaking system works by reflecting light, right?" Michael nodded. "Then what about if I shine a big light on it. Overload its sensors."

Michael pondered for a few seconds. "That can work. But we're taking a huge risk; if they copied my designs to an absolute they'll know that the sensors have cooling systems which stop them from shutting down. Then again they might have missed that part. Go on Rachel light 'em up." Rachel smiled and intensified her light shinning it down towards the sea. The water lit up as she scanned the area. After a few minutes of searching a spot of ocean began fizzling lightly. Michael immediately spotted the area and used his superhuman vision to see what was happening. He smiled gently and said. "Gotcha." There was more fizzling as the area suddenly began "breaking" apart. Michael saw bits of ship as the cloaking device failed.

Angel floated towards Michael and asked, "How many do you see?"

Michael began describing what he saw. "There's two ships guarding the carrier from what I can see they're…" Michael suddenly gapped at what he saw.

"Mike, what is it?" Angel asked.

"Angel, they're using LCSs."

Angel raised an eyebrow. "What?"

Michael didn't take his eyes off the ships. "A littoral combat ship; basically an upgraded destroyer. I'd heard that they were coming into service but not now."

Angel looked where Michael was looking. "Are they a problem?"

Michael threw his arms up in the air. "Of course they are. Normally they're armed to the teeth with missiles and everything. But if they're protecting something they'll probably be armed with more weapons, maybe even nuclear weapons."

Angel looked dumbfounded. "Nukes? You're telling me they're gonna have nukes? Mike we can't even think of letting them fire one of those; they'll fire them if they have to."

Michael nodded. "Not if they have a distraction."

Angel looked at him. "What are you thinking of?"

Michael pointed at the carrier. "I'm gonna land on it; once they see me they'll unload everything they have on me. And then you two swoop in and take care of the destroyers while I search for the weapons."

Angel placed a hand on his shoulder. "Mike, are you sure?"

Michael pulled a devilish grin. "I'm sure. Thick skin remember."

The deck of the *USS Nighthawk* was a busy place; flanking the carrier were two independence class destroyers, the *Knight* and the *Dark Runner*. The Nimitz-class carrier was travelling an average of 18 knots per hour and was making good time. Out of nowhere Michael landed on the deck gently. He looked around.

"Hi, can you help me?"

The crew suddenly stopped what it was doing and one of them shouted, "It's the prime target. Kill him."

Michael shrugged. "Well it was worth a try," he muttered. The control tower had a Phalanx CIWS or close-in weapon system which began firing on him. The turret was designed to shoot down missiles that would threaten the carrier. The armour-piercing tungsten rounds poured down on him. Michael barely felt the bullets; he activated his energy and shot towards the turret cutting down the bullets. That was one thing taken care of. A nearby Seahawk helicopter began firing its machine gun at Michael. Michael sped forward towards it and held it down. He lifted it up and threw it into the sea. The nearby destroyer suddenly opened its missile silos and readied itself to fire. Out of nowhere Dove flew towards the ship and created a massive light sword and swiped once at the middle of the ship. The blade cut deep into the hull but it still had missile capabilities. Firing off three missiles at Dove, she dodged two of them and blew up the third. She landed within the break of the ship and used her massive superhuman strength to push the two parts apart. The metal creaked and groaned as it was split apart. Dove put in more effort and finally the metal gave in and the ship was split in two.

Inside the *Dark Runner* the CIC was in shambles and water was bursting through the seams. The chain of command had been ripped apart after the ship had been attacked. An injured tactical officer crawled to his station; a large metal beam was sticking in his he leg. He knew he was going to die; but not before he took a few them with him. Pulling himself up, he began typing commands into his computer and readied one of the tactical Tomahawk missiles. For the purpose of the mission the two destroyers had been armed with nuclear weapons for the sole protection of what the carrier was conveying.

After finishing the launch sequence he chuckled. "Long live the new order." He slammed his fist on the launch button and finally succumbed to his wounds.

Michael threw a deck officer into another and felt more bullets smack into him. This was getting a bit too easy, Michael had expected a Kordite to be here but was thankful that they were not. A crowd of soldiers had jumped on Michael trying to pin him down but he simply shook his body sending them flying away. Composing himself he turned his attention back to the lifts used to bring planes up. Two F-35 fighter jets were getting ready to launch; one of them was almost ready. It powered up its engines and shot down the runway at take-off speed. Carriers used steam powered catapults to launch planes faster. The plane shot towards Michael. The plane appeared to be moving in slow motion as Michael moved out of the way. In a split second he reacted catching the tail and holding it back from its take-off. Michael roared with effort, the weight of the plane wasn't the problem it was simply the speed and thrust. Michael pulled harder and ripped the tail off sending the plane into the sea. Out of nowhere a missile thundered away, shooting into the atmosphere. Turning around he scanned the missile and recognised it as a Tomahawk and it was nuclear.

"Uh, Angel, Dove we've got a nuclear missile clearing the area. From its flight trajectory it's headed for the western seaboard," he shouted over the com unit. Dove was the first to react. Without speaking a word she shot after the missile chasing it down with ease. She redirected it towards space and began tearing it apart burning it with ease. The other destroyer, the *Knight* hadn't been attacked yet. Angel appeared at its bow; he waited for it to collide with him. As it did Angel grabbed the bow and began to flip it on to its side as he did he prepared his angel cry. His eyes turned a dark blue as he unleashed the cry. The sheer power of the cry began disintegrating the ship and tearing the metal down. The water behind it kicked up as if a sonic boom had pushed the water up. Angel stopped using the cry and flew up and then landed down on the surface of the hull. His angel cry pushed the ship further into the sea. That was that he thought as he flew towards the carrier.

Things on the carrier were proceeding to plan. Michael mopped up the rest of the deck crew throwing them into the sea. His incredible hearing picked up the pilot of the F-35's breathing; pivoting Michael watched as it shot off two missiles. Leaping off the deck he swatted one of the missiles away like a fly; his leap took him straight towards the F-35. Smashing his fist through the canopy he pulled the pilot out and kicked the plane down. Michael landed back on the deck and threw the pilot into the sea. Before he did anything he checked the carrier thoroughly making sure the carrier was intact and without damage. He began walking towards the control tower to open a door, as he did the door was shot off its hinges pushing him back slightly. A K human walked through the door and roared at Michael with malice. Michael readied himself and dodged the K human's punches. The last punch Michael caught and pushed him back into wall. The K human grabbed an assault rifle next to him and fired off a barrage at Michael. The bullets harmlessly bounced off Michael as he walked forward towards the K human. Grabbing the K human he threw him back outside. Michael sped down the tight corridors and found and steel bolted door. Scanning through the door Michael saw what he had been looking for. Pulling the door from its hinges he saw a lead package. Slamming his fist through the opening he pulled the nuclear material out of the crate. Michael instantly knew what it was.

"Angel, Dove you better get down here," he yelled. He felt two blurs rush behind him.

"Mike is that what I think it is?" Angel asked.

"If you're thinking it's uranium-235 then you'd be correct," Michael replied.

"Weapons-grade uranium? What the hell is that for?" Dove asked impatiently.

"It's for the drilling laser. The higher the power source the more powerful the output," Michael explained.

"Mike, why the hell were you using weapons-grade uranium?"

Michael shrugged gently. "I was 17 when I designed it and I was bored. I think I may have watched too much Star Trek but I only purposed the thing to cut rock." Michael bent down and reached into the crate pulling the newly repurposed X-5. "From what I can see they skipped a really important part. To compensate for the radiation I added nano lead shields bonded with the uranium. Without the shield you would have to have more lead which is why they're transporting it like this. The entire drill has been ripped apart and repurposed." It suddenly occurred to Michael what had happened. He stepped back while dropping the weapon. "That's why they want to use K humans." Angel looked at Michael quizzically. "K humans have a natural resistance to radiation. They can forsake the radiation shield because they won't need it."

Angel nodded in agreement. "But still how is their plan gonna play out? From killing K humans and taking our place, to taking over the world?"

Michael paced around the small room searching his thoughts. "It depends, maybe they're trying to get in with the president or maybe they're gonna be pushing for a new president one who will go along with their plans. Last time

I spoke to Nor he said that they were in control of a new president who will go along with their plans. In that way they'll be able to take over," Michael theorised.

"Are sure that's their plan?" Angel asked.

"Plan? I'm just spitballing, thinking aloud. I don't know. Right now we need to something about this radiation; it's a danger to the people around here. Dove can you put it in the sun?" She nodded and lifted the lead crate and flew into the space.

Angel looked around. "Do you think there are any other stores of weapons?"

Michael turned round scanning the areas. "No, this was the only one. Either that's a good thing meaning this is their first shipment or worst-case scenario this was their last shipment and they've got more weapons on the mainland." Angel nodded. Michael pondered about the different things he'd discovered.

In the torn down CIC the K human made his way through the tattered remains of the area. He had made his way back to the ship after being thrown from the carrier. His right arm had been crushed completely and was hanging from his socket. Approaching the console he began increasing the carrier's speed. The Nimitz-class had a top speed of 30 knots or 56 kph. Checking the radar he found a cruise liner travelling north around 200 kilometres from the carrier's present position. The needs of the many outweigh the needs of the few he thought as he put the carrier on course with the civilian liner.

"All hail the high father," he said. As he began to move he felt a white-hot wound within his stomach. He looked down at a sword made of light that had run him through. He felt death's embrace as he coughed up blood.

Michael and Angel were still thinking as Dove blurred in. "Guys we have a big problem back in CIC," she announced.

The trio blurred into CIC and checked the radar. Michael quickly scanned the console and put it together.

"He's put the carrier into its highest speed and a on direct course for that cruise liner."

Angel ran his hand through his hair. "We've gotta get to that cruise liner. I'm going to warn them. Dove with me. Mike, stop this ship."

Michael raised an eyebrow. "Stop the ship?"

Angel nodded. "This thing maxes out at around 100,000 tons; you can stop it. Believe in yourself."

Michael rolled his eyes. "Well at least warn them to either brace or speed up."

Angel smiled. "They won't need it," he said as he and Dove blurred away. Michael supersped on to the runway and leapt off into the sea. He stopped breathing and descended towards the ship's bow. Moving himself into the path of the carrier he braced himself for the weight. The weight hit him almost as hard as Nor or Kor. He pushed the ship back with his strength using his flight powers. The cruise liner was rapidly closing the distance with the carrier. Michael poured in the effort to slow the ship down even further. With one final titanic push the ship slowed down completely. Michael looked at the still moving cruise liner and realised his job wasn't finished. He flew towards the overturned carrier and supported its weight across his shoulders. The deepest part of the Pacific Ocean was 35,000 feet so there was no support holding the ship up. Michael readied himself and dropped it into the depths. Thanks to Dove flying the nuclear material into space the sea wouldn't be contaminated by the radiation. Michael flew back into the air and wiped water off his brow. Checking his watch he pulled up all the data Marcus had got from the carrier. As soon as Michael had set foot on the carrier deck he had asked Marcus to scour the ship for information. He began uploading the information back to his main computer at home.

Suddenly he heard cheers from the cruise liner. People were standing on the different parts of the ship cheering him on. Several of the people were recording the event. Michael had to make a hasty retreat; no way was he going to make it on the evening news. Soaring upwards towards space he stopped himself just above and took a few deep breaths. Though there was no oxygen up there the act of deep breathing calmed him down. Michael shook gently; he closed his eyes and shut himself off to the world listening to only his heartbeat. The shaking stopped after a few minutes as Michael calmed down. Out of nowhere two figures approached him. Michael knew it was Angel and Dove; the two handed him a face mask so they could talk.

Angel placed a hand on Michael's shoulder. "Mike, you alright?" he asked.

Michael shook his head no. "No, I'm not okay Adam. I... I can't find Charlotte and her family and all I want now is a Scotch. IT'S NOT FAIR," Michael shouted as his two twin beams of energy vision shot into the darkness.

"Mike, come on just calm down. This is not the way to deal with it. I know you're a genius and if anyone can find her you can."

Michael regained control and let his energy vision stop completely. "Look, Adam, I'm gonna go home and go through all the information I found on the carrier. If I find anything I'll give you a call." Adam nodded and received the face mask back from him as Michael shot towards home. Angel and Dove stayed where they were.

"Adam, he's gonna break in half; when he peeked into my mind I saw a bit of his reflection in mental vision. He's so close to breaking."

Angel nodded. "Sadly, I agree with you; the worst thing is that he's stopped drinking, he's gonna start going through withdrawal symptoms soon. The only thing that's gonna keep him going is finding Charlotte and we can only hope that he finds her soon."

Michael landed outside his manor and let Marcus open the titanium shield. Bernard hobbled over on crutches to be with him.

"You wouldn't have anything to with a near collision of a US aircraft carrier and a civilian cruise liner?" he said with a broad grin.

Michael shrugged. "Maybe? Although I did stop an aircraft carrier, it's probably one of the heaviest things I've lifted."

Bernard nodded. "I see. What did you find out then?"

Michael sat down and sighed heavily. Rubbing his black hair he leaned back against the sofa. "Not a whole lot. Other than a manifest the encrypted data that I found…" Michael was cut off by a single flashing light.

"Excuse me sir, you found?"

Michael smiled gently. "Okay, alright, the encrypted data that Marcus found," he said while enunciating Marcus's name. "Is still being decrypted, although I don't really know what were gonna find."

Bernard put his hands together while analysing the situation silently. "The weapon's system that they're using, can you track it?" Michael supersped to his lab and back. Holding the drill for Bernard to see, he began examining it.

"The drill was built for space rocks meaning that it couldn't have any holes. The small lead shield was the only place I left without complete sealant. I… I mean I could maybe track the radiation signal but even then I… I don't know Bernard. I really don't know." Michael felt the panic start. His arms shook visibly as Michael fell on his knees. He couldn't do anything; with all of his powers he couldn't save the one person he needed. Bernard hobbled over and held his wrist trying to stop the shaking. Bernard let Michael's head fall against his shoulder.

"Alright son, it'll pass. Listen to me; I know you can save Charlotte. I know you can, do you know why?"

Michael murmured, "How?"

"Because I saw it when you were young; you used to watch cartoons about superheroes and you'd run about, shouting that you would save people. I saw it and your father saw it that you can save everyone. Right know, you have to think hard and work hard; once Marcus has found the data you'll know where she is." Michael felt the shaking stop. He stood up and walked down to the lab.

"Marcus, use whatever you have and decrypt that data, now!"

Blue lights flashed rapidly. "I am rerouting every inch of power I have to decrypt it. I promise you sir, I will find her." Michael believed him. Even though Marcus couldn't actually feel human emotions he had been programmed to protect Charlotte and her family with everything he had. Michael sat on his chair and went into deep thought.

Kor was dressed in traditional Kordite wear as she walked through the military base. It bore the coat of arms for the Guild of Veer. It appeared to be a shield with Kordite glyph that resembled an X with two spears adorning it. One going down the middle and one going across. She entered her brother's office and found him meditating by hovering in mid-air. Deciding not to bother him she left immediately and went towards the holding cells. There were around three cells but most of the time they were never used; except for one. The cell housed the human female and her family. Kor didn't enter neither did she make a motion towards the door. Her uncle Zar was guarding the cell; the giant golem of a Kordite stood there like a statue and didn't even make a gesture towards his niece. Kor used her incredible vision to scan through the door and looked at the family. The two younger humans were asleep while the other two were watching over them. She listened to their heartbeats; they were slow despite the threat of danger looming over them. Zar still hadn't made a move, not even a breath; it scared Kor more than anything else. The two human females suddenly began speaking. Kor listened in.

Charlotte looked at her younger siblings; they were blissfully unaware of the danger that they were in as they slept deeply.

Looking over at her tired mother she said, "Mom, are you alright?"

Mary nodded gently. "I'm fine Charlotte, but you aren't; you should get yourself some sleep."

Charlotte shook her head briskly. "I'm fine and I want be ready for whatever these people are going to do us."

Mary smiled softly. "They won't hurt us at least not physically." Charlotte looked quizzically at her. "If they even think of touching either you or your brother and sister they'll incur the wrath of Michael." Charlotte smiled; but she was scared. While they had been in imprisonment she had tried to contact Michael over their telepathic link but for some reason it had been shattered. She missed Michael more than ever. She wanted him to save her; she knew he was doing whatever he could to save them. It reminded her of when she first had her accident. Though Michael was away for a long time he eventually returned and brought with him something to save her. She was sure that he would come for her. "Michael is strong but you can guarantee that this is hurting him though." Charlotte looked at her mother. "Before we were abducted Bernard was telling me about some of his nightmares. He told me about how he almost flew into the sun to protect you from him. From what I can see you are the only thing that has kept him together for the last few years. Without you, he must be truly feeling the pressure." Charlotte knew that she had made an impact on him and she could feel his pain. She had heard some of his nightmares; she had heard him whimper in the night. From the outside Michael appeared as a tower of power and indomitable will but inside he was broken, fractured and torn apart from what he had been subjected to. She had tried her best to heal the fractures but some things couldn't be properly healed. She loved Michael more than anything and she knew he was coming to save her.

Kor had listened back and forth between the mother and daughter. She could feel how much Ror meant to the family. She sincerely hoped that Ror would be here soon.

"Touching, is it not?" Her father's voice made her jump out of her skin. "How, mothers and daughters are always able to safeguard each other. How come you and your mother never had a relationship like that?" he asked, his words dripping with malice. Kor didn't answer her father; he knew perfectly why she and her mother didn't talk. When Kor was younger she and her mother were close but when she was to be trained her mother tried to stop Zor from training her. It culminated with Zor completely barring Kor from talking to her mother. She had not seen her mother in almost 20 years. "Ah yes I remember it, fondly," he almost purred the last word. He stepped forward and placed his hand on her shoulder. His touch sent shivers up her spine; it was more like icicles running up her entire body. "I want something from you, daughter."

Kor had to play the good soldier. "What is thy bidding, High Father?"

Zor smiled. "Torture the one he loves!" Kor stepped back; she couldn't, she wouldn't. "I can feel what you're thinking child and you must do what I say." Zor grabbed the back of her neck and squeezed gently. "Or should I get your brother to re-educate you again?" Kor swallowed deeply and shook her head no. Every instinct within her screamed at her to push her father through the wall and rescue the humans but she had to keep her cover; she hoped that the Guardians would forgive her. She entered the room and closed the door sharply.

Charlotte looked up at the Kordite soldier who had walked in; she was tall and was strikingly beautiful.

"I am going to torture you using my telepathic powers. Don't resist it will only make this harder."

Mary stood up and walked towards the female Kordite defiantly. "You will not touch my daughter!" Kor lifted her up with her telekinesis and pushed her back. She looked at Charlotte.

"I'm so sorry," she said under her breath. Her eyes turned silver and then everything went black.

Charlotte tried to adjust her eyes to the dark but it was darker than anything she'd ever seen before. Out of the darkness, Michael appeared, he was naked but specific parts were blacked out. The female Kordite walked out, she too was naked but was also covered in parts. She walked around Michael massaging his torso with her slender hands.

"You've always wondered why Michael wouldn't be intimate with you," she moved closer to Michael. "It's because you can't do what I can. You can't pleasure him like I can." It was clear to Charlotte what she was doing. They moaned passionately while the female Kordite looked deeply into her eyes. Charlotte desperately tried to close her eyes and hide.

"It's not Michael," she kept repeating. The moaning was loud and kept going on and on. Suddenly they finished; they

279

kissed deeply as Michael lifted her up into the air. "Michael please, it's me. It's Charlotte." Michael looked at her and his eyes glared red towards her. Then suddenly it started again, it was a never-ending dream. Charlotte finally gave in and screamed.

Kor couldn't even feel Charlotte's mom hitting her in her stomach. But she knew the mental torture was taking a toll on Charlotte. What she was showing her shouldn't ever be seen. She knew Charlotte would never forgive her for what she was doing to her. She hoped she could live with herself. Charlotte kept screaming in pain waking her younger siblings up who in turn began crying. Kor felt her eyes welling up with tears. She heated up her eyes to burn away the tears so they couldn't he seen.

"I'm sorry Ror, I'm so very sorry," she said softly.

Chapter 20: *I will destroy you all*

Blue lights flashed around Michael forcing him to exit his mind's reaches.

"Sir I think I have found something." Michael opened his glowing red eyes.

"What is it?" Michael was in a foul mood. While he had retreated into his mind he'd heard a scream that sounded like Charlotte's. Using both his superhearing and his telepathy he'd tried to narrow down the area but he had been blocked.

"Sir I have found a set of coordinates that the weapons were being delivered to. The coordinates are 37° 14' 6" N, 115° 48' 40" W." Michael immediately knew where that was. He sat up and activated the satellite logging in the coordinates. He waited a minute for the satellite that was over America to position itself above the coordinates. As the satellite began receiving the images the computer shut down.

"Marcus, what the hell is happening?" Blue lights flashed and then turned red.

"Sir I am being fought off by what seems to be the full force of the American hack defence systems. I'm shutting off our entries and back door to limit the damage to our own defences. I cannot relay the images; the satellite has been shut down."

Michael smashed his fist into the wall. "Dammit I was so close. I know roughly what the base is; it's a US airbase for R & D. Supposedly there were alien landings near there. I need to see what's really there and I think there is only one place that can show me what I need to see."

Marcus joined the dots together. "The observatory within the moon, sir." Michael paced the room thinking over what he could do. Last time he went to the observatory, his father tried to restrain him and then submitted Michael to the entire knowledge of Kord. Michael needed a way to protect himself from whatever his father could do.

"Marcus, scan every ounce of Kord technology I've seen. I need you to find a weakness so I can protect myself from whatever my father might do." Blue lights flashed repeatedly.

"Sir, from what I've seen Kordite technology is perfect. It has total protection from hackers and cannot be shut down from the outside. Although, it may have a specific weakness to electricity."

Michael looked around the room for something that could protect him. "When I was affected by the sword last time, you shocked me out of it," he said pointing at the holograms.

"Yes sir, I lowered your vitals long enough to stop the sword from affecting you. Maybe sir, you could build a taser capable of housing a massive amount of electrical power."

Michael thought deeply. "How much power?"

A single blue light flashed. "Maybe 2-3 gigawatts," Marcus estimated. Michael nodded; it didn't seem like the best plan but maybe that was a way to stop his father from grabbing hold of him. Blurring up to the "museum" room, as he put it, he found a taser in a drawer. The room had ancient swords and axes and other weapons. Michael's father had collected the weapons for artistic purposes. Each weapon had been cleaned and polished multiple times by Michael and Bernard. Michael removed the cartridge and fired it up. Sticking it against his skin he ran it once; Michael barely felt the sting, it didn't even tickle him. Blurring back to the lab Michael placed the taser within a workshop area. A metal shield covered the area as a set of robotic arms began working on the taser. Michael heard Bernard walking down into the lab.

He announced in a loud voice. "Every time you blur around the house I have to dust and vacuum even more. Please sir, stop doing it!" His tone was serious at first but then he started laughing softly. "What are you up to anyway?" Michael quickly explained his plan. Bernard sat down and sighed heavily. "While I have nothing but respect for your father, even I don't understand everything he does. I'm simply not smart enough for it." Michael started to protest but Bernard held up a hand. "Stop, I know I'd never be able to fully understand your father's schemes. Whatever he's doing is either to train or help you. Still you will have to protect yourself from what your father may be doing. Though he loves you and wants you save the people of earth, he may want you to sacrifice a few before you are ready."

Michael stood up. "No, I can't let that happen; she has to live." Michael looked at the small workshop. "Marcus, is the taser ready?"

A blue light flashed. "It is sir, although it will only have one or two shots. Be sure to aim for critical areas; and one more thing sir." Michael looked back. "Be sure to come back alive. I suspect Mr Smith does not like me that much," Marcus said with a twinge of sarcasm.

"He's right, son, I may have to brush the old double barrel off to put some buckshot into his core."

Michael smiled softly. "Behave both of you and I'll see you when I get back." Michael blurred outside and shot up into the air.

Michael reappeared on the moon's surface scanning for the entrance. He saw the small glyph and pressed it. The sensation of the teleporter didn't faze Michael like it normally did; he was a man on a mission. The area was lit up, the three shrines to the suits glowed in the brighter light. Michael moved slowly towards the console.

"Ah my son, you have returned," his father's ethereal voice echoed throughout the observatory.

"Yeah, I need to use some equipment," he said nervously.

"I can see the weapon in your hand, it will not be needed." Anger spread through Michael's mind like a wild fire.

"I don't need it? How about last time when you imprisoned me in a block of ice while they took Charlotte?" There was no response. "You've got nothing to say have you? It's because you know you were wrong. Now they have her and they will kill her and if they do. I swear I will destroy you all," Michael yelled as he smashed his fist into the observatory walls. The observatory walls cracked slightly and then almost instantaneously healed. Out of nowhere the hologram of his father appeared. Michael backed up but was not afraid. His father walked towards him with his hands behind his back. In a flash of movement Saar lifted him straight into the air. Michael tried to stop the grip but it was akin to Zor or Nor.

"First of all: Never touch this observatory in anger ever again. It is a shrine to your culture and you will respect it. Second of all: I was trying to help you by lifting your limiters." Saar dropped Michael. "While you were growing I imposed limiters on your abilities, psychological in nature, in order to stop history from repeating itself. You can break these limiters through intense training and mental preparation. However I... I didn't realise how truly you had been broken through the experiences you've faced. I owe you an apology, my son," Saar said while walking to the window.

Michael walked towards him. "Will you help me then?"

Saar looked at him quizzically. "Of course, my son. All I have done is to help you, just to make you a stronger and wiser hero. What do you need?"

Michael walked towards the console. "I need imagery data, thermal, infrared and anything else you have of a location."

Saar nodded. "Speak the coordinates."

Michael quickly remembered the coordinates. "37° 14' 6" N, 115° 48' 40" W." The window changed into a zoomed in image of America and then focused in on the area. The US base in question was Area 51 or as it was known in the military, Homey Airport. Mainly used for R & D it was the source of many conspiracy theories. Many people believed that alien technology was captured there. Michael chuckled to himself because of the irony. Saar suddenly looked at the area.

"Son, this is where Gar first set up his base. I always thought there could be some correlation between the supposed Roswell landings and Gar's followers." Michael pulled the holographic diagram of the base and began checking through it.

"Can you show up thermal imagery?" Saar nodded and the image changed. Michael was bewildered by the amount of signatures.

"My son, I can help you out with the differences between Kordite and human thermal signatures." Michael looked at him. Saar smiled a warm fatherly smile. "The brighter images are Kordite; we naturally have a higher body temperature

285

than humans." Michael looked back at the images. Michael saw a grouped number of human heat signatures.

"Can you zoom in?" The thermal images zoomed in and were almost clearly identifiable. The two smaller images were obviously Ryan and Amy; meaning that the other two were Charlotte and Mary. Euphoria rushed through Michael. He had found them and now he could act. He also spotted six Kordites. Michael's heart sank; six Kordites were gonna make this hard.

"Do not worry son, I'm sure you and the human heroes will be able to defeat them."

Michael smiled grimly. "You didn't see what happened last time, did you?"

Saar placed his hand on Michael's shoulder. "Do not worry my son, believe you will win and you will defeat them all."

Michael wished it was that easy. "Father, do you have a USB port?"

Saar looked quizzically. "You want to transfer data to your artificial intelligence?" Michael nodded. "Well why didn't you say so, I can transfer the data without you interfacing with the console." Saar smiled and activated the transfer. Michael realised what he had to do. He prepared to leave but before he did he embraced his father and held him close. Saar didn't feel like an image; he felt like a flesh and blood person. "What was that for, son?" he asked.

"I always wanted to hug my dad." Saar smiled at his son as he exited the observatory.

Michael put in a call to Bernard as he flew towards The Team's headquarters. "Bernard, Dad showed me a thermal image of the base I know what we have to do. Make sure you and Marcus get the data I've sent," he yelled over the sound of him flying.

"Understood sir, hope to see you soon!" Michael deactivated the phone and flew towards the ship. Landing on the balcony he headed for the CIC. The entire team was in there.

"Guys I've got something you'll wanna see." Michael walked to the main computer and began uploading the image data.

"What are we looking at, Mike?" Angel asked. The thermal image of Area 51 shot up. Michael explained about the differences in heat data between the Kordites and the humans. He showed where Charlotte and her family were being held.

The Team were quiet until Terrence spoke up. "We're gonna need backup. And I don't mean all of us; I mean an army of soldiers, tanks and attack choppers." Michael nodded. Angel stroked his chin gently.

"We'd need something like the US army."

Michael walked forward. "Normally I'd agree with you but I assume Zor has been in the army long enough to gain full control. If he asks them to stop they will stop."

Angel stood still. "Not if we have authorisation from the president."

Michael pursed his lips. "I doubt the president will back us with this one and even if he would hear our concerns he'd drag it out." Angel stroked his chin again and kept silent. Michael spoke up again. "Look Adam, I know you like acting within protocol but this time we can't do that. Assume the worst about anyone connected to the government. Who's the next best person to use?"

Angel held up his hand. "Norton's PMC is the best thing to use. They've all but cut ties with the government and don't take any contracts from them. We can trust them." Michael and Terrence nodded in agreement. Adam walked forward to the main computer and typed in Norton's number. A minute later and Norton took the call.

"Son, do I have to tell you not to call me every other day?" Adam and Michael quickly filled him in with the data about Area 51. Norton nodded. "I see. Well under the circumstances I will loan you two companies, four Ospreys all heavily armed, a group of Black Hawks and as many Little Birds as I can spare. I've got no fast movers or attack choppers so you'll have to make do. All the soldiers are trained with superhuman close quarters battle. And you know what, I'm coming with you," he explained and then turned his attention to Michael. "Sampson, how you feeling, son? Any jitters? 'Cos we're gonna need you with a good head."

Michael nodded. "The bastards are holding my girlfriend and her family, no withdrawal effects are gonna stop me from fighting these shitheads."

Norton nodded. "Good enough son. What's the signal?" Michael looked at Adam who let him proceed. Michael along with Terrence stepped forward towards the hologram projection of the base. Both Michael and Terrence were tactical planers; though Angel and the others were trained they didn't have as much as experience as Terrence did.

"Alright, the base is mostly underground and as far as we can see there's only one entrance meaning that a sneak attack is next to impossible. If I can get inside I can draw them inwards leaving the front entrance not nearly as protected as it normally would be." Michael looked at Terrence for confirmation.

Terrence took at chance to talk. "I agree with Mike. Norton, you'd have to get your men in close. You'd need some heavy firepower to keep the K humans down. Norton, I'm gonna get a bit tactical with you now. Do you have a variation of the Black Hawk like the MH-60L Direct Action Penetrator?"

Norton smiled. "I like how you think Terrence, the DAP Black Hawk is like a damned Apache when armed correctly.

Last time I looked we'd got some Hellfire missiles and Hydra rockets along with Vulcan cannons."

Terrence smiled. "Good, good. Have them and the Little Birds do attack runs clearing the area then land the troops using the Ospreys. As soon as the troops are deployed get them into a holding pattern out of the reach of the K humans and the Kordites. We'll need them for evac. Once you get sight of the civvies bring a Black Hawk down to get them out and away. Leave the rest to us and that should it." Terrence finished speaking; Dove, Angel and Tremor stood there amazed. Michael simply smiled.

Norton grinned. "Sounds like a plan."

Michael looked at the holographic base. "That distraction will have to be my department. I'll take as many of them out before they capture me."

Norton raised an eyebrow. "Captured?"

Michael looked grimly at the base. "They want me alive so they'll try and capture me. Once I'm out I'll give Angel a telepathic flash message and he'll give you the go ahead."

Adam stepped forward. "Mike it'll be four on one and you won't last long against them."

Michael shrugged. "I don't have to last that long." Without further speaking Michael blurred towards the coordinates. The Team brushed dust away. They looked at Angel.

"He does that sometimes."

After three hours of torture Kor decided that enough was enough. She walked outside the cell and tried to block out the sound of Charlotte's screaming. Her eyes welled up again. She looked around to make sure Zar or Zor weren't near and let the tears flow freely. What she had done would never be forgiven, not by the Guardians or by Ror.

"Dry your tears dear sister," Nor said softly.

Kor collapsed into Nor's shoulder. "I made her see such horrible things."

Nor nodded. "I know sister; I felt her and your pain. We only have to play this part for a bit longer and then we can act." During her sadness Kor suddenly felt a fracture from Ror's telepathic link. Quickly reacting she dove within in it to find Ror's plan. She stepped away from Nor.

"Brother, I know Ror's plan." She quickly explained the plan to Nor.

He nodded. "It is a good plan but you will have to report at least one part to father." Kor tried to protest but Nor calmly held his hand up. "Just tell him that he is coming for us nothing else." Kor and Nor set off to inform their father. Whatever happened next, they both knew it was going to be a busy day.

Chapter 21: *I'm not gonna help you with anything*

Michael hovered at around 10,000 feet above the ground. The bright, sunny day meant Michael was almost clearly seen to those below within Area 51. Michael felt the sun shine on him, giving him more and more strength. Anger flowed freely within him as he contemplated what was going to happen. Whether he lived or died he would save Charlotte. Using his amazing hearing he focused in on the base; for the first time in weeks he could hear Charlotte's heartbeat, smell her hair and listen to her breathing. This relaxed him slightly but still he could feel not all was well within her. They had done something to her, whatever it was it had made a deep impression within her. That was it Michael thought. Not making any motion to conceal his landing he hurtled towards earth crushing the ground beneath his feet. Sand whipped up around the area blotting out different parts. A deep depression had formed from where Michael had landed which had probably been heard by whoever was underneath in the base. The dust was getting in Michael's way. He clapped his hands as hard as he could; making a sound that was like thunder which pushed the sand away from him. Seeing the base in front of him, Michael began walking towards it. Using his incredible vision he focused in on the top of the base. Turrets stations had been set up and Michael could fully see Charlotte and her family surrounded by Zor, Nor and Kor. On the other part of the base Michael could see the giant Zar directing some snipers.

"Child of Vaar, you have finally arrived. Took you long enough, if you think we will go easy on you then think again. I may need you alive, but I will not be afraid to hurt you before I capture you. Maybe break a few bones, give you a bloody nose. Sound good, child?" Michael didn't bother to respond. He walked towards the base clenching his fists. He heard the order that was given next.

"Fire." Fifty calibre bullets spewed out of the turrets smacking into Michael. Pulling his jacket off he kept walking and responded with a blast of energy vision to destroy the turrets. Michael destroyed seven out of the twelve turrets. The rest felt silent. Michael kept walking. Out of the base four Humvees shot out towards Michael. Two of them were armed with grenade launchers while the other two were armed with heavy machine guns. Michael readied himself. He sped towards the first set of Humvees using his body as a sledgehammer to crush the vehicle. Grenades shot into Michael's indestructible body. He sped into the other one and lifted it up; pulling it apart like it was paper. Another one increased speed and drove towards Michael. Not bothering to move, Michael let the Humvee wrap around his body destroying itself in the process. Still walking towards the base four tanks came towards him. The M1 Abrams tank had been in service since 1980 and had no signs of slowing down. Its smooth-bore cannon armed and fired at Michael. Though the shot pushed Michael back it didn't hurt him. Michael broke out into a jog and kicked the first tank stopping it in its tracks. Lifting the structure by the gun mount, Michael began spinning it around as fast as he could sending it miles away. The other tank fired with its coaxial machine gun to try and push Michael away. Dodging it, like the bullets moved in slow motion, Michael shoved his fist straight through the depleted uranium armour. Moving his other fist into it he pulled it apart and threw the pieces away. The third tank desperately tried to run Michael over. *Idiots*, Michael thought as he held the tank steady and then threw it up into the air. Looking over at the other tank, his eyes glowed a brighter red and then twin streams of red energy sawed the tank in half. Michael kept walking forward.

Charlotte and her family had been given binoculars to watch the fight. Charlotte zoomed in and watched Michael as he tore apart the forces outside. She smiled gently as she saw that Michael was winning. Kor and Nor stood behind her and further from their father. They were interested in how Michael was going to get himself captured because from what they saw it looked as if Ror was ready to destroy them all. Zor smiled to himself. He could feel the child was happy that Ror was fighting them off.

"Stop smiling woman. Watch how he will fall." Zor looked over at the helipad. "Launch the choppers."

Michael was still about 500 metres from the base; turning his hearing towards the base he heard the helicopter squadron launching. Four Apache helicopters lifted off and flew towards him. The Apaches hovered first and fired their Hellfire missiles towards Michael. The missiles didn't even faze Michael; realising this, the squadron flew towards his position spraying the area with Hydra rockets and machine gun fire. Michael was getting bored of this; reactivating his energy vision he fired multiple shots at the helicopters. All but one of the helicopters survived. Michael looked at the broken Humvee, he walked over to it and pulled the machine gun off the mount. He threw the machine gun like a spear towards the tail rotor sending it crashing into Michael. That was it, no more Michael thought. He continued walking towards the base.

Zor growled softly. "Nor, take him now." Nor wanted to protest but he had to keep his cover up. Pulling the remainder of his sword out of the sheath he whipped it around him creating an air shield. Then he shot towards Ror.

Michael could see Nor heading towards him at full speed. He didn't bother running, he simply waited. Nor was on Michael in seconds but before Nor had a chance to swipe with his sword Michael punched him down to ground. Nor was stunned, Ror hadn't hit him that hard in their first fight. He was fighting to kill. Nor stood up gently and began swiping at Michael; stepping back, Michael caught his hand and pulled the blade away from him. Michael stabbed him in his leg and headbutted him back. Nor pushed him back and pulled the blade from his leg kicking Ror back. Michael quickly recomposed himself. He roared with anger and sped towards him, narrowly avoiding two swipes Michael punched him down to the ground. Nor desperately tried to get up but Michael was on him. Entering superspeed, Michael shot punches down at Nor causing a crater to form beneath them. Nor felt blood pour out of his nose, Ror was going to kill him. So be it he thought. Michael kept punching until his arm was stopped in mid-air. Michael looked up at Zar who was holding his arm. The mute giant growled at Michael. Growling back Michael hit him as hard as he could. The punch sounded like thunder and knocked his helmet off. Michael got a full look at Zar's scarred face. The giant's eyes glowed black as he pushed Michael and began smashing him down. Michael right hooked Zar as hard as he could briefly stunning him; while he was stunned Michael shot twin streams of heat at Zar's face burning it slightly. Kicking Zar off him Michael sped towards the base.

"Hold it right there, child of Vaar!" Zor shouted. Michael's heart sank at what he saw. Zor had a pistol aimed at Ryan's head. "Are you as fast as you really think you are?" Michael entered superspeed. Time was almost halted as he sprinted towards Zor and Ryan. Michael would never let anyone be hurt ever again. But suddenly he felt an assault on his mind. "*NO CHILD YOU CAN'T SAVE HIM. Witness all your fear made real.*" Michael's mind was filled with all the doubt he had ever felt. He felt his body shaking with fear. And then it happened. Zor pulled the trigger and the bullet flew into Ryan's head. His lifeless body fell to ground. Michael's superhuman reflexes enabled him to see the bullet crash into his head killing him instantly. Michael heard Charlotte's family scream in pain. Tears poured from his eyes, Ryan was dead and he was responsible. He barely felt the two spears that were thrust into the sides of his body.

Nor's jaw and leg had healed completely from the damage cause by Ror. Kor had felt like crying, when she saw the child die. Nor was rocked by it; maybe they should have acted now instead of later. They could have saved the child. Accompanied by Zor and Zar they made their way to the holding cell which housed Ror. Inside Ror was held up by two spears and chained up to some incredible weights behind them. His eyes were red raw from crying and they still shone red. Kor's heart sank at the sight of Ror. His mind had been broken from what had happened to the child. Michael looked up at the four Kordites. He desperately tried to power up his energy vision but it was to no avail. Zor smirked at the effort.

"Don't bother child, your wounds and powers will not work down here. The two spears are close to your heart and every time the wounds try to heal they are split apart again by the metal. So, no burning my face off like you did to my brother over there." Zar growled deeply at Michael who responded with a smirk. Zor drew a sword and placed the blade through the necklace and observed the dog tags. He smiled psychopathically. "Do you know what your rank is in our society?"

Michael looked up, his eye shining red. "I'm a prince."

Zor laughed. "In human society yes, but in Kordite society you are a Royal Sentinel." Michael raised an eyebrow. "In Roman society a sentinel stood guard for a city and warned of danger. In Kordite culture a Royal Sentinel is one of the main protectors of family and the guild. Your job is to watch over your guild when the Guild Master and Guardian are away with different missions that require their attention."

Michael kept his eyes red. "So? I've never been to Kord. I've never even seen it."

Zor smirked. "It doesn't matter because you will always fail at that task." Michael spat some blood on to the ground. He didn't care about anything; he'd failed at protecting Charlotte how could he take care of a guild? "So child, do you want to know the reason why I have hidden myself within the military?" Zor asked.

Michael looked up. "I'm gonna die either way. So, wow me."

Zor smiled. "Earth is a junkyard, a place full of death and idiocy. When I first came here in the early 50s I joined the military to see what these humans were like. Some of them had honour and respect. I rose through the ranks and then found myself fighting in Vietnam. The war was long and bloody and many young soldiers lost their lives." Zor stopped for a second. "Have I lost you yet, child?"

Michael turned his eyes red. "Still here."

Zor continued. "When the war was over I returned to America. And do you know what I saw? I saw what humans were truly like. These so-called peace lovers shouted obscenities at us calling us baby killers and other such filth. Do you have any idea how disgusting that was? On Kord and in the Universal Committee soldiers are respected and treated fairly. The next biggest thing was in 2001 and New York was rocked by the Twin Towers being brought down. Do you remember it, child?"

Michael looked. "Of course I do. The Team hadn't been formed yet so there was no one to help."

Zor nodded. "Yes you do. Days later what happened? The public turned on us and demanded that we admit to flying those planes into the towers. Do you know what that felt like? I was in a room with other soldiers who broke down in tears because of what had happened. So we waged war again to find the culprits and in May 2011 we had intelligence that the one responsible was in a small house. So what did we do? We sent in a Special Forces group to kill him. We found him there and killed him. What happened next? Another outcry that we had faked it and that there was no mission."

Michael said through gritted teeth, "Get to the point."

Zor punched him as hard as he could. Michael could feel a loose tooth. "The point is that humans are ridiculous. They have no respect for anyone or anything. The youth of today believe they know everything; they sit behind computers and write how they can do things better than any of us can. This is not what life is about. So we are going to erase these humans from the earth and let life start again but not without you."

Michael let his head fall. "I'm not gonna help you with anything."

Zor smiled darkly. "Of course you won't but when you're broken and have lost everything you will help me. You see history is about to repeat itself all over again. Once I have unleashed you of your limiters you'll be the weapon you were meant to be. You will be like the original nuclear bomb: a weapon of incredible power shocking the scared humans into finally giving up on their pathetic lives."

Michael spat some blood out. "I'm not helping you and I'm not gonna let go of my limiters. I'm gonna let go now and let myself die."

Zor smiled. "No you won't." He walked towards Kor. "Torture him."

Kor didn't want to do this, she'd almost destroyed Charlotte's mind with her telepathy and now she was being asked to destroy an even weaker mind. Ror's mind was almost fractured and after failing to save the young boy Kor didn't know how much he could take. She felt tears again but quickly burned them. She bent down next to Ror. As soon as she came close enough Michael suddenly awakened with anger. His eyes flickered red with anger.

"GET OUT OF MY HEAD," he roared, his words dripping with pure malice. Kor almost flew up into the air.

She faltered and looked back at Ror. "Please, forgive me." Her eyes turned silver and Michael's eyes faded into black.

Michael was on his knees surrounded by death and destruction; dead bodies littered the area and parts of the ground were blanketed with blood. Michael's eye's flickered red as he saw Kor walking towards him.

"This is New York, Ror, or what's left of it, after you destroyed it."

Michael stood up shakily. "What is this?"

Kor smiled. "This is your future; you don't become some saviour. You are a destroyer just like your brother before you.

You'll slaughter billions of humans around the world." Out of nowhere Michael's doppelgänger appeared. He smiled at the destruction and then at Kor.

"I like this, it's better than anything I could ever imagine." He pointed at Kor. "I like this girl as well; much better than Charlotte. How's her brother?" Kor winced at that; Ror's psyche was already breaking, that statement might push him over the edge. Michael's eye twitched with anger.

"DON'T SPEAK HER NAME. Leave me alone." The doppelgänger sped over towards Michael and lifted him up.

"No Michael, I'm not leaving you alone. I am you and you are me. Give in to this and things will be much better." Kor didn't care if her father found about this. She sped towards the evil Ror and pushed him away. The doppelgänger looked at her. "Like I said Mike, I like this one she's got some bite to her." The doppelgänger kicked her back and then proceeded to beat her down. Kor tried to block but it was overwhelming even her telepathy. She couldn't let Michael lose and become this. She concentrated and ended the torture.

Sweat poured off both Michael and Kor after the event. Michael sobbed with pain and tiredness. Kor heard him keep repeating, "Make it stop". She crawled over to him and let his head fall on her shoulder.

"I'm sorry, Ror, me and my brother have decided to rebel against our father. When you strike out against our father we will join you. Please forgive me and him." Michael heard the words and struggled to believe them but he listened to her heartbeat to check to see if she was lying, and she wasn't. Kor made a hasty retreat out of the room. Michael let his head fall; he was physically and mentally exhausted. He never normally felt like this, his almost inexhaustible stamina always came through for him; but not today. Michael thought he'd got a respite until Zor walked back into the cell.

"Enough rest, it seems your mind is broken enough to push out my daughter's powers. It seems that you are ready." Zor pointed at the ceiling. "In this ceiling there are over a hundred reflectors that will feed solar energy into your body. I understand that since you are a pure blood the more energy I pump into your body the more power you will gain and your brain will begin to switch to a more primal form. Your limiters will simply dissolve from the amount of power."

Michael grinned grimly. "You're not a pure blood, are you?"

Zor sped towards him and grabbed his throat. "Very few know that secret, you do not deserve to know that secret."

Michael spat in his face. "That's why you hate me so much, right? Zar, your brother was one of the experiments to make a stronger pure blood and root out the second blooded Kordites. But then you were born a second blood; the Guild of Veer encourage strength, you must have been shunned; it's pathetic." A backhand slap made Michael spit out more blood.

"Genetic engineering, enhancement and healing are not needed. Look at me: I am a second blood and I have become a High Father. You deserve nothing that you have." Zor smiled a terrible smile that could crack mirrors. "Now, be a good boy and relieve those limiters for me." As he walked out the reflectors activated and shone over him. Michael's eyes turned red and his veins turned yellow as the energy flooded his system. Everything returned to him, his strength, his stamina and his healing. But it didn't matter; he still couldn't do anything. The chains that held him down were almost immovable and the two spears that dug into his sides wouldn't move at all. For the first ten minutes, Michael restrained himself from giving into the pure intoxication. It felt better than any drink in the world and Michael felt like he was floating. The pain had gone away finally and his mind was clear. Then it started happening; his eyes glowed a brighter red and his veins lit up as well. Michael wanted to move, the energy didn't hurt him but he wanted to run and lift weights. He groaned quietly and spat out. No he thought no giving up; if he lost control for even a second the other side could take control. Michael gritted his teeth and forced himself to try and turn the absorption power off.

Behind the one-way glass, Zor stretched watching the child try to fight against the energy. The superhuman corporal who was manning the reflector control panel looked up.

"Sir, the subject seems to be resisting the energy flow."

Zor looked down. "He will break soon; his mind can't take it for much longer."

The corporal checked her screens. "Nevertheless sir, the reflectors are running down on energy and need to recharge. It'll take around three hours."

Zor nodded. "Very good."

Chapter 22: *Show time*

Michael roared with pain as the energy kept rising through is body. His mind almost wanted to crack but Michael held on.

"NOOOOOOO!" he yelled. "I WILL NOT GIVE IN." The reflectors switched off again and Michael let his body fall gently.

Zor walked in. "I grow weary of this child; give yourself to the primal side of your mind or I will take further steps."

Sweat dripped off Michael. "No... No I will not give in."

Zor sighed. "So be it. But remember you are putting me in this position." Zor walked out. He returned momentarily with a girl with a black hood on her head. Michael suddenly woke up in pain when he realised who it was; it was Charlotte. She was wearing the same clothes that Michael had seen before. She cried in pain as Zor lifted her up by her neck and held her steady with a gun pointed to her head. Michael shook his head no and pleaded.

"Please, I'm begging you Zor don't touch her."

Zor smiled and dropped her to the ground. "I will not hurt her if you give in!" Michael looked over Charlotte, his eyes dripping with tears.

"Charlotte, baby I love you but I can't let them use me."

The hooded face looked over at him; Michael could make

out the features, she was pleading with him. Michael looked back over at Zor. "I'LL KILL YOU IF YOU LAY A FINGER ON HER!" he spat.

Zor smiled again. "I'm going to count to three; I will expose you to as much solar energy as possible. If you give in I will spare this poor wretch if not another innocent will die by your hands." The reflectors charged up and began beaming at Michael; he began sweating again. His eyes glowed pure crimson, part energy, part anger. "One." The word rang out as Michael realised what was happening again. Michael roared with effort to force his body to absorb even more solar energy; but he couldn't feel any difference. No please not now he thought; he couldn't keep it up. "Two." Michael roared more desperately trying to lose control.

"Please, don't do it!" Michael exclaimed at the top of his lungs; he had to lose control. A gunshot rang out. Michael closed his eyes as tears ran from his eyes; he looked over at the body as it fell on to the ground.

"NOOO!" The word turned into a roar as he lost control; anger and hatred flowed freely through his body.

Zor sped into the other room. He whispered, "Show time." He wouldn't have believed it if he hadn't seen it first-hand. A vicious yellow lightning bolt struck Ror and shattered the chains holding him down. He had heard the rumours and even seen some evidence but he hadn't expected it to happen like this.

Within the lightning bolt, Michael stood up and felt power surging through him. The twin spears were forced out of his body and sent into the walls. The windows fractured from the force and splintered glass all over the people behind it. Michael felt his body start to change from the stress of the lightning. He felt his arms grow larger and become far more defined as if to accommodate new strength. Bone protrusions lined his arm and were as sharp as blades. He grew to nine feet tall and his eyes blazed crimson with power. He had lost all notion of reasoning and logic as if his body was acting on a more primal mindset. The only constant that remained in his mind was rage, pure unadulterated rage. He was going to kill all of them, every last one on of them.

Kor helped up a human female soldier who had been covered by glass. The lightning bolt had drilled through hundreds of feet of concrete and metal to find Ror. She dusted herself off as she watched her father grin maliciously as they watched Ror give in to his power. The telepathic link with him had been shattered after she'd tried to torture him. Zor was flanked by another civilian woman with a hood on; at first Kor didn't recognise her and then Zor pulled the hood off.

She gasped. *Oh no*, she thought, *it's Charlotte.*

Zor reopened the door and pushed her through. "Now he will kill her and whatever mangled remains of his humanity will be destroyed." Kor wanted to intervene but her brother held her back.

"*Not yet little sister, we will move soon,*" he said over their telepathic link.

Charlotte was in handcuffs; she desperately tried to pull them off. She looked over at the dead body and let out a shrill gasp; the dead body had been wearing almost the exact same clothing. The body had been badly burnt by something that had left a lasting impression on the small room. She looked around at the back and saw what looked to be Michael. His body was bigger and he appeared to be far taller. He looked over at her and roared. Michael stepped forward towards her. Charlotte screamed and flew to the corner of the cell; she'd never been scared of Michael but now all she felt was pure fear. She instinctively called his name.

"Michael." The name brought Michael back from the depths of his insanity. He looked at Charlotte, the real Charlotte, and backed away. Michael held his head and summoned the will to change back to his former self. He fell on his knees and roared with effort as another yellow lightning bolt struck his body. For some reason the lightning didn't affect Charlotte, instead it stayed focused on Michael. He felt the sense of power leave and his body began changing back to normal. He sighed softly as the lightning splintered and crackled away. He had expected to feel tired but instead all the anger and rage was still there. He still had the power but he was free of the primal madness that once gripped him. No more he thought. He looked over at Charlotte and almost burst into tears. He didn't want to cause hurt, he would never hurt her again.

Zor's face turned to a scowl as he saw the results of the second lightning bolt. The concrete and metal were still hot in fact Zor could feel the heat from it even from where he was standing. He looked at the human female who had crawled up to her computer station. "What is happening?" he asked her in an irritated state.

"Unknown sir, it appears phenomena that occurred has destroyed the reflectors and left a giant hole through the base. I'm getting reading that the subject's energy levels are not running lower from the stress. In fact they are higher than when he was brought here. The hostage also seems not to have been damaged by the subject or the phenomena."

Zor's eyes turned crimson. "Impossible, she should be a bloody pile of entrails now."

Kor smiled softly. *Go on Ror*, she thought, *fight back*.

The mental struggle felt like an eternity but Michael was getting control. His body felt normal but all of his wounds had been healed perfectly. Charlotte ran over and held Michael while he shook. She kissed him gently.

"Mike, I'm here now just let it go."

Michael shook even more. He telepathically reached out to Angel. "*Angel, the mission is a go.*"

Angel and Dove hovered with the Black Hawks, Little Birds and Ospreys which had been flying in a holding pattern. Angel suddenly got the message. He spoke into his microphone.

"All players, this is team leader prepare for phase line alpha. Send the choppers in now."

Michael stood up shakily. He looked over at the one-way mirror and grinned manically. Turning his eyes red he saw Zor, who was surrounded by more armed soldiers armed with a variety of weapons,

"Zor, I'm may have been down but I am not out. I'm going to bring this building down around you and gouge out your eyes." He activated his energy vision and incinerated the soldiers in the room. The remaining soldiers began firing on Michael; the bullets bounced off him and snapped dangerously close to Charlotte. He turned round and looked at her. "Charlotte, get behind me and stay there." She quickly moved herself behind Michael. Closing his eyes he concentrated on the guns and made them fly away. The soldiers pulled out their sidearms but Michael was already on them. He lifted two of them up and threw them into a wall. Focusing his energy vision, he fired a barrage at the soldiers sending them back. Zor had beaten a hasty retreat away from where they were. "Charlotte we're safe, let's go find your family." Charlotte followed him and picked up one of the sidearms and they set off through the smoke.

Mary held Amy close as she heard gunfire outside the cell; she hadn't stopped crying since Ryan's death. Michael hadn't saved him but she knew she couldn't blame him. It was something that bastard did to him; she and Charlotte had heard Michael's screams before. He had been tortured all the while that he was there. Out of the erupting gunfire the door began to creak and crack. Out of the smoke Mary smiled at the figure.

Michael yanked the door with one final pull and threw it down. The interior was dimly lit so Michael lit up the room with a shine of his eyes. Mary and Amy were huddled up and hiding but they smiled slightly as Michael and Charlotte walked in. Michael couldn't face Mary, her son was dead because of him; instead he walked outside and checked the area with a sweep of his superhuman vision; no one in sight. Mary suddenly tugged Michael's arm.

"Hey, Michael, look at me and turn those damn flashlights off." Michael let his eyes dissolve to black and looked at her.

"Mary... I'm so sorry, I understand if you hate me."

Mary shook her head no and reached up, wrapping her arms around him. "I don't hate you Michael, I know you did everything you could but now I need you to focus and get us out of here." Michael nodded and walked outside. As suspected the guards had retreated inwards to stop Michael from escaping. Good he thought the helicopters would be lining up for their attack run now.

The two DAP Black Hawks closed in on their targets.

"Arrow 2-3 this arrow 2-4 I'm going in for the attack follow me close," the pilot said.

"Roger, 2-4 I'm coming in behind you." The two helicopters flew towards the main door and armed their Hellfire and Hydra rockets training them on the door. The missiles flew towards the door blowing it apart.

"Arrow 2-3 good hit repeat good hit. Let's clear the area for the Ospreys." The helicopters peeled away as the three Ospreys pulled up behind. The Ospreys descended towards the ground and stopped around ten feet before it. PMC troops dropped out and secured the area, ready to invade the base.

Michael led Charlotte and her family through the remains of the tunnel making sure his hearing was working at full blast to detect any threat. He was surprised that Nor and Kor hadn't appeared to stop him. Maybe they had really defected from their father. Out of nowhere Zar tackled Michael into the wall.

"Charlotte, continue down the tunnel and get out of here," Michael shouted. Zar smashed Michael into the wall again. Charlotte looked back and fired two rounds at Zar's head trying to get his attention. Zar turned and glared at her; before he had a chance to move Michael burned his face again and followed with a right cross. "GO!" Michael shouted confidently. Charlotte ran with her family out of the tunnel. Michael defiantly stopped Zar's fist and headbutted him twice pushing him back. Dropping to the ground Michael coughed and before Zar could react supersped him into the wall. He pulled him back and began superspeeding around him, trading strength for speed and used his energy vision blast to put him off balance. Zar took multiple beatings until he stopped Michael dead; lifting Michael up Zar smashed him into the ground. Raising a giant foot, Zar began stomping him down until a blur smashed into Zar. Nor stood in front of Michael welding his blade, Kor appeared beside him.

She turned around. "Ror, we will try and deal with our uncle." She helped him up.

"No, can you shadow Charlotte until she and her family get out of here." Kor looked over and zoomed in on Charlotte. She nodded and blurred away. Michael stepped forward to help Nor but he held his sword in front of him.

"No, Ror. For the last few years I've willing gone ahead with my father and his plans; but no more. You fight off the remaining forces. I will deal with my "uncle"." Zar roared at Nor. "Go!" Michael nodded and supersped away.

Nor let his uncle make the first move, a barrage of jabs. Nor ducked down and kicked Zar back sending him hurtling backwards. Following him through the rubble, Nor lifted him up and threw him through the roof. Nor knew that in a straight fight he would lose, no matter if he was a pure blood he could not match the millennia of combat experience Zar had. Nor activated his energy vision and burned Zar down to the ground. Dropping to the ground he used a barrage of blows to push him off balance. He heard multiple soldiers shout, the ones who were still aligned with Zor, began firing on him. Nor couldn't stop focusing on Zar, a one second loss of concentration could mean Nor's death. Zar roared again and smashed Nor down but he was ready as he kicked Zar up. There was only one solution; Nor had to get Zar out of the area. They hurtled out of airspace; Nor could only hold him still for so long. Zar began to pull him down and angle him towards the city of Los Vegas. They crashed on to the main road and through a building. Nor stood up gently shaking off the dust; while making sure there were no civilians left Zar rushed him into the wall. Nor got up quickly and supersped towards Zar, moving with lightning speed Zar moved and pushed Nor down. Lifting him up Zar threw him into another building. This wasn't how it was supposed to happen Nor thought. Zar lifted Nor up and rushed him through the building like he was a bulldozer. Nor pushed Zar away and lifted himself up gently levitating in the air. The building was practically coming down and most of the civilians were dying or had moved out of the way. His attuned hearing suddenly heard a scream from a room above him. Looking up, he saw a human male reaching out towards his child and a female standing next to him. Nor turned his attention to the family and shot up towards them. As the ceiling above them began crumbling Nor grabbed them and shot down towards the street. Placing them down, they stood in awe of him.

"Go, now, take your family and warn others to get out of this area. The beast is about to destroy the city, I will do my best to stop him. Go now." The family still stood there; the child in particular stared at Nor. *Hmm*, Nor thought, *I should take a less polite stance.* "Move, humans and get the hell out of here, now!" That shook the family up as they sprinted away from him. "Peasants," he muttered under his breath as they ran away. Nor breathed a sigh of relief as he drew his mangled sword from his sheath; he turned to see Zar emerging from the rubble. The relief was limited as Zar showed no signs of slowing down. Nor flew towards Zar, pushing him through the remains of the building. Freeing himself from Nor's grip, Zar pushed him down and repeatedly beat him into a crater beneath him. Desperately trying to block the giant's attacks, Nor held his hands up in front of his face. Blood poured out of his mouth but he held on, Nor waited for his chance and headbutted Zar off him. Levitating up, Nor rushed Zar into the road pushing him down the street rippling the tarmac. Entering superspeed, Nor attacked Zar as much as he physically could. As the blows landed Nor gained confidence but suddenly Zar stopped his fist. Pushing him he away, he supersped towards him and began smashing him into different parts of the rubble. Nor coughed as he tasted blood; he smirked at his uncle.

"No matter how much you hurt me, I will fight you and kill you."

Michael pushed two K humans into a wall killing them instantly. Outside the base Michael saw the superheroes moving in. Multiple PMC troops moved in formation firing on specific targets. The attack choppers sporadically fired; Angel landed in front of Michael.

"Hey Mike, took you long enough," he said as he fought off different K humans. Michael killed one by turning his face into ash with his energy vision.

"Knock it off Adam I'm in no mood." Angel nodded. Out of nowhere the other two Kordites appeared. One flew into Angel sending him back into the base. The other charged at Michael; time slowed down as Michael turned and grabbed the Kordite by his cape and slammed him into the ground. Michael stomped on him repeatedly desperately trying to gain the upper hand. With a flash of movement the Kordite fired a barrage of energy vision. The energy vision blast to Michael's face caused him to cry out in pain. He wiped away at his eyes as quickly as he could but he was too late; the Kordite pushed Michael back. They engaged in hand-to-hand combat; the Kordite's strategy was completely unique compared to Michael's. He struck first then countered; Michael's brain analysed the battle to find faults or loopholes for him to exploit. It was almost foolproof, their punches connected with such force that sand was whipped up around them. Michael incorporated his energy vision, blasting at the Kordite's fist and chest. Gaining an advantage Michael jumped up and brought both of his fists down on to him. The Kordite fell on his knees; Michael kneed him in the head. Putting him into a headlock Michael held the Kordite down. Before Michael wouldn't have been able to hold him but now he realised that he had to fight to win.

"No more holding back," Michael said as he twisted his hands breaking the Kordite's neck; letting the body fall he suddenly saw the Kordite's aura fade away. Michael looked away to the rest of the battle and rejoined it.

Angel finally stopped himself from crashing through the walls using his massive wings. The Kordite sped towards him but Angel was ready; he sidestepped him and delivered a crushing blow to the Kordite's skull. The Kordite recovered and delivered several blows to Angel the last one broke Angel's skin. Recovering quickly, Angel pressured the Kordite on to his back foot. Entering superspeed he sent a barrage of blows raining down on him. The Kordite realised that he was losing; quickly lifting Angel up they flew through the roof of the base. Angel began headbutting the Kordite causing him to bleed and finally broke his nose. The Kordite lost control for a second and Angel responded with everything he had. *Finally an advantage*, he thought but it didn't last long, the Kordite fired on Angel with his energy vision. The power pushed Angel back but he finally flew above it. Angel had one last thing to do. His eyes became a dark blue as he powered up his angel cry; he released it with everything he had. The power pushed the Kordite down towards the ground; Angel followed him keeping up the pressure. The Kordite tried to stand up but he couldn't; Angel increased the power to as much as he possibly could. The area behind the Kordite vaporised; the armour began fading and disintegrating. Angel let it all out, he didn't hold back and as he did part of the base suddenly crumbled and began collapsing. The Kordite tried to walk forward but the angel cry suddenly vaporised him. Angel fell on his knees panting giving his energy a moment to recycle. He'd never let go of his power like that before and this was the result. The part of the base had been totally vaporised and the Kordite was completely gone. Angel shook off the consequences and rejoined the fight.

Michael kept fighting as hard as he could, Kor appeared by him pushing a K human away from him. He looked at her and nodded, she smiled back at him.

"*Ror, I know this is not the time but I have to say it: I'm sorry for what I did to you and Charlotte. I didn't know how to make my father believe that I was still with him.*" Michael didn't respond at first as bullets crashed on to him but then he did.

"*I read about what happened to you, how you were indoctrinated and how you had to follow or face death. I forgive you, in another life I may have loved you but right here, right now, we need to kick your father and his brother off this planet.*" Michael could sense she was smiling as she sped in front of him to stop a missile from hitting him. Michael engaged his energy vision taking down three different enemy choppers. Out of nowhere Zar appeared carrying Nor and landing on the ground. Michael heard Kor whisper his name; speeding towards Zar Michael hoped he could catch him off guard, but it didn't work and Zar hit him with Nor's body. Two close by air support Little Birds appeared and began firing on the trio. The bullets harmlessly bounced off their bodies; Zar had had enough of the helicopters. He launched the remains of a Humvee towards the pair of helicopters. A gunner on one of the choppers was sent flying from the helicopter. Michael leapt towards the gunner catching him and landing safely on the ground. Nor came around, shook off his unconsciousness and caught the two Little Birds landing them carefully.

"You okay?" Michael asked the gunner.

"Fine friend, I need to rally with my choppers." Michael nodded as the gunner sprinted off. Nor pulled the two battered pilots out of the choppers.

"Soldiers, are you hurt?" he asked. The pilots shook their heads while gaping at Nor. One of the soldiers stood up and pulled his rifle from the wreckage.

"We're fine, thanks for the assist. Rangers lead the way." Nor nodded.

Michael shouted towards him. "Nor, you better get over here. Your uncle's waking up." Nor casually looked at his uncle removing a ton of wreckage from his body. He walked towards Michael and placed his hand on his shoulder.

"Can you hold him?"

Michael nodded as his eyes turn red. "I'll do my best." He shot off towards Zar; Nor telepathically called out to his mangled sword and caught it. He looked to see more soldiers land on the ground from helicopters. K humans were joining the battle in force. Nor sighed as he swiped his sword around and charged off to engage them. It was time for him to display his full amount of combat experience. All of the K humans had enhanced speed, meaning they could move, think and react at speeds that baffled ordinary humans. But Nor was known for his speed among his kin and he could dispatch them within seconds. He closed his eyes and felt time slow down to the point nano seconds passed like minutes. He reopened his dark green eyes and moved between each K human, slicing them without a second's hesitation. He appeared behind them as they all took one step forward and fell dead on the ground. He reopened his eyes and sheathed his shattered sword.

Chapter 23: *I will not die*

Michael was thrown through some rubble; he hadn't got time to wipe the dust off him as Zar chased him back. Michael flew towards Tremor, who was powering up another earthquake attack. At the last second Michael flew upwards and let Tremor hit Zar with the attack. Michael and Tremor fist bumped as he handed him a comm unit.

"Angel, where is Charlotte?" Static crackled.

"They're on arrow 2-2, I'll patch you through to them." Static crackled again.

"Michael, are you alright?" Mary's voice echoed over the comm unit.

"I'm fine Mary where's Charlotte?" Static crackled.

"I don't know, I thought she was on another chopper but I haven't heard from her since." The words hit Michael like a freight train, he'd lost Charlotte again.

"Oh god no, listen Mary I'm gonna find her just stay calm." He didn't have time to listen to her reply as Zar threw Tremor at Michael. They got up gently; Michael looked at the base.

"Don't worry Mike we heard the last transmission go look for Charlotte. We'll hold them off." Michael nodded. As Zar stepped forward gunfire peppered his armour. Michael looked up at the Little Bird and saw Norton and Bernard firing at Zar. Michael smiled and supersped towards the base.

Tremor prepared himself for another punch by the giant Kordite readying an earthquake shield to ward off the attack but the giant's blow sent Tremor hurtling back. Spitting blood out, Tremor stood up and leapt at Zar with a haymaker made of a 10.5 earthquake blast. Zar fell back as Tremor leapt upon him and landed multiple blows. The last blow missed its target and Zar pushed Tremor down. Tremor had nothing left to give; he was tired and knew the end was coming. As Zar stood up, Tremor prepared for the worst but suddenly a blur crashed into Zar. Tremor looked up and smiled as Angel appeared throwing Zar down.

"Tremor, regroup with Dove and Bolt and push forward into the base. I've got this." Tremor jumped up and sped off. "I think," he muttered, as the giant stood up. Angel didn't give Zar a chance to even think about moving; he smashed into Zar dragging him into the terrain. Zar pushed Angel away and tried to blast him with energy vision. Dodging it Angel sped forward and struck with everything he had. The giant stepped back smiling like a creep as he wiped spittle from his mouth. He sped forward and grabbed Angel; leaping high into the air he headbutted Angel repeatedly drawing blood from his nose and mouth. Angel struck out with a right hook and then a kick towards Zar's ribs. Zar held firm and began pulling at Angel's arm. Angel realised what was happening; the psycho was trying to pull Angel's arm off. Angel used his other hand and dug his fingers into his eyes.

"C'mon you bastard let go." Zar grinned. Angel's eyes glowed pure blue as he readied his angel cry. His voice distorted as energy thrashed Zar down. Parts of his armour began to vaporise but the bastard held on. Angel put everything into it, his hatred for them for causing Amy's death. The energy physically began ripping the ground apart underneath them; feeling the burning of his skin, Zar let up and pushed Angel off. Angel breathed deeply; he couldn't beat him. Zar walked forward preparing to deal a final blow. Suddenly two blurs shot into Zar pushing him away. Nor and Kor appeared and helped Angel up.

"Human hero, we will attend to this. Return to the battle."

Kor struck first as she landed a flying kick to Zar's scarred face. Nor followed up with a blast from his energy vision and a one-two combo. Zar growled at them and rushed them both.

"*Sister, we must push Zar out of this area.*" His telepathic message was acknowledged by Kor as she grabbed Zar's arm and flew up. Nor followed suit; they flew away. Reaching supersonic speeds the trio entered San Francisco in seconds. The public below most likely assumed a fighter jet was performing manoeuvres above them as the trio soared through the city, high enough to not cause damage. Kor and Nor couldn't hold Zar for much longer as they crashed towards the defunct Alcatraz prison. Breaking through the walls, Nor pushed Kor away from any danger and continued tackling Zar through the building. Nor stood up gingerly, spitting blood from his nearly broken jaw; he scanned the area for his sister. Zar had been hurt slightly but he easily shook it off; he sped over towards Kor and lifted her up. She desperately tried to fight him off but she couldn't pull herself from his vice-like grip. Zar began to speak.

"You were to be the next generation of fighters for the Guild of Veer. But you were weak, unlike me or your father you were not ready to do what was needed for the guild," he said in a deep guttural voice.

Nor laughed. "Don't make me laugh, you bestial moron. We were not doing this for the guild neither were we doing this for the honour of Kord. We did it because my father grew mad with rage at not being a pure blood. He wanted to prove himself to the Guild Master and the Guardian that he could be better than them all. And to do that what; what was he going to do? He was going to obliterate a race who didn't even know we existed. He was going to kill men, women and children because he was insane," Nor said in his unmoving calm tone; even with the stress of the moment his voice was always cool and collected.

Zar sneered at the injured Nor. "You are not a true guild member. She would be disgusted in you."

Nor's eyes turned dark green with anger. "You do not mention her, ever."

Zar laughed a disturbingly deep laugh. "What can you do now, child? You're injured and now I will take your sister away from you." Zar took a small cylinder from his belt and pressed the side. A four foot spear emerged and he aimed it at Kor's heart. Nor's eyes widened; he had seconds to react. Entering superspeed, it looked as if he had almost teleported over to Kor. Grabbing her from his grip, he took the spear blow and managed to push it into his stomach. Kor's eyes were wide in amazement as her brother held her tight. She felt like she was baby in his arms but she realised the amount of damage that had been caused by the spear. Nor fell on his knees, his long black hair covering his eyes as he breathed labouredly. Pulling out the spear he dropped it to the ground; blood flowed freely from the wound and splashed over the ground. Kor was still in shock.

"Brother, why? Why would you save me?"

Nor breathed deeply. "I never cared about you properly, I never took care of you, and I never even held you when you were scared. And even through all this you still loved me as your elder brother. Even though I tried to drive you away, I always cared for you. Hurting you was something I never forgave myself for. But now, in this day and time, I will never let anything hurt you again." Kor blinked back tears as she looked at her wounded brother. She looked up at the approaching Zar and her eyes turned harsh silver. Twin beams of energy smashed into Zar sending him deeper into the prison. She lifted the spear from the ground and flew towards him. Zar may have been injured but he was still incredibly powerful. He parried away Kor's spear swipe with his gauntlet. He tried to use his reach to grab her but she dodged with extreme speed. The second spear swipe caught his chest and cut diagonally through the armour like it was butter. Zar stepped back and tried to grab Kor with his giant hands. Kor again dodged and this time stabbed directly into his stomach. Zar spat blood on to the ground as he fell to his knees. He tried to power up his energy vision but it faltered; the tattoos under his cuirass shimmered faint and failed as energy leaked from his body. Kor stabbed him again with the spear. She stood behind him and placed him in a headlock.

"This is for my honour and for my brother." She pulled and then broke Zar's neck. She walked over to her wounded brother who was healing as he absorbed energy. "Brother, we must go back to the main battle." Nor stood up slowly and breathed deeply. The deep wound in his stomach had completely sealed up. He walked towards Zar's lifeless body and lifted it up. Together they flew back to Area 51.

Michael pushed a tank at a group of K humans, he'd searched everywhere for Charlotte but he couldn't find her. Searching the area with his superhearing he tried to listen for Charlotte's voice.

He had one choice; focusing with his telepathy he connected with Kor. "*Kor, I need your help; is there any other place Zor would have taken Charlotte*?" There was no reply for a minute and then she echoed in his mind.

"*There was a second level beyond the one we were allowed to go, she might be there.*" Michael nodded and supersped back to where he was held. The area was dark now because of the damage dealt to the base but it didn't impede Michael. He found a sealed titanium door; gripping the sides he wrenched and pulled the door from its hinges. Moving inside the area he found an elevator and peeled the doors back. Dropping down he smashed into the elevator car and shot through the doors. Another door revealed a massive spaceship; bigger than any plane and shaped almost like an arrowhead. On one side Michael saw a walkway on to the ship. He focused in and saw Charlotte being carried in by Zor.

"Charlotte, RUN NOW!" he yelled as he superleaped towards Zor, smashing him into the rock walls. Michael burned him with his energy vision and battered Zor into the ground. Switching to a different method of pain, Michael headbutted him repeatedly. While Zor tried to recover Michael noticed a blur sending Charlotte into the ship. Another Kordite he thought. As he turned around Zor produced two daggers and stabbed Michael. He then lifted him by the neck and burned his face using his energy vision. Michael desperately tried to form a telekinetic shield over his face. Zor threw Michael back into the door.

"It's no use child, I am taking your beloved and you will never save her," he said as he boarded the ship. The craft's massive engines hummed and began to power up. Michael sped back up to the surface but lost control; the pain in his stomach was intense. Michael dug the blades out gently. He coughed up blood as The Team appeared. The base suddenly blew apart as the ship launched into the air and shot off towards space. Michael was spent; the fight had taken almost everything he had left. Angel looked back at the ship then back at him.

"Mike, what are you waiting for go, now!" Michael looked up at him as Kor and Nor landed back with the dead body of Zar.

"I can't I haven't got anything left." Kor supersped towards him and held his head next to hers.

"Ror, I know you're hurting and I know you're tired but you are the only one left now. We must keep the fight going. Here…" Kor held him close and her veins started to glow; Michael suddenly felt a jolt of power wake him up. His eyes turned red. Kor looked tired but smiled. "I've lent you some of my energy. Now go and rescue your beloved!" Michael smiled softly as he walked through the crowd. Thunder cracked around the area as a figure shot on to the ground, Michael realised it was the hologram of his father.

He smiled warmly at him. "She is right my son, you can save her, you can save all of them. I will begin entering the ship's systems and help you deactivate it." Michael nodded, took a deep breath and leapt up towards space as he reached higher he let the ground fall from him. Flying faster than ever Michael shot towards the ship; grabbing on to the engine Michael let the heat smash into him. He easily ripped apart the armour and shot through. The area was a giant engine bay and it was pristine. As long as Michael had the element of surprise things would go easily. Michael made his way towards the door and peeled at it but before it came off a fist sent him hurtling. Michael grabbed the piece of metal he'd ripped apart and then shot himself back into the bay. The Kordite walked through and made the first move striking with incredible speed. Michael dodged and then countered the last punch with a strike to the Kordite's throat. Following up with another barrage of punches Michael gained the upper hand and blasted him with energy vision. Flipping over the Kordite Michael grabbed the Kordite's neck and snapped it with sheer precision. Tossing the body out of the ship, he shot towards the small hangar and found Charlotte in a cryogenic pod. Her skin was light blue as Michael began to deactivate it. Out of the darkness Zor punched Michael away; he blasted away at the areas of the ship trying to hit Michael. The last shot blew part of hull away.

"You will not save her," he said as he launched Charlotte's pod out of the ship. Anger surged through Michael as he pinned Zor to ground. Unleashing his full strength Michael began smashing Zor down. With every punch Zor kept looking back at him, laughing and spitting blood out. Michael landed one final punch. A hologram of his father appeared and placed his hand on Michael's shoulder.

"My son, go after her, I will deal with the ship." Michael looked up and obeyed. He fell out of the ship drifting back towards earth. The ship suddenly flashed out of the area. Turning back he looked for and then focused in on the cryo pod and heard Charlotte screaming. A stray bolt of energy vision had hit part of the pod. Shooting down towards the capsule, Michael broke the hypersonic barrier as he desperately tried to catch up with the pod. Landing on the vessel Michael held it tight. Slowing it down was useless as the pod was already increasing speed. Charlotte looked up at Michael.

Michael activated his telepathic link with her. "*Do you trust me?*" She nodded rapidly. Michael's reflexes slowed down time as the ground sped up to meet them. In the last second Michael ripped the door off and pulled Charlotte out. The capsule blew up and Michael held her closely as fire hit his back. They were low enough so that Charlotte could breathe. Michael looked at her and then remembered her brother's death.

"Oh god, Charlotte I'm so sorry," he said, his lip quivering. Charlotte started crying and buried her head in Michael's chest as they descended towards the ground.

Chapter 24: *This is your home*

Michael, Kor and Nor stood on the moon's surface with the bodies of the Kordites. As soon as they had mopped up the rest of the K humans, Kor had sent a communiqué back to Kord calling a few representatives from the Guild of Vaar and the Guild of Veer. Norton's men had set some charges to blow the complex up from within. The Team had flown to Washington DC to inform the president of what had happened. Charlotte and her family had been flown back with Bernard to prepare for Ryan's funeral. Michael had kept his distance from them; he couldn't even look at Charlotte. Tears welled up in Michael's eyes but he evaporated them before they even fell. The area in front of them suddenly began distorting and opening up before them. Three Kordites appeared; two of them were wearing the symbol of Veer and one was wearing Michael's symbol. He focused in on the female; she had almost crystal white hair and pure blue eyes. She suddenly looked at Michael and smiled speeding over towards him she grabbed Michael in the tightest hug he'd ever had.

"Brother, or should I call you cousin, it's so good to see you," she said joyfully.

Michael smiled. "I... uh don't know you properly."

She smiled at Michael. "Well of course you don't you were only a baby when I first saw you. I never had time to see you again."

The two representatives from the Guild of Veer were slightly sterner. They took the bodies of the Kordites and instructed their two guild members to stand where they had teleported in.

Michael pointed at them. "What's gonna happen to them?"

Her face grew dark. "They may be sent for punishment yet, I don't fully know."

Michael shifted on his feet. "They shouldn't be punished they were indoctrinated from a young age to believe that what they were doing was right."

She nodded. "Oh I'm sorry my name is Lara-Vaar and I need you to come back with me."

Michael raised an eyebrow. "Back to Kord?"

She nodded enthusiastically. "Of course, the High Father and Guardian of Vaar want to meet you. They are your family." She pointed at the bracelet on his arm containing his suit. "And you will need to wear that not this strange garb you have on."

Michael sighed and pressed the button on the bracelet. The suit flooded over his body sealing it against his skin. Lara smiled and led him over to the teleportation spot. The two representatives from the Guild of Veer activated their teleportation devices and Lara activated hers. In flash they were teleported away disappearing towards the stars.

The group reappeared over Kord just above the atmosphere. Michael gaped at Kord; it was beautiful, not like earth which appeared as a jewel in space, but something about Kord took Michael's breath away. The planet oozed beauty but an almost destroyed beauty. There were massive land masses and crystal blue oceans but some parts of the planet appeared destroyed; no doubt caused by the wars that had raged on its surface. Outside the planet there were many space stations and the planet had around seven moons in total. Massive warships patrolled the moons; Michael was absolutely astounded at the sizes, some ranged from three miles in length to around ten miles. In deeper orbit there were sentries posted wearing full armour. The sun was a bright yellow but Michael hadn't absorbed that, there was a different type of energy; it was pure and refined.

Lara looked at Michael and smiled. "You can feel it, can't you?"

Michael nodded at her. "That's not from the sun, is it?"

She shook her head no. "No the energy surrounding and within the planet is part of the Infinite Source Pool, a primordial energy that has existed before the big bang itself. Unlike solar energy it is pure and unfiltered giving us more of an edge."

Michael smiled. He accelerated his absorption of the energy giving him a boost. His eyes turned a brilliant red as he fed on the energy. The group descended towards the planet and through the atmosphere. As soon as they entered multiple sentries surrounded them.

"State your business." Lara went to talk but the representative from Veer spoke first.

"Fool, we are officers from the Guilds of Veer and Vaar. Know your place." The voice sounded like thunder and was filled with authority. Having been put in their place the sentries immediately retreated to their patrol areas. As they descended further they broke up; Kor and Nor were sent in an opposite direction.

Michael tried to speak to Kor but she shook her head no. "*Do not worry Ror; we will see each other again,*" she told him. Michael smiled and followed Lara down towards a giant fortress. Michael stood in awe of the huge building. There was a holographic picture of the guild symbol which looked almost real. The vast surface of the fortress was maintained by different drones. Lara didn't even have to look at Michael to see his reaction.

"Amazing, is it not? This landscape was where the original members of the Guild of Vaar lived. They built this fortress with no intention of finishing it; instead it is constantly being upgraded with the latest technology or artwork. Inside is full living quarters for all the members."

Michael looked over at a mountain nearby. "What about those mountains? In a vision I saw Kordites living there especially the original Guardians."

Lara nodded in agreement. "Yes, some of our members do live there, including the High Father." Lara suddenly lifted up and they floated towards the giant doors.

"Where are you taking me?" he asked.

"Well the Guardian wants to talk with you but first I want to take you to see your mother and sister."

Michael sped in front of her. "What!"

Lara gently placed her hand on his shoulder, her voice was soothing. "I am taking you to the holy memorial – a graveyard as the humans call it. But here you will see your mother." Michael nodded and followed her into the fortress.

The inside of the fortress was beautiful and beyond anything Michael had ever seen in his entire life. He followed Lara towards the memorial; as they entered Michael started shaking. He fell on his knees begging it to stop. Lara looked back and sped towards him; she held him close and set up a telepathic link with him.

"*It's alright Ror, you are with family now. I can feel your pain but nothing will happen now.*"

327

Michael responded. "*Take me to see my mother.*" She nodded and they moved towards the memorial. Michael took more deep breaths and went with her. They entered the memorial. One sentry was posted, he wore full armour and instead of a firearm he had a lance. He nodded at Lara as they moved further into the memorial. It was beautifully quiet and there were fires in front of different grave areas. Lara floated up and Michael followed suit. She pointed at the one in front of them.

"This is where your mother lies in death." Michael floated forward and placed his hand on the grave. "Reach out to her," Lara said softly.

"But... She's dead."

Lara smiled. "Nothing ever truly dies brother; the Infinite Source Pool reclaims us when we die. That is what we believe." Michael focused on the grave trying desperately to reach out to his mother; but there was nothing.

He looked back at Lara. "I can't feel her." Lara floated and placed her hand on the grave; her eyes closed and she smiled. She placed her hand on Michael's shoulder. Michael suddenly felt clear, he could see his mother.

"*Mother, I am here,*" he said. She turned towards him and smiled warmly.

"*Son, I knew you would return. I cannot stay long. Know that I love you more than anything else,*" She suddenly disappeared out view. Michael wanted to talk more but they turned back. He looked at Lara who appeared tired but she smiled at him.

"Fear not, brother I am fine. But we need to meet the Guardian now." Michael followed Lara out of the memorial and up through the atrium towards the Guardian's chamber.

The room was pure white with different mosaics across the walls. In the centre a figure was levitating and was in deep meditation. Lara kneeled and instructed Michael to do the same.

She spoke softly. "Guardian Vaar, I have brought the child of Saar and Lira to see you." The Guardian opened his eyes which glowed an electric blue and focused on Michael. He smiled warmly.

"Welcome child, it is nice to finally meet you." The voice was pure and had an almost fatherly tone. Michael didn't know whether to speak. "*Child, you can stand and speak.*" A telepathic sentence echoed through Michael's head. He stood and was speechless.

Finding his voice he said, "It's nice to meet you, sir." The Guardian landed gently on the ground and walked towards him. He stood around 6 foot 7 and had the weight of an oak tree.

"Please child, I am as a human would call, your uncle. Your father was my older brother and he was originally to become the Guardian." He looked over to Lara. "Daughter, you can leave now." Looking at Michael's suit he laughed gently. "It looks good on you child. I suppose you never wanted to wear it?"

Michael let a smile out. "I didn't really want to wear it, but father said that it would look iconic to the humans."

The Guardian smiled. "Yes it does." Michael looked down. "What is wrong, child?" Michael looked desperately trying not look at him in the eyes.

"Zor told me that I am an aberration to the Kordite people because I was genetically engineered. I... I suppose I wasn't expecting such a warm welcome."

The Guardian placed a hand on his shoulder. "You are our family, no matter what you are or how you were born. You were born for a special reason child; your father believed that you could help guide the humans. At the moment the earth is somewhat of a hot topic. Some of the Guardians wish to destroy the humans and restart. But others, myself included, wish to give them a chance to see if they can correct themselves. You are our ace in the hole. With you we wished to guide the humans in a correct manner. I will not lie to you child; the task will not be easy and will sometimes seems impossible but in time they will meet our expectations." Michael took it all in. One of the things Michael had noticed was that the Guardian radiated power.

"Uncle, what about the Ziborian threat?"

The Guardian's face darkened softly. "It is another topic that is up for debate."

Michael walked forward. "This seems wrong; forgive my candour, but when I learned about the Guardians, once they saw something was wrong they did something about it. It's in the Scroll of the Guardians, isn't it?"

The Guardian smiled. "Strong-minded just like your father. Yes you are correct; in the old days once we knew something was wrong we intervened. But some of the Guardians have raised objections to the Scroll's... usefulness. They believe that the scroll was written in difficult times and that it is not relevant for today." Michael started to protest but the Guardian held up a hand. "Let me finish child. That is not an opinion that I or the Guild of Veer believe in. But the other Guardians from Zaren, Marion and Acardion believe that our time is a time of diplomacy rather than force."

Michael looked down. "But haven't the Ziborians already destroyed billions of lives and quite a few planets?"

The Guardian stroked his white beard. "Yes they have and many from the Guild of Veer and a few sentries from our guild stopped their armada temporarily. But they need more support and they won't get it until it's too late. We are stuck in an endless loop."

Michael frowned until his superhuman hearing picked up an explosion outside. The Guardian had also sensed it and walked towards one of the walls. It suddenly polarised and revealed a balcony that they walked on to. The serene skyline was disrupted by fire and explosions. Michael picked up multiple humanoids zipping through the fort's city. Sentries lay dead on the ground as civilians tried to run from the beings. The Guardian's voice hummed with power and anger.

"Ziborians. They dare attack our planet."

Michael's eyes turned red. "What should we do?" The Guardian gave him a rod which Michael took. The rod lengthened and became a hammer-like weapon.

"We must join the fight." Moving with speed that baffled Michael he shot over towards one of the Ziborians. Gripping the warrior by its throat lightning surrounded them and incinerated the Ziborian. Michael was in awe at Guardian's power. Leaping off the balcony he flew towards one of the Ziborians. It was holding a Kordite civilian and was trying to rip it apart. Michael increased speed, swung the weapon at the Ziborian and attacked with a kick to its stomach. The Ziborian recovered and delivered three blows to Michael's face. The strength was incredible but Michael brought the hammer back down on the Ziborian's face causing it to bleed profusely. This was useless; though the weapon was powerful it was taking too long to kill the Ziborian.

"Child, the weapon is a Guardian weapon, summon the power from the Source Pool. It will kill it." Michael focused and is veins turned yellow he refocused the power into the hammer. The weapon glowed with power; electrical energy appeared over the weapon. Michael smashed it into the Ziborian finally killing him.

"Brother." Michael looked over at Lara who held a dead Ziborian in her hands. Michael smiled. "Don't look so surprised, I know how to fight," she said. "Now you go we can handle this."

Michael shook his head no. "No, these are my people and this is my planet and I will defend it." She smiled. Another pair of Ziborians flew towards the duo. Michael gave the hammer to Lara and telekinetically summoned a fallen sentry's lance and sped forward towards him. Michael battered the Ziborian down to the ground; the Ziborian moved with incredible speed and tried to kick back at Michael. Dodging the kick, Michael stabbed the lance into the Ziborian's gut.

"*Brother, the Ziborians have a thing for dismemberment. Be careful of them.*" Michael understood he had seen what the Ziborian had tried to do; they were dangerous. Out of nowhere three Ziborians fell out of the sky; dead. Two massive sentries from the Guild of Veer descended out of the sky. Another figure appeared behind them. Michael supersped over to Lara.

"Who's the big guy?"

Lara's face grew dark. "It is the Guild Master of Veer; his presence is... troubling." Two sentries from the Guild of Vaar landed in front Michael and Lara. The Guild Master was in full armour with the symbol of Veer on his chest. He was at least eight foot tall and walked with military precision. He pushed through the two Vaar sentries and walked towards Michael. The Guild Master looked as if he was about to hit Michael; and he did. Michael dodged but didn't counter. Lara tried to intervene but was stopped by a sentry. Michael dodged again and didn't dare hit back.

"Come child fight back." The Guild Master unleashed a barrage of blows. Michael dodged and finally went on the offensive; he pushed his fist down and shoved him back. "No child I want you to hit me. Let me see what all the fuss was about," he said as he landed more blows on Michael. Dodging the fist he unleashed two punches on to the Guild Master. The Guild Master responded with another punch but Michael reversed it and responded with a blast of energy vision to his chest. Michael had no illusions that he could beat the Guild Master; to be Guild Master a Kordite had to train for hundreds of years and especially for the Guild Veer, they had to fight in many different wars. Michael noticed that the Guild Master blended both the brutal style with the elegant style. It was mesmerising how the Guild Master could blend the styles and use them to their fullest. The Guild Master directed a nerve strike to Michael's right shoulder which went completely dead. Michael was down an arm and had to think of another tactic. Using his left arm, he tried to throw him off balance with a telekinetic blast and follow up punch but it was all for nothing; the Guild Master pulled the blast apart and trapped Michael's arm. Michael's brain began to analyse a way out of the trap; he pushed back and floored the Guild Master. Breaking out of the lock he moved back.

"Enough," Michael shouted.

The Guild Master stood up and pushed the sentries away from him. "It ends when I say it will." The Guild Master flew into Michael crashing him into the ground. Michael headbutted the Guild Master and pushed him off him. Reactivating his energy vision Michael blasted his fist and then his chest. Speeding forward Michael landed a barrage of blows on to the Guild Master. The Guild Master was toying with Michael; grabbing Michael with a giant hand he lifted him up and began slapping Michael. Michael spat blood on to the Guild Master's visor; he activated his energy vision and tried to blast the Guild Master back, but it was to no avail. Lightning-like energy surrounded the Guild Master as he summoned it to wear Michael down.

"ENOUGH!" The voice sounded like thunder as the Guardian of Vaar landed. The Guild Master continued to strangle Michael until the Guardian physically pulled him away and slammed him to the ground. The Guardian stamped his foot on to the Guild Master's neck and held him down. "Will you yield?" The Guild Master nodded and the Guardian let him up slowly.

"My apologies, Guardian I simply wanted to see whether the child was worth all of the mess." The Guild Master looked back and Michael. "He is a talented fighter." The Guild Master walked towards Michael; the Guardian was wary but didn't intervene. The Guild Master held his hand out; Michael shook it. "I am proud to have met you. You have the guild's apologies for the events of what happened on earth." Looking from Michael to the Guardian he bowed slightly. "Forgive me for my... harsh demeanour but I must leave for my fortress. The Ziborians have breached our planet and have caused damage. I must draw up a military plan."

The Guardian nodded and turned to Lara. "Send the child home." He looked at Michael. "Child, it was nice to see you but now you must leave and begin your father's plan." Michael nodded and turned to Lara. Tears welled up in Michael's eyes; he would have to face Ryan's funeral.

"Do not be scared brother, I know what you are going through. And if this Charlotte loves you almost as much as she appears to do from your memories, she will forgive you."

Michael smiled and hugged her. "It was nice to meet you, sister."

She smiled at him. "You too, brother." Activating his bracelet, Michael was sent back to the lonely surface of the moon. He broke down shaking and trying to fight back the tears; but he couldn't.

Chapter 25: *I need to leave*

It was raining in New York; the funeral was reserved. Bernard was there along with Adam, John, Terrence, Rachel and Andrew who all watched as Charlotte and her family cried. Andrew stood with Sarah who was desperately trying to hold back tears. She buried her head in Booker's uninjured shoulder and let the tears flow. Booker held her close and even started getting misty eyed himself. Adam held Charlotte close while she cried. Bernard swiped a tear away and looked around. Michael was nowhere to be seen; no doubt reeling from the guild that he felt. Bernard was sure that Michael was there but hidden from view. The priest continued the burial service. Charlotte broke into tears again. Bernard walked over towards her.

She pleaded with him. "Bernard, where is Michael? Why isn't he here?"

Bernard pulled her close. "I'm sure he is here, Miss but he's probably too sad to stay. He blames himself for everything that happened."

Charlotte wiped tears from her eyes. "But I don't, none of us blame him."

Bernard nodded. "I know but he doesn't know that." While she continued to cry Bernard noticed something peculiar. He saw a figure wearing a white shirt with black trousers and a black jacket and wearing black sunglasses. A tear came down his right eye but red circles formed in the lenses. Charlotte looked up and saw the figure; she instantly recognised him. She wanted to reach out to him but it was too late; the figure blurred away. Bernard held Charlotte close as the priest finished the ritual. The silence was disrupted by a sonic boom across the area.

Bernard smiled and muttered, "Be careful son but know that we all will miss you."

Michael landed on the manor's lawn; the mansion was still destroyed but multiple drones sped around trying to rebuild it. Entering through the main door, several blue lights flashed.

"Sir, I have begun reconstruction of the manor and I have new protection details set up for Miss Charlotte and her family. Sir, what are you doing?" Michael had listened to Marcus but was packing a bag. Taking the essentials, he almost left a tablet that he had found in his father's lab. Michael knew what he had to do now; he would let his father train him and mould him into the hero he needed to be.

"Marcus I'm going away for a bit. You can't tell Bernard or anyone else, this is priority alpha."

Lights flashed. "Confirmed, sir. Might I enquire where you are going?"

Michael smiled softly. "That's the problem; I don't know where I'm going. I need you to keep an eye on Charlotte."

Lights flashed again. "Do not worry sir; I will take care of them. I wish you well on your journey."

Michael smiled and flew up through to the stratosphere. Closing his eyes he let himself land wherever he could. Once he landed he looked up and started walking.

Printed in Great Britain
by Amazon.co.uk, Ltd.,
Marston Gate.